PRA[ ]
THE ACCID[ ]

"Ms. Cassidy's knack for the out[ ] out the story . . . Has a laugh-out-loud twist. I could not put this one down."
—Fresh Fiction

"I have to admit that Dakota Cassidy is one of my favorite authors. I haven't come across any of her books that didn't deliver a strong, funny, and fabulous story line packed with passion, and *The Accidental Human* is no exception. You won't want to miss this one!"
—Fallen Angel Reviews

"A delightful, at times droll, contemporary tale . . . Dakota Cassidy provides a fitting twisted ending to this amusingly warm urban romantic fantasy."
—Genre Go Round Reviews

"A paranormal romance with a strong dose of humor . . . The characters are fun as hell."
—Errant Dreams

ACCIDENTALLY DEAD

"Funnier than hell. If you like the writing styles of MaryJanice Davidson or Katie MacAlister, then you will love Dakota Cassidy. She's in a class all her own!"
—Bitten by Books

"A laugh-out-loud follow-up to *The Accidental Werewolf*, and it's a winner . . . Ms. Cassidy is an up-and-comer in the world of paranormal romance."
—Fresh Fiction

"Jumping from one supernatural species to another . . . Cassidy's snappy dialogue and outlandish situations ensure snickers aplenty."
—Romantic Times

"An enjoyable, humorous satire that takes a bite out of the vampire romance subgenre . . . Fans will appreciate the nonstop hilarity."
—Genre Go Round Reviews

continued . . .

THE ACCIDENTAL WEREWOLF

"Cassidy, a prolific author of erotica, has ventured into MaryJanice Davidson territory with a humorous, sexy tale." —*Booklist*

"If Bridget Jones became a lycanthrope, she might be Marty. Fun and flirty humor is cleverly interspersed with dramatic mystery and action. It's hard to know which character to love best, though—Keegan or Muffin, the toy poodle that steals more than one scene."

—*The Eternal Night*

"A riot! Marty's internal dialogue will have you howling, and her antics will keep the laughs coming. If you love paranormal with a comedic twist, you'll love this book." —*Romance Junkies*

"A lighthearted romp . . . [An] entertaining tale with an alpha twist." —*Midwest Book Review*

MORE PRAISE FOR THE NOVELS OF DAKOTA CASSIDY

"The fictional equivalent of the little black dress . . . Funny, sexy, and a must-have accessory for every reader."

—Michele Bardsley, national bestselling author of *Over My Dead Body*

"Serious, laugh-out-loud humor with heart, the kind of love story that leaves you rooting for the heroine, sighing for the hero, and looking for your own significant other at the same time." —Kate Douglas

"Dakota Cassidy is going on my must-read list!" —*Joyfully Reviewed*

"If you're looking for some steamy romance with something that will have you smiling, you have to read [Dakota Cassidy]."

—*The Best Reviews*

"Ditsy and daring . . . Pure escapist fun." —*Romance Reviews Today*

ACCIDENTALLY DEMONIC

DAKOTA CASSIDY

BERKLEY SENSATION, NEW YORK

THE BERKLEY PUBLISHING GROUP
Published by the Penguin Group
Penguin Group (USA) Inc.
375 Hudson Street, New York, New York 10014, USA
Penguin Group (Canada), 90 Eglinton Avenue East, Suite 700, Toronto, Ontario M4P 2Y3, Canada
(a division of Pearson Penguin Canada Inc.)
Penguin Books Ltd., 80 Strand, London WC2R 0RL, England
Penguin Group Ireland, 25 St. Stephen's Green, Dublin 2, Ireland (a division of Penguin Books Ltd.)
Penguin Group (Australia), 250 Camberwell Road, Camberwell, Victoria 3124, Australia
(a division of Pearson Australia Group Pty. Ltd.)
Penguin Books India Pvt. Ltd., 11 Community Centre, Panchsheel Park, New Delhi—110 017, India
Penguin Group (NZ), 67 Apollo Drive, Rosedale, North Shore 0632, New Zealand
(a division of Pearson New Zealand Ltd.)
Penguin Books (South Africa) (Pty.) Ltd., 24 Sturdee Avenue, Rosebank, Johannesburg 2196,
South Africa

Penguin Books Ltd., Registered Offices: 80 Strand, London WC2R 0RL, England

This book is an original publication of The Berkley Publishing Group.

Copyright © 2010 by Dakota Cassidy.
Cover illustration by Katie Wood.
Cover design by Diana Kolsky.
Interior text design by Kristin del Rosario.

PRINTING HISTORY
Berkley Sensation trade paperback edition / February 2010

Library of Congress Cataloging-in-Publication Data

Cassidy, Dakota.
  Accidentally demonic / Dakota Cassidy.
    p. cm.
  ISBN 978-0-425-23228-6
  1. Vampires—Fiction. I. Title
  PS3603.A8685A67 2010
  813'.6—dc22   2009038687

PRINTED IN THE UNITED STATES OF AMERICA

10 9 8 7 6 5 4 3 2 1

ACKNOWLEDGMENTS

Thanks to the usual suspects; Renee George, Michele Bardsley, Terri Smythe, Jaynie Ritchie, Vicki Burklund, Erin, Qwill (you rock the mod, baby), Kaz, Sheri Fogarty, my group of "Accidental Fans" and "The Babes." Also to my son's friend Terrence. Dude, I love your accent so much I based a character on you, who has one that I hope reads just like it. So in your honor—"Fo sho, you da bomb-diggety!"

Mucho thanks to the makers of Guitar Hero World Tour and Rock Band—uh-huh, you read that right. I know what you're thinking: but she's too old for video games. Ah, but old people rock, too. Just not as hard, or nearly as long before we need Ben-Gay massages and warm milk. Anyway, you have no idea how many plot issues have been solved while I beat those drums during the Foo Fighters "Everlong"—or the utter and pathetic joy I feel when pretending I'm the drum player for Boston.

Picture me, fist held high, index and pinky finger skyward, my tongue hanging out à la Gene Simmons and hear my rebel yell, "Rock and Roll, Hoochie Koo!"

Next up to conquer: Dancing with the Authors.

Huge, huge thanks to my editor, Cindy Hwang, who gives my whacked sense of humor a forum. Elaine Spencer, my agent, and everyone at The Knight Agency. Crystal Jordan, whose librarian skills bar none.

And always the fans. You gave the accidentals a shot—you're the reason I can't go to a reader convention without someone asking "Is *this* in my color wheel?" You crack me up when you let your heads hang low and sheepishly tell me narrowed of eye with hushed defiance, "I *like* the color yellow—so—so *there!*" That my crazy has spread speaks devotion—and forever I'm beyond grateful to every single person who's picked up a copy of one of my books, shared it with a friend (you brave warriors), got it from the library, or even bought it from a bargain bin. Thank you, thank you!

Never to be forgotten, Rob—a man who loves me even when I wander around in my pajamas with greasy hair, bemoaning my lack of word count, and worrying I've written myself into a corner. A man who totally understands that this profession means sometimes he takes a backseat. With my dirty laundry revealed publicly, it only goes to show you that true love really *does* exist, even if it needs glasses and a thorough psychiatric evaluation.

Dakota ☺

forum.wordreference.com
www.vikinganswerlady.com
www.tshirthell.com/hell.shtml
www.speakjamaican.com/jamaican-slang-glossary.html
www.straightdope.com

CHAPTER
1

"Wandaaaaa!" Casey Schwartz whispered low and harsh into the mouthpiece of a black phone attached by—of all the demeaning, degrading things—a rusty *chain* to its base. It was debilitating. No, that wasn't the right word. It was debasing. *Debilitating* meant to incapacitate.

Oh. My. She was officially so freaked she had the disease known as contextual error.

Though, in her defense, and despite her almost sickening anxiety, this situation could very well be debilitating, if, say, Big Sue next door decided to make good on her threat to yank her intestines out through her belly button.

"Casey?"

Her gulp was undoubtedly audible, but she refused to allow her voice to wobble. If Wanda knew just how hysterical Casey was, she'd only get hysterical, too. The Schwartzes hysterical together equaled hysterical to the millionth power. "Ye—" She cleared her throat, wiping away the squeak and hoping to keep the tremor of her bottom lip in check. "Yes, Wanda, it's me. Your long-lost sister who never calls you." Well, except when she's in some deep doody. Like now. Yes, now would be the kind of doody one might call deep. Either way, that wasn't exactly how she'd hoped her opening line would come out.

If she'd ever felt like complete shit for not calling Wanda and her parents more before today, it would never compare to the steaming pile that was her remorse right now.

"Oh, honey." Wanda's tone grew gentle and admonishing all at once. "Don't be like that. I told you to call me whenever you're able, didn't I? No strings attached. I know your life is busy and getting away from that tyrant you work for is difficult. I totally understand your not being able to even so much as pick up a phone until maybe as far into the future as when Mars and Venus align. Really, I do. But believe it or not, I can't talk right now. I'm on my way for a girls' weekend in lovely Connecticut with Marty and Nina. We're off to a B and B for some quality girl bonding."

"Yeah." Casey heard a disgusted grunt in the background. "Quality girl *bonding*, Wanda. Is that what we're calling dragging me to stupid-assed antique store after antique store to look at overpriced junk while in between hunting garbage we stop at quaint little sidewalk cafés and order prissy tea with names I can't even pronounce—or drink—then have massages by some weird guys with weirder names like Bjorn who really just wanna see chicks naked."

"Nina!" Casey heard yet another voice interrupt, much sweeter in tone. "First of all, no one forced you to come, whiner. We only invited you to scare off anyone who might potentially want to become our friend anyway. Because honestly, the idea of adding someone else to our friendship mix when we have you is about as appealing as inviting the devil himself to play Russian roulette with the gun of his choice. Second of all, she's on the phone with her *sister*. You know, the one who lives in Manhattan and doesn't *visit much*. Just shut up, already!"

Casey sighed into the mouthpiece, avoiding at all costs letting her lips so much as graze the black, marred surface. Another pang of regret settled in her stomach knowing Wanda's friends were apparently aware she was a total slacker when it came to keeping in touch with her family. She'd dwell on that if there weren't more pressing matters at hand.

Like her life.

Or, at the very least, her wool socks—which, oddly enough, they'd let her keep and were no doubt warm and desirable in a place like this. But definitely not worth the threat of sawing off your feet with a nail file for.

Nausea turned her stomach in waves. Casey pressed a hand to her belly.

Her orange-clad belly.

A rustle of what sounded like material scraping against the phone ensued; then Wanda growled with a snap, "Nina, Marty, knock it off, *now*! You know damned well I'm not kidding with the two of you, either."

Growled? Wanda had *growled*? Had the second coming of Christ been scheduled, and she'd missed the memo? Wanda didn't growl. She didn't swear, either. Wanda always went in whatever direction took her as far away from growling and swearing as she could get. Baffled at her sister's confrontational tone, Casey cocked her head to listen more closely.

"Casey, honey?"

"I'm still here." Still. *Here*.

"Did you hear me? I can't talk right now. Especially with these two beasts in the car. If you only knew what road trips are like with the two of them. Hell, I tell you. Utter and complete hell. Like total submersion in the ninth level of Purgatory. How about I call you when we get back from Connecticut on Monday? We can set up a time that's convenient for you. Maybe when the Big Dipper's in full view?"

Panic rose to lodge in her throat despite the fact that Wanda was taking a potshot at her. She peered over her shoulder at the line forming behind her. "No! No, you don't understand, Wanda—"

"No, sweetie, I really do. I'm just teasing you about your utter lack of communication and acknowledgment of any and all familial ties. Honest. Now, you go do all the important things that keep you from pressing my number on speed dial and we'll talk next week—or next year—your call."

"Wanda!"

"Casey?"

"*Please* just listen to me."

"Of course I'll listen, but wait. Hold on for just a second."

Hold on? Sure. She could hold on. She could hold on for as long as she could hold off the very angry mob of people closing in on her. A rather imposing, large woman with a small head and square shoulders like a linebacker butted up against her and whispered so the guard wouldn't hear, "Hey, four eyes, hurry it the fuck up or you'll be reading Braille." Casey self-consciously pushed at her glasses, glasses a very nice guard had given her a Band-Aid to hold together after they'd been viciously stomped on with a red stiletto worn by a woman with a thigh the size of a tree trunk. She clamped her fingers firmly above the rims in case the hardened bully behind her decided to make good on her threat. "Wanda?" she squeaked, fighting for composure.

"One more sec, Case. Nina!" Wanda bristled once more. "Give Marty the frickin' map and give it to her now. You know good and well you couldn't read a map even if your IQ suddenly shot up fifty points. Hand it over, and hand it over this instant. I knew we should have taken Marty's car. She has GPS." More rustling occurred; then she heard her sister's exasperated sigh. "Do you see why I can't talk now, baby girl? It's just madness when the three of us try to do anything like normal girlfriends do. An all-consuming trip into insanity."

"Wanda!" She'd resorted to a whisper-yell to get Wanda's attention. And really, who, in the position she was in now, wouldn't at the very least whimper?

"I'm just not getting through to you, am I? What's this sudden need to talk all about, Case? You almost never want to talk. Not willingly, anyway. And to reiterate, I'm not blaming. I'm just stating a fact. I only wish you'd chosen a better time to call. If the timing were right, I'd yak with you for all of the three seconds you devote to saying the words *I'm fine*. But I just can't right now. We're lost somewhere in New York City, and believe me when I tell you: no one wants to be lost with Nina and Marty. No one. In fact, I'd bet the man upstairs himself would rather have a do-over of World War Two than he would be lost with Marty and Nina."

"One minute remaining," an automated voice boomed in her ear.

"One minute remaining?" Wanda queried. "Are you calling me from a pay phone, Casey? Do they even still have pay phones anymore? Where's your cell, honey? I didn't even check my caller ID to see who was calling. I—"

"Wanda! Quit talking and listen closely!" she yelped, finally blurting out the most heinous statement she'd probably ever make in her entire life. "Seventh Precinct, lower east side of Manhattan. Come get me—please, please come bail me out!" She realized her voice had risen to stratospheric proportions, but her mounting hysteria couldn't be contained.

"Bail you out?"

A click in her ear meant the one minute she'd had remaining

was up, but it wasn't up before she'd heard the disbelief Wanda's voice left ringing in her ear.

Yes.

Bail her out.

Of jail.

Of the poe-poe.

From the big house.

From the hoosegow.

For assault and battery.

Of an off-duty police officer.

A half an hour later, Wanda showed up just in time for the scheduled visitation with her two friends in tow. "Oh, Casey!" her sister fairly shrieked, gathering Casey in her arms and hugging her tight to her slender frame. Despite her dire circumstances, she couldn't help but notice how pretty and healthy Wanda looked these days. Since she'd married Heath, her cheeks were always glowing and her eyes were bright. More ugly guilt ate at Casey's gut. Seeing Wanda reminded her she hadn't been able to take time off to attend Wanda and Heath's wedding on the Island. Noooo, she'd been too busy catering to the grown women she literally babysat.

Wanda pushed a strand of Casey's tangled chocolate brown hair from her forehead. "Are you okay?"

"Don't ask her that, Wanda. Of course she's not okay," a blonde with shoulder-length hair, and a chic sapphire blue, formfitting sweater dress with a gold chain-link belt draped casually over her hips, chastised. "She's wearing orange—a color I assure you isn't even close to her color wheel. It makes her look sallow and almost yellow around the gills. And she's in"—the blonde leaned in and whispered—"*jail*. Jail, Wanda. There's nothing okay about jail."

Another woman, as dark as the blonde was light, and a stark

fashion contrast to her in faded jeans and a sweatshirt that read, "Yellow Sucks," nudged the blonde hard with a flat palm to her shoulder and an irritated look. "Shut the fuck up, Marty. A—the color wheel bullshit is now a thing of the past. Or did you forget Heath, the director of marketing *you* hired, shot that shit all to hell and renamed it an 'Aura Arc' or some such crap? B—stop whispering the word *jail* like it's the plague or something, and quit acting like you're all above this, Miss Hoity-toity. Jesus! Don't you think the poor kid feels bad enough without being reminded her color wheel's out of whack, and she's in jail? Sometimes you're so fucking insensitive."

The blonde—Marty, from what Casey had distractedly gathered—gasped and fiddled with the black coat she had draped over her arm, clenching tight fingers on the collar as though she was warring with the idea of a little physical violence. "Excuse me, but if you remember, I voted Heath down on the ridiculous idea a color wheel should be anything but what it is. A *color wheel*. And me? Insensitive, Nina? Um, helloooooo, Miss Potty Mouth. Who's insensitive? Wasn't it you who just the other day—"

"Nina, Marty, knock—it—off!" Wanda intervened with a stern look, putting a hand up between both women. "Now, my sister's in crisis. This isn't the time to have a knock-down, drag-out about arcs and wheels—especially here where I just might allow the nice policeman in the corner over there to haul you both off to cells. You know those dank, dark cages where you all have to share the facilities and some woman named Inga makes you her cellblock missus? Cut it out and behave accordingly."

Wanda turned back to Casey, plastering a forced smile on her lips, but it didn't hide the disgust she just knew her sister was undoubtedly experiencing. Casey could see it in the wrinkle of her pert nose and the pinch of her glossed lips. "Now, back to you. Are you okay?"

Casey glanced at the other prisoners in the gray, institutionally colored visiting area and blanched. *Oh, Jesus, oh, Jesus, oh, Jesus*— she was in jail. She fought for the calm, unruffled demeanor that was almost always her outward appearance. She liked to call it her "work face." The face she used when someone had to remain calm in the midst of all the chaos and madness her employers' twenty-something daughters created.

How you did that in the visiting room of the pokey while surrounded by criminals with something called a "grill" in their mouths was going to be a primo effort. Casey gathered what was left of her sane, levelheaded self and laid it right out there for her sister to see. "I'm about as good as can be expected in jail. Did you pay the bond? I know it was a bundle of money. I swear I'll pay you back for all of it—every penny. I have most of it in my savings account. The rest I'll make payments on every month. Promise."

Wanda threw up a dismissive hand as though money was no issue. "Don't be silly, honey. The money isn't the problem at all. I took care of it, and I know you're good for it. Here's the real problem—you assaulted an off-duty officer, Casey—in a bar. What the *ef*, young lady? You're standing here in front of me all stoic, like this is no big deal. I don't even know who you are. You were always so studious—thoughtful—quiet, and I can't ever remember you going to a bar. Don't you remember how we were always saying, 'That Casey, always with her nose in a book. She's so quiet.' So quiet in fact, now we hardly ever hear from you. Since when did you go all vigilante?"

Good question. If someone had the answer, she'd be all in for hearing the explanation. "I don't know." And she didn't. She couldn't remember past . . . well, she couldn't remember. Period. Fear rose again like the swell of froth on a freshly tapped beer. "I don't even remember what happened, Wanda," she blurted out, then silently damned herself for not thinking before she opened her big mouth. Shit. Casey let her head hang low, dropping it to her chest to hide her eyes—and, okay, her shame.

But Wanda would have none of that. She tilted up her sister's chin and forced Casey to gaze into blue eyes so different from her own. "You can't remember? But you always remember—everything. Details are your thing. Wait . . . were you . . . drunk?" Wanda frowned with distaste, whispering the word so no one would hear her—as if that was the worst offense you could commit in a place like this. Wanda's nostrils flared in an obvious effort to find alcohol on her breath.

Hah. Drunk.

As if there was ever enough time to so much as breathe the air designed especially for her when she was too busy breathing it for the Demonic Duo, Lola and Lita—her boss, Calvin Castalano's, twin daughters. Spoiled, self-centered socialites who did virtually nothing but plan their eyelash-curling time around their next Botox injections and drive-by implants. Though drinking wasn't a vice she heartily pursued—if anyone could drive someone to become a shoo-in for AA, it was Lola and Lita.

Casey focused on Wanda's face again and replied with as much succinct calm as she could muster, "No. No, I wasn't drinking or drugging or doing any of the things that would make me forget how I ended up here in jail for . . . assaulting an officer." Casey cringed, folding her fingers together to rest at her thighs. She'd hit a police officer. Her. Casey Louise Schwartz.

And she hadn't just hit him. According to what she'd overheard, she'd slammed one Arvin Polanski up against the far side of the bar's wall—with just a single, delicate hand.

Oh, and then she'd hurled herself at him, suspending him approximately three feet above the ground, but not before she made an extra special effort to threaten to sacrifice the heart she'd rip from his chest in a ritualistic offering of satanic worship.

And sheep.

There was also a reference to sheep she neither understood nor wanted clarification for.

That the two arresting officers had even been speaking with the smallest, most remote reference about her and satanic rituals might just mean a psych eval was in her very near future.

She'd never raised a hand to anyone in her life, but clearly, when she chose to throw down, she did it with a thundering hand and wild abandon. And that could be handy info to have on her side should she ever encounter, say, a mugger.

Or a brutal serial killer.

Whichever came first.

Yet those moments she'd only heard bits and pieces of as they were booking her remained a complete blur. The only thing she did remember was the aftermath. The aftermath that included hog-tying her and hurling her like a sack of potatoes into the back of a police car while Lola and Lita stood mortified on the outskirts of the biggest crowd she'd seen since the last Flock Of Seagulls concert she'd gone to as a teenager.

"Casey? Care to explain that statement?" Wanda pressed, giving the visitors area the once-over with a scathing glance. "Because here you are. In jail not remembering how you got here."

"Here I am," she confirmed. In jail. To say anything else, to defend herself without all the details, would just be stupid. She'd clearly blacked out, but the how and why was a big, honkin' blank.

"Did you have a drink?" Marty asked, her eyes warm and clear with concern. "I read an article a long time ago about how dangerous it can be to set one down in a bar. Freaks put all sorts of things in them—like maybe psychotropic drugs or something. You can't ever be too careful these days."

"I didn't have anything to drink," Casey said, thwarting that idea. There was never enough time to do anything as self-indulgent as get your own drink when you were too busy finding the best champagne in the house for the demon twins.

Wanda's one hand went instantly to Casey's forehead, prying one of her eyes wide-open with the other to gaze into it. "Did you hit your head? Are you having some kind of neurological issues you haven't told me about?"

She shrugged off her sister's fingers, forcing down her irritation. "No."

"No," Wanda repeated plainly. "That's all you have. Just no."

Yep. That about sized it up. "Yes."

Nina stuck her head between the two of them. "Am I outta line here or would it be too much to ask you two to worry about the explanations and memory recon missions later? You know, after we get the fuck out of here," Wanda's friend Nina said, saving Casey from having to offer any further explanations. "I hate to rub salt in the wound, but we are in the slammer. And I'm not much likin' the seedy dude over there in the corner who, if he keeps eyeing my booty and thinking the shit he's thinking, is gonna be pulling my fist from his throat by way of his ass. I know I said I'd almost rather do anything than go to that fucking spa slash B and B with you two wing nuts, but this wasn't high on my list. So can the interrogation, Wanda, and let's get Casey home before I beat the fucking snot out of that freak."

Wanda gave Casey one last sympathetic glance before she nodded her head in agreement. "For once, Nina, you have a point. They have to out-process you or something police-ish like that, is what I'm told. Paperwork, I guess. We'll meet you out in front of the *jail*," she said with intended emphasis. "In the parking lot."

Casey watched her sister tuck her purse between her arm and side, her short, quick steps brisk and efficient as she and her friends exited the visiting area's locked doors. Just as Nina passed the "seedy dude," she leaned in with a narrow gaze of her black eyes, letting loose an odd, menacing sound from her throat.

A shiver ran the course of her spine.

The Nina chick was scary.

How she'd become friends with her sister, meek and about as confrontational as Mother Teresa, escaped her.

When she broke out of the big house, Casey made a mental note to make nice with the scary chick at all costs.

"OFFICER?"

"If you're here ta file a complaint, sit over there." The police officer pointed a finger to the left without looking up, his Brooklyn accent distinct. "If you're here ta bail somebody out"—he thumbed over his shoulder—"it's the room on the right."

Clayton Gunnersson stuck his hand under the officer's nose, giving him a cheerful grin. "I'm not here to file a complaint."

"Then it's the room on da right, buddy," he offered distractedly.

"Actually, I was wondering if the Unabomber has visiting hours. I baked a cake for him. Chocolate. It's his favorite."

The officer's head snapped upward, eyeing Clayton. "Yer a funny guy."

"Now that I have your attention, I'm not sure exactly where I need to be. So before I take door number one or two, I was hoping you could help me."

"Look, pal . . ." He drifted off when Clay captured his eyes, holding them in a stare.

Clayton leaned over the high desktop and smiled. "I only need a moment of your time. Promise. I'm looking for someone who was involved in an incident at Crimson Lips. I don't have her name, but there was only one arrest, so it shouldn't be difficult to locate her."

The policeman began to move his head in an "absolutely not"

fashion, but Clayton caught him, directing his attention back to his eyes. "Nuh-uh-uh, now, don't go all rules and regulations with me. Be nice and help a guy out. Ready?" Clay motioned his fingers up and down, and the officer's head followed with obedience. "Nice. Now, where's the girl who was arrested at Crimson Lips?"

His eyes were shiny and glazed, but his lips moved in a sluggish response. "Posted bail—her sister, I think."

Clay smiled once more with approval. "Excellent. And what's the young lady's name and address?"

"I can't give you that inf—"

Clayton gave him a mock pout. "Oh, Officer Kilpatrick, you do know it's pointless to deny me, don't you?"

Kilpatrick nodded, transfixed by Clayton's stare.

"Perfect. Now, do me this—look it up on your computer, and then write it down on one of those sticky things for me. I forget a lot lately, and this is important." Clay pointed to the stack of sticky notes, his eyes never leaving the officer's face. "Use a yellow one, please."

Officer Kilpatrick gave him no trouble at all, typing in a few words, then transferring the information to the sticky note Clay requested. He took the note from him, sticking it to the front of his jacket and holding it out to show Kilpatrick. "So I'll remember."

He nodded again, slow and wooden.

Clay reached over and slapped him on the shoulder. "You're a good egg, Officer Kilpatrick."

Looking down at his shirt, he glanced at her name, saying it with a silent movement of his lips, then cringed.

He'd done a bad, bad thing.

With a grimace, he pondered this Casey Louise Schwartz.

She was in for a surprise.

Though the throwing of confetti was probably inappropriate.

CHAPTER 2

Casey led the women to her apartment off the main living quarters and though they remained silent for the most part, the occasional grunt from Nina bounced off the cavernous walls of the Castalano residence.

"Nice digs out there," Nina commented with a thumb over her shoulder as Casey flipped the light on, illuminating her small living room.

Marty set her purse on the coffee table. "Wanda? Did you see the Picasso? I think it's real. Like, really *real*."

"It is," Casey confirmed, flopping on the couch, drawing a worn blanket over her shoulders. "Worth millions, I think."

Nina snorted. "That big-assed thing hanging in the hallway? It looks like a kindergartner finger painted it after slam-dunking too many gummy bears."

Marty sat on the arm of the chair Nina had positioned herself in and flicked Nina's dark hair. "You're such a heathen,

Nina. You wouldn't know real art from the pictures in a comic book."

In anticipation of Nina's response, Wanda raised a threatening finger. "Shut. It." She turned to Casey, tucking the corners of the blanket under her chin. "Now, what do you say we talk about how you landed in the pokey?"

A groan escaped her lips. How could she possibly explain to Wanda that she had absolutely no clue how she'd found herself in jail? How could she explain threatening an officer of the law if she didn't remember doing it? In fact, she only remembered what happened just before she'd apparently offered to kill an innocent man, and she was so embarrassed by the lengths she'd gone to protect Lola and Lita, she for sure didn't want Wanda to know what she'd been trying to prevent before she'd blacked out. When she finally spoke, her shame kept her words simple. "Let's not."

"All right, then. How about we talk about what's all over your shirt?" Wanda pulled apart either side of the blanket to point at the angry, dark splotch on her white, tailored blouse. "It looks like blood, Case. So what is it?"

The proverbial broken record continued to play when she repeated, "I—I—"

"Don't know," Wanda finished in that uppity older-sister tone. "Right. Got that part. If you don't know what happened—and blood was involved—I hate to be the one to point this out, but that's a pretty big 'I don't know.' Blood was shed, Casey. You know, the stuff that runs in your veins or, say perhaps, drips from your finger when you have an owie. From the looks of your shirt, there was a lot of it, too. How could that have happened without your knowing? There were witnesses who *identified* you. People in the bar who saw you accost this officer 'like you were possessed,' as one man described it. It's obvious we need to talk."

Indeed. Talking would be fine, but pointless if she couldn't remember a damned thing about how she got blood on her shirt. Plus, she just didn't know if she had any words left in her to talk with. She'd been up all night, hovering in the corner of a damp cell filled with angry hookers and female knockoffs of the Zodiac Killer. All while she gnawed her nails to their cuticles, trying to make herself as small and unnoticeable as possible. "There's nothing to explain," she said once more, for lack of anything valuable to offer.

Wanda pursed her lips. "Um, wasn't it just me who paid a butt-load of money to get you out of jail? It costs a lot of money for the kind of bail you're given when you *assault* an off-duty officer and end up in jail. *Jail*, Casey Louise Schwartz. I think I deserve at least an attempt at an explanation."

Which seemed to be the ever-elusive most popular quest of the day. An explanation. "If I don't have one, then I can't give you one, Wanda." Which was a very logical answer, considering her very illogical position. She avoided her sister's eyes by scrunching farther into the couch and bowing her head, then found herself face-to-face with the ugly stain on her shirt. How she'd missed that when they'd out-processed her could only be chalked up to exhaustion.

Wanda wasn't buying it. Her eyes grew determined and her tone no-nonsense. "How could you not have an explanation for being arrested? What happened before you beat the off-duty officer up?"

Cutting Wanda off, Nina snorted with a grin she obviously fought. "And threatened to sacrifice some organ or other while you fed it to a sheep. Believe me, I don't say this often, kiddo, but I'm not worthy of your kind of creative threats. You da man." She tilted her head at Casey in apparent admiration.

Marty slapped at Nina's black leather-clad shoulder again. "That was not what they told us at the police station, mouth. They said she threatened to sacrifice his heart in some satanic ritual that involved sheep. God, Nina, get the facts straight. Don't make things worse than they already are."

Her mortification made her slide to the edge of the couch, preparing for a quick exit if necessary. Jesus, Joseph, and Mary. It *was* true. What those police officers had said was accurate. A farm animal? She didn't know the first thing about farm animals. The only pet she'd ever had—still had—was a goldfish, for shit's sake. Not to mention the fact that she knew absolutely nothing about satanic rituals.

This had to be some huge mistake. Huge. Ginormous. Monumental. A disastrous case of mistaken identity.

"And please don't embarrass yourself by telling me there must be some mistake," Wanda said, reading her mind.

Hookay. No denial. Instead, she opted for more uncomfortable silence while each of the women stared her down, waiting.

A knock at her door almost made her sigh with relief until she realized it would probably be her boss, who would no doubt fire her. After last night, she shouldn't much care, but there was the issue of eating. Something she sort of needed to do if she hoped to get all crazy and not *starve to death*.

Casey popped up, racing to the door as fast as her loafer-clad feet would carry her. She cracked it open to peer out only to have Lola, reed thin and dressed in a tight, pink belly sweater, shove her way in. "Omigod, Casey! Thank God you're okay!"

Crap. She didn't want Wanda to know the kind of degradation she suffered chasing after her employer's grown children like she lived in servitude. And she sure as shit didn't want her to know what had happened before she'd suddenly become a candidate for Amnesiacs Anonymous.

"Yeah," Lola's twin, Lita, dressed identically, agreed, stroking the ends of her thick, platinum blond ponytail. "We were soooo worried about you."

Huh. Last time she'd checked, when you were worried, you didn't let the cops drag the person you were worried about off like a hog to slaughter without saying word one about *why* the worried for had done this heinous thing she'd done and she couldn't remember. However, instead of losing her cool, she did what she always did, no matter the trouble the twins caused—even if the trouble now had involved her. She stared blankly at them and waited. It always freaked them out when she expected them to complete a sentence.

Lola played with the earring in her eyebrow, nary an ounce of remorse on her face. "We totally couldn't believe you were encapsulated."

Someday she was going to handcuff these two to a chair and force them to read the dictionary. Every frickin' word. "*Incarcerated*. I was incarcerated, and no, I'm sure seeing me pepper sprayed and handcuffed wouldn't tip you off that maybe, just maybe, I might be *incarcerated*." Casey clamped her lips shut to keep from going any further. Again, the eating issue, and maybe even the fear of ending up in a homeless shelter, kept her silent.

Lita frowned with a cutesy innocence that might work on their father, but only pushed Casey closer to the edge of a place she couldn't remember even coming close to. The girls definitely brought her their fair share of grief, and yeah, this was an extreme case of it because she'd ended up in jail, but the angry niggle that had begun as Wanda grilled her began to increase with hot pulses along her spine. "We tried to tell them what happened. They just wouldn't listen." Lita pouted her full lips prettily. The way she had when she'd mutilated her father's vintage Vette.

Wanda was up off the couch in a shot at Lita's statement, glaring down at the two twenty-two-year-olds who held her paycheck in their destructive hands. Marty and Nina, too, gathered right behind her, planting themselves in the small entryway, leaving Casey suddenly feeling oppressed, like if she didn't get air to her lungs, she'd explode.

"What did happen?" Wanda eyed the girls with a hawkish glare.

"Oh, I love your sweaters, and they match. Sooo cute," Marty cooed to the twins. "Where'd you get them?"

Nina rolled her coal black eyes. "Shut the fuck up, Marty. This isn't a trip to Neiman Marcus. Leave the Double-knit Twins alone, and let Wanda find out what happened, seeing as Casey"—she swiped two pairs of index fingers in the air—"can't remember."

"No!" Casey roared, then clamped a hand over her mouth when several surprised glances cast her way.

"Dude," Nina barked, hovering over her with a suspicious frown. "If they know what happened, and you don't, why the fuck wouldn't you want them to tell your sister? The sister who fucking spent a lot of greenbacks to get you the hell out of the slammer."

Because, you interfering, meddlesome piece of trailer-park trash—it's no one's business but mine. Casey slapped her hand over her mouth again to fight a gasp, her eyes wide. Where had *that* thought come from? And had she just thought that about *Nina*? Lest she forget how scary Nina was. Hello, badass in da house. She threw an apologetic glance at Wanda's friend. Even though she hadn't spoken the words—that she had merely thought them appalled her. "I just—"

"So, ladies, why don't you tell me what happened?" Wanda interjected again, sending Casey's anger up yet another spiky notch.

Nary a warning came before that little niggle of irritation turned into a heated push of irate, irrational fury. "Goddamn it, Wanda, I said—*no*! Now stay the hell out of it!" Casey fairly howled, her words gravelly and deep to her ears as she grabbed each of the girls by the arm and gave them a shove out the door. Her chest throbbed, but she managed, "I'll talk to you two tomorrow." She slammed the door with a harsh slap of her hand and cheeks that grew hot, then eyed Wanda. "When I tell you to stay out of it, you'd friggin' better stay—out—of—it! Got that?"

Wow, wow, wowee. Once more, surprise at her harsh, down-right ungrateful words to Wanda, who'd been nothing but good to her, made her want to crawl out of her own skin.

Silence pulsed between the women. Nina looked at Wanda, who looked at Marty, who looked bug-eyed at Casey.

Gawking.

Awkward.

Nina was the first to speak, closing in on Casey and cornering her. Her words were threaded with quiet intimidation, spat from clenched, incredibly white teeth. "What the hell is wrong with you? Look here, exorsistah, you ungrateful little whiner, you'd better start spilling and stop wasting our friggin' time. I don't have all fucking night to sit around and listen to you piss and moan like some pansy-ass about how you don't remember what went down. Especially after Wanda, you know, the sister you don't spend two minutes on the phone with unless it's a *timed* phone call from jail, begging for cash—the one who just spent an ass load of money to bail you out. Now spew, Sybil, or I'll beat it the fuck out of you."

"Nina!" Both Marty and Wanda yelled.

Casey felt her eyes narrow, her chin jut upward, her posture stiffen, all while she stared up at Nina—who, lo and behold, she quite suddenly wasn't so afraid of.

Well, huh.

A shot of pure adrenaline rocketed through her veins with such a swift surge it jolted every muscle in her body—invigorating her. As if the opportunity to spar with the menacing, überscary Nina was a full-on smackdown she'd invite.

What. The. Fuck?

But abruptly, her mouth opened and words spilled out. "Were I you," Casey said in a tone that was deep and filled with condescending arrogance, "I'd back off, *bitch*." She pointed up into Nina's face, letting her index finger rest just under her nose.

Casey heard the room fill with more gasps, but her vision had narrowed to nothing but Nina's beautiful face. A face she wanted to ram her fist into—but good.

Nina's eyebrow rose to a perfect arch, but she didn't budge. "Were I you, I'd watch my hindquarters, Miss Priss. I so know you didn't just call me a bitch. You'd better hope I didn't hear right, *bitch*, because I'll shove my fist so far down your throat they'll have to get the Jaws of Life to extract it." Wanda and Marty hovered behind Nina's right shoulder, but she held her hand up with an angry flip of her palm.

Casey crossed her arms over her chest in defiance. "Oh, but you heard me per-fect-ly."

Nina's lips thinned. "Hookay, I'm gonna to give you one last op to shut that yap of yours because your sister's my friend. But if you don't knock it the fuck off right now, it's on, Princess. Got that?"

For the briefest moment, she warred with herself, an odd struggle of socially acceptable decorum and the need to take Nina out so rife it was palpable. Casey fought it for all of maybe two seconds before the rising fury, so unexpected and uncharacteristic, consumed her. Her last semi-sane thought was, omigod, she was totally going to call her sister's friend a bitch to get a rise out of her. And then—she did—with a roar so earsplitting and fierce, Nina's long, wavy hair ruffled from the *whoosh* of her breath. "I'll say it once more for those in the room who struggle with English comprehension—*back—off—bitch*!"

So it was on.

Nina planted her hands on either side of Casey's smaller frame and let her face loom mere inches away. Her mouth, tight and pinched, sneered; her next words became a snarl. "You do know we're game on, don't you?"

Cockily, she jammed her face in Nina's. "Guess what, badass? This is me not afraid of you. Yeah. That's right—I went there!" She flicked a finger in the air, grazing Nina's hair.

Nina snarled. "This is me telling you, you should be very afraid, little girl."

"Nina! That's enough—you know better!" Marty yelled, yanking at her shoulder from behind while Wanda tried to get between them. "Back off! You'll hurt her if—"

"Bring it, *bitch*!" Casey bellowed, shoving at her so hard, she heard the crack of her palm against the leather of Nina's jacket. Out of nowhere, Nina was easily ten feet away from where she'd been almost plastered up against her.

And Casey was staring *down* at her.

Which was undoubtedly odd because Nina was at least five inches taller than she was.

"Nina! Noooooooooo! You'll kill her!" Casey heard Wanda scream.

Yet, she found she cared little because she pointed her finger at Nina again when she attempted to round on her once more. "What about *back off, bitch* don't you get, *biiitch*?" Somewhere, way deep down, she knew she'd tacked on that extra *bitch* because it would make Nina freak. And she liked it—reveled in it—relished it with lip-smacking anticipation.

Somewhere, way deep down inside, she also knew her ass was so in for a lickin'. Yet, also somewhere way deep down inside— she didn't give a flying fuck. So she emphasized that way deep down inside disregard by pointing at Nina again and screeching, "Bitch!"

At the top of her lungs.

While Casey Louise Schwartz, always the calm in the middle

of chaos, watched flames, bright orange and crackling blue, shoot from her fingertips and headed straight for her sister's "not as scary as she once was" friend.

And then . . . oh, holy Heaven.

Set Nina's hair on fire.

CHAPTER 3

So pandemonium and four women became one swirling, writh-ing entity of high-pitched screams, foul language, and tangled appendages.

Wanda, eyes wide, limbs slicing through the air at a freakishly blurred, breakneck speed, launched herself at the blanket Casey had left on the couch. Throwing it squarely at Nina better than any rodeo-roping cowboy, javelin-throwing Olympian, she managed to envelop her friend in it. Wanda became a distorted ball of color, catapulting herself onto Nina's smoking head and knocking her to the floor with a hard grunt. Straddling her friend, Wanda tamped out the crackling flames with haphazard thwacks of her palm to Nina's skull while Nina flapped her arms and swore.

And a frantic-eyed Marty, mere nanoseconds behind Wanda, scanned the room. Her feet beat a thumping path to the small table in the corner of Casey's living room. Marty's eyes honed in on what she was apparently looking for, and, wasting no time, her fumbling hands reached for the desired item. Grabbing Casey's fishbowl, containing her beloved goldfish, Shark, Marty promptly dumped it over a smoking, screeching Nina with a triumphant howl.

A gush of water and colorful rocks splashed over Nina's head, compressing the blanket flush to her face and leaving an ominous sizzle of extinguished flames in its wake.

Casey viewed this with an almost out-of-body observation while she lingered.

In the atmosphere.

That observation was mingled with an eerie calm. Vaguely the thought flitted through her mind that she should be more than a little panicked. Be it her on-the-job training, or maybe that her feathers didn't ruffle very easily, she simply took in the scene below her feet, versus allowing the kind of hysteria one should experience when they levitated to flip her out.

"For Christ's sake, Nina!" Wanda hollered. "Stop fighting me and hold the hell still or I'll knock your teeth in!" Clutching the lapels of Nina's leather jacket, Wanda gave her an almost violent shake, laying Nina flat out and pinning her to the floor.

Casey—from her vantage point still ten feet off the floor and now rising—gasped, breaking her strange, cloudy haze of indifference. Who was this Wanda? A Wanda who not only took the Lord's name in vain but had managed to wrestle the scariest woman Casey had ever encountered to the ground with nothing more than a hard shake.

Never mind that, her conscience called. *Who. Are. You? All floating in the air like you're the newest member of Cirque du Soleil.*

Right. There was that. The panic she wasn't experiencing just moments ago made a sudden appearance—spiky and resonant.

Casey's fear and surprise by this turn of events were only sidetracked by some of the most creative cussing she'd ever heard.

Nina heaved her hips upward, shoving at Wanda to no avail while she tore at the sodden blanket plastered to her face. "Wanda, get the frig off me now, you fucktard! When I get up off this floor, not only will I kick the shit out of your mouthy, ungrateful sister, but I'll whip your ass while I'm at it, too." Droplets of water flung in all directions from lips that had anything but their happy on.

Casey shivered.

While she floated.

Continually moving upward until she had to press her hands against the ceiling to keep from banging her head. Her cheek kissed the frigid, lumpy plaster, allowing her vision from only one eye, but it was enough of a view to see how feral her sister had become. The half of her mouth that wasn't pressed to the ceiling became slack at her sister's next words.

Wanda leaned in low, letting the tip of her nose touch Nina's. Her whisper was sinister. "Don't make me, Nina Statleon. You know darn well the kind of damage you could do. It's an unfair advantage I won't allow." Her sister spat the warning with thin lips and a throbbing pulse to the right side of her forehead Casey worried might bust the vein that held that angry pulse in check.

Whoa. Exactly what kind of unfair advantage did Nina have against screaming fireballs? Was she some kind of killing machine? A ninja? Because from where Casey stood—er, floated—it would seem she was the one who'd been advantageous in this smackdown. It was *Nina* who was on fire, wasn't it?

Remorse washed over her. She'd set someone on fire. Fire. She'd felt the flames shoot from her fingertips, purposely directed them with the intent of zinging Nina in a rage she'd never before experienced. Casey looked toward her fingers pressed against the ceiling—fingers that looked like they always did with nails that were trimmed short and neat—half expecting to see some kind of remaining residue, like soot.

Marty refocused Casey's attention to the scene down below when she planted a foot on Nina's abdomen, folding her slender arms across her chest. "We're not letting you up until you promise not to annihilate Casey. Got that, Mistress of the Night?"

"Fuck you, Marty," Nina shot back, but slowed her struggling.

Marty smiled glibly with a shake of her head. "Promise to behave."

"The. Hell," Nina said with a glare so fierce Casey felt the heat of it.

From all the way up near her entryway light fixture. Crazy that.

"Shark," Casey managed to mumble just as her legs cracked against the ceiling, forcing her head to point fully south and look down at Nina, where she caught sight of her fish. Her eight-year-old carnival goldfish flopped by Nina's head, desperately seeking air. "Shark! Water—he needs water!"

Quite contrary to her red-hot anger of earlier, tears began to form in the corners of her eyes over her fish. He'd managed to live far beyond expectation, and though he wasn't a cat or a dog to snuggle with, Casey was attached to him.

Nina scrambled to her elbows. "Fuck you and your fish, you brat! I'll fillet your goddamned guppy for dinner and sop him up whole with a biscuit."

Marty toed Nina with a smirk. "Oh, quit, badass. You know you can't eat foo—" She cut herself off as quickly as she'd begun, but not before Casey saw all three women exchange glances that screamed, "Can it."

Which was strange indeed, but not nearly as strange as floating around in your apartment like a hot-air balloon. Stranger still, not one of these women seemed to find the very fact that she was floating—*floating*—even the least bit disturbing.

Wanda was the first to recover when she ordered Marty to fill

Shark's bowl back up and put him in it immediately. She hovered over Nina, jamming a finger under her nose. "I'll say this once, Nina. If I let you up and you so much as lay a finger on my sister, I'll take you out. Got it?" Her sister's face hardened, and her eyes gleamed dark and threatening.

Nina's lips grew thin, but her features relaxed an increment, making Casey take a deep, grateful shudder of breath. "Let me just make myself clear. If she wasn't your sister, I'd lasso her ass, hog-tie her, and jam a fist into her piehole while I fished around for her tonsils." Her eyes rolled upward to glare into Casey's. "Got that, Princess?"

Casey gulped. All of that fierce bravado she'd been spewing earlier went the way of leg warmers and she decided to beg. For mercy. Because the "fishing for her tonsils" part of Nina's state-ment was just this side of heinous. "I'm so sorry, Nina. Oh, my God. I don't know—I don't understand how . . . I—"

"Yeah, we know. You don't know. Seems that's the ongoing theme for tonight." Wanda slung her leg over Nina and rose to cock her head at Casey, planting her hands on her hips in her big-sister way. The one where she silently demanded an explanation without actually asking for one.

Which brought Casey again to the thought she'd had earlier. Was she just bat-shit crazy, or was levitating a class she'd missed at the Y—like yoga or Pilates? Was it all the rage and she just wasn't aware of it because all she did was chase after two airheads day and night? Why wasn't anyone freaked out? In fact, why wasn't she freaked out? Why didn't hovering ten feet above the room, pressed nearly flush to the ceiling, *feel* like she was doing nothing short of a Houdini-ish act?

Yet Wanda wasn't much impressed. On the contrary, she ap-peared rather irritated. Nay, she was annoyed. Casey knew Wanda, and her expression said she was aggravated that Casey had the audacity to be on the ceiling, and it was becoming damned inconvenient. "Okay, enough of this. Get down here now, Casey." She pointed to the spot on the floor by her feet. "So we can discuss whateverthehell this is."

Discuss. How rational. How did one even begin to discuss the notion that she was mushed against the ceiling with no outside influences—like recreational pharms? "Wanda?"

"Yes, Casey?"

"I had a thought."

"And that is?"

"My thought is this—is it me, or is the fact that I'm hovering up against my ceiling just a smidge alarming—especially when not one of you seems too troubled by my sudden predilection for feats attempted only by David Copperfield. Add to that the fact that you all but ordered me to 'get down here' as if you'd ordered me to do something ordinary like go to my room, and I think it's time for me to render your mental stability questionable."

Wanda's cheeks puffed outward in a breath of exasperation. "Just get down here, for Christ's sake, Casey."

Casey took another hard swallow, rubbing a hand over her grainy eyes while keeping the other planted with a firm palm against the ceiling. "Just so we're clear, Wanda. I don't know how I got up here. I can promise you, I have no idea how to get down."

Marty reentered the room from the kitchen with Shark safely ensconced in his bowl again and shot Wanda another of those secretive looks. "Here." She handed Wanda some pantyhose.

Wanda's right eyebrow arched upward. "What are these for?"

"I found them in your panty drawer, Casey. Forgive the intrusion, but in case you haven't noticed, Wanda, she's floating—or whatever, and call me crazy, but it appears as though she's not exactly the grand master at it."

Exactly! Floating.

"And some fine silk hosiery's going to help that how, numbskull?" Nina asked. Clearly recovered from her blaze-filled battle, she came to stand near Marty with her arms crossed over her chest.

Marty shrugged her shoulders. "I thought maybe we could tether her to a chair or something until we figure this out. You know, like a helium balloon. Pantyhose are pretty strong, and this pair does have the reinforced-cotton crotch . . ."

Not typically prone to histrionics, and exceptionally skilled in the art of calm, even Casey started to experience the beginnings of sheer terror rise like a killer wave along her spine. She'd gone all *Crouching Tiger, Hidden Dragon* and her sister and her friends were concocting DIY ways to tie her to a chair with nylons with nary so much as a raised eyebrow.

Wanda slapped Marty on the back, smiling with warmth. "Good idea. Casey, honey?"

Casey fought to unstick her lips from the ceiling. "Uh-huh?"

"Got a ladder?"

"Only a stepstool. In the closet by my bedroom."

Wanda was instantly all business. "Nina, grab it, please."

Casey heard the shuffling of feet and the scrape of the metal legs on her stepstool when Wanda positioned it beneath her, but she'd closed her eyes due to the onset of the potential to blow chunks as her predicament settled deeper in her brain.

The air below her stirred. "Give me your hand, Case," Wanda demanded in the same no-nonsense tone she'd taken earlier.

Fist clenched, Casey forced her right hand to dangle while the nails on her left hand scraped against the ceiling, unsuccessfully attempting to grip a surface that just couldn't be latched onto. Wanda secured the pantyhose around Casey's wrist and began to tug, but her body seemed intent on staying rooted to the ceiling.

"Nina!" Marty shouted. "Grab Wanda around the waist to keep her feet on the stool and I'll do the same with you."

Casey heard a grumble that was all Nina, but she must've complied because the shift of her weightless body began to reposition itself.

"Watch your head, Casey." Wanda grunted with a yank that almost dislocated her shoulder. Casey bit the inside of her mouth to keep from crying out, and suddenly, she was seeing the world the way it was intended.

The way normal people who didn't levitate saw it.

Right side up.

Her head bobbled for a moment until she righted herself, while Wanda and Nina stretched one leg of her pantyhose to its limit, securing it to the leg of her La-Z-Boy recliner.

Wanda brushed her hands together in an act of completion. "Now, that's much better, don't you think, Case?"

Probably almost anything was better than being smashed on your ceiling. "Yes, thank you." In a lifetime, how often did one thank another for keeping them from floating away?

Nina, Marty, and Wanda plopped on the couch facing the recliner with synchronized huffs. Wanda, sitting between her two friends, crossed her legs and leaned back to look up at Casey, who dangled like a human marionette. "So. Maybe you have something to tell me," she coaxed in a gooey-sweet tone Casey identified from their childhood. The tone she'd used when Casey had stolen Wanda's Barbie doll's shoes and threatened to swallow them if she didn't let her play with the golden-haired doll.

Casey's mouth fell open while the left half of her body strained against the nylons and fought to tip her back upward. Something to tell *her*? Her? She wasn't sure what she couldn't believe more. The idea that she was tied to a recliner—or the thought that not one of these women was having an apoplectic fit and calling her the live edition of *The Exorcist*. Still, she hung on to her calm. "Okay. This has gone kinda kooky for me. So I'm just going to make a few points that seem obvious to only me, but not before I tell you one more time I don't know what's going on, Wanda. I don't know how I ended up in jail after threatening to sacrifice a sheep's heart—"

"An undercover cop's heart in a sacrifice that involved sheep," Nina corrected with a narrow-eyed snort.

A prick of irritation fluttered square in Casey's belly, but she beat it back down. She handled the paparazzi all the time for Lola and Lita, she could definitely keep her cool with a "poke at you with a stick" novice like Nina. It took a lot more than a wisecrack to trip her trigger. Well, except for earlier tonight, but she was determined not to let that become a factor right now. "Right. I don't know how that happened, Wanda, because I swear to you on my life I don't remember it. I swear it. And I don't know what just happened. I don't know why I can shoot fireballs from my fingertips or why I can float—am floating—levitating—whatever this is. The only thing I do know is this—you're all sitting on my couch, looking up at me while I'm suspended *midair* and acting like I'm doing something average, dare I say, normal. So my question is this—and I have to tell you, I'd really appreciate an answer, because I think I'm just a butterfly net and tranquilizer gun shy of losing my mind here—why am I the only one in the room who finds fingertip-shooting fireballs and levitation just this side of insane?" Casey took a deep breath, pressing her free hand to her chest to quell a heartbeat that was rapidly becoming jittery.

The three women looked at one another again, and their eyes held the same secretive glint they had each time Casey proposed the idea that they were whacked for not losing a nut over what was happening right in front of them.

Marty rolled her tongue in her cheek as though she were pondering something, then slapped her hands on her thighs. "It's like this—"

Wanda clamped a hand over Marty's lips with a clap of flesh

against flesh, but Nina pulled at her sister's fingers, dragging them from Marty's mouth. "She has to find out sometime, Wanda. She's your sister, for crap's sake. I think it's pretty obvious some freaky-deaky shit's going down that we don't have the skills to handle. She needs to know."

Casey bobbed to and fro like a float in the Macy's Thanksgiving Day parade, confused. What did she need to know and how did it relate to what was happening to her? Instead of wondering, she decided against her better judgment to ask. So she asked, "What exactly do I need to know?"

Wanda grimaced, passing Nina a stern look. "This isn't the kind of information you just dump on someone, Nina. You can't just hammer them over the head with it. There has to be a subtle entry to telling someone about . . . us. A buffer of some kind."

If she hadn't been intrigued before when no one batted an eye at her setting Nina's hair on fire with the point of her finger, she was certainly all in now. Though she didn't say as much for fear they'd clam back up. Who were these women and what had they done to her sister? Wanda wasn't anything like she'd once been. *Nothing* like it.

She was edgy, and seemingly unafraid of much these days. Casey knew so little about her sister's friends other than the passing comments Wanda had made in their phone calls that lasted no more than mere moments. And that made her sad that she was the shittiest sister ever and worried all at once about exactly whom Nina and Marty really were.

Nina rolled her eyes, pushing a lock of her now-damp hair behind her ear. "Oh, and how we told Lou was subtle, Wanda? Jesus Christ in a miniskirt—you almost gave her a fucking heart attack when she caught you fangs deep in Heath's—"

"Nina!" Wanda yelped, yanking Nina's freshly burned hair. "Shut it."

Casey's head fell back on her shoulders. Levitation. Fireballs. And now fangs. Hookay. Full-on disturbing had arrived. And who was Lou?

"Oh, please, Wanda. Lou survived it, and she's no spring chicken." Nina gazed up at Casey, drifting back and forth with an invisible breeze, jaw nearly unhinged, and cackled. "Casey's young, aren't ya, Case? Her heart can stand hearing about us."

Us. What was this "us" they spoke of? Like they were some sort of cult. And seriously, what could they possibly tell her that was any worse than what was already occurring? As Casey swayed, not just her discomfort but her fear mounted.

Marty shook her blond head. "You know how much I love to agree with Nina, Wanda—like, never—but she's right. So either you do it or I will—or, God forbid, big of mouth will." She pointed a finger at Nina. "I get the feeling it'd probably be a whole lot less stressful for Casey if *you* did the talking here."

Casey had to remind herself again—she wasn't prone to histrionics, nor was she the kind of girl who panicked in an emergency. She dealt with emergencies, scandals, tabloids, and paparazzi almost every day. She was paid to keep her wits about her at all times and never create a scene, not to mention minimize the ones the girls continually made all on their own. And she'd done that until now—she hadn't panicked once. Not when Nina was a bonfire on her floor because her own fingers had apparently turned into Bic lighters, and not even when she'd risen like a phoenix to the highest high of her apartment ceilings.

But that was all over now. As was evidenced by her rising tone. "What the hell are you all talking about? Somebody just tell me what's going on and what it has to do with me being tied to a chair with pantyhose!"

Wanda's face grew pensive. "I wish you could sit down for this."

Yeah. Casey looked down at Wanda, straining against the nylon tied to her wrist to stay upright. "Uh, me, too."

Her sister's fingers went to her temple, massaging the area between her eyes.

Nina sat back into the couch and snickered.

Marty bit her lip.

"What?" Casey almost screamed the question.

"Okay, it's like this, honey. We're not freaked out by—by—by whatever this is because when I tell you we've seen some stuff over the past couple of years that'd curl your eyelashes, I'm not kidding."

Nina chuckled, making the hair on the back of Casey's neck rise up and tickle her like soft tentacles. Her heart began to pound as her mind raced—but she still didn't get it. "So explain, please. Just tell me whatever it is."

Wanda rolled her head on her neck and cracked her knuckles. "What's happening to you has to be something paranormal. We know that because we've experienced the paranormal."

"Have we ever," Marty muttered, tucking her chin to her chest with a yawn.

Okay, that, she could almost wrap her brain around. "Are we talking ghosts here?" Maybe Nina and Marty were part of some ghost-hunting club and Wanda had taken an interest in it and joined a group they were both in?

"Well, not yet, but I wouldn't rule that shit out." Nina's comment was dry.

Wanda flicked Nina's thigh with her finger. "Not ghosts, Casey. Do you know anything about vampires and werewolves?"

"Or were-vamps, for that matter?" Marty chimed in.

Were-whos? "I'm almost afraid to answer that."

"Vampires and werewolves. A were-vamp is half vampire, half werewolf," Wanda supplied.

Good to know. She'd just tuck that away for later use. Until then . . . "How do vampires and werewolves that're half vampires explain why you three don't seem at all surprised I'm being kept in check with a pair of pantyhose?"

Wanda popped her lips, giving Casey a hesitant look. "Okay, no more soft shoe. We're not surprised by your fireballs and levitation because, well, we've seen stuff—*experienced* stuff—in the past couple of years that makes what you're going through seem like an afternoon at a day spa."

Her mind swirled.

"Hey, Casey?" Nina called up to her.

"Uh-huh?"

"Gird your loins."

She swallowed—hard. "Girded."

"So, when I say we've experienced things, they're the kind of things that at first you won't believe. You'll go through a range of emotions most likely beginning with denial, then disbelief, and then fear. . . ." Wanda winced, then confirmed her assessment with a nod. "Yes, fear. It's sort of like the five stages of grief minus the bargaining stage because believe me when I tell you, you won't want to swing a deal with us . . . though I can definitely see depression happening." Wanda shook her head again with a wry look. "Never mind. Anyway, we have proof. We can prove to you what we're saying is true—"

"Oh, dude—can I be the one to show her the proof?" Nina interrupted, her tone very clearly riddled with maniacal glee.

Wanda narrowed her eyes at her friend. "No, you absolutely cannot. You're just being spiteful and despite the fact that Casey set you on fire, I won't let you exact revenge. Not on my watch."

Nina flipped her palm up in Wanda's face. "You're always harshin' my vibe, Wanda. She did set my fucking hair on fire. I owe her one."

Wanda ignored Nina, gazing back up at a bewildered Casey. "Where was I?"

"Grief," Casey reminded her. "The five stages."

"Right. Well, then I suppose you'll be angry that I didn't tell you, but it's not like I haven't tried. You're about as easy to get in touch with as a Tibetan monk."

Casey didn't know much about these stages, but laying on the guilt must be one of them.

"And then there's acceptance. Which"—her sister swept her hand around the room—"is what we've all come to. We're all very happy."

Centered. Stay centered. Casey reprimanded the half of her that wanted to punch Wanda and her butt-ass long-winded explanation in the head. And clunking her sister over the head had absolutely nothing to do with her prior, uncontrolled anger. Even Job would consider bodily harm as a mandatory point of action at this juncture. "Wanda?"

"I'm lingering?"

Casey puffed a long-held breath from between her lips, leaning to the left to counterbalance the constant tug of gravity. "Yes, and I'm being truthful when I tell you, I'm tenuous at best."

"Sorry. Okay, so here we go. Ready?"

No. "Yes."

"I'm not the person you once knew. Not mentally and most especially not physically . . ."

At the word *physically* Casey instantly eyed Wanda's breasts. Implants? No, definitely not. Then what? What? What, *whaaaaaat?*

"I'm not the same because I'm a were-vamp. Half werewolf, half vampire. I shift into what humans call werewolves, and I have fangs. And how all those things happened has a very long story behind it. Oh, and for the record, Nina's just a vampire, and Marty's only a werewolf. But I'm a were-vamp. Two for the price—"

"Wanda?"

Wanda exhaled. "Yes, Marty?"

"Rambling."

"Stopping."

A small giggle-snort erupted from Casey's mouth before she could stop it. Well, that explained everything. Just everything. Of course that was why Wanda wasn't disturbed by fireballs and floating. She was a were-vamp. All good were-vamps surely must be trained or at least have born witness to the art of fireball lobbing. "You're fucking crazy," Casey said before she could censor her almost always carefully planned words. Chalk it up to exhaustion, the mortifying notion that she'd been in the actual pokey—not the kind you see on TV in *Prison Break*, but the real thing—and it made for a combo pack of wildly swinging emotions she could no longer squash.

Nina rolled her shoulders as though a bell only she could hear had gone off in her head, signaling another round was due. "You got some set of gnads calling *us* fucking crazy. Was it us locked up in the big house after beating the shit out of an off-duty cop? No, I think that was you, mouth. If I were you, I'd be really careful about where you take this, 'cause it doesn't look like too many people are lining up at your door to help you the fuck out. We're sort of it."

Which had proved hugely beneficial thus far. But Casey was all out of energy and a verbal response.

"Nina! Lay. Off. Don't you remember how freaked out and scared you were after Greg bit you? Cut her some slack," Marty chastised.

Who was Greg and why was he biting Nina? In fact, how did he get close enough to Nina in order to bite her before she bit him first?

"I was so not scared, Marty."

"Were so."

Nina's eyebrows, naturally arched and dark, crunched together. "Listen, you furry, Milk-Bone lover, I was not scared—"

Wanda slid to the edge of the couch. "Cut it out! Both of you. God, the two of you are the bane of my existence, and to think I have to put up with you and your constant bickering for an eternity."

Casey nodded in silent agreement with her sister. Indeed, an eternity was a long, long time. So if she were mentally organizing everything that had been said thus far correctly—biting, eternity, vampires, werewolves, were-vamps, and fur were responsible for their less-than-hysterical attitude toward her levitating.

Wanda rose and grabbed Casey's hand. "Look, honey, trust me when I tell you I know what I'm talking about. We're not crazy, and whatever's happening to you has to be something that has to do with the paranormal. Just stay put and hear me out. Deal?"

As if escaping were a remote possibility when she was being held captive with a La-Z-Boy and a pair of Leggs. Casey merely nodded, seeking the kind of composure she'd needed when Lola's video vixen days had caught up with her on the Internet.

Wanda began to pace as she explained while Casey drifted, Nina smirked, and Marty nodded from time to time with sympathy in her blue eyes.

And the facts were these: Marty, when she and Wanda and Nina were all Bobbie-Sue Cosmetics recruits, had been accidentally bitten by a werewolf while walking her teacup poodle Puffy . . . no, Muffin. That was it. Muffin.

The man who'd bitten her fell in love with her, but not before she was kidnapped, had to adjust to becoming a werewolf, and learned to fit in with her pack. They got married. Marty's packman's name was Keifer—or Keith. *Keegan*. Uh-huh. It was Keegan.

Nice.

Lovely, in fact.

Then Marty found out she was heir to Bobbie-Sue and skipped off through bright yellow fields of buttercups to live in Buffalo with her werewolf, pack mate, person of hairy origins who owned a rival cosmetics company called Pack Cosmetics. Obviously, someone out there in the universe had a killa sense of humor.

They now had a baby—a little girl.

Lovelier still.

Then Nina, the ultra-scary, after quitting Bobbie-Sue because she'd sucked at selling cream blush, got a job at a dentist's office. While prepping a guy for some anesthesia, the guy accidentally bit her, turning her into a vampire. Now she drinks blood and stays up all night with her husband slash life mate, most likely concocting ways to kill people and take over the world.

But Casey didn't want to judge.

Then came Wanda. Her sister, so different from the woman she'd once known, who claimed she was a were-vamp. She'd become a were-vamp because she'd been dying of ovarian cancer and in the process of dying she'd met her now husband, Heath, who applied to her ad for Bobbie-Sue Cosmetics. And Casey had to agree with her sister when she said it was strange—a man wanting to sell cosmetics. But there was a reason he'd wanted to join Bobbie-Sue, and Wanda informed her she'd explain that part of this Wes Craven story later.

Anyway, finally finding the man of her dreams at the worst possible time in her life, Wanda decided dying wasn't an option she fancied, and she'd called on her friends to help her live—eternally.

Because they could—being vampires and werewolves and all.

In a rush of words Wanda fired at rapid speed, Casey had parsed out this: both Nina and Marty had bitten her because Nina thought

Marty had done a shitty job of it, and it wasn't working. When a vampire and a werewolf both bite you within a twenty-four hour period, the changes in your body overwhelm you and due to that, Wanda had become rabid.

Or snarling and drooling, if you listened to Nina's version of it.

Heath, once a vampire himself, but then a reverted human, yet another story Wanda said was for another time, sacrificed himself to save Wanda. Because when you're snarling and drooling, you need a human's blood to set you on the path of the righteous. Ah, but when you sacrifice your human self, you also end your mortality.

Very dramatic.

That act of self-sacrifice on Heath's part might have summoned a big, dreamy sigh from Casey if it wasn't so completely whacked.

While Wanda claimed they still didn't quite understand what happened the night of her "turning"—clearly another supernatural adjective—Heath somehow managed to come out of it okeydoke. The theory being that some of his vampiric traits had lingered and protected him from total annihilation. Now Wanda and Heath were mated for life, too, due to some ritual involving a vein and some blood.

So now here they all were, one big, fat paranormal meeting of the minds.

"Casey?"

"What?"

"Are you okay?"

This time, she really had to rock the calm, but someone had to in the midst of all this lunacy. "Oh, I'm fine. It's the fucked up trio that is you women I'm worried about. I find it sort of uncanny that you enable each other the way you do. It's kind of cute to the extreme."

Wanda swatted her hand. "Casey! Watch your language, and we're not effed up. We're telling you the truth."

"In what alternate reality does your truth exist?"

Nina popped up off the couch, lifting her sharp chin up to pierce Casey with her olive black eyes. "That's it, powder puff—I'll show you fucked up—so fucked up you'll slink off to a corner and curl up in the position you were in for nine goddamned months. Get ready to cry for your mama when you have a look at *these!*"

Before anyone could stop her, Nina hissed as her mouth became a gaping hole.

With lots of teeth.

Unlike jail, which hadn't been anything like TV, Nina's teeth—or fangs, if you will—bore a striking resemblance to the kind of teeth you did see on TV. On someone who was, like, say, Dracula.

In closing, that was when Casey officially slipped over the metaphoric edge she'd been teetering on since this night had begun.

And then she did what all sissified, namby-pamby girls do when they're confronted with the suspension of their safe, warm realities.

She screamed.

CHAPTER 4

Nina clapped her hands over her ears. "Shut her the fuck up, Wanda, or I will!" she bellowed.

Wanda gave a hard yank to the length of nylon securing Casey's wrist, jolting her with the strength of a linebacker, and catching her full attention. "Casey! *Shhhhhhhh*. Nina's ears are very sensitive to sound—especially the kind of caterwauling you're doing. Vampires have superhearing. Knock it off!"

A fissure of pain shot up her arm and rooted in her shoulder. "Damn it, Wanda, that hurt," she moaned, but it had nipped her full-on freak in the bud.

With her terror semi in check, Casey sprung to action—or as much action as one can spring to when they're being held hostage by three fruitcakes and some Leggs. Tugging back, she flapped her one good hand at Wanda, pointing a finger at her in warning. "You stay away from me, Wanda Schwartz Jefferson *were-vamp*! I don't know what's happened to you, or what kind of crap you've been up to with these two women, but keep them the hell away from me!" Wrapping her free hand around her wrist, Casey pulled, trying to free herself of the knot Wanda had tied like a Girl Scout.

Nina stuck a finger in her ear and wiggled it, looking to Wanda. "You do know she forced my hand, don't you?"

"Jesus, Nina. Leave it to you to find the harshest possible way to introduce Casey to the paranormal. Sometimes—no wait, what am I thinking—almost all the time, you're like a bulldozer with a vajayjay," Marty jabbed.

Okay—she was out. Casey put her teeth to her wrist and began to tear at the nylons out of desperation, sticking her fingers under the tight knot Wanda had tied to try to free herself. If she levitated right out the window of this high-rise and sailed over Manhattan, it'd still be better than being in this room with these three women who apparently needed more psychiatric help than was available in the free world.

Wanda latched onto her forearm and snatched Casey's fingers from her wrist while Marty jammed a finger between her teeth, and Nina tugged at her feet to keep her at eye level. "Casey! Get a grip. Please. Relax. If you don't stop this right now, we can't help you."

Frothy saliva had begun to foam at the corner of her mouth, snatching her hand back from Wanda; she ran her thumb over her lip to wipe it away. "Help me? Help me? How is what *she* just did helping me?" she spat at Nina. Gazing at the two of them with hard eyes, she accused, "What have you done to my sister? What kind of sick psychopaths are you? Wanda—what the hell have you gotten into? Did you do that to your teeth, too?"

"Oh, Casey. I didn't do that to my teeth. It just happened when I was—"

"*Turned*, right? Is that the word you're going to use? Is this some kind of cult you joined where they use crazy catch phrases like *turned* and *bloodletting*? I thought I'd seen everything there was to see with the two undisciplined, spoiled-rotten brats I babysit, but this beats even that place called 'The Dungeon' they talked me into going to by telling me it was a cool medieval fair. So you know what, Wanda? I don't think I'm the one who owes you an explanation at all! It's you who owes me one because whatever you're into is sick. It's sick, Wanda—do you hear me? And if I ever get down from here, I'm calling . . . I'm . . . I dunno, but it'll involve an intervention and a long stay somewhere tranquil with lots of medication in big syringes."

Out of nowhere, Nina threw her head back and laughed, right in the middle of Casey's meltdown. "You know, I gotta give you your props, Casey. You're sort of at a disadvantage here, and still you're all feisty from way up there. And you didn't even pass out when I showed you my teeth. I thought for sure you were the kind of chick who'd need a cold washcloth and a wake-up slap to the head. So I'm going to cut you some slack because I admire your stick-to-itiveness. So here's the thing: my teeth are for real, dude. I haven't had implants, and I sure as hell didn't have them filed. I'm a vampire. Marty's a dog, and Wanda's half vampire, half dog. If you want, I can latch onto a vein to prove it to you, or Wanda can shift into her werewolf form. So let's get over this 'Oh, my God, you're all nuts, what did you do to my sister' bullshit and get to figuring out what the fuck is going on. In other words, suck it up, buttercup, and let's figure this shit out so I can get the hell away from you tards."

"I *can* show you, Casey," Wanda offered, her words solemn and low. "And I'm not a dog. Neither is Marty. There's a huge difference between werewolves and dogs. Nina's just rude and likes nothing more than to create chaos, as you've already seen. Now, are you going to lay off the crazy and cooperate so we can try and figure this out, or are you going to continue to go the route of cults and brainwashing? Honestly, I'm having trouble with the fact that you're having difficulty believing us. You are the only one in the room levitating."

Score one for team bipolar.

She was indeed hovering like a hot-air balloon with absolutely no explanation. She had to give that much up.

"Don't forget the fireballs," Nina reminded. "Which brings me to another point here, sunshine." She held up a lock of hair on the side of her head that had been totally fried not twenty minutes ago. "You did set my hair on fire. You did see that it was burnt like a forgotten hot dog on a barbecue on the Fourth of July, didn't you?"

Casey's eyes widened. She had.

Nina twirled the glossy, totally unfried black length around a slender finger. "Now? Not so much, right? So how do you suppose that happened? Wanna know why that happened? Because I have healing properties. All vampires can heal themselves when they're injured."

"Well, unless they're staked through the heart with something made of wood and their heads are chopped off in one simultaneous act of depravity," Marty offered helpfully, smiling.

Oh.

Score two.

"So how about you suspend your disbelief for the moment and we try to figure this out?" Wanda took Casey's hand between hers and rubbed, warming the frigid tips of her fingers.

"O-okay." Her ears seemed almost surprised at what her mouth had just agreed to. Casey rolled her head on her neck to loosen her stiff muscles while stalling for a moment to rationalize. On a somber note, what choice did she have? Wanda was right on all counts, and if—*if* what they said was true, it explained why they weren't running around calling on the Lord and throwing holy water at her. If what Nina had shown her was real—really real—it was only another piece of evidence to back up their story.

Wanda's smile was determined. "Okay. So let's put our heads together." She turned to her friends. "She's obviously not vamp or were because none of us can levitate or shoot flames from our fingers. Though, Nina, you can fly."

Bet that'd piss Superman off.

Hold up. Fly? Nina could fly. Panic began to rise once more, and it was all Casey could do to force it to back down.

"Yeah, but I can't hover like she does. She's been up there for-ever like the Goodyear Blimp, Wanda. Did you guys see her eyes when she had her back up? Dudes, they glowed—red."

Marty gasped, nodding her head. "Yeah, they did. Oh, Jesus . . . maybe she's possessed? It was sorta shades of Linda Blair. The only thing she didn't do was spin her head around."

Casey blanched. Of all her fears in this lifetime—being mugged, losing a limb, dying a long, drawn-out death—she'd never consid-ered possession had the kind of potential to make all those other things seem like frolicking on a white, sandy beach.

Wanda nudged Marty. "Stop. You're freaking her out. We're just talking this out, Casey. Don't panic—"

Wanda was interrupted by the buzz of Casey's intercom. "Miss Schwartz?" a deep baritone called.

"Shit," Casey whisper-yelled, "that's Roosevelt. He's the door-man downstairs. Damn it, damn it, damn it, if Lola and Lita are at it again, I swear, I'll kill them. Wanda, press the button and let me answer him, please. Hurry, before he calls Mr. Castalano." Oh, Christ on a skateboard, if he woke up her boss, the shit would fly.

Wanda zipped to the door and pressed the black button. Casey called out, "Yes, Roosevelt? Is everything okay? Is it the girls?"

"Right as rain, Miss Schwartz," his ever-so-slight Southern drawl assured.

"Then what's wrong?"

"There's someone here to see you."

To see her—or someone pretending they were here to see her but really wanted to see one of the "blonde-tourage?" The twins had pulled that crap on her more than once, using her name to sneak someone upstairs. It better not be that rapper with the gold teeth, or, given the op, she'd set more on fire than just his hair. "Who?"

"A man. A big man, Miss."

"A man?"

"Thass what I said."

"What man?"

"A big one."

She sighed. "His name, Roosevelt. What's his name?"

"He says his name is Clayton Gunnersson."

Nina ran to the door, pulling Wanda's finger from the button. "Clayton's here?"

"You know him?" Casey asked.

Her glossy head dipped. "Yeah, he's my husband's best friend. Oh, shit. Maybe something happened to Greg?"

Casey's eyes sought Nina's. "How could he know you were here?"

"Grab your panties again, fruit cup—vampires can read minds. It's sorta like a GPS, and if we need to contact each other for help, we send out a signal. A brain wave or some crazy shit, and if Clay's here, it's urgent. Unless you're mated, vampires don't send out signals unless shit's going down, or it's an emergency."

Concern riddled Nina's features, prompting Casey to ignore the surreal nature of one more paranormal detail and urge Wanda to let her tell Roosevelt to send this Clay up. "Send him up to the back elevator so he won't disturb anyone, please."

"Yessss, ma'am, and you have a right fine evenin', Miss Schwartz."

"Wait!" Casey held up a hand to the women. "We can't let him see me like this. I'm floating."

"I told you, he's vampire. He gets it," Nina said over her shoulder, running for the door.

So really, who wasn't? But the worry written all over Nina's face kept Casey's mouth glued shut.

Nina pulled the door open, stepping to the side to allow a tall, sandy-haired man into Casey's apartment.

Casey's eyes went wide when he stepped out of the shadows and into the entryway light. Her stomach shifted to the point of discomfort and her heart began to pulse.

Shazam.

"Is it Greg, Clay?" Nina asked, her expression vulnerable, a stark contrast to the seething fury of before.

Clayton Gunnersson's eyes said surprised when he saw Nina at the door, but then he placed a hand—a big brawny one—on Nina's shoulder, making Casey twitch with an odd emotion she didn't know how to compartmentalize. "Nope. He's fine. So, heeeeeey. Funny meeting you here?"

Nina sagged against the door in clear relief. "Christ on the crapper, you scared the hell out of me, Clay."

"Everything's fine. Greg's playing poker with some of the clan. Aren't you supposed to be getting mud baths and seaweed facials this weekend?" Clayton's throaty question to Nina made Casey fairly glow. It wasn't the question that did it, either. It was the scratchy, throaty tone to his reassurance.

"Yeah, and do you remember when I told you and Greg I'd rather do almost anything else than go to some stupid-ass spa?"

The corner of his lips lifted in a smirk. "I do."

"I fucking lied."

Clayton chuckled, but as quickly as he let loose that sensual growl of amusement, his lips returned to a thin, grim line. "What are you doing here, Nina—with her?" He tipped his head in Casey's direction.

"She's Wanda's little sister, Casey—and we have a problem."

Clayton's eyes strayed to Casey's, locking with her bewildered stare. Shards of heat rose from the tips of her toes to land on her cheeks. "Yeah. I guess her floating midair is problematic—or cool, depending on if your glass is half full, or half empty, but color yourself relieved of the problem. Now she's *my* problem."

"Excuse me?" Casey finally found her voice.

"I said you're my problem," he answered back, all man, all serious, but then he grinned. "I'm here because I did this to you. You're floating because of me." He paused, watching Casey's eyes react, then nodded. "I know, right? It's crazy, but it's true. I'm sure right now you don't like me much, seeing as you're tied to a chair, but maybe, in a week or so, you'll thank me, because you have to admit—it *is* wicked cool."

"What are you talking about?" Wanda crowed, reaching around Nina to give Clayton a quick hug and a questioning glance.

Clayton winked at Casey's sister with a casual smile as though a woman floating was all part and parcel of a vampire's day. "Hey, Wanda, how's Heath?"

Her eyes brightened at the mention of Heath's name. "He's good. So how is my sister your problem?"

"I'm the one who did this to her." He said it as if he owned it, and again, Casey twitched with a discomfort that might be described as deliciously decadent. And that was ridiculous.

Nina was the first to respond with the slap of her palm to forehead. "Go figure. In how many lifetimes do ya think shit like this goes down not once, but four times? Un-fucking-believable," she muttered.

Marty turned to Clayton, her blue eyes deep in confusion. "So is she a vampire? Because, hoo boy, is Nina ever going to be pissed that Casey can shoot fireballs and she can't. That's some neener-neener, huh, Elvira?"

Nina flipped her the bird.

But hold the phone. "I'm tied to a chair because of *you*?"

"That you are—with pantyhose. My deepest apologies."

As much as she wanted to be hacked off about that, who could be hacked off at a guy who looked like this Clayton did? He was stone-cold fine. As fine as fine could be, and while she should be focusing on his declaration, she wasn't. Things were beginning to get distorted internally again—totally out of whack. Wobbling, she asked, "What exactly did you do to me? I don't even know you." That sounded completely lucid and held together despite the inner boil of her intestines.

"True enough. We don't know each other, but we did bump into each other the other night in a club called Crimson Lips. Know it?"

Marty looked up at Casey. "Wasn't that where you were arrested, Casey?"

Clayton didn't let her answer. "She was. It was bedlam. But you look like you're okay—well, except for, you know . . ." He waved his hand upward along the length of her body.

Casey frowned. "But I don't remember seeing you. . . ."

Rocking back on his heels, he wrinkled his nose and squinted his dark eyes. "Yeaahhhh." He let the word draw out, adding some drama. "I'm guessing that's because you were otherwise occupied with a photographer, a man who was only trying to help you, and a wall. But to your credit, you were awesome in action. Very Jackie Chan." He whipped his hands around in a karate move.

Closing her eyes, Casey forced herself to try to remember the visual he created, but she came up dry after the photographer. "I don't remember much from that night."

"That's what I figured, and that's why I'm here. To explain, and hopefully, to help." He took two strides, holding his hand out to Casey. "Take my hand and I'll get you down."

The. Hell.

On the outside, she shrank away from his touch. Ah, but on the inside, her girlie bits were all woo to the hoo. Wait. What were her bits, or for that matter, any bits, doing showing up at this soiree? She'd forgotten she had lady parts; it'd been so long since she'd last had time to even pay attention to a man.

"He won't hurt you," Nina reassured.

Casey's lips tightened and a spike of fury rocketed along the back of her neck. "And you know that how? By your vampire GPS—or did your fangs tell you that?"

"My fangs'll tell you something, all right, you pain in my ass—"

"Nina." Clayton's resonant tone was soothing, and not just to Nina, who instantly calmed when he spoke her name. "She knows?"

"Like we had a choice, Clay," Marty defended. "She did wonder why we weren't all that impressed when she started a bonfire to rival any high school rally with Nina's hair from the fireballs she was shooting from her fingertips."

"And she's done shit else but whine about how crazy we are since we told her," Nina provided.

Clayton put his hand back on Nina's shoulder. "She's upset. She has every right to be. Wouldn't you be upset if you were tied to a chair with pantyhose? While I'm applauding your resourcefulness, I can see her distress. Even *I* might whine in her position. So cut her some slack. Besides, you know as well as I do, she needs time to digest."

Casey looked down at them, fixing her eyes on him. "*She* has these things called ears, and *she* can hear you, but *she* agrees with what he said."

Clay rolled his tongue in his cheek. "I apologize. I realize this is probably pretty scary, but if you'll give me your hand, I swear I can get you down—no lie. Don't you think you'd be more comfortable?" He held out his hand once more, cool as a cucumber, like butter wouldn't melt in his mouth.

Casey's brain said no, but her hand didn't want to play well in a team setting. It drifted into his, creating a riotous frenzy of hot and cold chills along her arm.

His fingers, callused and long, entwined with hers while little bolts of electricity zinged along her skin.

She descended as easily as she'd risen, almost without realizing it, falling into Clayton when she touched the ground. Long, solid, well-muscled arms caught her by the waist, with a light press of her length to his.

The moment their bodies touched, something—wait, honesty check, it wasn't just something. It was her *libido* that came out of its quiet, dark closet. In no time flat, she was eagerly, albeit internally incredulous about it, leaning into his sumptuous frame.

And it would be nice if she could chalk that up to the need for a steadying hand after being suspended for so long. But that wasn't the case. Not at all.

She *wanted* to be near him.

Hoo boy.

A war of words began in her head while she struggled to force herself to unglue her body from his. Clayton was an attractive man. No, attractive was downplaying the reality. His lickability factor was high—from head to toe, he was the bomb-diggity. Not classically handsome, but hard-edged and almost broodingly so— like he had this fine line he walked and if you set him off, he'd be a scary guy to tangle with. It was in the tic in his jaw, and the clench of his teeth. In his deep-set black eyes, smoldering beneath thick, dark eyebrows. He had a razor-thin scar over his left eyebrow, and rough stubble covering his sharp cheekbones that gave him a dark, forceful presence. The dimple in his chin was like the final stroke of a paintbrush on the canvas of the perfect male specimen.

However, all that aside, never in the entirety of her thirty-one years had she ever been this aware of a man's good looks—this stirred by them—after what, maybe five whole minutes in the same room with him?

As quickly as that notion came, it was gone when she found her fingers, the traitorous digits, walking their way up his arm— which, just FYI, felt damned familiar.

Odder still was Clayton's reaction, but it wasn't via words; it was his eyes that reacted. At first his glance was undoubtedly filled with surprise, but it turned to what she'd for sure call suspiciously wary. "I think we'd better talk."

"I think you're right," Wanda intervened, poking her hand between the two of them with eyes that held suspicion.

Casey instantly backed away, bumping into the edge of the chair. The hard knot of pressure in her belly eased some when she wasn't so close to him. "Good idea. Let's talk. I'll make coffee or something," she offered, casting her eyes toward the kitchen and anywhere but at Clayton. She had to do something—anything to quell this anxiety. Action was always the best remedy. Casey began to head out of the room, but was yanked harshly back against the chair. Holding up her arm to Wanda, she pointed at the nylon still around her wrist.

Wanda grimaced, then obliged by untying her. "Don't go to any trouble, Case. The only person who can drink coffee is Marty, and she never has it this late at night."

Casey clung to her sister's arm, pulling her aside and almost

forgetting her earlier mission to have Wanda locked up. "Wanda—
do you have any idea just how completely nuts this all sounds?
Vampires and werewolves, and fangs, and self-healing and . . .
it's outrageous. This is all crazy. How could you have not told me
about something like this? If this is all really true, how could you
not have called me on the phone and *made* me listen to you? Am I
supposed to believe you've been living this way since before you
and Heath got married and you didn't say one word to me?"

Wanda's hand cupped her chin. "You have no idea how well I
understand the 'this is crazy' sentiment, and I guess it just made it
easier—not being able to get in touch with you much. We hardly
talk anymore, and when we do, I spend a lot of time on hold or
rushed with clipped answers. I should have made you listen to me.
You're right, but you have to admit, this isn't exactly an easy pill
to swallow."

Duly noted.

Clayton tapped Wanda on the shoulder. "We really have to sort
this out."

A glance at the watch on her wrist made Wanda nod in consent.
"It's getting late, and if we don't wrap this up, you're stewed by
daylight, right?"

He grinned, wide and breathtaking. "Right. You know how it
goes. Sunlight plus me could equal a vampire version of *Dawn of
the Dead*. Just a heads-up."

Casey snorted, tamping down a severe case of the slaphappys.
"By daylight? Wait. No. Stop. If you tell me that you'll sizzle if the
sun shines on you, I swear I'll pass out. Right at your feet."

His eyebrow rose in Wanda's direction and the corners of his
lips tilted upward. "I guess I'm the best candidate to catch her. Me
being the only man here."

A gasp fell from Casey's lips and her hand went to her belly.
"Sit. I need to sit."

Marty came up behind her and directed her to the couch, where Wanda dragged her coat off the back of it and tucked it under Casey's chin. "I know. Believe me, I know how you feel, but let's just figure this out. Clayton's a good guy, and I'm sure he has a good explanation for what's happening. I know for a fact if he's owning this, he'll do whatever it takes to help."

That notion might have given Casey some reassurance, if not for the fact that she still wasn't sure Wanda wasn't nuttier than squirrel shit.

Clayton stood before the women, hands deep in the pockets of his dark blue jeans. "So here's what we're dealing with."

Casey found herself leaning forward in anticipation right along with her sister and her friends—ears wide-open.

"I think, and I use that word loosely, you're a demon." After he spoke, he hunched his shoulders inward; his eyes squinted in obvious preparation for some screeching denial on her behalf.

Nina's sharp bark of a laugh made Casey cringe. "No fucking way, dude! What a rush. Oh, Jesus. I've never had so much shit go down as I have since I met the two of you. Seriously, every time I turn around somebody else is hip deep in horse puckey. Never a dull frickin' moment."

Marty nudged Nina in the ribs. "How about you dig somewhere deep in that nonexistent, black place where your heart used to be for some sensitivity, would you? As I recall, you didn't think it was such a scream to be turned into a vampire, and we all walked around on eggshells while you bitched about it at every turn for close to a month. Just shut your trap and give Casey a break. As a matter of fact, give us all a break from that mouth of yours."

"A demon?" Casey whispered with surprise. Almost like she'd just been told she was only the first runner-up in the Miss America Pageant. She'd expected to hear she was a vampire or a werewolf. Why couldn't she be a vampire or a werewolf, too? The way Wanda and her friends talked, it appeared they had that supernatural bent all figured out. If she weren't one of those things, whom would she turn to for help . . . and therapy? "So what does that mean and how did it happen?"

Clayton's coal eyes became evasive, but only for the most minute of seconds. "I had a vial. I'd just collected it and was heading out of the bar when I crashed into you. From where I stood, it looked like you were in the process of trying to keep some photographer from snapping a shot of a young girl who was . . . um, behaving badly—exposing herself."

Yes! She remembered that now. Lola'd had far more than her fair share of booze that night, and for whatever reason, a few chocolatinis always made her want to be naked. The problem was, it was never from *behind* her bedroom door. Casey had seen the photographer was from a ragmag and, as was her job at all costs, was going to prevent him from getting a pic of Lola that would only end up all over the Internet, minus the modest black dots covering her most delicate of girlie bits.

The photographer had gotten pretty pissy when Casey tried to get Lola the hell out of there.

"Another man tried to help you when the photographer pushed you out of the way, and right into me. That's when I spilled the vial's contents on you." He looked at the front of her shirt. "It made some mess, huh? I hope it's not dry clean only—that'll cost you—or me if you're the litigious type. Anyway, you . . . ah, you, within seconds, lost all reason and went after the guy who was trying to help. That Jackie Chan thing I mentioned," he reminded her.

"That guy was an off-duty police officer," Wanda said, running a hand over her hair.

Clay dipped his head up and down. "That I watched be single-handedly thrown across the room. Even I was impressed with the air she got on that toss. But then things went from bad to worse. I know all about what happened. I went to the police station—saw the report, through devious means no doubt, but for a good cause, and found your address. So here I am."

Casey ran a hand over her greasy, tangled hair while her cheeks flushed. She let her head hang in her hands, but asked, "And how does spilling something on me explain why I have fingers of fire and the ability to hover even a helicopter would envy?"

Clayton's answer was measured. She could see it in the way his eyes darkened. "I have serious doubts my explanation's going to turn your frown upside down."

Oh, he was a comedian, huh? She was tired. Ass-fried, and despite the fact that this Clayton had her fragile emotions in a tizzy, her practicality was coming back into focus, and apparently, so was her temper. Popping up off the couch, Casey circled Clayton. "So how about you get to the point here, because I'm pretty unclear as to your involvement, and quit dickin' around about it!" Oh, my. She hid the surprise of her insistence by narrowing her eyes like she made demands like this every day.

Wanda reached for her sister's arm. "Casey—"

But Casey turned on her, feeling perfectly justified. Yet at the same time, equally horrified. "Get off my ass, Wanda, or I'll knock your teeth in!" Shaking Wanda off, she sneered at Clayton. "If you did this to me, explain what *this* is. What was in that vial that could possibly result in this?"

Yummily reserved, he answered with a concise reply. Yet he looked as though it was a fight to keep his expression serious. "Your reaction to that off-duty cop was because of what was in the vial. You were able to fling him across the room with one hand because of what I spilled on you. It's heavy duty."

Cold chills slipped up her spine. She looked down at her dirty shirt. "What did you spill on me?"

His ultra-hot lips thinned. "I know how this is going to sound—

bad, really bad. And it is, but it isn't as bad as you might think. I mean, look, you *can* float. I just want to point that out once more—that's pretty cool."

Now Casey's lips thinned. "Say. It."

He winced almost comically. "Demon blood."

"Demon blood?" three voices chimed in unison.

Casey cocked her head, an eyebrow shooting upward in skeptical disbelief. "Demon blood." She dropped the words flat.

Nina popped her lips, breaking the silence. "Well, I guess that explains it, then, huh? Hookay, I say we go and let these two scream this out. I'm beat, and I don't think I have anything left in me for antique shopping or lame mud baths. I'm going home to Greg. So, peace out and all that shit." Nina rose on slender legs and looked at Marty and Wanda expectantly. They both looked back at her and scowled.

"Sit back down, Dark Mistress," Marty ordered, pointing to Nina's former spot on the couch. "We're not going anywhere until we know Casey's all right. Just like we did with you. Or have you forgotten all the self-sacrifice and cheerleading we did on your behalf?"

But Casey didn't care at this point whether they stayed or left— what she wanted to know was what in all of fuck was Clayton, or *anyone*, doing with demon blood? "Is it me, or does anyone else think having demon blood on your person at any given time is just a tad out of the ordinary?"

Nina looked to each of her friends, then shrugged with a light lift of her shoulders. "Um, nope."

Pinching the bridge of her nose, Casey tried another tack. "Okay, how about this—does anyone else think this joker's cheese is sliding off his cracker because he believes he actually had a *demon's* blood?"

"Clayton has to drink blood in order to function, honey," Wanda soothed. "I know what you're going to say—this is crazy—but in our world, it's like taking your vitamins or eating your vegetables, you know? It's what Nina, Clayton, and myself included, need to survive." She bit her lip and winced when Casey gawked at her. "It just is—though I can't say I've ever heard of anyone we know drinking demon's blood. I didn't even know demons truly existed other than the occasional gossip I've heard at parties, which you can't always trust. But after the past couple of years, there isn't much I'd doubt at this point. So no, I guess there isn't a whole lot we find very surprising at this point."

Clayton's jaw twitched, but his expression remained poker-faced. "Demon's blood is a delicacy—a exceptional one. In your world, Casey, it's like a human's one-hundred-year-old Scotch or a Cuban cigar. It's something to be savored. But I think, although I can't be sure, my spilling it on you somehow left you with a manifestation of some demon traits. It's the only explanation for your levitation, which—I'll say once more—might seem inconvenient now, but in the long run could be really cool."

"And her fireballs—don't forget those," Nina reminded them, holding up a strand of her self-healed hair.

And so there it was. Four rational adults, talking about demons and blood like it was normal—nay, like it was sane.

So okay, insanity aside, at least she knew what she was dealing with, and some of what they all said had to have some kind of merit. There was absolutely no denying what she'd been doing before Clayton Whateversson had shown up.

Now all they had to do was fix it. Surely if she could fix some of the debacles Lola and Lita got into, she could find a way to fix this. It was what she was good at—making everything better, cleaning up sticky messes. The only thing was, this time she couldn't clean it up with a chunk of Mr. Castalano's cash or his lawyer—which could prove problematic but maybe not impossible. Nothing was impossible.

Squaring her shoulders, Casey summoned all of her hard-acquired skills, and made a desperate, internal plea for patience. Rolling up her sleeves, she stood before Clayton, disregarding the wonky tingle he evoked that made her light-headed, and instead, dug into her reservoir of determination. "Okay, so let's just say, for argument's sake, I'm a demon. Yay me. You're nothing short of upstanding for rushing over here to tell me you were the one responsible for my—my issue. It's obvious I can't deny *something's* happened to me, though I admit to a great deal of reluctance believing what's going on has to do with demon's blood, but that's neither here nor there. You all seem to speak a language I don't understand. Either way, it's not a language I want to speak.

"What I do want to know is what we do next. I think you probably get that I don't want to levitate or shoot fireballs from my fingertips. There's a certain amount of discomfort and awkward moments to be had if you can set someone's hair on fire just because they made you angry. So if you know you did this to me, and you know how it happened, you must have a solution or you wouldn't have taken the risk in coming over here when daylight is rapidly approaching and you vampires melt in the sun." She fought the urge to snort. "So go ahead and do whatever it is that you have to and make this all go away. Just let me know if I should prepare for an act that's painful. I have a pretty high tolerance for pain, but I'm sure I have a limit that can be exceeded."

No one spoke.

Or moved.

Or did much of anything but stare at her with blank expressions.

Casey rolled her hand in the air to motion that Clay should get this show on the road. "Well, c'mon—let's do this. I have a long day tomorrow and now, to my utter humiliation, that you've all heard exactly what it is I do for a living, you can see I need a lot of rest to keep up with the kind of job I have."

Was that the sound of crickets chirping?

Casey clapped her hands together under Clayton's nose. "Hey! C'mon—let's go." When he didn't budge, and no one else did, either, that panic she'd so successfully beaten down all night long began to rise. And then a thought hit her. Demons. When one thought of demons, one thought of what? She was a voracious reader. Church. Yeah, church. Heaven and Hell at war. Angels. Ouija boards. Ooooh, scary. Raising the dead. And—and—oh, Holy Mother of God—*possession*. If she really was a demon—if she could shoot fireballs and float, and was just shy of speaking in tongues—though the night was young, who knew what else might happen—she had to be possessed.

That meant she had to be exorcised—and not in an elliptical fashion. "I'm possessed. Is that what you're all avoiding telling me—that you have to exorcise me?" She lost the ability to breathe after voicing that fear, but she suctioned in a much-needed gulp of air and forged ahead. Okay—it would be okay. She knew lots of priests. Her boss was a devout Catholic and if Lola and Lita did anything on Sunday—it was only after they'd attended morning mass. She let out a shaky sigh of relief, and looked up at Clayton square into his delicious, dark eyes. "Do you want me to get some rope and a chair?"

Puzzled was definitely how she'd describe the look Clayton gave her back. The deep dimples at either side of his mouth standing out when he compressed his lips before speaking. "But we just met. Don't you think it's a little soon to bring out the *toys*?" His eyebrows wiggled with a lascivious upward slant.

Her face flushed all sorts of red. "You're a real riot, huh?" She waved a hand to dismiss him. "Just get the stuff . . . *please*."

"For?"

She'd have never guessed he was such a dim bulb—he didn't come across that way at all. "So you can tie me down, of course. You know, when you say prayers and throw holy water on me—or whatever it is you do when you exorcise a demon. Forgive my lack of knowledge on the subject, but I only have a couple of movies under my belt on the subject, and one PBS documentary."

Wanda was behind her in an instant, gripping her shoulders, kneading them, attempting to relax her. "Casey, you have to listen. I think what Clay means when he says you're a demon is that you're a demon. You're not possessed by anything."

The rustle of his hair against his collar pricked Casey's ears when he nodded his head. This time there was no playful glint to his eyes, either. "Wanda's 100 percent accurate. That's exactly what I mean. You absorbed demon blood into your system, Casey. That means you're now half demon—"

Nina was back up again, cutting Clay off as she stuck a finger in Casey's personal space. "Hold up—I know this part of the conversation—it's like putting on an old pair of comfy jeans. Here's what they're trying to tell you and there's no Vaseline to make the point of entry any less painful. It means there ain't no goin' back, kiddo. Believe me when I tell you, I know your angst. It's a total harsh to your life buzz, but that's just what it is. You're a demon forever. So adjust. Oh, and Wanda and Marty are really good at the sympathy thing. I'm not so much into the candy-ass crap."

Marty used the heel of her hand to knock Nina in the arm. Her blue eyes narrowed. "You're as helpful as a bull in a china shop. And I hate to be the thorn in your gangsta side, but you did your share of candy-assing, and of all of us, you were the one who took the longest to adjust. Again, I refer to endless days and nights of trying to make Greg take the vampire in you back while we ran behind you, offering more support than a 1-800 number for

Microsoft desktop users. Just back off and leave the consoling to the people who can speak an entire sentence without the use of the word *fucktard*, okay?"

A cloud of fear cast a hazy glaze on the clear head Casey had clung to, making her heart crash and her tongue thick. This couldn't be permanent.

Yet Clayton didn't seem to notice how she struggled to maintain an even keel.

Where Wanda's hands had once been, his larger ones replaced them, forcing her to look at him. Which so would have been an "angels singing a chorus of hallelujahs" moment but for the severity of this situation. "What they say is true, Casey. You're not possessed by a demon. You *are* a demon. Half a demon, anyway. If part of you weren't still human, you'd have scales, horns, and from what I understand, you'd have to learn how to take on a human form again. . . ."

Scales—if nothing thus far had turned her into a suicidal train wreck, scales should certainly be the defining affliction. However, his voice—deep, scratchy, cultured—slipped away as the swinging pendulum her emotions had become arced with a wild shift she experienced by way of an infuriatingly hot itch on the top of her skull, and the semi-familiar jolting sting of electricity to her fingertips.

Her head bent low, gearing up for what she decided was probably another attack of blistering anger by the feel of her blood boiling, but a synchronized gasp from all parties concerned had her head propped rightfully back upward.

Eyes, four pairs, wide and blank, stared back at her.

There was a mouth or two open, but their returned silence became an entity all its own. One she knew meant another horrifying occurrence was in the making.

"Whaaaaaaaat?" she yelped.

Nina was the first to comment. "That is some shit, my friend. I don't think Bobbie-Sue makes a fucking single thing that can cover that up, Wanda."

Marty's hand flew to her mouth, where she stuck a knuckle between her teeth. "I can't believe I'm doing this twice in a night, but Nina's right, Wanda. We don't even have anything in preproduction to help *that*."

Help. She needed gobs of that lately.

Clayton whistled, long and low. "Okay, so maybe you won't find *that* as cool as levitation."

Wanda tilted Casey's chin up into the light, then gave the sides of her hair an upward swoosh. She blanched. "No words—I'm out. All out."

Casey pulled her chin from Wanda, shaking her off with a shove. "What, what, what!"

Lips pursed, Wanda looked around, scanning the walls of the room, then, obviously making a quick decision, tugged Casey into her kitchen. Clayton headed up the rear, stopping short in the doorframe while Nina and Marty dodged just shy of crashing into his back. They each poked their heads around his arms. "Wanda." Clayton's gravelly warning rang in the small space. "Maybe you should—"

Wanda's hand was in the air with a *whoosh*. "Let me handle this, Clay." She held up her silver toaster. "I'd do this with less abrasion, but this lifestyle doesn't always allow for it. It's like ripping an old Band-Aid off a wound—you can't peel slowly or it'll just hurt more. So remember this, when I rip your metaphoric bandage off, Case. I love you, and I'm only doing it this way because there really is no other way."

She held up the toaster.

Casey looked into it—confuzzled.

Wanda offered assistance by repositioning her sister's head so she might have a primo view of the top of her head.

Oooo.

Life really was like a box of chocolates, Casey reflected.

You never did know what you'd get.

Although, when you reached into a box of chocolates, you mostly got some species of chocolate. Maybe it wasn't always the kind you liked most—like the chocolate-covered truffles, or even the caramel-covered chocolate. Sometimes, you got the buzz-kill kind—like the orange gooey-centered chocolate. Bleh.

But she was pretty sure, when you reached into that box of chocolates, you never, ever got the kind of rare chocolate treat she'd just acquired.

The chocolate with horns.

CHAPTER
5

Lifting her chin, Casey turned her head to the left and then right, watching the distorted image of herself in the toaster, silently reciting Hail Marys. "No. Those can't be what they look like, they are—it's—impossible." The word whispered from between her lips with horror.

"Welcome to stage whateverthefuck Wanda numbered it. This is stage denial," Nina said.

"Hush, Nina," Wanda chastised. "Okay, so maybe we can figure out a way to disguise those, you know, Case? I was really good at my job with Bobbie-Sue."

"Please, Suzy Sunshine," Nina cut her off. "Knock off the optimism and stop feeding her false hope with a silver spoon. Here's the reality, Casey. I have fangs. Wanda does, too. Both Marty and Wanda shift into something even the most diehard bleeding heart would pass over at the local pound on adoption day, and they have tails. We learned to adjust. I learned to keep my fangs to myself and your sister learned to shift without scaring society at large. Don't let anyone tell you it's ever gonna be any different from here on out because they'd be full of shit. And don't try to convince yourself you can be changed back. That maybe there's some magical cure or whatever you do in your head to pacify this craziness—because then *you'd* be full of shit."

Wanda held her palm up to quiet Nina while Marty clamped a hand over her mouth and Clayton frowned at her to quiet down. She ran a finger along the side of Casey's face with a sympathetic smile. "Nina's just bitter because her entry into the world of the paranormal wasn't without a lot of kicking and screaming. It took her a while to accept her fate, and it was a long, ugly process because, as you can see, Nina's anything but rocking horses and rainbows." Wanda paused for a deep breath. "But even though I know next to nothing about demons, we *can* help you. We do know everything you're going through right now—every single emotion, every single fear. I know shooting fireballs and shifting into a werewolf are two totally diff things, but the shock of the reality that this exists is the same. The fear is the same. You have a lot of changes coming your way, but I'll help you, sweetie."

Casey, speechless for far too long, finally ponied up, swatting at Wanda's interfering hands, which without notice felt like small intrusions to her personal space. "So what you're telling me is that I'm always going to be like this. The chances I'll scare small children with my horns—*horns*, people—and fry my manicurist are high. How do you suppose you can help me with that? And you." She pointed a finger at Clayton, accusation blazing in her eyes. "If what you say is true, and that vial of blood is what did this to me, what kind of lunatic takes a chance like you did going to a crowded bar with something so damn dangerous? It's like running with scissors or—or carrying around a saltshaker full of anthrax, you—jackass! It's careless and stupid, and—and fucked up!"

Clayton's mouth opened, but Nina—go figure—got there first.

"Oh! Anger. I so get this one," Nina called from the doorway. "You're just whipping through those five stages like Marty here whips through a clothes rack at Macy's, ain't ya, powder puff?"

Casey's eyes grew hot and so did her delectable anger. In fact, the stage had a certain amount of freedom to it she rather enjoyed, thus deciding, not entirely of her own volition, to test again—in Sybil-like fashion—on Nina. "Do you ever shut your mouth? Really, you're the rudest species of cow."

Wanda was instantly in Nina's path. "She doesn't know what she's saying, Nina. Her hormones, not to mention her emotions, are raging—you know this. How about you try and be the bigger paranormal here and back down first?"

Nina was obviously giving thought to that, but it just wasn't enough contrition for Casey. Nah. She instantly, and once again, quite illogically, wanted a piece of Nina's ass to chomp.

Casey sauntered up behind Wanda's back and peeked over her shoulder with a smug smile just as Nina's chin lifted and her eyes bored holes in Casey's. She wanted to make damn sure Nina knew she knew *exactly* what she was saying. "Moooooooooo," she taunted.

Once more, chaos erupted as Nina reached around Wanda, grabbing at Casey. "C'mere, demonlicious, I'll moo your lungs right out of your fucking chest!"

"Ladies!" Clayton roared, pushing past Wanda and Nina, and scooping up Casey by the waist. He gripped her to his side like she was light as a feather, wrapping her struggling legs around the back of his waist, and securing her by clamping her ankles together with one hand. He looked down at her, his face tight with how fed up he was. "You need to get ahold of yourself. All of you either sit down in the living room and shut up or go the hell home. Got it?" His sudden serious turn made everyone take notice.

Clayton stormed past the women, carrying a bouncing Casey with him. He shoved open her bedroom door with a booted foot and dropped her on her bed like a sack of potatoes.

Infuriated, she popped right back up, her fists in a death lock. "Who the hell do you—"

"I said," he grated out with a throaty warning, "enough. And when I say enough, you'll learn you'd better cut it the hell out, or I'll *make* you cut it the hell out. The latter will be anything but enjoyable if you don't." Placing both hands on either side of her body, he stared her down. "Do we understand each other?"

Instead of cringing to the far corner of the bed, Casey found she'd far rather move closer to him. So while her brain told her to knock it off with the slutty, her womanly parts sang a very different tune. An arm, so obviously not in her control, draped over his wide shoulder. "You. Are. Hot." An internal gasp as loud as the howl of a January wind sounded in her head. She'd just called him hot. Out loud.

Because he is.

Yes, yes, yes, he was. Oh, Heavenly Father, he was.

So what's the gripe?

It was forward.

Which is better than backward.

Clayton picked up her hand by her fingers and dropped it to the bed. "While I'll admit that's still nice to hear after all these years, you're not yourself. So any and all compliments by you about me are going to be taken with a grain of salt. Now, it's time we talk about this without interference. Sit down, still your mouth, and listen to me." He backed away, standing in front of the window with his arms crossed, all forceful and powerfully brick shithouse.

Reason returned with a swift kick to her innards, followed sharply by embarrassment for her very vulgar display of wanton lust. Her cheeks grew as hot as she'd just thought he was. "I'm not sure what we have to talk about."

"How do you figure levitating isn't worth an ear?"

Score team vampire. "So talk."

"There are things you need to know as a new demon."

"But you're a vampire."

"So I hear."

"My uneducated, paranormal guess is that's totally different than a demon."

"Astute."

Casey ignored his jibe—as long as he stood across the room, she was back in control of most of her female faculties. "So what can you tell me about being a demon if you're a vampire?"

Clay's eyes fixed on her face. "I know enough to know that you'll need to control that rage you just displayed out there with Nina, who, as I'm sure you've already witnessed, has some anger-management issues and never backs down from a confrontation. That rage you're experiencing is something you'll need to harness. You're a mix of emotions right now. Part of that is due to the changes your body is going through, but you need to learn to control them. You can't set fire to just anyone—especially a human. People talk. It's a surefire way to be discovered. Not to mention the fact that if you tangle with the wrong entity . . ."

Casey's chin lifted. That sounded ominous. "Entity?" There were more entities? What kinds of entities was he talking about? She shook her head, holding up a weary palm. "No, don't say it. I'm on mystical-information overload. I think I need some time, maybe. Time to let this just sit. Please. Maybe you could come back tomorrow—or next week." It would be a battle, but if her anger was what was triggering these off-the-wall magical powers, she'd chew her fingers bloody before she allowed herself to rip anyone's head off.

Lips thin, Clay pinned her with his intense eyes to convey he wasn't joking anymore. "You don't have time, Casey. I think that's obvious after tonight. Well, unless you're a thrill seeker and you get off on the element of surprise. If that's the case, I can just go home. Which would be fine with me. TiVoing a Giants game sucks out all the fun."

Frustration turned ever so rapidly into irritation. Sliding to the end of the bed, Casey rolled up the sleeves of her dirty, wrinkled shirt. "I'm trying really hard to keep a grip on this, but here's where I'm at. I hope you don't mind if I just get it all out so we have some sort of understanding about my emotional status."

Clay nodded his head in consent as though he was *allowing* her a moment of self-indulgence. "By all means."

Casey rose from the bed and paced before Clay, staying far enough away that she couldn't be tempted to touch him against her suddenly wayward better judgment. Her voice was tight, but her thoughts were crystal clear. "So here's where I am. I've been locked up in a place where criminals roam dank, dark cells and threaten to make spaghetti out of your intestines and sop it up with your small bowel. I haven't slept in thirty-some-odd hours for fear I'd lose, at the very least, a finger and I smell like the inside of a dirty outhouse. I was in that dank place because of *you* and your penchant for aged blood—or whatever." She stuck a knuckle in her mouth to keep from screaming her horror, sucking air into her lungs.

But she wasn't done. Facing him, she blew her wad. "I attacked an off-duty police officer like a rabid animal because you had something so dangerous on you, you may as well have had a ticking time bomb. If that wasn't bad enough, I had to call my sister—a sister I hardly ever get to see or talk to because I have the job from hell that I'm too much of a chump to demand time off from—and beg her to bail me out of *jail*. And it wasn't cheap—in fact, it'll probably take me a lifetime to pay it off. I come home, thinking this is all some crazy nightmare, only to find out the nightmare's just beginning. I not only float like a helium balloon, but I set fire to possibly the most frightening woman with clear homicidal tendencies this side of the Mason-Dixon. And if the rumors are true, my eyes glowed red while I did it. As if that wasn't the icing on my triple-layer cake, I sprouted horns. *Horns!* So if needing just a little time to gather my wits is too much to ask—tough shit!" Somehow, she'd landed right in front of him, an accusatory finger waving under his long, straight nose, her voice bordering on a screech.

However, it appeared not much daunted him by his dry response to her impassioned plea. "We don't have time, Casey. First, there's the issue of the literal time. I only have a few hours until sunrise. Second—you didn't see that guy fly across that bar like I did. I say this with all seriousness. After that, you could be drafted into the NFL. The point here is, you had no control over it—you don't even remember it. And don't think I'm so callous I don't understand this has been traumatizing for you."

Ya think?

"We just don't have time to indulge in your trauma, but I promise, later, if you want, we can hold hands like they do in therapy; you can give your testimonial and put it toward earning your demon chip."

Casey watched his lips toy with another smile, infuriated by it. "In what way is this at all funny?"

His eyes flashed a small hint of sympathy. "I'm sorry. I'm not trying to make light of your situation. I'm just trying to impress upon you that we can't allow your emotions to hinder our progress. You've already displayed signs of demonic powers. It's pretty crucial you get them under control. You can't afford to hurt someone."

Those words deflated her rant, leaving her feeling exhausted with defeat. She would never willingly hurt someone, and she'd done it not just once, but twice, in twenty-four hours. If she walloped someone innocent with an errant fireball by mistake, she'd never forgive herself. Just the crazy in that thought alone should make her throw every single one of these supposed turning, shifting, flying paranormal lunatics out of her apartment.

Her fingers went to the top of her head, feeling her horns— *oh, Jesus, horns*—and she knew her options were few. The general consensus was that she'd been officially inducted into this super race of paranormals, and her new state of being wasn't going to change. Ever a realist, odds clearly stacked against her, she had to face this practically.

Casey backed up, setting herself on the edge of her bed. Cradling her head in her hands, she asked, "So what can you, the vampire, do about me, the demon?"

"I can help. Or I know of *someone* who can help."

"Really? Is this someone in possession of the *How To Be a Demon* playbook?"

His laughter drifted through her small bedroom, husky and low, surprising her with the ease it displayed. "No, but it will involve you trusting me enough to come with me. *Now.*"

Her eyes glanced at the alarm clock on her nightstand. It was almost two in the morning. "I can't go with you. I have to get up in four hours for work." If she wasn't in her downstairs office at seven sharp every day, Mr. Castalano would shit day planners. She couldn't afford to lose her job.

Clay held out his hand to her, sticking it under her nose to prompt her to take it. Oh, no, brotha. She wasn't touching him ever again. Evah. "You'll just have to take a sick day."

"I don't have sick days. I haven't had one in five years." Not even when she'd had bronchitis and all but hacked up a lung on Mr. Castalano himself.

"Today you will." He said it as though it was a demand versus a request. "Of course, there is always the chance you could levitate in front of your boss, and then you won't have to worry about a job at all. So I think you don't have a choice."

Casey snorted her displeasure. "Yeah. Choices seem to come my way in a limited quantity as of late."

"I did apologize."

"Magnanimous should be a hyphen on your name."

"Casey . . ."

She jumped up off the bed, moving around his offered hand, but heeding the warning in his tone. "Okay. Fine. I give. I'm not so unreasonable that I don't see I obviously have a problem. But I have a couple of questions before I go anywhere."

"Make it quick," Clay ordered, glancing outside her window, his eyes fixed on the skyline.

She might have made a stink about how bossy he was, but then she remembered a vampire fact. "Right. Daylight or whatever."

"Right. A sizzling one at that, but it isn't as much of a problem as it once was. When sunscreen was invented my horizons broadened. The problem is what's known as *vampire sleep*. Come dawn, no amount of NoDoz can stop it. So unless you want to free-fall until the sun sets tomorrow, I'd suggest you hold it together for just a little longer. Not much can wake me once I'm totally under."

Vampire sleep. More new catch phrases. She'd have to leave the eleven billion questions that phrase brought up and put them on the back burner.

There were other things that troubled her.

Some thoughts had begun to slowly form as this demon thing sank further in—images, not to mention the folklore surrounding demons, brought with it some frightening memories from her Catholic school days. Images and tales she couldn't believe she hadn't given any thought to at the onset of this debacle. Casey well remembered the book about demons Sister Theresa Ignatius had on her desk. She'd peeked at the pictures when Sister Ignatius was with Father Hoolihan. She'd also had nightmares about those pictures for most of her elementary school days. Her stomach took a hard dive. "Demons are—are—well, they're evil. They're not exactly winning any Nobel Peace Prizes. . . ."

He fingered the frame of a picture of her and Wanda on her dresser. "No. That's true, but not all demons are in it for the sheer joy of destruction. Some are just mischievous, nothing more, nothing less. Some were tricked into choosing Hell as their eternal resting place. Some were too weak to deny themselves the remote chance the promise of eternal goodies really does exist in Hell, and they bailed due to fear of retribution from above for past indiscretions. The flip side of that coin is, some are most definitely evil, and you'll have to learn to watch for the difference. Closely."

"And that makes me which side of the coin?" If her performance thus far was any indication—she was on the downhill run to felonious acts.

"You weren't pegged for Hell, and you weren't coerced into making a deal with a demon. You certainly didn't shun the light. This was an *accident*. I don't know exactly where that leaves you. That's what I hope to find out, but I can't do it while we stand here." His impatience with her pesky questions was clear. His "time's a-wastin' " attitude irked her.

Casey's hands found their way to her hips, where she planted them, sticking her neck out and pursing her lips. "I'm sorry to be such an inconvenience, Mr. Vampire. I'll try harder to keep my silly girlie fears to myself from now on."

Clay's face held another flash of sympathy, but it faded to the harder, more serious expression he'd worn earlier. "I think this is a man-woman thing. Venus and Jupiter—"

"Mars—Venus and Mars. Just so you have your planets all aligned," she cracked.

"Mars, whatever. Women like to talk their problems out—men like to solve them and move on. It isn't that I don't want to hear you freak, or address it, Casey—it's that I don't have a lot of time to do that in. I'd really prefer not to fry sunny-side up for lack of sunscreen, while you're feeling conversational and time ticks away. Or worse, pass out and be no help to you at all. Because when I sleep, I'm told I look like a body at a crime-scene investigation. I wasn't joking when I told you that."

A shudder crept over her arms and along her shoulder blades. If he was telling the truth, and he really would fry when the sun crept over the horizon, it was something she didn't want to take a chance on having a bird's-eye view of. Instantly, she was contrite— even if contrition was the last thing he deserved for being such a dumbass that he'd been skulking a very public place with demon juice. "Sorry. I keep forgetting—but just one more thing."

"One more thing. Any more than that, and I'll have to follow through with my evil plan to rule the world and bite you, turning you into one of my minions."

Her eyes widened.

"That was a joke." Shooting her an amused smile, his eyes glittered, and his jaw twitched.

"Don't be sad if Kimmel doesn't call you for a guest spot."

"I'll try to keep my disappointment on the inside. Now, that one more thing?"

"Where exactly are we *going*? Do demons live in subdivisions behind white-picket fences with two-point-five kids like everyone else?" Because her mental image was of a dungeon with an eerie glow created by thousands of candles and a room with a sacrificial altar where a mesmerized virgin in a white flowing gown lay beneath a pentagram on the wall, all hosted by a man in a hooded red robe.

His smile was wry. "I imagine some do, but not this demon. And we're going to see someone who can help you," he tacked on.

Casey gave him a pensive look. "Who?"

"Darnell."

"The demon."

The corner of his luscious lips lifted. "Yep. *Darnell the demon.*"

Heh.

"We can bring Wanda with us if that will ease your fears. She won't add any hysteria to the current situation, at the very least. She knows enough about the paranormal to not be too surprised about whatever Darnell tells us."

Wanda, her sister the were-vamp. Unfazed by anything extraordinary. Right. But there were Nina and Marty to think of. Just the thought of Nina made her fingertips grow warm. "Thoughts on how we exclude Nina from our little adventure without upsetting her? She and Marty seem to be a package deal, and while I like Marty, unfortunately Nina sets my teeth to grinding." She frowned, still unable to quite grasp why she had such trouble dealing with someone of Nina's caliber. "Though I can't explain why. I'm usually pretty tough to rile. As erratic as I've become, I can't promise she won't end up with a sawed-off wooden spoon imbedded in her chest. I'm clearly a danger to her, and I don't want anyone else hurt. Especially people who can't self-heal, or . . . whatever."

Clay laughed again. "Can't say I thought I'd ever see the day Nina would meet someone who can rival her brand of pissed off, but I'll make sure she goes home to Greg. He never likes when she's away anyway. He complains too much for my taste about it, something about not being able to get comfortable in bed without her to spoon with. This gives him the perfect excuse to keep his pride intact instead of calling her every hour on the hour because he *misses* her."

His scathing tone regarding Greg's abundantly clear love for Nina made her wonder if it was because Nina had to be a hard woman to love, and he didn't get it—which FYI, neither did Casey—or if it was just love in general that put that sarcastic mocking lilt to his words.

Not that it was any of her business. It was time to put her good-decision jeans on and stop waffling. "Okay—then let's do this and get it over with so I know what I'm up against." Or what new, unsightly appendage she might sprout.

He nodded, heading for the door in two long strides of his booted feet, his departure easing the tight ball in her stomach. "I'll talk to Wanda and the girls. And, Casey…you're a better sport than I expected."

She blushed, then caught herself just shy of visibly preening because he thought she was a good sport.

"Oh, I dunno if I can be called sporting. Doesn't everyone take the news like a champ? I can't imagine *anyone* complaining about being turned into a demon. How silly and shallow."

Clay chuckled once more.

And she preened because he chuckled.

Bleh.

CHAPTER
6

Loud rap music spilled from the open window at the top of the apartment building Clayton pulled up in front of. The black cement front literally shook from the pump of the bass, though the street itself was eerily devoid of any movement. Barren of much but a streetlight with a fluttering bulb and a fire hydrant that was peeling and had seen better days, the building was dark and lone against the purple, inky sky.

Casey gave Wanda a quick worried glance over her shoulder. Wanda responded from the backseat with a reassuring hand to her shoulder. "I'm here. Trust me when I tell you, I can play the badass card if need be, Casey. You're safe with me."

For the thousandth time, Casey wondered who this Wanda was. The badass card? This from the woman who'd once spent almost an entire day hiding in the playhouse on the playground because Mary-Margaret McGooken had threatened to beat Wanda up for talking to her boyfriend after catechism.

But the illusion of safety beat the reality she'd been vividly creating in her overactive imagination on the ride here.

Clay came around to open the door for her and Wanda, and Casey couldn't help but be struck by how wildly he made her heart thrash. She slid out, careful to avoid contact with the big hand he offered her.

No touching, she'd decided. None. Since she'd acquired her demonicness, her estrogen levels had risen to inferno proportions, and her body wanted nothing more than to plaster itself to Clay's—whether she wanted it to or not. During the ride over, after she was done summoning stark, frightening scenarios that involved sacrificial rites of passage involving the blood of like a wildebeest, she'd found herself all but drooling over Clay, leaning into his arm for no other reason than to feel the pressure of it against her own. Her emotional state had narrowed to but two gears. Off-the-charts sensitive and irritable—or angry and owning it like fury had been created just for the likes of her.

Inhaling a shuddering breath of icy air, Casey hopped out of Clay's pickup truck—a very large truck that also had her pondering such an odd choice of vehicles for a vampire. A sleek sports car or a luxury sedan seemed more vampire-ish, dark with tinted windows and leather seats. Definitely stereotypical, and without a doubt movie related, but this big monster truck didn't fit the mystique surrounding a night dweller, which was what Wanda had informed her Clay was, and she herself was half of. His truck was nothing like what she'd anticipated. It was a silvery blue, and according to him, in his color wheel as per Marty, and from his rearview mirror dangled a rope of garlic—fake, he'd told both her and Wanda as a sort of karmic screw you.

"I like big," he commented with a gleam in his eye, stepping aside to allow her space.

Yeahhhh. Me. Too. Casey looked up at him with guilty eyes as though her thoughts had been shared out loud. "Sorry?"

"My truck. I can tell you're wondering why a vampire would drive a truck. I like a big vehicle." He slapped the hood of the shiny truck and smiled. "It's useful—for, you know, the bodies. A big bed like this pickup has can hold a lot of 'em."

Her eyes glazed over. "Bodies?"

A snort flew from Wanda's glossed lips. "If you could see your face," she said on a giggle. "He's joking, Case. Vampires don't collect bodies. In fact, most don't even drink from an actual human—only each other. Where'd your sense of humor go?"

I set fire to it along with your stupid, psychopathic, homicidal friend. You wanna go, too? She rubbed her eyes with the heel of her hand, hoping to eradicate her horrible thoughts, giving them both a tight smile. "Sorry. I'm obviously not myself, and I'm having some rather unusual responses to situations I'd normally take with a grain of salt. I mean, I did get so angry with Nina I set her on fire. I think it's fair to say, you know me well enough to know I'm not normally so edgy or so easily provoked. But that's all gone the way of big hair and Tears for Fears. My only excuse is it's been a long two days."

Wanda threw a comforting arm around her shoulders. "I get it. C'mon, let's go see what this Darnell has to say."

Casey held Wanda back while Clay made his way to the red steel front door of the building. "Do you really trust this Clay, Wanda? Because I'm only being truthful when I tell you that I still don't know if I'm over the nuts part of this night. Vampires and werewolves? I'm just not 100 percent sure I believe you, let alone this man who says he did this to me."

Wanda's tongue rolled along the inside of her cheek, a sign that she was growing impatient. "I told you I could show you. You want fangs or fur?"

Casey licked her lips with a nervous, darting tongue. "No! I'm sorry. I am, but you have to at least remember what it was like not to believe any of this was true. You couldn't have just accepted it and not at least had a few moments of doubt." And if Wanda hadn't, she might have to rethink the butterfly net where her sister was concerned.

"Of course I did. When Marty first shifted in front of me I spent several days afterward denying what I'd seen with my own two eyes, kiddo. I was just shy of the corner of a room and the fetal position. But we don't have time for denial, Casey. You've got something going on that will keep you from doing that slave labor you call a job, and just in general living your life. You had at it with Nina. *Nina.* Not only is she bat-shit crazy, she's a hundred times more fearless than a kamikaze pilot. Even I, on my best days, shudder to think what she'd do to me if she were ever to call me on one of my many bluffs when I shoot her down, and I'm technically twice as strong as she is. You saw in the jail what she was capable of when she did nothing more than growl at that man ogling her back end, and still you chose to poke her. Whatever triggered that kind of anger has to be dealt with before you hurt yourself or someone else."

What was worse was that she'd reveled in the chance to provoke Nina. Like, a lot. She'd wanted to wrap herself up in antagonism like a weenie in a blanket. "All that aside, what do you really know about this Clay? How do you know he's really bringing us to meet a real demon? I mean, c'mon. . . ."

Wanda's head cocked and her lips pursed. "How do you know he's not?"

Valid. "I don't. I don't know anything anymore. I just know that this is so surreal, so Stephen King, I just can't seem to wrap my brain around it."

Her sister's grin was wry. "Yeah. Been to that rodeo. But I do know one thing—Clay can be trusted. He's Nina's husband's closest friend, and a really good guy. They have clan rules that strictly forbid them from harming anyone purposely, Casey. If Greg found out this was something he'd done on purpose, Clay would be shunned. Shunning's a hot mess not many would risk—especially someone like Clay who's next in line to run the clan if something happens to Greg. And he's not too shabby on the eyes, either. How he's eluded a mate all this time and continued to exist is beyond me."

"A mate," was Casey's wooden response.

Wanda's shoulder-length brown hair whispered in the breeze when she shook her head. "Forget it. Another paranormal deet that pertains to vampires and werewolves—of which you're neither. It doesn't matter if this guy turns out to be some hack, Casey, or even if he's dangerous. I'm here. I'll protect you."

"Wanda?"

"Yep?"

"Do you remember when you were in middle school and I was still in elementary school?"

"Vaguely."

"Do you remember when Nunzio Titaglioni pulled your hair when we were walking home from school and made you cry?"

"Yeah, I think so. Why?"

"Do you remember who punched him in the head with her Strawberry Shortcake lunchbox for it?"

"You did."

"That's right. *I* did. The *I* in the sentence being the operative word. I always protected *you*, Wanda. When did you go all fierce?"

Her wry laughter cloaked Casey in the dark night, swirling around her head in circles. "When I met Marty and Nina. I didn't realize how much I needed a spine until I met those two. A lot's changed for me, Casey. I'm not the wimpy woman who was married to an asshole podiatrist. Some of those changes are because of my friendships with Marty and Nina—I learned more than just how to be tough because of them. I learned what it is to have someone's back. And now I've got yours. Nowadays, I don't so much let life roll over me, I roll over *it*." She grinned. "But it isn't just that, Casey. I'm half vampire, half werewolf. That has some serious advantages that leave me unafraid of much. Not to mention, if anything ever happened to me, Heath and my clan members would be so on this Darnell the demon's ass, he'd wish the devil himself had taken him directly to Hell without passing go."

Stabs of guilt needled her. She'd have known about all of the changes in Wanda's life if she hadn't been so selfishly absorbed in doing a job that was so meaningless. To find out that Wanda had battled something as severe as ovarian cancer, that she'd turned to her friends for help, and had never said a word to her own flesh and blood, left Casey chilled to the bone and so filled with sadness. Yet here Wanda was, offering her help as if their relationship of late had consisted of more than just three-minute phone calls and a Christmas card. Straight up, she was a shitty sister and not even that stopped Wanda from being selfless.

Casey threw her arms around Wanda's neck and squeezed her hard. "I trust you. And thank you. I'm not sure how I would have handled this if not for you and your—your—"

"Paranormal skillz?" Wanda's question was muffled against Casey's shoulder. Gripping her arms, Wanda set her from her and smiled, her white teeth flashing in the deep of the night. "It definitely helps to have someone in the know. Now let's go find out what's next and how we can make this manageable."

Clayton was already at the door when a large, very round man opened it with a wide, gleaming white smile. His multiple chains, or swag, as she'd learned it was called in the holding tank, rested beneath two—no, three chins. He topped Clayton by at least three inches, putting him in at least the six-foot-five range. "Yo, yo, yo, Clayton, my brotha! Whass good?"

Clayton gave him a half smile, shaking his hand and pulling him in hard for a quick shoulder bump. "I think it's safe to say, not a lot is good right now, my friend. Though, I gotta admit, I'm a little green with envy over the levitation."

Darnell, clad in a large football jersey and baggy jeans, eyed Casey. "Sho nuff. Ain't nuthin' good about what's gone down. That her?" He pointed a burly finger at Casey, giving her a good, hard stare.

"That's her. Every floating, fireball-throwing inch of her."

Oh, label, label, label, why don't you?

Darnell paused for a long moment, taking a lengthy, squinted look at her. The silence between them pulsed with a life of its own, making Casey pause, too. His scrutiny was done in increments until she was left feeling naked and exposed.

Dramatic.

Out of nowhere, Darnell's eyes opened wide in terror. He held up two fingers in the sign of a cross, backing away with stuttering steps and emitting a terrified wail so loud, Casey grabbed Wanda's arm, her fingers digging into the material of her jacket. "She's the devil! Evil, I say—she's eviiiiil! Eviiiil! Oh, Lawd Jesus—save yourself!"

Oh, Christ. She *was* the devil. All her worst fears on the ride over confirmed, her stomach gurgled and rolled in protest. It could happen, right? If her sister and her friends could be vampires and werewolves, why couldn't she be possessed by the devil no matter what Clayton had said? What the hell did he know about demons anyway? He was a vampire. Why would possession be any nuttier than what had already transpired?

A warbled chuckle of laughter followed, deep and resonant, and it came from the black, gaping hole of the entrance to Darnell's building. When he came back into view, he was doubled over with laughter, placing his hands on his ample belly and wiping tears from his eyes with a thick thumb.

Clayton shook his head like he was indulging a small child's antics. His eyes glimmered in the dark night and it was obvious from his profile that he fought a grin. "Enough, Darnell. She's had a tough enough time as it is. I need to get this show on the road. It's late. So let's hit it."

Darnell held the door open for them, sweeping them inside a foyer swathed in deep red with only the dim light from an ornate chandelier to guide their way. "No sweat, man. Let's get it on. Tell me everything."

As Casey passed this "way too happy to be a demon," teddy-bear cuddly, large man, he sniffed her. Her gaze shot to Wanda's in question as Clayton and Darnell turned to climb a long staircase. "Smell is very important in my world now, sweetie. I can tell a human from a paranormal, vampire from werewolf, in just a whiff. I'm guessing demons can do the same. C'mon." Wanda motioned, looking up the staircase with determined eyes. "It's okay. Well, all right, it's not totally okay, but it beats not knowing, right? So let's get it over with." She held out her hand. Casey took it, fighting her fear and instead focusing on the graffiti that lined the stairwell walls.

Big swirls of loud colors bled into shapes that intrigued her, yet she couldn't identify one as any particular geometrical form.

Clayton and Darnell spoke in hushed tones when they entered Darnell's apartment with a reluctant Casey and a clearly fearless Wanda in their wake. Pictures of famous rappers hung on Darnell's walls above a purple velour sectional that took up almost the entire space of floor. The white shag carpet under her feet was cushioned and immaculate.

Darnell slapped Clay on the back, shaking his dark head.

"Didn't I tell ya to stay away from temptation? Now look what you gone an done. So you spilled that shit on her, man? Oooo-wee, and now you say she's shootin' fireballs and levitating—*already*? Righteous—a noob, too. Huh." His perplexed surprise was evident in the crinkle of his wide, heavily wrinkled forehead.

From what Casey could gather, it would seem she'd somehow managed to excel at this demon thing, skipping right through the harder powers to master, such as levitation, and had moved to the head of the class without even trying.

Her parents would be so proud.

Casey's voice, or maybe it was just the recent occasional trance she found herself in, was almost lost to her. But not quite. "So I'm not supposed to be able to shoot fireballs yet?" was the first question out of her mouth. Not "How can we make these ugly protrusions poking out of my head go away? Or, even, "Are you sure there's nothing we can do to, oh, I dunno, fix this?" No, she wanted to garner a pat on the back for best novice shot with a fireball.

Darnell rubbed his jaw with fingers covered in shiny rings. "Took me near eight months to get that shit right. Fo real, I musta set fire to half of the Bronx before I nailed that. I don't even wanna talk about how long it took me to figure out the summoning of vermin thing, and levitating? Shoot. I still get dizzy. Fo sho, you got somethin' crazy-ass goin' on. That's all I'm sayin'."

Vermin. How four-legged and long-tailed. Casey shuddered. She wasn't interested in summoning anything but a way out of this mess. According to Nina, there was no way out, and if that was true, it was time to face the music. "I have a question before we get any deeper. Feel free to tell me if I'm being inappropriate."

"Go." Darnell nodded, and for the first time, Casey caught sight of his initials shaven into his closely cropped hair.

Gripping Wanda's arm, her gaze was hesitant, but she met Darnell's chocolate brown eyes head-on. "Maybe this is too personal. I mean, I don't know if demons feel uncomfortable talking about their . . . choices. But how—how did—you, you know, become a demon?" Clay had said that sometimes trickery was involved when you didn't choose the light. Where Darnell was concerned, his reasons would go a long way in making her at least feel a bit less like she'd gone to Genghis Khan for advice on how to be a demon—a *good* one. And not good in the sense that she'd rival demons far and wide when it came to her skills for eval. The kind of good that meant no one would end up chicken-fried.

Darnell stuck his hands into the pockets of his sagging jeans, crossing his high-top-sneakered feet at the ankles when he leaned against the wall for support. His grin was sheepish. "You know who Hank Aaron is?"

Casey relaxed a bit, shoving her hands into the pockets of her coat. "The baseball player?"

His sigh was wistful. "That's him. Shoulda been me. 'Cept I was a broke-ass baseball player back then—still am. Even now, couldn't hit a ball if I drove my Escalade straight into it. Just no damn good at the game was all, but I loved it just the same. Long story, but here's the score. Some dude told me if I signed a piece of paper, I could be in the majors just like Hank. Maybe I could make some money to help out my family. I was poor. Quit school in the seventh grade. I wanted to help out Mama and my sisters."

Casey didn't know a whole lot about baseball, but she didn't remember ever hearing about a Darnell anyone playing baseball who was as famous as Hank had been. She winced in sympathy. "I have a bad feeling things didn't go according to plan."

His snort was husky. "Oh, I made it to the majors all right—as a bat boy. I was tricked by that jacked-up muthafucker! 'Scuse my language, but it still makes me hot he took advantage of me that way. Anyway, I got hit in the head with a baseball that took me out. When collectin' time came, that dude had the piece of paper

I signed, all wavin' it up in my face. Told me I owed him my soul, and now I had to pay that shit up." His chuckle made Casey's open mouth snap shut. "S'all good now. I might never get upstairs, but I do what I can to help out a demon in need. Feel me?"

A fist lodged firmly in her stomach, twisting her intestines, increasing a newly found fear. She wasn't 100 percent sure when Hank Aaron was in the majors—she definitely was no sports aficionado, but she was pretty damn sure it hadn't been, like, last year. "*When* did you die?"

"1966. Was a nice day to do it, too. Spring training, birds were chirpin', weather was just fine for practice." Darnell's expression grew wistful.

1966. Darnell had been dead for more than forty years. Yet here he was, upright and mobile. Her fingers reached for the outlandish purple velour couch for support. Clayton was instantly at her side, placing a hand at her elbow to steady her, but she brushed him off. "So you've been dead for more than forty years."

"And counting. I didn't mean to scare ya, but Clay told me you want this shit straight up. So straight up, I'm a demon. It ain't no thang to me anymore, and I can help you learn what needs to be learned. If you want, that is. I know plenty a demons like me. Dudes who didn't know what they was gettin' into. Just 'cause Satan's got my soul, and I hafta live like this forever, don't mean I gotta do no harm."

Clay must have seen Casey struggling and immediately took the reins. His rakishly handsome face, pale in the dimly lit room, held questions. "What does this all mean, Darnell—for Casey? What's going to happen to her because she's a demon? This wasn't something she chose. It was an accident—*my* accident. Nobody asked her to sign anything, and no one made promises to her. Her soul wasn't up for grabs. So where do we go from here?"

Darnell's immense shoulders shrugged. "Best I can figure is the blood you spilled on her absorbed into her skin. I told you that shit was toxic, didn't I? You spill it on a human, and that's a bad thing. Does some jacked-up shit to 'em. Now, I smell *some* demon on her, but she ain't full demon. Yer right. She can't be if she didn't give up her soul, and I don't even know if that means she's got eternal life either. Course, that don't explain her powers bein' so strong so soon. Takes a while to learn all that. Might help if you knew what kinda demon that blood you was nursin' like an expensive Cuban cigar came from."

Clayton's head popped up with a sharp motion, his large frame became ramrod straight, the muscles beneath his jacket rippling with tension. "Why?"

"If I knew where it came from, I might be able to figure out what kind of a demon she got runnin' through her pretty veins. Good demon, bad demon—in between. If she got all those powers in such a short time, musta been some powerful shit you hooked up with. I hafta go with the idea that this is like transference, ya know? Like the blood she absorbed—which, like I said, for a human is bad mojo, kicked her powers up a notch because it came from another demon. Gave her a head start nobody I know had. When you a noob, you gotta learn how to do all the shit she's already doin' in just what—twenty-four hours?"

Thirty-one, but what was seven hours among demons? Casey held up a hand, looking to Clay with eyes that had grown grainy. "Okay, so I'm going to assume the blood you had was from a source who doesn't identify his donors—so I won't ask. That's neither here nor there because the point is moot. I'm half demon. End of story, right?"

Darnell's nod was solemn, his next words, more so. "Yes, ma'am. You in now, whether you like it or not."

She'd already known the answer, but hearing it was still no less painful. The full impact might take a while to absorb, and maybe she'd have a delayed reaction, but for now, all she wanted to do was figure out what would become of her as a half demon. "Okay. I'm in. There's no going back. I get it. I won't try to kid myself into believing this can change. I won't cry and carry on, though I can't promise that won't be something I might contend with at a later date. Right now, this is what I want to know. Where do I go from here? Will I live forever like you?"

Darnell's shoulders scrunched in indecision. "Can't say fo sho. You didn't sell your soul like me. I dunno how that'll all play out. I could ask around. . . ."

A moment of horrifying clarity struck her. If she lived forever, she'd spend a lot longer single than was right or fair for an average girl like her. How unjust. Damn all eternal life. "So do I just go home and go right on living my life like this never happened until I levitate while I'm in the middle of the House of Hwang's flaming the joint because they yet again screwed up my order of crab Rangoon, and I'm so pissed I want visible carnage?"

"Hah!" Darnell barked. "That's somethin' you gotta learn to control. You're gonna have mood swings that'll make the end of yo mama's birthin' years look like one of those fancy balls. Those powers you got ain't for no beginner. That's why they're so strong—because you have someone else's shit. Now all you gotta do is perfect 'em."

"So being half demon is what made me want to see my sister's friend lit up like a sparkler on the Fourth of July?"

"Yep."

"But I didn't even know I could do it. One minute I was just feeling out of sorts, and the next I was hovering like a Black Hawk while I torched Nina's hair. Clay said it was the same in the bar. I guess, considering the air the police officer got, I must have been feeling like I did with Nina."

Clay agreed. "Should have seen it, Darnell. I'd pit her against Tom Brady any day of the week."

"And how did you *feel* when you did it?" Darnell inquired.

"Like the bitch deserved it."

She wasn't the only one who gasped at her harsh words. Wanda joined her, but Darnell laughed again with that deep gurgle. "Boooooyyyy, you got some stank on you. You were mad, huh?"

Casey's cheeks flamed while her head fell in shame. "And I don't even know why. I'm not prone to fits of temper, and I'm anything but confrontational. I'm always reasonable—always. I just remember thinking I wanted to make Nina angry. Wait, that's not entirely true—I enjoyed poking her. I've never wanted to seriously hurt another person in my life, but it's like I suddenly have this switch that turns on and off, and when it's on, well . . ."

"It's on," Darnell confirmed.

"In all senses of the word," she agreed. It was on in a million other ways, too, but how could she possibly ask Darnell why her libido was all but doing basket tosses? He was a man. A demon man. He didn't have ovaries.

"There's somethin' else you should know, Casey." Darnell's tone held a warning she wasn't much liking.

"If your next statement revolves around a pitchfork, I'm out." She only half joked, pressing a shaking hand to her abdomen.

"Nah. They banned pitchforks in Hell sixty years ago. This has to do with your . . . it has to do with your—your, um . . . I hope you know I don't mean to offend, but I told Clay here I'd just be straight with ya, and this is important while you get used to bein' a demon. So here goes." He paused, running his fingers along his bulldoglike jaw, obviously preparing next his words with care. "You know when you're feelin' amorous? Like you need a little visit from . . . uh, the doctor of love?"

Wanda, silent since they'd begun this, ran one hand over her face, clamping her purse with the other closer to her side. Her lips pinched and her shoulders squared as though she were bracing herself for something.

But Clayton was the first to speak through lips that fought a curl of a smile. "Doctor of love?"

Darnell popped his mouth, giving Clay a secretive glance. The man-card secretive look. "C'mon, man, you know what I'm gettin' at. Like when you gotta get your groove on. When you have needs that *need* meetin'."

Everyone went silent.

Clay winced again.

Darnell's head dipped down and back up. "Yeahhh, that's what I'm gettin' at. If you think the fireballs are powerful, your womanly desires will knock you on yo ass."

Swell. This just got sweller by the second. So she wasn't imagining her hormones had grown to monstrous proportions. They had. Fighting the tremble of her lower lip, she asked, "So not only can I start my own backyard barbecue with my fingertips, but up next for me is hunting penis?" Instantly, two fingers went to her lips, tugging at them in strange wonder, as if they belonged to someone else entirely, and she was just borrowing them momentarily.

"Casey!" Wanda nudged her with a sharp elbow to her ribs.

Her knees grew rubbery. She leaned on the arm of the couch for support. "I'm sorry! Obviously, I have more than just my fingertips and levitating to control." The sigh that followed was shaky and ragged. "So what do I do about it? You keep talking about control. How can I control my hormones and my fingertips and my sudden rages? I don't get a lot of warning. Things I wouldn't dream of saying spill out of my mouth before I can stop them."

"Demons have strong sex drives, Miss Casey. I can only hope you ain't got some succubus blood runnin' through your veins. Lawd, that'd be bad."

Was that like the equivalent of a deviant demon? Mary, Mother of God, how many subspecies of these loons were running around? "Succubus? There's more than just one kind of demon?"

"That's a sex demon. We got all types. Just like humans. But even if you ain't, your drive will still be bigger than it ever was. It's like bein' sixteen again times a million. I can't help ya with that part, 'cause I'm a man, and men don't get the bad rap women do when they fulfill their . . . *needs*." He whispered the word like it would burn his tongue if he said it any louder. "But that's not everything. This is really important. You gotta be real careful now, too. Bein' a demon means you gonna attract others who're like you— some not so good. You have to learn to smell the difference—feel the vibe of a bad dude and a good dude. You gotta get you more skills."

And a vibrator.

Oh, thank Jesus and all twelve *that* hadn't come out of her mouth.

Clay, though still silent, put the back of his hand over his mouth to obviously fight a bout of laughter, but he straightened when she scowled at him, slapping a serious look on his face.

"It's real important that you remember you don't know what kind of demon blood you got in ya. If the demon was a bad one, there'll be other demons that smell your scent and maybe mistake you for somebody else. Somebody they caused a ruckus with, maybe even, you know, had *relations* with." Again, he whispered the word.

That was absurd. "How can they mistake me for someone else when they see I'm *not* someone else?"

Darnell shook a beefy finger at her. "Don't matter what you look like on the outside, Missy. Demons can take on lots of different human forms. I don't know if you can do that because you're only half a demon, but if you can, you can look like whoever you wanna look like. When I was alive, I was maybe a hundred and ten soaking wet." He looked down at his belly, spilling over the top of his low-cut pants, with a grin. "But look at me now. Lookin' like this helps me livin' here in these parts. Nobody messes with old Darnell, and that keeps me from havin' ta mess with them back. Keeps me on the right path."

Wanda brushed her hands together, clearly ready to attack this head-on. "All righty, then. Fireballs, levitation, horns, and a killa sex drive. I think it's obvious you'll need someone to stay with you while you—you—"

"Adjust," Clayton offered helpfully with evident forced cheer in his tone.

"Right," Wanda agreed. "So I'll call Heath and tell him what's going on, and have him send me some clothes."

Casey shook her head. "Wanda—no. You're newlyweds. You can't leave your life to come and babysit me. It'll be okay." Or not. But she was a big girl, and she couldn't ask Wanda to come and stay with her while she tried not to set things on fire and fought off these wild urges for some dick.

"Oh, the hell I won't, Casey. No way am I leaving you on your own. Not until I know for sure you have a grip on this. I can't impress upon you enough exactly how many changes you're going to experience, and if what Darnell says is true about you attracting demons that are—"

"Bad dudes," Darnell cut her off.

Wanda's head bobbed up and down with purpose. "Right, bad dudes. You'll need someone who knows how to take care of business. That someone is me."

"And me," Clayton said, his eyes finding Casey's and penetrating them with his dark gaze, making her shiver. And then they lightened again. "You don't seriously think I'd let you do the testimonial thing alone, do you?"

Oh, sure. He'd be the perfect babysitter. It was like having your older brother's hot friend come over and babysit you. Except, she wasn't little, and neither were her womanly desires. No. They were big and loud and begging for attention. Casey threw a hand up between them. "I can't have you at the apartment." She pointed to Clayton's broad, appealing, oh so wide chest. "My agreement with the Castalanos is clear— no men. My job is to be available to the twins at all times. I get phone calls in the middle of the night, early in the morning, at all hours about the girls. My job is pretty demanding, and the two of you definitely don't want to have to go to some of the places I do because of the girls and their . . . antics."

Darnell came to stand in the middle of the small group. "I hate to be rude again, Casey, but your sister's right. You need babysi-tin'. It ain't gonna be easy without help. I already told you, you ain't startin' at the bottom like the rest of us. You at the top. It's like givin' an AK-47 to a preschooler who had too much Mountain Dew at snack time. In fact, I think it'd be good to have Clay here with ya. He knows what to expect when it comes to demons." Darnell finished his statement with a sly look at Clayton, whose face all at once was visibly strained and unreadable, yet defiantly agreeing with Darnell.

And that left Casey suspicious. "Okay—so how do you suppose I'm going to keep you hidden from my boss? The girls? I can't lose my job. It affords me that thing called food and electricity." *And ulcers and headaches.*

Wanda and Clay glanced at each other. "They'll never know we're there," Clay assured her. He held up one hand in a Scout's honor. "I promise. I do stealthy like nobody's business."

Well, if he excelled at stealthy the way he excelled at demon making, it was good. But Casey was skeptical. "How can you be stealthy in a tiny apartment like mine?"

Clay's face went cocky. "Just trust me when I tell you, I got it."

"Please don't tell me you have the ability to be invisible. I really don't think there's a whole lot more I have left in me in the way of comprehension."

Wanda rubbed Casey's back with slow circles and a sisterly smile. "Don't be silly, honey. We just know how to lay low. So it's settled. Clayton and I will keep you company. Now, we need to get back because"—she yawned—"I'm due for some shut-eye and so is Clay. And just because I'm nosy, on the drive home, I think I want to hear all about the kind of boss who won't let you have a man in your own apartment. Not to mention the kind of things you do for this family." She turned to Clay. "Do we have everything we need here? Or is there more?"

Darnell stuck his fist, knuckles facing out, toward Wanda and chuckled. "I think you all good for now, but if you got problems you don't know what to do with, you call ole Darnell, and we'll see what we can see. There might be times she'll be too far gone to think to get in touch with me. I feel better knowin' you're with her, it'll help to have someone to talk her down. Don't be afraid to call me. Aiiight?"

Wanda cracked his knuckles with hers. "Done."

Too far gone. Where exactly would she go?

"Do you two mind giving me just a minute alone with Darnell?" Clayton's request might not have appeared so out of place if it weren't for the hooded gaze he sported or the evasive way he avoided their eyes.

Right now, she didn't care if he was up to something. Exhaustion seeped into her bones with a fell swoop. She just wanted to lie on her bed with her patchwork quilt from a thrift store and not think about anything. She didn't want to think about what *too far gone* meant, and what talking her down involved.

Casey stuck her hand out to Darnell, and he enveloped it, surrounding her smaller hand with his meaty one, then surprised her by yanking her against him and giving her a bear hug. "I'm sorry you got all mixed up in this, but I'll do the best I can to help look out for ya."

"Thank you." Her reply, muffled against his armpit was almost weepy. Darnell so didn't seem like the kind of guy who deserved eternal damnation.

Come to think of it, she wasn't the kind of girl who deserved eternal damnation, either. But that was sort of up for grabs seeing as she was the first ever "accidental demon." If what Darnell said was true, it was unclear whether she'd have an eternity, but it was apparently possible.

Which meant she was an overachiever. So take that, Maria Theresa Gambini. Miss Head Cheerleader, and a constant boil on her ass throughout her entire high school years. She'd always been one step behind Maria.

But not anymore.

Who needed a spot on the cheerleading squad when you could torch a pair of pom-poms from a hundred paces?

CHAPTER 7

"You thought about what'cha gonna do?"

Clayton ran a hand over the back of his neck to relieve the tension he could no longer feel but completely remembered from his human past. If there were ever a time that tension should be present, now was it. "Do?"

"Uh, yeah, man. What'cha gonna do about"—he cupped one hand to the side of his mouth—"you know—you know who?"

His nod was curt. He knew exactly *who* Darnell meant, and it wasn't Casey. "There's nothing to do, Darnell. 'You know who' doesn't know anything's any different than it ever was."

"Yeah? Well, if I know 'you know who' like I know 'you know who,' won't be long now 'fore 'you know who's up your ass like a bleedin' hemorrhoid. Ain't the name we ain't sayin' out loud due for a visit soon anyhow? Ain't your year almost up?"

Jaw clenched, Clay fought the urge to put his fist through a wall. "Yup."

"That's all you got? Yup?" Darnell scrubbed a palm over his cropped head. "Maaan, you in some serious shit if what you told me on the phone's true. 'You know who' ain't gonna like what's gone down. That ain't fair to Casey, neither. She deserves to know what you mixed up in. *All of it.* Case 'no name' shows up. You know what that's like—that's some scary shit. 'Specially when the person we ain't mentionin' gets mad. Lawd, that ain't nuthin' I'm gonna forget anytime soon. Casey needs to be prepared, Clayton Gunnersson. 'S only fair."

Yeah. It was definitely some scary shit. "You're right. But I'm looking at it this way—she's been in jail for the last two days, unintentionally set her sister's friend on fire, levitated, sprouted some horns, found out her sister and her two friends are paranormal, then found out she's half demon and it's never going to be any other way. It's been a helluva couple of days for her. Maybe the rest of this mess can sit until she's had a good night's sleep." Which was utter and total bullshit. He knew it, and so did Darnell.

Though, if just saying it out loud might make his words true, then he wanted to offer that much to Casey. Casey, who'd caught him off guard with how innocently appealing she was. Casey, who looked at him with big brown eyes and soft, full lips while she attempted to piece together something practically that was completely impractical.

Darnell's left eye scrunched up. "Maybe, but I'm thinkin' not so much. I'm thinkin' you buyin' time, and you ain't tellin' ole Darnell the whole story. Like where you got that blood you spilled all over her. Shoot, man. You don't drink no demon's blood. So who you think you're kiddin'? I know you wouldn't drink from a demon just 'cause a where you been and how you got where you got to. What'chou doin' with shit like that anyway?" Darnell's forehead wrinkled just before his broad face lit up with realization. "Oh, hellz, no! You finally figured it out, didn't you? After all this time . . . Oh, Jesus, save us all. That's what you dumped on Casey, ain't it?"

He shook his head before Clay could answer. "No, don't answer me. I already know. Dude, that was 'you know who's blood. That's why Casey's so powerful so quick." He backed away, one hand spread across the place where his heart once beat. "Oh, no, no, no, no, no. You gone and done it now. I don't know what you thought you had, or who talked you into believin' that blood could help you with your predicament, but you gotta tell Casey. If she got 'no-name's blood in her, I ain't properly prepared her for what's comin'. If she's anything like 'you know who,' you better hope her human half fights back."

Was there really any preparing Casey for what was to come? Fuck. "Look, Darnell. I'll be with her and so will Wanda—wherever she goes, whatever she does. I've been around a long time—and Wanda's no slacker when it comes to taking care of business. Nothing can happen to her if we don't let her out of our sight. And if 'you know who' shows up and wants to fuck with Casey because of me—I'll handle it."

"Oooooo-weee, boy. 'You know who' shows up, there might not be time to handle it. That one's got a jealous bone."

"Damn it, Darnell! I was this close to ending this fucking nightmare. This close," Clay spat. Fucking hell. He'd been so near an end to this miserable existence he'd been forced to live with for more years than he could count he wanted to bash his fist through a wall.

Now, in his rush to rid himself of something that had stalked him for far too long, he'd only made things worse, and not just for him, but for someone innocent. Coupled with the disaster he was already in, he now had to try to find the kind of focus he'd need to protect Casey until her demon ears weren't so green, while looking out for his own ass. The monumental mistake he'd made could only be deemed careless, stupid, and bumbling.

Running a hand through his hair, Clay asked, "The still-human half of her, you think it can cancel out the half that's malicious demon?"

Darnell's finger wagged at him. "You damn well better hope so. I'd like to think yeah, because she's a good person from what you found out about her, but she's gonna have some times when she'll battle it. 'S up to you to try and keep that shit on the down low and help her channel it for good. Takes time to work it all out. Sometimes you so overrun with the power, you figure people owe you—'specially if you was like me—always bein' taken advantage of. You get all jacked up with it. If you ain't careful—ya lose sight of what's right."

Goddamn it. "Do you think I've doomed her to eternal life? Is there a way you can find out?"

"I told you, man, I'll poke around and see what I can see. I'll call ya if I hear somethin'."

Then that was that. Clay held out the top of his fist to Darnell, signaling his impending departure.

"Hey, wait. You still *feel* 'you know who' all the time like you used to?" Darnell looked around with clear caution. As though 'you know who' would pop up at mere mention—which, unfortunately, wasn't exactly an exaggeration.

Clay's grunt was of eternal exasperation. "Like a goddamn ax lodged between my shoulder blades." *For centuries.*

"Look, you pay close attention to Darnell. You be careful. Bad enough you got problems. That poor kid don't need 'em, too. If I get a heads-up 'bout anything, I'll let you know. You do the same. I'll keep my ears to the ground case I can maybe hear anything that can help you or her."

Clay slapped him on his linebacker-wide shoulders. "Thanks,

Darnell. I have to go—the sun will be up soon, and I'll be no good to Casey if I'm in vampire sleep."

"Uh, yeah, 'bout that. You give any thought to how you're gonna look out for her durin' the daytime, vampire?"

"Wanda's not full vampire. She's part werewolf, too. I figure she can take the day shift."

Darnell winked one twinkling dark eye. "Man, yous all a crazy bunch. I thought us demons was bat-shit, but ain't nuthin' like bein' a vampire. You take good care a her. I can tell you think she's pretty, but you better leave that shit alone." Darnell knocked fists with him before he made his way down the long stairwell to his truck where Wanda and Casey waited.

His cell phone chirped a tune he recognized and, at this stage of what was going on, dreaded hearing. Flipping it open, he said with impatience, "I told you I'd call you later, and I will when I'm settled in."

The response was nothing short of what he'd expected—difficult and argumentative.

"I'll call you later," he repeated, shutting the phone and instantly regretting his cranky response.

Clay grimaced when he hoisted himself into the pickup, avoiding Casey's pretty, round, fearful eyes. Yeah, there was nuthin' like being a vampire.

Nuthin'.

"WELL, well, well. I didn't think I'd ever see you again."

"I'm sorry?"

"Don't be sorry, sweetheart. I'm not."

"Um, I don't believe we've met."

"Oh, we've more than met," a male voice slithered into Casey's ear from behind her. "We've been—*carnal*," he whispered, harsh and throaty and way too familiar for her liking.

Goose bumps trickled along the back of her neck. "No, I'm pretty sure we haven't."Well, okay, she wasn't positive she hadn't. But the word *carnal* made her about as close to sure as she could be. She hadn't been "carnal" in a coon's age.

A hand, large and warm, grabbed a fistful of her butt from behind. His lips, so close to her ear they left the residual heat of his breath curling around the outer rim of it, moved in tickling increments. "*Now* do you remember me?"

"I'm probably being exceptionally rude when I say, um, no. I also hope I don't go too far over the line when I say this as well. If you don't remove your hand from my ass, I can't promise there won't be some hot coffee involved and the potential scalding of your most personal assets."

His chuckle was warm and silky in response. Like she was playing a game with him she didn't remember choosing a playing piece for. "That's not what you said the last time I was behind you like this. Remember the—what was it called? Oh, wait. Now I remember—'Bendy Bob.' As I recall, you begged for more."

Hookay. Bendy Bob . . . She might have had some pretty kooky shit happen to her in the last few days, some of it she couldn't much remember, and she was definitely, guiltily, up for almost anything carnal since this had gone down, but the last time a guy was behind her with even the slightest hint of carnality was when that B-list actor had tripped over her at a party the twins had attended in Hollywood. By mistake—because he couldn't see without his contacts and it had nothing to do with a Bob who was bendy. "No. No, I'm pretty positive I don't remember that. Which means you have the wrong girl. Which also means if you don't back off, a scene, ugly and very, very public, could happen right here in the middle of a crowded Starbucks full of people who just want their morning dose of caffeine minus a rather loud, possibly fiery throw-down."

And fiery wasn't exactly an overstatement on her part. The fingers that clutched her purse tingled with sharp pinpoints of electric currents. Oh, God. Please, please, please. Not. Here. Every single person behind the counter knew who she was. Knew her so well, they didn't even have to ask what her order was. She'd placed the same one for the twins each morning for four and a half years. The day didn't begin unless Lola and Lita had coffee waiting for them on their nightstands.

The unknown hand on her ass tightened its grip. His tone became suggestive, as though they'd ruffled some sheets with wild abandon, and she'd somehow missed it all. Every slick-with-sweat, hot, from-behind moment. That would make her almost a little sad, seeing as sheets and a man—one in particular—were all she could think of, if she wasn't so sure it was the one thing she could remember *not* doing.

"I think I like this whole new guise you've acquired. It's sort of no-nonsense and bookish with only a hint of the vixen you really are. It's hot, hot, hot," he purred.

Self-consciously, her hands ran over her simple but warm, brown down-filled jacket. Out of habit, her fingers went to the bridge of her nose where she pushed up her black, square-framed glasses—glasses she didn't seem to need as often since she'd been turned into a demon. She'd been many things in her lifetime—been called many things—vixen wasn't one of them. Neither was hot. Though her temper certainly was moving apace toward hot. Yet for the moment, she couldn't bring herself to indulge in trying to understand just what he meant when he said she'd "acquired a guise."

Who'd want to acquire a guise like hers? Boring, predictable, and so far left of a vixen, it was laughable. No matter, there were other things to focus on. Like her burgeoning lust to fry this man's love sacs. Not quite as sudden this time, but definitely bearing down with the potential for a gale-force flip-out. Darnell had said she'd need to control her more primal urges. So far, in the almost two days since she'd found out she was a demon, she'd successfully mastered the art of not claiming Clay as her very own vamp love toy, and she hadn't touched him once. There should be some kind of restraint award for that alone. So she tried to heed Darnell's words with teeth clenched and her spine rigid. "I don't have a clue what you're talking about, but if I turn around, and you're still here when I do—I can only hope you shaved this morning."

"Shaved?"

"Shaved—and I don't mean just your five-o'clock shadow."

He pulled her in closer. "I'm intrigued. Why would I need to have shaved?"

"Because if you don't get the fuck off me, I'll torch the ever-lovin' shit out of every hair on your body! Now, hands off my ass before I—kill—you!" Whirling around, Casey glared up into the face of a strikingly good-looking man who wore a look of amused surprise.

And clearly, from the gasps that flew on astonished wings from several patrons' mouths—her voice had risen, and that control thing she'd bottled up like a fine wine had popped its cork.

Wanda's carefully highlighted head sprung up amid the throng of people. "Casey!" She pointed two fingers at her eyes. "Look at me and calm down. Say it with me now. I'm calm and centered. C'mon."

Oh, fuck calm and centered. She'd much rather be fired up and crooked. "Go back to the apartment, Wanda. I'll handle this." And she would—after she ripped this mutant's balls off.

The man's eyes, a gorgeous, unlikely blue, narrowed. "I think you're the one who needs to be handled," he growled, the crinkle of his black leather trench coat piercing her ears when he moved ever closer. Dressed in black from top to bottom, he had a Goth feel to his attire. Three lines were shaved into his right eyebrow. Adding to his dark persona was a tattoo of a snake wending its way along his lean neck.

Casey, feeling as though she were in someone else's skin, using someone else's lips, yet completely aware of what was about to occur, felt the stirrings of a good freak. "I'm not sure you'll be singing the same tune when I tear your balls off and eat them Rockefeller style."

"Casey!" Wanda was between them in the blink of an eye— pressing a hand to her sister's shoulder, forcing her way into Casey's line of vision. "Look at me, Casey, and focus before you go too far. Try and think about yesterday when all the maid did was ask you where you put the mail. Did she really deserve to have you set fire to her spare pair of shoes because she disturbed you while you were watching *American Idol*? It was mean-spirited and totally out of character for you."

Yeah. Poor Magda. But by hell, it was the only two hours she had free while the twins were holed up in the exercise room with their yoga teacher. Still, it had been sucky mean on her part, and yes, incredibly out of character for her. The moment she'd flicked her fingers was the moment she'd regretted this crazy impulse she had no control over until it was too late. "I bought her a new pair before she ever knew they were missing."

Appeasing and doting was how she'd describe Wanda's smile. "And that's good, honey. Contrition is good, but your temper was what brought that on. We absolutely have to learn to control your bouts of rage. I vote we don't make a scene we can't fix by just going to Payless. A scene that could cost thousands of dollars you don't have. A scene right here in Starbucks—where *everyone* knows you and your boss."

Casey leaned in close to Wanda as though she were going to share a secret. "Fuck everyone, Wanda. It isn't everyone who had their hand on my ass. It was just him." She reached around Wanda and jabbed a finger into the presumptuous prick's chest. His sharp, slanted cheekbones sprouted two red spots on his otherwise cool, angular face.

"Casey." Wanda let off that warning she'd become so gifted at. Not the older-sister one, but the half werewolf, half vampire one. The one that said no matter how demon-ish Casey was, Wanda was still the badder ass.

And still, that didn't stop her. "Wanda. Move." Because if Wanda didn't move, she'd move her—then she'd spike this asshole through the eyeball with her nail file.

"Casey. No."

"Girls? I see our daily dose of mayhem and madness is well under way," Clayton drawled, tilting his sunglasses downward for a brief glance at the two women.

All of her attention, all of her focus, instantly centered on Clay. His words, no matter how sarcastic, were like divine music to her ears. His tall frame, dressed in jeans and a tight-fitting black thermal shirt that accentuated every muscle she'd fought so hard not to touch, blocked out everyone else in the small space. Placing a hand on Casey's shoulder, he pushed his way into the threesome, kneading her flesh as he did.

"Wanna lend a girl a hand?" Wanda pleaded up at him.

"That's why I'm here. You"—he pointed at Casey—"settle down. And you"—he leaned down toward the shorter man, clamping his other hand on his shoulder—"get the fuck out of here or I'll be forced to suck you dry—very unpleasant experience I'm told."

"Clay!" Wanda looked around, her wide eyes full of caution and worry. "Watch what you say," she muttered almost under her breath.

Clay's broad hand only gripped the now-wary man's shoulder

harder. "No need. We understand each other, don't we, friend?" he asked the now-cowering, not so arrogant after all, man.

The unidentified man was quick to nod his agreement, the look of confidence he'd worn shriveling into a weak smile of apology. "Completely." But his eyes sought Casey's. "So I guess I'll see you around, *kjæreste,*" was his last suggestive remark before he slunk out of the coffee shop, leaving Wanda and Casey with bewildered gazes lancing his back.

The anger that had so consumed her fizzled, but the million questions she had running through her brain didn't.

Yet Wanda was the one to voice them. "What did he just call you? What language was that?"

"Scandinavian—Swedish, I think. Maybe Norse." Clay answered the question from between stiff lips, then turned his rapt attention toward the front of the store.

Casey directed her gaze at Wanda, irritation littering her response. "You ask that like I might actually have an answer, Wanda. I have no answer for why he thought I was anyone other than mousy Casey Schwartz—or why he seemed to think he had a right to plant his hand on my . . . butt like we've always known each other. And I definitely don't know why he seemed to think we had prior, uh, *knowledge* of each other. If I'm honest, there are very few who do know me in *that way*, and they definitely don't frequent coffee shops talking about it because it probably wasn't nearly as memorable as the encounter I supposedly had with that man. An encounter I either can't remember, or forgot in a fit of passion, because, you know, I'm supernatural now and can't be held responsible for what happens during my blackouts."

Clay put his hand on her lower back, propelling her forward in the line while whispering in her ear. "I did warn you there'd be those who'd recognize you as a demon, didn't I? Yep, yep, I did. And that was exactly why I told you not to leave the apartment without one of us. But nooooo, instead, you take a chance like maybe setting a coffeehouse on fire—or worse. You're a real walk-a-tightrope kind of girl, huh? FYI, he was a demon."

In Starbucks? "No shit?"

Clay looked down at her from behind his dark glasses. "Nope. No shit."

"So that was about the thing Darnell told us about? You know, the bit about me attracting other demons?"

"Yes, and you have to be very careful who you incite, Casey. Threats of bodily harm might only provoke a wrath you can't yet handle, and I might not be around to take care of it. If I'd known you were going to be this hard to keep track of, I'd have hand-cuffed you to my side. Under any other circumstance, I guarantee that'd be fun. But I get the impression you're not into that."

Said who? Her mental gasp whistled through the corridors of her brain. She was not the kind of girl who—who—used paraphernalia.

But how do you know until you try?

Casey pressed her fist to her lips in an anxious move.

"So in other words, when I say can it, you damned well bet-ter can it, young lady!" Wanda admonished, swatting her on the shoulder. "I tell ya, kiddo, you're almost as bad as Nina is when she rages. It's like you can't hear or see anything but how angry you are. You have some serious tunnel vision. If we're ever going to get control of this, you're going to have to start trying harder and help me help you."

Babysit her was more like it. Casey was beginning to under-stand why Lola and Lita were so resentful of her constant pres-ence. Their father had hired her to escort them wherever they went because they got into constant trouble, and it was always public. She was damage control. How ironic that Clay and Wanda now held the same tedious position she did. "I didn't want to wake

you, Wanda. You were sound asleep and you looked so comfortable. You've been sleeping on an uncomfortable couch, missing
Heath, and babysitting me day and night for almost four days now.
I figured you deserved a break—and who knew I could get into
any trouble with a quick trip to Starbucks? I mean, honestly, who
would ever suspect that me, Casey Louise Schwartz, would have
some strange man accost me and my ba-donk-a-donk in broad
daylight like he had every right to?"

Clayton stuck his head around her shoulder. "What's a *ba*-donk-
a-*donk*?"

"My ass."

"He touched your ass?"

"Like he'd done it a million times before."

"I'll *kill* him."

Casey made a face at him. "If you would have just left me alone,
I could have done that myself. So how is it you're helping me?"

"No," Wanda intervened, shaking her finger at Clay. "You won't.
I don't need the both of you as a tag team to deal with, okay? He's
gone now. Casey knows what he looks like, and if she ever en-
counters him again, she can turn the other cheek—or cool her
fingertips in a bucket of ice—whatever it takes."

"That's part of the problem, Wanda. He could show up in another form and Casey'd never know. It's pretty important she begin to learn to smell another demon—and soon. That's why you
shouldn't go anywhere without at least one of us, because we can
smell a demon." Clay yawned on his last words, making Casey feel
enormous guilt that he wasn't getting the kind of vampire beauty
sleep he claimed he so needed.

"What are you doing here anyway? Last I saw you, you were
sound asleep on the floor in my closet. I think I even bumped into
you when I was trying to find my loafers, and you didn't budge."
The eerie sleep Clay fell into was almost comatose. There was no

breathing involved to begin with, but to see him immobile like that was too much like dead for her. Of course, he was technically *dead*, and she couldn't dwell on that or she'd probably never come back from the place called crazy.

Wide shoulders, thickly muscled, rippled beneath his shirt when he shrugged his shoulders. "I don't know. I just woke up and had a sense you needed me. So I came. But it's a good thing I wasn't alseep more than an hour or so, or there'd be no waking me and you'd have ended up making a morning coffee run an affair to remember for these people."

On tippy toe, Casey rose to whisper in his ear so no one around them would hear her. His incredibly sexy, dreamy ear that was right near his thick fall of hair, hair she wanted to grab between her fingers and tug hard at while he . . . whoa, Nellie. Clearing her throat, she asked, "Is it that vampire GPS thing?"

"Don't be ridiculous, Casey. You're not vampire. Clay can't sense you the way he can another of his kind." Wanda said it with a cluck of her tongue like Casey should know all the paranormal rules and edicts just because she'd been inducted into demonicness.

"Is there some kind of rule book you two might want to loan me? So I can maybe study all these magical powers you have, and I won't always feel like odd man out?"

Wanda's blue eyes rolled up into her head. "No. You just learn as you go, and I learned a vampire can't track anyone else unless the other person's a vampire, or their mate. Neither of which you are."

Casey couldn't see his eyes behind his sunglasses, but she felt Clay's body stiffen. Which was a lovely event that she should stop thinking about right now. "No. Wanda's right. It wasn't GPS because you're not a vampire, but it did disturb a perfectly good sleep. I'm old. Really old. I need eight or I'm just not the same vampire," was all he offered before he ushered Casey to the coun-

ter where she placed her order, fighting to keep her words clear
with his hand at her back.

Coffee ordered, the trio left to head back to the apartment.
Clay's cell disturbed her deep train of thought. She watched him
flip open the phone and it was obvious he recognized the caller.
His face softened in a much different way than she'd seen so far,
and the smallest smile touched the corner of his lips. "Can't talk
right now, but I promise to call you later, okay?" He smiled again,
like he was sharing some secret with someone special.

The green-eyed monster's hand gathered up her gut and twisted
her intestines. What she'd seen of Clay thus far had been anything
but soft and cuddly—funny, quick to crack wise, yes. A gooey
inside? It just didn't compute. That he shared that secret tone of
voice and that good-natured smile so easily with whoever was on
the other end of the phone made her want to scream. Ridiculous,
no doubt. They hardly knew each other.

But still . . .

When they made it back to the apartment, Clay and Wanda
took the service elevator up while Casey made like everything
was as normal as normal could be so as not to raise suspicion.
"Morning, Roosevelt." She waved one hand cheerfully while jug-
gling the carrier of coffee and heading for the door he held open.

Roosevelt tipped his hat in her direction, tucking his free hand
between the folds of his uniform jacket. "Mornin', Miss Schwartz.
You catch your early-mornin' visitor? I told her I wasn't sure if you
was up yet."

"Visitor?" There hadn't been any scheduled interviews for today that she could recall. She'd checked her day planner the night
before to be sure. No one came in or out of the building for the
Castalanos who wasn't authorized unless she was aware of it. "Was
it someone for the girls?"

"No, ma'am. Said she was here for you."

"Me?" Maybe Nina or Marty had shown up? They'd both promised Wanda they'd come take her away from her Casey-sitting duties for lunch and shopping.

"Yes, ma'am. Said she wanted to talk to you—that she was a friend. I didn't let her up 'cause you didn't give me the okay, but she said she'd call you."

Nina was closer to Manhattan than Marty was. "Was she tall with long, dark hair—really, really pretty in a scary, sort of thug way?"

His eyes crinkled when he smiled, almost swallowed whole by his puffy, pinchable cheeks. "Oh, no, ma'am. She was a blonde, but not like those blondes who ain't really blondes, if you know what I mean. She was so blonde, it was almost white, real pretty and tall, a sturdy-lookin' gal."

Definitely not Nina, or even Marty. "Did she leave her name?"

He pulled a slip of paper out of his coat with gloved fingers and read the word on it. "Yes, ma'am. Hildegard, no last name. Funny name, huh? If she comes back around again, you want I should send her up?"

Hildegard. What an odd name, but saying it in her head set her gut on fire with an odd intuition. Keeping her face as serene as possible so as not to alert the doorman, she nodded. "Please do, and thanks, Roosevelt. I can always count on you." Casey gave him a pat on the arm.

"You okay, Miss Schwartz?" His eyes cast downward to his shiny, black shoes as though he were embarrassed. "I know you had some trouble the other night, and I been meanin' to ask if you was okay. But I know you, Miss Schwartz, and I know you was only lookin' out for those two wild ones. I'm just about as sorry as anybody can be it landed you in the pokey."

Yeah. Sorry. Everyone was sorry for poor Casey. She shot him a grateful smile. "I'm fine, Roosevelt. It's all okay."

His head dipped low and he frowned. "I hope you don't mind me sayin', and I almost don't care if you do, but it ain't okay if you got a po-lice record because a those two. Bad enough you ain't got no life to call your own, a nice, pretty young girl like you, but to go to the pokey for them without even havin' some fun before ya did is just plain wrong."

His sympathy touched her. She hadn't been aware anyone noticed how little she did without the twins—or for that matter, cared. "Really, Roosevelt, it's okay. I was just doing my job. It's over for now, and I absolutely have to get these up to the girls before they wake up, but thanks for your concern." Smiling again, she headed for the elevators. She had bigger fish to fry than Lola and Lita. And the fish had a name.

Hildegard.

Pressing the button for the penthouse, Casey gnawed on her lower lip. She just knew this Hildegard had to do with Clay. Why, she had no explanation. No one ever showed up here for her—especially not sturdy, blond gals. Forgetting about delivering the girls' coffee, Casey headed straight for her quarters the moment the elevator doors swished open. Rushing into the living room, she dropped the coffee on her kitchen table and cornered Wanda, snuggled on the couch with one of her romance novels. "Where's the vampire?"

"Vampire napping."

Turning on her loafer-clad heel, Casey headed for her walk-in closet, a surprising luxury in what was termed the "servants' quarters," where Clay chose to sleep because it was almost big enough for him to lie completely flat on the floor, and dark enough for a vampire to get some shut-eye. She didn't knock before she pushed open the door, letting the light from her bedroom spill over him.

Fuckall if, even though she absolutely knew he had something to do with this Hildegard, she couldn't catch her breath when she found him fast asleep, using her duffle bag for a pillow. He lay with his arms straight out at his sides. Strong arms that gave way to hands she wanted all over her out-of-whack body. Navy blue boxer-briefs were all that was between her and him—naked. His chest didn't rise or fall, but his pecs begged for a tired head to rest on them. His chest was hairless but for the patch of dark, wiry curls that narrowed to a frustrating point on his belly and slipped beneath his underwear.

Damn his night-dwelling ass for being so beef-cakey.

Sitting on her haunches, Casey poked his chest with a quick finger. Where Clay was concerned, it was best not to linger. When he didn't stir, she leaned in farther, putting her lips as close to his ear as she could without touching it.

Whatever cologne he wore, it was an olfactory orgasm. Casey took a deep whiff before whispering, "Clay. Wake up. I need to talk to you."

His lips tilted upward a fraction of an inch, but still he didn't stir.

"Claaaaaayyyy," she singsonged again, breathy and light.

Nothing.

Bracing her hands on the floor, she moved in closer, keeping the impulse to bury her nose in his hair to herself. "Hey! Vampire—get up!"

Clay bolted upright, smacking into her, knocking her flat on her back into a pile of dirty laundry. His eyes were instantly open and searching hers while he hovered above her. "What the hell?"

"We need to talk."

"Now?"

"Now."

"Is that asshole back? I swear, I'll kill him if he doesn't leave you alone, goddamn it. Are you okay?"

Okay had so many variables when a man so fantastically gorgeous, rugged, and simply divine was hovering over top of you, your bodies just centimeters apart, as your hormones danced uncontrollably on steroid-injected feet. Casey gulped, restraining the impulse to wrap her thighs around his waist and body-slam him. "No, the asshole isn't back. But I think I have a question you need to answer."

His lip curled. His pouty lower one that she simply knew would be a sinful treat to run her tongue over. "Didn't we just go over the sleep thing and me? This couldn't wait?"

"No."

"I was almost asleep."

"Boo-hoo. I wasn't. And quite frankly, I'm not sure I ever will be again after the past few days. So suck it up, pal."

He gave her an indulgent smile. "Fine. I'll let you play the pity card. I owe you. Get to the point."

"Hildegard."

There was a peculiar, almost unnoticeable stiffening of his muscles. And she might not have noticed if his thighs weren't pressed to hers. Like, really pressed to hers. So pressed to hers they rippled, casting currents of deliciousness along her skin. "The point," he demanded.

"Who is she?"

"Why do you ask?" He was clearly hedging.

"Why don't you answer?"

"There has to be a reason for the question."

She cocked an eyebrow at him. "Says who?"

Clay volleyed a cocked eyebrow back. "Says me."

"I don't care what you say," Casey countered.

"She's no one who should concern you."

Her eyes narrowed. "Aha! So you do know her. I saw your reaction to her name."

"And if I do?"

Her eyes clouded with confusion. "Do what?"

"*Know her*, Casey."

"It means something." She felt it in her gut.

"Like?"

"Like, apparently Hildegard came calling."

"Said who?"

"Roosevelt. The doorman. And she came calling for *me*."

Clay's silence was all she needed to confirm her suspicions.

Casey pointed a finger at him. "Aha, again!"

"Aha, what?"

"You know this Hildegard, don't you?"

Clays lips thinned. "I do."

"So who is she?"

"A woman."

She pursed her lips. "Never would I have imagined."

He smirked. "You're funny."

"You're not." *Hot? Yes. Funny? Not.* "*Who* is she?"

"Someone I know."

Hugely helpful. "Then why isn't she asking for *you,* Mr. Cloak and Dagger?"

"I don't have an answer for that."

"Then riddle me this—*how* do you know her?"

Clay shifted positions. "We socialize in the same circles."

"So you're friends?"

"No."

The sigh she expelled was aggravated. "How long do you suppose we'll keep circling the airport?"

Out of nowhere, Clay grinned down at her. "Probably not much longer. I'm pretty tired."

"Answer the question and you can go back to your coma."

"I did."

Shaking her head, she said, "No, you're being evasive and avoiding the question, but if you don't answer it within the next two seconds, I'm going to be forced to light your fire, and while I realize being a vampire, you can self-heal, I take pleasure in the fact that it'll at least be an inconvenience. So answer the question, Clay. Who is Hildegard to you, and what does she want with me?"

"She's my life mate."

Casey's head swiveled at the gasp she heard from behind. One she knew all too well. Wanda's.

If Wanda was gasping, and getting Clay to spit that bit of info out had been like her trying to get into a pair of size-four jeans—whatever this life mate thing was must have some drama and a side order of serious implications surrounding it.

"Life mate."

"Yep."

"Which means?"

"Exactly what it implies. We're mated—*for life*," he said between gritted teeth—like it hurt.

Wait. Hadn't Wanda wondered why no woman had snatched Clay up when they'd been at Darnell's? "I don't get it."

"It means," Wanda drawled, her lips thin, her expression hard, "that Clay's somehow managed to avoid ever letting on that he's mated to someone none of us knew a thing about. It means he's essentially married—for *eternity*."

CHAPTER 8

Harsh.

These vampires didn't fuck around. They took marriage like a cardiac patient should take a heart attack. Crazy serious.

For all the thoughts Casey had, there was one that pushed its way through her crowded brain to the forefront. And it wasn't pure.

Clay was off the market. Unavailable. Hands off.

How goddamned irritating. How bloody inconvenient.

How dare he be so lust worthy and connubial?

Ah, but that definitely explained why Hildegard had come to call.

Yup.

She wanted to kill Casey for gettin' up in her matrimonial business and monopolizing her hunky man's time. He was, after all, sleeping in another woman's closet—in another woman's *bedroom*.

With all these rules for vampires and werewolves, would that mean she was in for a staking at dawn because she'd had inappropriate thoughts about Clay? Hopefully, they couldn't keep a tally of just how many inappropriate thoughts she'd had about him. She could be brought up on at least a thousand charges of indecent thoughts with misdemeanors ranking in the double digits.

Did this GPS also include a mate alarm for when others had thoughts about your spouse that were erotic in nature?

Either way it didn't change the fact that Clay was married, and Casey couldn't remember ever being so disappointed about anything as she was that he wasn't single.

Boo to the hoo.

"I think you'd better explain, Clay." Wanda stood above them, her tone demanding, her stance wide and stiff. The wide bow on her silk shirt trembling.

Yeah. He'd better explain.

To her libido—which was, at this very moment, preparing to sit Shiva.

Though she'd only known him but three days now, she felt as though she'd been slammed in the stomach with a Louisville slugger at this new bit of information, and that was ludicrous. So he was cute. There were boatloads of cute guys. It didn't upset her one iota that they might be otherwise romantically entangled.

But it burned her knickers that Clay was.

Glancing up at Wanda, she saw that she had that "do not fuck around with me" look on her face, which, as of late, meant an answer better be in the offing. "So?"

Yeah, so?

Clay pushed himself off the floor with strong arms, rising to stare back at Wanda, and he did so with clear irritation, like he didn't owe anyone anything. Crazier still, he did it in his boxer-briefs without any obvious embarrassment. And really, who would be ashamed to be half-naked when they had a body that was so hot-diggity? Thighs that were so—so thick and bulging with muscle? She'd grocery shop in her underwear if she looked that good in them. "I wasn't aware I had to explain anything to you."

Oooohhhh, indignation. Nice. Very nice—especially when you could pull it off in your underwear and with Wanda, who was bearing down on him with angry, flashing eyes. He was right. He didn't have to tell Wanda anything. His personal life was his personal life. She just wished he'd given her libido a holla before she'd spent so many wasted hours fantasizing about him. Not that it would have made a difference. Someone like Clay would never be interested in someone like her, but at least, if her urges had gotten the better of her, and she'd made a complete ass of herself, she wouldn't be labeled an infidel on top of being an ass.

Wanda's neck stuck out and her finger began waving in various directions at Clay. "I think you do have to explain if you're here in my sister's apartment, sleeping in her closet, and you have a mate you have to atone to who won't be too happy about you spending time with a young, attractive woman. Don't get indignant with me, Clayton Gunnersson. The last thing Casey needs at this point is to have to deal with an angry, jealous mate. So spit it out or I'm going to Greg."

Nina's husband and head clan-man. Right. Casey remembered from Wanda's explanation the other night. Oh. Clay was so going to be grounded or something.

His tongue rolled along the inside of his cheek. "Greg knows."

Wanda's brow furrowed. "He knows you have a mate?"

"Yep."

Casey finally scrambled to her feet, too, avoiding looking at the lower half of Clay, but deciding it was time she took care of her own business instead of letting Wanda, who seemed to have developed the steamroller gene, do it for her. "How about we forget all of the mate stuff?" Because she'd like to keep her weeping on the inside. "Okay, so Clayton's married—mated—whatever you people call it. That's not the issue. Why did your mate come here and ask for me?"

"I don't have an answer to that question, Casey. If she should be looking for anyone, it definitely should be me. Maybe she asked for you because no one knows we're here and she didn't want to create trouble for you." His answer was beautifully executed and smacked of bullshit. Though she wasn't quite sure why it smacked of anything but what he claimed it was.

Casey cocked her head, pushing up the sleeves of her prim button-down sweater. "So here's the bigger question, then. Why don't you just call up your mate on the phone, or contact her with your Vulcan mind meld, and ask her?"

Wanda joined her in that sentiment, bobbing her highlighted brown head up and down.

"We don't speak."

"Is this a case for Judge Joe Brown—like, divorce vampire style?"

"There are no divorces of any style when you're a vampire, honey."

This time she rolled her eyes at Wanda, pushing her mussed hair out of her eyes. "Again. Isn't there some kind of vampire handbook or informational pamphlet you pass out that answers all of your vampire questions?"

Clay shook his head. "What Wanda says is true. Once you're mated, you're mated." But he didn't add anything to enlighten her any further, either.

Interesting. "Sorry. I wasn't trying to intrude. Is this mating thing something we should just chalk up to another kooky by-product of your being a vampire?"

Clay's face lightened, his stance relaxed. "Kooky isn't a bad choice of word."

Closing her eyes, Casey ran her fingers over them. "Look, I don't want to pry. Your marriage, mating, whatever it is, is your business. I just don't understand why your wife would want to see me. And I have to admit that my fear comes from this: I'm a little worried she's going to take issue with me and, like, I dunno, crack open a vein." She made light, but it was a cover for the sheer terror she felt at the idea that a vampire might set her in the sites of her crossbow, fangs, whatevs. Though, damned if she didn't want to know why they were estranged. Not at the expense of her ass, mind you, but she was definitely curious.

"You have nothing to fear from Hildegard as long as I'm here." His words were reassuring, but hidden behind those dark, unreadable eyes was something she couldn't put a finger on.

Yet something about this was totally wrong. Call it a vibe, call it premonition, but something was missing and she wasn't going to be left in the dark if some jealous she-vamp came calling. "Then why is she asking for me and not you?"

"I answered that."

Hands on her hips, Wanda went for it. "Well, Casey may not want to pry, but I don't have a problem with it. How is it you're mated and none of us had even an inkling?"

Clay's face changed, but only a little, and Casey wasn't sure if the expression he wore was defensive or defeated. "You know how the mating thing goes for us, Wanda. Sometimes it isn't always what we want, but a necessity for survival."

Instantly, Wanda's face went from granite hard to concerned and sympathetic. Her hand went to the front of her white silk blouse, circling her slender throat. "Omigod—you were down to the wire, weren't you? Oh, Jesus. How awful." She looked at Casey. "That happened to Greg, as of course you know, Clay.

What a frickin' nightmare that was, but you're actually living it."

Casey raised a hand in the air. "Uh, noob demon here. Care to explain?"

"Vampires have a rule. They have to mate by the time they're five hundred or they turn to dust. I just couldn't cop to that. Dust is pretty harsh, don't you think? So I did what I had to do."

Grim. "So you *can* die in a fashion that doesn't include wooden stakes and sunlight? Color me befuddled."

"Mating ensures the longevity of the clan, the integrity, if you will, and the power it creates makes us stronger as a whole when we mate. It's a protective measure. I don't know where the rule came from, or how long it's been in existence. I just know. I've seen it, and it blows." His expression soured.

"So instead of turning to dust you mated with someone you knew you'd have to spend an eternity with—someone out of necessity, but someone you don't even like?" She had to say it out loud for it to make sense. This paranormal existence was mind-boggling, steeped somewhere back in the Dark Ages.

His dark eyes drifted off to a spot on her closet wall. "Again, your spot-on observations are startling. Yes, in essence, that's what I did."

What kind of Neanderthals ran this vampire thing, for the love of God? How prehistoric. And yet, at the same time, promising. It was obvious Clay and Hildegard had no love lost between them.

Wheeeee. Things were looking up.

Oh. Bad Casey. It doesn't matter whether they like each other or not. Marriage is marriage—paranormal and premeditated or not, you slut.

Wanda's lips were at her ear with a harsh reprimand. "Wipe that look of hope off your face right now, Miss. Once a vampire's mated, they can't ever mate with anyone else—ever, or you're shunned, and while I'm still not exactly sure what that entails, I just know the mumblings I've heard about it, and it ain't pretty. I've seen you look at Clay with those big, moony eyes and I was okay with it until I found out he's mated. Now knock it off. Put the panties in your mind back on, and break out your chastity belt."

Guilty, guilty, guilty. Casey looked down at the floor, studying her brown loafers, hoping Clay hadn't heard Wanda with his vampire hearing.

His snicker said otherwise. "Look, my mating wasn't by choice—I do what I want, go where I want, and so does Hildegard. That's that. Now, if you both don't mind—I really need to get some sleep." With that, he gave Casey a shove out of the closet with a gentle hand and closed the door firmly shut, ending the possibility for a more thorough investigation.

Turning to Wanda, her eyes were wide. "Is that really true? If he, you know, does it with someone else, he can be shunned?"

Clay popped the door open again. "Yes. It's true. So I'm hoping you'll take pity on me, realizing that sort of rule can be a lot of stress for a guy like me—exhausting, in fact—and let me get some damned sleep." He winked before he shut the door again.

Casey grabbed Wanda's hand and dragged her back into the living room. "So he has to live forever and never have sex? Ever?" How depressing. She might not be having sex this very moment, but she had high hopes for the future—like someday, when she found the right person. But to be denied eternally? People joked all the time about not having sex in forever, but it was metaphoric. If Clay said it, it was literal.

How abundantly crappy.

"First of all, I've heard about some of these arrangements between vampires, and yes, they're all out of necessity and the desire for eternal life. Personally, I think I'd rather just off myself than be tied to a man I didn't want anything to do with. But I don't judge because I haven't been around as long as some. Second of all, how do we know Clay's not having sex with this Hildegard? She is his wife, essentially, and he is a *man*. You know how that goes. Sometimes it isn't about love, but need."

While Wanda spoke, Casey's fingers had latched onto a pear in the fruit bowl she always left full on the coffee table. Hearing her sister's words, toying with the idea that Clay was possibly bedding this woman, made her insane.

Unjustifiably insane.

"Sometimes it's just about scratching an itch," Wanda continued, "and unless this Hildegard is butt ugly, I guess whatever differences they have Clay manages to overlook when he's, you know, wobbling her eyeballs. You don't have to talk or even like each other to wonk."

Rage, pure and sweet, blinded her to everything else. Where it'd come from or how it had gone from zero to sixty in such a short amount of time, Casey couldn't say—but it did make a hella mess.

Because she'd crushed the pear with her hand.

Just one hand.

Juice and the pulp of the green fruit ran down her wrist and onto the floor.

"Casey?"

Immediately, she was contrite. "Shit. Sorry."

"What is wrong with you?" Wanda called over her shoulder, making a beeline for the kitchen. The slam of a drawer was like cold water being dumped over her head. Wanda came back with a dish towel and began to sop up the mess. "So what set you off this time?"

Clay and Hildegard locked in an embrace filled with passion, long limbs with her flowing white-blond hair tangled around them. No. She couldn't admit that. That she had anything to admit at all left her incredulous. So she turned the tables. "Do you have to live by the same rules, Wanda? Because you're only half vampire."

Kneeling down, she scooped up a handful of exploded pear. "Yep, I do."

She held her hand up while Wanda wiped it off as though she were a child. "But that's insane. What if you and Heath drift apart two hundred years down the road and you want out? We're not talking about signing on for the average human marriage of maybe fifty years. We're talking forever. Like, love you long time, Joe."

When Wanda stood back up, she smiled. "First of all, if you go into marriage thinking there's always a way out called divorce, you might as well not get married. Second of all, who would evah want to part with the man who sacrificed his life for yours? And third, Heath rocks the sheets. My sheets didn't rock much when I was first married—I don't plan to give that up. Not now. Not ever. And if Heath were to want out—I'd hunt his ass down, and drag him back home. Oh, and I'd make Nina come with just to make sure I did it right." She grinned.

Laughter burst from Casey's lips for the first time in what felt like days. "Wow. That's pretty deep. You didn't ever talk about the ex like that."

"That's because the ex never made me feel like that. I didn't know you *should* feel like that. The bonding ritual is deep, sweetie, and yes, it's a forever thing—but with the right person, someone who fulfills all of your needs, yet lets you be who you are without interference, and, let's be real here, boinks like a dream . . . Well, there's nothing like it, bar none."

Her breath caught in her throat. That kind of devotion, or longing for it, wasn't something she spent much time dwelling on since her college days. But seeing Wanda's face when she talked about Heath, hearing the conviction in her voice about her choices, made Casey feel very lonely.

Her sister had this life, albeit unconventional, and it was filled with rich textures and bright hues she could almost reach out and touch when Wanda spoke of them. She had good friends and a husband she was so obviously wild about.

As isolated as that made her feel—it also made her smile. Wanda deserved only great things after the kind of divorce she'd had—the type of man she'd been married to. It made Casey so glad tears stung her eyes. She reached out for Wanda and hugged her hard. "I'm sorry I missed out on so much, Wanda. I'm sorry this was the way we ended up seeing each other again. I'm sorry I didn't see you get married, and I'm sorry I wasn't there for you when you were sick. If I had known—I would have told you how sorry I was—am."

Cupping her cheeks, Wanda winked a blue eye at Casey. "Well, we're together now, and I think I can almost understand why it's so hard for you to do much but take your next breath with those twins. I didn't think that cell phone would stop ringing yesterday for the amount of times they called you. Do they do anything on their own?"

The embarrassment she felt about the lengths she had to go to in keeping the twins out of trouble and in line was mortifying on so many levels. But that feeling hadn't ever been as acute as it was now. Her laughter was tinged with bitterness this time. "Not often, and if they do, it's usually bad and ends up in a four-page spread in *Star* magazine. But I love them regardless—even if that means nothing to them."

"So how did this happen? I mean, this job. I thought after all the bouncing from major to major in college, when you found teaching, you'd finally made a decision. What happened to getting your teaching certificate at that private school?"

"That's sort of where it started. I was working as an aide at the very exclusive school Lola and Lita attended. They were always in

131

some kind of trouble, but for whatever reason, I was able to stay one step ahead of them most of the time. Their father, my boss, Mr. Castalano, took notice of it and made me an offer I couldn't refuse. My money was running out. I wasn't going to be able to get my degree at the rate I was going because I did so much of that bouncing—so I bit, thinking I could work days and go to school at night." And that *was* how it had started—sort of . . .

"Who could shit at night when those two are always up your ass?" Wanda's face screamed distaste.

Casey shrugged in response. "I didn't realize how demanding it would be. At first I was just shuffling them back and forth to school, and making sure they did their homework—I was almost like a nanny—but when the girls graduated and had some freedom, it became a free-for-all. Time slipped away, and here I am." Yeah. Here she was. Ashamed, undereducated, belittled by two women who had everything handed to them on a silver platter via her hand. Yet they had no purpose, no plans for the future other than the next party given by their newest fascination—rappers. The hotter on the music charts, the better.

Wanda brushed a strand of hair out of her face. "Casey. You don't have to do this—be treated like some gofer. You went to *jail* for those young women, and they didn't do a damn thing to stop it. I want to know why they didn't call your boss and have you bailed out. He certainly has the money. No, wait. I know exactly why those two didn't do a single thing to help you, and you do, too. Because it was easier to let you take the fall than have to deal with their father. And that's bullshit. Look, I can help you go back to school. I'm not poor. So tell me where, when, and how much. Please. No amount of money is worth those two."

The shake of Casey's head was firm. "Nope. It was me who spent far too much time dicking around about choosing a major. Mom and Dad told me I needed to get it together, and I didn't.

They only had so much cash to throw around, and I used my fair share. I don't want handouts." She'd had those—just once in her foolish youth. They'd brought a misery she'd rather not revisit. They were part of the reason she worked for the Castalanos to begin with.

"Then call it a loan."

"I'm not calling it anything. I don't want your money, Wanda. I got myself here, I'll get myself out." Someday. Though, since she'd been in the big house, her patience for someday had come to a screeching halt. She'd gone to a lot of extremes for the twins, but being holed up in the slammer for a night, not to mention now having a criminal record for defending them, was above and beyond. It was time to reevaluate.

Once she was done figuring out this demon thing.

And speaking of—the almost unbearable itch on the top of her head drew her clean hand to her scalp. Good. Fantastic. Her horns had arrived. She went to the kitchen in humiliated silence to wash her hands.

"I gotta say those are even stranger than Marty's tail. I thought I'd seen it all until I saw those." Wanda leaned over her shoulder, handing her a fresh towel.

A tail . . . No. Not going there. "Speaking of strange. I just had a thought—care to explain the five-hundred-year rule?"

"Vampire tradition says you must mate when you reach the age of five hundred—in vampire years, that is—or you turn to dust."

"So when did Clay turn five hundred?"

Wanda frowned. "You know, I don't know. I don't know a whole lot about Clay other than Greg trusts him, and as a result, we all do, too. But I think I'll poke around a little and find out."

"Don't do that on my account," Casey said with far more haste than she was comfortable with.

Wanda was quiet for a moment until her hand came to rest on

Casey's forearm. "I know you find him attractive, but I'm going to give you a really serious warning. This isn't just from your older sister, but from another vampire. Do. Not. Canoodle. With. Him. Understood? I don't know who this Hildegard is, or what kind of temperament she has despite Clay's claim they each do as they please, but I can tell you, if she's easily cranked, hell could ensue. Think Nina. . . ."

Yeah. Nina. Casey shuddered. "About Nina. You said Greg had been in the same predicament Clay was. Did he have to marry Nina to save himself? I can almost—*almost*—see his imminent death as a good enough excuse."

Wanda barked a laugh. "Nina made him mate with her, yes, but he was already head over heels for her anyway. When they met, he was nearing his five hundredth birthday. He just neglected to tell Nina that until almost the eleventh hour. So she forced his hand, but it wasn't just to save him—she was in luuuuurve." Her chuckle was the kind reserved for a fond memory.

A strange one, but fond nonetheless.

Casey's cell phone chirped to the tune of Kenny G, signaling the girls calling, probably wanting their coffee. She sighed, racing for her phone. "I have to run, Wanda. If the twins don't have their coffee the moment they wake up, things get off to an ugly start."

Wanda hurried behind her as Casey made her way to the door, pulling a colorful scarf off her blazer. She tossed it at Casey. "It's a good thing I'm not their personal assistant. Things would get ugly all right, right after I took them over my knee and spanked them. Here, put this around your head—you know, to hide your—"

"Oh, Jesus. My horns!"

"Slow down, Case. The world won't end if those two don't have their coffee handed to them the moment they realize they're still breathing." Wanda grabbed her arm, demanding she catch her breath.

Casey's smile was crooked. "No, the world won't stop, but I'll hear about it until I want to take my own life just to get away from them. So in the interest of keeping them pacified—I gotta go. I'll see you later. Oh, and if you still think I need a babysitter, I hope you're up for a long night. The girls have a party to go to this evening—a club opening downtown. Some rapper or another. So put your dancing shoes on, and bring earplugs. If your ears are as sensitive as Nina's, they're in for a bass-thumping smorgasbord."

Gripping her shoulders, Wanda gazed down at her sister. "You be careful, and don't leave this building unless you tell me. And don't forget about what I said about Clay. If this Hildegard shows up—send her to me. I'll take care of it."

Flying out the door, Casey had just enough time to say a quick prayer that Hildegard wouldn't show up—for her or Clay. She didn't want to see her blond bit of fabulousness.

It infuriated her that this woman simply existed—like, to the depths of a place she didn't understand. An emotion she couldn't quite recall ever having over a man who wasn't available. A man she'd known just a few days.

And that made no sense.

No man was that hot—or worthy of that kind of all-consuming jealous anger.

Yet, Casey now found that the fear she'd experienced at the idea Hildegard might come and throw down with her was gone.

All that was left was an insatiable need to wrap her fingers around the throat of the woman who'd ruined her chances of ever slamming Clay.

She looked around with caution before entering the main apartment, as though someone could hear the naughty thoughts she was thinking.

And then she turned red.

* * *

"HOLY ho—would you look at your little sister, Wanda? All
grown-up. What happened to your knee socks and plaid skirt, little girl?" Nina crowed from the middle of Casey's living room.

Casey sauntered out of her bedroom to stand in front of Nina
and Wanda, half marveling that she was actually able to remain upright in four-inch red stilettos. But at the same time, not amazed
at all that she could strut in them like she was working a catwalk.
And yep, that was frickin' odd—and not. Again with the same
mixed, warring emotions churning inside of her, she came to
stand in front of Nina. "They're in the same place you apparently
rummage for all of your clothing, Nina. You know, the Dumpsters
out back?"

Wanda flung up a hand at Nina to keep her from responding,
and then her head cocked to the left, her eyes scanning Casey's
outfit from head to toe. She stopped at the button she'd purposely
left open between her breasts. The button she'd paused at in the
mirror and flicked back open with two fingers like she'd always
done it. "Uh, wow."

She smiled, slow and with a hint of coy. "You like?"

"Well, I'll give you this much, that red shirt is definitely in
your color wheel. Do you always dress like this when you have
to tag along after those spoiled brats?" Wanda asked, bending at
the knees to tug down the very short, black miniskirt Casey had
poured herself into.

Don't. Be. Ridiculous. She faltered. "Not always. No. But it is
a club opening, and I'll stick out like a sore thumb if I dress the
way I usually do. So I spiced it up a little." She'd come back late
this afternoon with a strange, driven purpose to shed her predictable, "worn out of ease" clothes for something more grown-up.
Something that said she was all woman. All while she'd curled her

hair so it fell in soft waves around her face, and even while she'd put on a damn near cement mixer full of makeup, Casey'd been determined to spruce up her assets. Looking down at her breasts, ensconced in a torture device called the Miracle Bra, she decided her assets were cooperating.

"Whore-up, spice-up. Same diff, right?" Nina asked.

Casey cast a scathing glance up and down Nina's body, smirking at her well-worn jeans and a sweatshirt that read "I Fucking Love to Cuddle." "To the crass like you, Nina. Yes. Yes it is."

Wanda must have made Nina promise to be on her best behavior. It was evident in the way she scrunched her face up and clenched her fists, but made no move to play Mr. Potato Head with her face and put her nose where her eyes should be.

Wanda clucked her tongue in warning. "Both of you—quit. Casey, be nice to Nina. I know she pushes your buttons, but she's really good at spotting trouble, and she can help handle any problems that crop up if we need to deal with another one of these demons. Her sense of smell is much better than mine is at this point in my paranormal journey. So consider her an ally, and shut it. Nina? You lay off the insults, and do what you came here to do—be scary."

Casey gave Nina a catty smile. "Let me grab my purse and we'll go."

"While you're at it, maybe you should grab a needle and thread to sew up the front of your shirt," Nina mocked.

Pivoting on her thin high heels—yes, *pivoting*—she still couldn't get over what a pro she was at this—Casey sucked in her cheeks and, thought, yeaaaah, she was going there. "While you're at it, maybe you can stop at the local homeless shelter, and see if they're open to bidding for a night with you? While you're there, you might find something to wear, too, eh?"

Nina was on her in the second it took to almost get out a

full mental pat on the back she was going to give herself for her quick, snark-o-licious response. "Wanda," she spat between white, clenched teeth, cornering Casey. "I know I promised to try and remember Princess here's in a bad way, but she really needs a beat down."

And then in a flash, Wanda was on Nina, a hand on her collarbone. "Back off this instant, Nina! And Casey, once more, shut it. I can only handle one mouth at a time." She gave Casey a sharp shove toward the door just as the doorbell rang.

Shaking off the desire to make Nina wish she were still capable of dying, Casey yanked the door open to find an exasperated Lola and Lita. Their faces held sour expressions until they perused her outfit. "Omigod, Casey. What *are* you wearing?" Lita looked confused.

"Clothes." Of course they'd have something to say about her crude attempts to look less like a spinster and more like she actually belonged at a party featuring the elite company the twins kept. Why she hadn't given thought to what the girls would say about her attire escaped her when she'd dressed.

Oh, wait. Now she remembered. When she'd decided to add some flava to her wardrobe, she hadn't given a single fuck what the girls would think.

Lola chewed at the tip of her fake nail. "Yeah, what happened to those ugly shoes and your navy blue sweater with the butterfly embroiled on it?"

"*Embroidered*, you twit," Casey chastised almost as rapidly as she regretted calling Lola a rude name.

Lita puffed her cheeks out, stroking her platinum ponytail. "Whatever, Casey. If you wanted to play dress up, you could have at least asked to borrow something of ours. This"—she plucked the sleeve of Casey's red fitted shirt with the upturned collar—"is so trailer park."

Lola nudged Lita with a sharp elbow and a scrunch of her pert, freckled nose. "Don't be a tard, Lita. She can't wear our stuff because she's not a size zero."

"Well, if I could, at least then I'd match your IQs," Casey drawled, "added together, that is." She came so close to cracking Lola's twiglike leg, her pump had lifted an inch off the ground before she even realized it.

Nina was beside her in what must have been the equivalent of a vampire second. "Oh, look, Wanda. It's the Double-Knit twins. Wonder twin powers activate, and all, right, kids?" she snarked, but the joke fell on not just deaf ears, but ears that would never in their wildest dreams imagine someone was cracking wise about them.

Lola piped up. "And *who* are you?"

"Your new bestest friend, blondie. Hope your limo has enough room so I can sit riiiight between you two. You know, so we can be all girlie on our way to this club." Nina threw an arm around Lola and grinned, running her knuckles over Lola's perfectly coifed hair.

Lita's round blue eyes, decked out with false eyelash extensions, rolled. "You have to be invited, and I'm pretty sure Lil' Milf wouldn't have someone like *you* on the list."

Nina caught her pert nose between two fingers and yanked. "Oh, you'd be surprised. Me and Lil' Milf are pretty tight. So c'mon, let's do this." Giving a slight shove, she sent Lola out the door. But not before Casey could mouth the words *thank you*. Because Nina had kept her from throttling them, and if she throttled them, she'd be fired. This not five minutes after she'd wanted to rip Nina's head off her neck.

God, she was an absolute train wreck.

Wanda threw on her coat with a glance at Casey. "I did tell you Nina was a strong ally, didn't I? If anyone can handle those two bitches, it's Nina."

Yadda, yadda yadda.

Wanda's face held impatience and a tinge of haughtiness when she gave Casey a final once-over. "Let's get this over with. Clay said he'd meet us there and be inconspicuous."

A shiver of anticipation zinged up her spine.

How exhilarating to ponder what Clay would think of this kittenish Casey.

Me-ow.

Even if he had a wife.

"So I'm guessing you don't approve of my outfit," Casey said as they stepped onto the elevator. There was still a vestige of the levelheaded Casey in that question, and while she recognized it, that recognition went as quickly as it came.

"I don't have a right to approve or disapprove, Casey Schwartz. You're thirty-one years old. You can do as you please. Even if what you please is revealing and incredibly *obvious*." Her lips compressed into a thin line, and her perfectly arched eyebrow cocked upward.

"Says the woman in the turtleneck and linen slacks."

"No. Says the woman who doesn't dress like she needs the money."

Ouch. Okay. So this wasn't the norm for her, but to a degree, it felt right. It felt like a second skin. Or maybe that was just because her skirt was so tight.

"So can you still breathe when your ta-tas are under your chin?"

Casey threw her head back and laughed, briefly relieved. "It's definitely an all-out event."

When the doors of the elevator popped open, Wanda grabbed her arm just as they exited the elevator. "You watch yourself tonight, Casey. You don't much look like a personal assistant dressed like that. I imagine Nina and I will spend more time fighting men off you than protecting you from potential demonic harassment. And mind your temper. If you could see the look on your face when you go full-on freak . . ."

Casey waved her off with two fingers, heading toward the lobby doors, and winking at Roosevelt, whose placid smile exited his face when she winked.

She just didn't get what all the worry was about. It'd be fine. She'd go—do her babysitting duties—run to and from the bar until the wee hours of the morning like the lackey she was—come home and collapse, only to begin all over again in the morning.

Nobody would notice little old Casey Schwartz. Dressed all slinked out or not.

No one ever did.

CHAPTER 9

It'd be fine. Yep, that was exactly what she'd thought before getting off the elevator and into the limo with the girls.

Probably, this wasn't so fine, she mused.

But alas. She didn't much care, either.

She was having way too much fun to care.

In fact, she'd stopped caring where the twins were, and if the paparazzi was taking pictures of them butt-ass naked, holding crack pipes while they snorted white lines of cocaine from one of the snazzy glass tabletops cluttering the outskirts of the dance floor. She didn't care where Nina and Wanda were, either. Though last she'd seen them, a very large, lanky man with many, many rings on his fingers was teaching Wanda how to do Destiny's Child "Bootylicious." And she hadn't seen the very married Clay anywhere.

That was probably just as well due to the fact that she was feeling very much alive, very empowered, and especially decadent.

Decadent and Clay was a combo that was ripe with the threat of her potential death if Hildegard found her.

The throb of the music had taken hold of her, pulsing in the pit of her stomach until all she could hear was the heavy beat and the call of its cadent rhythm.

Sipping on her festive pink drink with the multicolored paper umbrella, she took another turn around the pole, wrapping her leg around it as though she'd greased some steel in her time. Which, for the record, was so inaccurate. Oh, sure, she'd seen them at different parties. They'd been all the rage for quite some time now—poles and cages where guests danced, or hired dancers to entertain partygoers.

But she'd never, ever actually considered trying one on for size.

Who knew it would be such a perfect fit?

Who knew swinging around on one of these could be so freeing?

"Caseeeeey!" Wanda yelped, pushing her way through the crowd of gyrating bodies to clear some room for her to stand in front of the stage the pole was on. "You get down from there right now! You're behaving like a—a—"

"Hootch, Wanda," Nina yelled, staring down Casey, who gave her a catlike smile over the rim of her glass. "Go on. Call it like you see it. I got yer back if she gets feisty." She crossed her arms over her chest and popped her lips.

"If you make me get up on this stage, Casey Schwartz, I promise there'll be bloodshed!" Wanda pounded her hand on the stage, slapping it with a rapid thump.

But Casey paid no never mind to Wanda, or even Nina. She was too lost in this new discovery. She might have just found a new way to make a living that didn't entail chasing after grown women who couldn't wipe their own noses if she wasn't running behind them with a box of tissues.

And it was exhilarating.

Taking another swing around the pole, her eyes scanned the crowd that had begun to gather, comprised mostly of men.

Rich, available men.

Boy howdy.

Wait. Whoa. Since when had she placed a price tag on a man? She'd never, in all the time she'd worked for the Castalanos, ever abused the kind of wealth and privilege she was exposed to on a daily basis. She met all sorts of mega-bucks in her line of work. Bankers, lawyers, celebrities, and it had never occurred to her to entertain the idea that one of these men could be hers.

Until tonight. Until this very second.

As the mob of men began to cheer, she teetered over to the edge of the stage and set her drink down. Looking over her shoulder, she placed a coy finger between her red, pouty lips and winked, eliciting a roar of thunderous approval.

And if she were to be honest with herself, it had a certain bangin' adrenaline rush to it.

Each step she took back toward the pole, each swish of her ass, was a sure sign she was a step closer to imminent disaster. The problem was, this place she was in was a place where she didn't give a Flying Wolenda.

And fleetingly, she then thought, that—yes, *that*—was a bad, bad thing.

But that was just two seconds prior to her launching herself at the pole.

Suddenly, she was one with the steel, twirling around it like she was fingers on a swizzle stick. Speaking of fingers, they'd latched onto the pole as though they'd come home again. Each digit worked its way along the cool silver, climbing higher with expertise, all while stretching her free leg out to swirl downward. This from a woman who had been booted out of ballet class because she couldn't get her feet into something as simple as first position without falling over—and that was while she held on to the ballet bar.

Heh.

Eyes closed, head thrown back, Casey relished the swell of cries from the audience she'd gathered at her feet, opting to ignore the ones littered with screeching panic from a wide-eyed Wanda.

Well, until she hit bottom and landed on something hard and pointy, that is.

Stretching her neck upward, her eyes took in Clay.

Oh. He was pissed.

"Rethinking your career path?"

Her eyes scanned the floor beneath her, now littered with a sea of dollar bills. Casey's hand slid along the floor, scooping up a handful of cash with a demure pout. "Are you here to poop on my party?"

His face was hard in the flash of the strobe light. "Oh, I don't think I'm the one who's going to be the poop in this equation. But if I were you, I'd get up now. You know, before any more, how should I say this, uh, unflattering pictures are taken of you. Though, the lighting is very flattering to your coloring."

Lightbulbs flashed everywhere, raining the glaring reality of what she'd been doing down on her parade.

With the grace of a cat, she swung her legs around behind her and pulled herself up, using the pole for leverage, giving the crowd a broad smile and a quick curtsy before grabbing Clay's hand and dragging him down the back exit stairs.

He halted her just as they came to a long, dimly lit hallway, whirling her around to press her to the wall with a not-so-gentle shove. Lips a thin line, sultry dark eyes narrowed, Clay bore down on her. "What the hell is wrong with you? Jesus Christ, Casey—do you have any idea how bad that looked?"

Her grin was mischievous. Holding up her hand, she crinkled the wad of cash she'd gathered. "I'd say it must've looked pretty good."

Clay's hand yanked the money from her fist and threw it on the ground, where it fell with an echoing rustle of paper against concrete floor. "Listen up, little girl. Making a spectacle of yourself at a high-profile rapper's party isn't exactly showing a whole lot of self-control, now, is it? Not only will you lose your job, but if I can't get my hands on everyone with a camera, you'll be splashed all over the front of some ragmag. You'd better goddamn well hope the three of us can get ahold of those photographers, Casey. They ate your raunch up like it was an ice cream sundae."

His anger sent a wave of shivers from the tips of her heeled toes to the top of her teased head.

Rawr.

While momentarily she thought about how insane provoking him and being turned on by it was, she also wasn't able to stop herself from wondering what it would be like if he ate *her* up like an ice cream sundae.

"You know," she drawled, slow, sensuous, accentuating each word, "you're spankin' hot when you're angry."

His jaw lifted, revealing the sharp edge to it—a hard line of flesh she wanted to nip at. "You know, you're not when you're behaving like you're vying for the top spot in a 'Paranormals Gone Wild' video."

The chuckle she let go came from deep within while her finger traced a line down the lean length of his cheek. "I don't think you mean that." She followed her bold statement with a flutter of her overly mascara'd eyelashes, fleetingly grateful they didn't stick together.

His teeth, white and clenched, allowed little room for words, but the words that followed were succinct and punctuated with an angry growl. "I think you'd be mistaken."

Even before the words were out of her mouth, she knew she sounded like some kind of schizophrenic out on a day pass, but it didn't stop her. "I think you think I'm just as hot as I think you are."

If he was at all surprised by her blatant display, it didn't show. The cocky look he gave her was cool and chock full of confidence. "I think you need to give a great deal of thought to the kind of fire you're playing with before you open your mouth again, Casey."

"Oh, Clay. I think you're full of shit," she replied with just as much confidence, drawing her calf along his tightly muscled ass, reveling in the silk of his trousers against her naked leg.

He reached a hand around his back, clamping it onto her leg to keep it still. "I think you're going to be in deep shit if you keep this up." Yet that wasn't what the southerly parts of his body were saying, but whatever.

"Is this the part where I should be scared?"

"This is it."

"Surely you know me better than that." Her statement whizzed from between her lips before she could even comprehend how utterly ludicrous it was to ask such a thing of a man she'd known but a few days.

"But I don't know you at all, Casey."

Point. Though, right here, right now, she felt like she knew him. Like he knew her. In fact, it was a familiarity she experienced in her very core.

And that was some jacked-up shit.

Yet, that was when her breathing became shallow, and the continuation of his "you've been a bad girl" speech became nothing more than a garble of slo-mo words from Clay's lips.

The tight bra she wore grew tighter when her breasts pressed against Clay's chest. The heat between her thighs pulsed with a raging request to be sated. His lips moving enticed her until she could no longer bear to not have them on hers.

With a thrust of her hips, she captured him by wrapping her thigh more firmly around his waist, relishing the grunt of surprise he gave, the sculpted press of his torso to hers.

Casey's lips moved in, hovering over Clay's for but a second before capturing them, consuming them, locking them to hers. Her arms wound around his neck, her nostrils inhaled the spicy scent of his cologne, her tongue slid into his mouth, cool and silken, seeking, tasting.

For all his talk about not knowing her, and all the stank she'd be in if she kept up her cat-and-mouse shtick, reluctant wasn't a word she'd apply to his lips. Lips that took total and full control, gliding over hers, demanding she submit. Clay's arms curled around her, dragging her closer, pulling her flush to him. His hand splayed over her spine, bending her lower body to meld with his. His deliciously long fingers first cupped her jaw, tracing a pattern of exquisite circles before settling in her hair, gripping a handful of it, drawing her deeper into the kiss.

Their lips tangled, their tongues dueled, her eyes rolled to the back of her head from the exquisite stroke of his mouth. His hands were infuriating and exciting all at once, running along her ribs, yet skirting the undersides of her breasts.

A hot groan of longing whistled from her lips when he pulled her head back, exposing her throat, curling his large hand around it to caress the sensitive flesh with his thumb. Wet heat gathered between her thighs, making her lift her hips, seeking the hard pressure of his lower body against hers.

She couldn't get close enough to him, couldn't get enough of his lips consuming hers. Images of Clay naked, driving into her with hard abandon, made her squirm closer.

With every fiber in her body she wanted to rake her fingers down his naked back, dig them into his flesh as they both screamed for release.

"Casey. Louise. Schwartz!"

That scream. The one where her sister used her full given name, the one that had just emitted from lips Casey knew when she opened her eyes would be puckered, was not the scream she'd just been so desperately hoping for.

The release of their mouths resounded with a suctioning slurp throughout the corridor, making Casey cringe.

Frozen in place like two dieters caught hitting the fried chicken wings at Hungry Hal's All U Can Eat, neither of them moved.

Wanda's eyes pinned them to the wall, her ramrod-straight posture never faltered when she stomped toward them. "You know what, Miss? I've had just about enough of you tonight. First, I can't find you anywhere. Then, I find you on a pole—a *stripper's* pole, Casey, working it like you were a hired hootch earning her keep at a virgin's convention! And to top everything else off, your charges, the ones you ditched us with for greener pastures, were better behaved than you!"

Clay held a hand up to thwart Wanda's tirade. "Wanda—"

But her finger under his nose was faster. "Do. Not." She clamped her fingers together to signify he should shut up.

Casey placed a hand on his arm to keep him from defending her, and he apparently sensed her need to handle this by the thin line of his lips going silent.

And then Nina was in the mix. "Yeah, and you know what else, buttercup?" She rolled up the sleeves of her jacket before driving her hands into her pockets and pulling roll after roll of camera film out, letting them rest in her fist. "I had to use my powers of persuasion to get these, you walking hormone. I fucking hate using my powers of persuasion. It's work. It makes me tired and cranky. I'd rather just beat the shit out of them to get what I want, but no, Wanda here told me I had to tread lightly, and where are you while I'm hunting down sleazy dawgs with cameras? In a hallway, shoving your tongue down Clayton's throat like you're at the eighth-grade dance. I want no part of that, sistah. I hear Clayton has a mate, and there's no way in hell I'm going to some shunning because you can't keep your panties on. You know, I might just beat the shit out of you for the fuck of it."

Wherever she'd just been, she was back—big. Her saucy attitude and devil-may-care manner slunk back to the dark place inside her. Her arms fell to her sides, and her leg dropped from around Clay's waist like it was made of lead. Casey hung her head, but before she did, she caught Wanda's eyes. "So you're mad?"

Arms crossed over her chest, eyes blazing, Wanda's hair literally shook around her face when she spat, "Mad because you're accosting a man who's mated in a dark hallway at some party filled with drugs and booze, prancing about like you're Belinda Bubbles? Noooooooooo, don't be ridiculous." She waved her hand for emphasis. "I'm in love with the idea. So in love, if Nina doesn't get to you first, *I'm* going to beat the shit out of you!

"Didn't I tell you not to leave my sight? Didn't I?" Wanda's eyes were full moon–sized and her face was an unflattering red. Casey decided *seething* wasn't a word she'd rule out. "You were going to the bathroom, Casey. The next thing I know, you're sliding up and down on a pole like you were born to grease it, and I'm fighting off some man-child with a gold tooth named Cherry-Ice—"

"I thought it was Rainbow-Ice?" Nina interjected.

"Whatever!" Wanda howled, clenching her fists. "How, in the name of all that's holy, is what you've been up to even remotely like making an effort to get a grip on yourself? Did you even *try* some of the calming techniques we've practiced?"

Well . . . okay, no.

"Stop, Wanda." Clay cut off any opportunity Casey might have taken to defend herself. His jaw set with a stern grind of teeth. "I was a part of this, too. Casey's obviously not herself. It won't happen again."

On the inside again she was weeping. Because "it wouldn't happen again."

On the outside, she raised her eyes and gave Wanda a look of ashamed apology. "This was my fault. Clay didn't . . . he didn't . . . Look, I know I've said this before, but once it happens, I can't seem to stop it. I don't even know how I get where I end up. I just do, and I'm sorry." Her eyes then went to Clayton, still standing far too close for her comfort. Each nerve in her body was rubbed raw with sexual tension, every bone teeming with embarrassment. "I—I—apologize. I was rude and forward and nothing like the person I am . . . was . . . used to be . . . really, really want to be again." She found her favorite spot on the concrete floor once more, fastening her eyes to it like her life depended on it.

"Casey!"

She caught sight of two pairs of feet wearing expensive shoes. The clatter of their heels clacked around in her addled brain.

Shiny.

The twins had arrived.

They crowded into the hallway, forcing Clayton to press back against her very fragile, so raw and cagey she just might explode, body.

Drinks in hand, Lola planted her hand on her waiflike hip, taking a long sip from her straw before eyeballing Casey and Clay. "I can't even believe this is you! I mean, you lecture us all the time about our inappropriate behavior, but hellloooo. You're always nagging us to show some de—de—"

"Decorum," Casey filled in Lola's blank spot on a shaky breath.

Her head dropped back to its proper place—hung in mortified shame.

"Uh-huh, that. Wait until Daddy finds out. He's going to be so pissed when he finds out what you've been up to."

Clay made a move to usher the girls off, his face tight and angry, but Casey stopped him. She knew how to deal with the girls without any help.

Lita nodded her agreement with a bob of her vacant head. "Yeah. Like, wait until he sees the pictures the 'razzi were taking of you. Holy shit, are you screwed. Where'd you learn to do that, anyway, Case? You were, like, a conformist, all twisting around that thing."

"You know." Nina stepped between the girls, slapping an arm around each pair of shoulders, trying to steer them out of the tight confines of the hallway. "Aren't you two scheduled for belly shots at the bar or something? Isn't there a rapper out there with your names on him?"

Casey's head popped up when Nina attempted to derail the twins. Anger was always the best defense when you were knee deep in humiliation. It showed spunk and balls. "No, Nina. I've got this. Oh, and it's *contortionist*, Lita. And I can't imagine what I did was any worse than what the two of you did. Remember the thing that landed me in jail. *Jail,* you spoiled, self-absorbed children! Wouldn't *Daddy* just love to hear about the bullshit I've gone through to hunt down bottom-feeding photographers and all of your dad's lovely money that I've spent paying them off to shut them up. What I did tonight doesn't even come close to the kind of crap I've put up with from the two of you. So if your father's angry because of what I did tonight, maybe he'd like to see some of the messes I've gotten the two of you out of—messes he never had a clue about. Messes that are documented in living color!"

Lola gasped, her doe eyes astonished. "That's—that's—absorption!"

Casey's eyes glazed over, only this time it had nothing to do with a demonic state. This was all Casey, eyeball deep in fed-up. She rounded on them both, pushing her way between them. "No, Lola, it's *extortion*, and yeah, you can bet your size-zero ass I'd be happy to tell Daddy I went to jail because you two oversexed, brainless, boozing fuckwits haven't a shred of moral fortitude! And again, so you don't confuse yourselves, I said *fortitude*. Look it up in that crazy thing they call the dictionary and while you're at it, look up the word *resignation* because when I'm done telling your father the kind of crap I've put up with for more years than I'm willing to cop to—it's what I'll be handing him tomorrow in the morning!"

Shooting past Wanda, whose mouth formed a perfect O, and Nina, who appeared to give her a begrudging thumbs-up, Casey flew down the narrow hall. Her feet in these ridiculously high heels, so confident merely an hour ago, caved at the ankles, making her exit less than swift.

Clay's footsteps thundered behind her, while the outraged babble of the twins mingled with Nina's sharp tongue.

She heard Clay call her name and insist that she wait for him, but she wanted no part of ever having to look him square in the eye again.

In fact, should death befall her at this very instant, she'd go willingly. She'd even offer to throw herself under the bus if it meant she didn't have to face Clay or her sister again.

Zigzagging her way through the crowd, she swatted at pairs of drunken hands grabbing at her as though they had the right just because she'd all but screamed out loud she was up for a good time. Remarks about her chastity, or lack thereof, were made when she shoved her way toward the exit sign.

The need to hide under her covers for the next century kept

her feet moving, pushing her to get to the door located at the far-thest corner of the whole damned club.

Not to mention the tingle in her fingertips kept her focused on her goal. After everything she'd done tonight—she didn't need arson as her nightcap.

Her heart crashed when she slammed into a much larger woman than herself.

Tall and striking, the woman pulled Casey toward her, shelter-ing her from men who slung lewd remarks as they shot through the crowd. Yanking Casey by the arm, this large, imposing woman shoved her way to the exit, cracking the door open with just a push of one pink-tipped finger.

Incredulous might have been her first emotion, but grateful to be hurled into the cold night air won out.

Taking deep, shuddering breaths, Casey stumbled out along the uneven pavement, bobbing and weaving in heels that no longer represented sexy, but instead resembled a ball and chain. Placing her hands on her thighs, she bent at the waist and fought the dizzy rush drinking always left in its wake.

Supermodel long legs in a wide stance shuffled in front of her. "Well, you certainly know how to cause a scene, don't you?" Gravelly and deep, throaty and rich, the voice that asked the ques-tion followed up with a chuckle that was like ribbons of dark choc-olate, all hot and melty.

Casey might have laughed, too, if her words weren't the blatant truth of the matter. She blew a strand of hair out of her eyes. "Yeah. I seem to have a way."

"You know what else you have a way with, darling?"

Well, in light of recent events, she hoped it involved a knack for panhandling. Straightening, she cocked her head, gazing up at the blondest woman she'd ever met with the longest pair of false eyelashes on the market. "No. What?"

Her blue eyes sparkled the kind of sparkle that matched the coppery gold glitter dress she wore that showed off her broad yet lean shoulders and highlighted her long, thick braid. "Getting into the kind of trouble you don't stand a chance of getting out of."

If that wasn't the fucking truth.

In just four days she'd managed to land in the pokey, turn into a demon, find out her sister was super-paranormal, sprout horns, reinvent 101 Ways to Use a Stripper's Pole, and lose her job. How uncanny that this Nordic goddess towering over her had picked up on that vibe.

She snorted, letting her head fall back on her shoulders. "Tell me about it. You have no idea the kind of week I've had. You'd never believe it." Casey began to walk, shivering when a gust of wind shook the surrounding trees. The tall woman followed behind her, finally falling into step beside her, and matching Casey's much shorter strides.

"I understand exactly what you mean, darling." Her voice was sympathetic.

Now that was just plain silly. How could the average human being know exactly what she meant? Especially one who looked like she did? Casey shook her head. "Oh, I disagree, and if I had enough breath left in me, I'd tell you why I disagree. But I'm too tired." She paused for a moment, looking up and down the street in the hopes she'd find a cab.

"No. I really do understand what you're going through. I've had a bad week, too," she insisted.

Pu-lease. But the woman *had* rescued her. The least she could do was acknowledge that she wasn't the only person in the world facing a crisis. "Did I thank you for getting me out of there? You were incredible. I don't know how you opened that door with just one finger, but I'm awed. It was the stuff amazing's made of."

She waved a long-fingered hand dismissively, the thick diamond bracelet on her wrist glittering under the twinkle lights that lit the trees lining the sidewalk. "Oh, it was no trouble. No trouble at all."

Yeah. That thing she'd done with her finger didn't seem like it was much trouble. It had seemed eerily easy. "Well, thank you. I was in deep back there." And because she didn't want to seem ungrateful, Casey asked, "So you had a bad week, too?"

She pouted, pushing her red, shiny lower lip out. "Dreadful."

Casey let out a sigh that made her shoulders lift and release. "That sucks. What happened?"

"I found out my ma—er, husband was cheating on me."

Bumma. Maybe that did trump being turned into a demon. Casey cast another long look at her. She was gorgeous. Every long-limbed, graceful, perfect, platinum blond, at least six-foot inch of her. Who, in their right mind, would cheat on this specimen of beautaciousness? Men could be such bottom-feeders sometimes. "That's awful. I'm really sorry. But if it's any consolation, you're a beautiful woman with a good heart who was nice enough to save this woman who was in distress. You won't be single long. I mean, that is if you don't plan to reconcile. I watched a show about infidelity not long ago, and the therapist said that some marriages actually do recover with time and counseling. Maybe you can work things out?"

"Or I could just *kill* the other woman."

Casey giggled, patting the woman's slender arm. "I'm sorry. I don't mean to laugh. I know you're just turning a phrase because you're hurt and angry."

"Oh, I'm very hurt and very, very angry."

"You should be. What is the matter with men, anyway? I know every marriage has troubles, but jeez. Why do some men think cheating is going to solve the problem better than just telling your wife you're unhappy? I just don't get it." Casey slapped her hand against her thigh to emphasize her point. "I mean, really, isn't it just easier to be honest and leave the marriage before you go sticking your private parts in someone else? Doesn't that just seem so backward to you?"

"Decidedly backward."

Casey shook her finger in the air, nodding her head. She knew all about this. "You know why they don't leave first? Because they're chickenshits. They don't want to risk losing everything, their houses, their cars, their money—their status—before they're sure they're doing the right thing. Which to me seems foolish. If you have doubts about the other woman being right for you, why would you do it in the first place?"

Her porcelain face, clear and smooth, lit up in total agreement. "That's exactly what I've been asking myself since this all began."

A small crowd of people wandered behind them, making Casey take notice that they'd walked until the view of the club was almost out of sight. It reminded her she needed to get home. Look through the want ads. Find out where the local homeless shelter was. "Well, either way, I sure hope things work out for you. Whatever you decide. I really have to get going now." She turned to stop on the sidewalk, sticking out her hand. "Thanks again. You really were a lifesaver."

Her laughter floated, tinkley and light. "It was nothing."

A rustle of feet behind the woman startled Casey.

It was Wanda.

And Nina, too.

Wanda was holding a finger up to her mouth, signaling Casey should be quiet.

Casey rolled her eyes, ignoring her sister and taking the hand the woman had put in hers with a warm smile. "You know, I never got your name. I'm Casey."

Wanda's hands began to flap with wild, broad gestures.

Like they were playing charades and Casey was supposed to guess Wanda was Big Bird.

Nina was busy rolling up the sleeves of her long trench coat.

That was never a good sign. It meant she was preparing to lay the hurt on someone.

"And you are…" Casey prompted, furrowing her brow at a bouncy Wanda.

"Me?" She smiled. "Oh, I'm Hildegard. A pleasure. Truly."

Wanda squeaked.

Nina narrowed her eyes.

Refusing to allow them to distract her, Casey said, "What an unusual name." *Hildegard*. Very unique.

Yet so uncommon.

But rather familiar.

Oh.

Realization hit.

Wanda slapped her hand to her forehead in a "duh, you dumbass!" kinda way.

Nina stepped around from behind Hildegard.

To Casey's dismay, it just wasn't quick enough to stop Hildegard from yanking her up by the front of her shirt. Her feet dangled and her head was forced to rest at an odd angle. The force Hildegard used to gather her up took her breath away, but she managed to hold up her hand to keep Nina from pouncing. She'd had enough violence for one lifetime.

Think, think, think, Casey! There isn't a problem you can't solve when you use your reasonable tone and your words. "So you're upset, and definitely I can see why. But this is just all some big misunderstanding. Clayton and I—we're not—I mean, we wouldn't—I would *never*—"

Her smile was bright, glowing, just this side of lunaticky. "You stutter. How endearing."

Hey. Hold on there. "No, it's just that it's a little uncomfortable way up here. Now, if you put me down, I just know we can work this out." One of her shoes clopped to the ground as though it was an exclamation point at the end of her statement.

Hildegard gave her a good shake, making her eyeballs rattle and her teeth clack together. "I just don't see that happening, darling."

Nina, never one to wait anything out, reacted. "Put her the fuck down, you goddamn giant, or I'll beat the blond right out of you."

Hildegard's face soured. Not good. She eyed Casey. "Is this your friend?"

She bit her lip. If she answered wrong, Nina could be hurt. While she'd once put her own brand of hurt on Nina, she hadn't meant to. Nina wasn't afraid of much, scratch that, she wasn't afraid of *anything*, but what if in this paranormal mayhem, demon beat vampire? Oh, carefully. She had to tread carefully. "Well, *friend* is a relative term. If you mean friend like we shop together, have the occasional lunch or some late-night chatty time on the phone, no. But—if you mean friend like we know each other and see each other from time to time, then yes, she's my friend."

"Then you won't mind if I kill her, too? Seeing as you're not the late-night-chatty-on-the-phone kind of girlfriends."

And thus, the volcano known as Mt. Saint Nina erupted.

She grabbed Hildegard's silky braid, yanking her head back so hard, Casey thought her long neck would snap. "If you don't let her go, bitch, I'll jack you up so far you won't remember where your ass starts and your elbows begin! Got that, She-Ra?"

Wanda, proving she still held the badass card in her hand, latched onto Hildegard's ear and whispered low, "Do what she says, or I'll tear it off and shove it down your throat."

Now, them was fightin' words.

Hildegard's creamy throat worked, the tendons in it bulging when she laughed—all scary and crazy.

That was just before she flicked her wrist—one small shake— tossing Casey into a festively decorated tree.

With lots of twinkle lights.

So many, in fact, they got caught in her hair.

Hair she'd worked on for an entire hour to perfect.

Fuck it all if that didn't piss her off.

Looking back, the appearance of her flaming fingers sure would have helped *before* Hildegard had thrown her across the street.

But she couldn't complain.

Because they'd ignited just in the knick of time to launch a real screamer at Hildegard.

Gazing down at her volatile fingers, Casey smiled.

Her aim was damn good.

She'd totally meant to fry Hildegard's false eyelashes.

CHAPTER 10

"Hildegard!" Clayton roared down the street with a loud snarl in a blur of color and motion.

Somehow, Casey had managed to hop down from the top of the tree like she'd acquired bionics, landing on her feet with a feather-light descent.

In one heel, no less.

Yay, all things demony.

The prickles of rage that had made her fingertips emit a screaming fireball now lit every part of her body as she stormed Hildegard, whose eyelashes no longer burned but sent wafting pencil-thin tendrils of smoke in the air. Hildegard quite casually pulled a hankie from her clutch bag, gave it a lick, and patted at her eyes like she was completely unaffected.

Casey went straight for her, circling her imposing frame, her breath puffing in short, raspy clouds of steam while Hildegard remained clearly undaunted. She'd decided that her words—

the ones she always used to solve any kind of discord—were fruitless.

She'd much rather see the giant bitch dead.

"Casey!" Wanda screamed. "Back off, Casey! Back off now."

"Oh, shut the fuck up, Wanda. Let her kill the bitch," Nina said. "Because if she doesn't, I will."

"Casey. Listen to my voice—back off. Take a cleansing breath and let go of your anger," Wanda soothed.

In increments that relaxed each part of her body one muscle at a time, Wanda's voice penetrated the thick veil of her anger. One minute she was up—the next down and horrified she'd torched Hildegard's eyelashes. Again, still as bewildered as she was the first time she'd set Nina on fire, Casey looked at her fingers with a dismayed groan. "Egads."

"Oh, fuck this, Wanda," Nina hollered. "You're always trashing all the good shit with your sappy breathing techniques and warm squishy shit. You know, there's nothing wrong with a good ass-kicking, and if anybody needs one, it's this fruitcake here. So why can't you just let well enough alone, knock off all the Hare Krishna, beatin' your tambourine bullshit and let Casey kick her ass from here to Boise?"

Clay jammed his body between Casey's and Hildegard's, his eyes fixed on Hildegard's face while Casey's view of her was blocked by his broad back. "Nina! Enough. You know what could happen if you get involved. Stay out of this and go home to Greg. Wanda—take your sister home. *Now*. I'll deal with this."

The. Fuck. Casey tapped him on the back.

"Casey—*go*," he seethed.

How had she come to a point in her life where it seemed everyone was either telling her what to do or saving her from doing something reeealllly bad? No way was she leaving without clearing some of this messiness up. "That's easy for you to say, pal. It wasn't you who almost had the ass whooping of a lifetime. I'd really kind of like to work this out so we can all move on. If we just explain to your wife what's been going on, I'm sure she'll understand, and everything will be right as rain." She gave Clay a hard shove with her shoulder, but he didn't budge. His rock-solid frame was unmovable. As a matter of fact, it was like she hadn't touched him at all.

Ducking from behind him, Casey positioned herself in front of the two of them, but it was almost as if she wasn't there.

"Goddamn you, Hildegard. If you touch one hair on her head, I'll see you in Hell," Clay threatened, the warning no more than a snarl.

Holy hacked off. Clay wasn't kidding when he'd said their marriage was one of convenience. He was just short of rabid and drooling. Which gave Casey pause. If theirs was an arrangement born out of circumstance, what the hell was up Hildy's ass? Like she should care if Clayton was doing a whole harem of women all at once while they rode tricycles and blew "Yankee Doodle Dandy" on their harmonicas?

Hildegard's ice blue eyes glittered. "You'll see me there eventually, won't you, my love?"

"Leave, Hildegard. Or I'll kill you myself."

Phew. Death. Destruction. Killing. Maiming. Paranormal people had such a hard-on for serious threats. They didn't just threaten to do a little damage. They went straight for a shot at capital punishment.

Her response was dry and snide. "Oh, darling. No, you won't. You can't, remember? Clan law or something, isn't it?"

Had Clay tried to kill Hildegard before? Jesus Christ. Had a man with a predilection for murder been sleeping in her closet? Hadn't Wanda said he was trustworthy? He was such a strange concoction of light and dark. She was alternately amused by his wiseass responses and freaked out by this newly seething, exposed half of him.

"But I will. Now get gone, and if you come near Casey again, it'll be your end."

Again with the final.

As Casey watched this scene between two married people play out, she found herself unbelievably curious about how they'd ended up together.

"Hey, you two?"

Their heads swiveled in her direction, as though they hadn't even realized she was still there. "Tell me something?"

Clay sucked in his cheeks. "Go home, Casey. Wanda, help me out here."

Casey raised a palm in her sister's direction. "Don't you dare, Wanda. I just want to ask a question and then I'll go."

Hildegard gave her a sly smile, then sent Clay a secretive glance. "Certainly."

"What is the problem here? Okay, yeah, I get that you had to get married because you vampires and werewolves and lions and tigers and bears have rules. Fine. But what's the uproar about? I mean, I don't get the big deal. It's obvious you're married in vampire only—or whatever. So even if Clay was, you know . . . and before you get that freak on again, he isn't—wasn't—won't— with me, what's the crime? He'd only be screwing things up for himself, right? It'd be him that's shunned or whatever horrible fate you people cook up when someone breaks their marriage vows. It wouldn't hurt you at all, Hildegard. In fact, it would work in your favor. You'd no longer be strapped to a guy you obviously hate. Then maybe you could find the vampire of your dreams and have baby vampires. So all I'm saying is this—calm down, already. If Clay screws up, you win. Game over." Even as she said those final words, she cringed. He would die—*die*—if he stomped any other mattress but Hildegard's, and that troubled her.

Deeply. What troubled her more was she couldn't just chalk it up to the injustice of it all—or even the sort of compassion one human being feels for another whose fate was so precarious. It wasn't the kind of "oh, too bad" feeling you had when you saw a tragedy on the news.

It, like, seriously had her stomach in a knot that Clay could lose his immortality and fall off the face of the planet.

Nina flicked Casey's arm. "Jesus, you're a twit. Shut up and let's go. Let the two of them work this out. Alone, without that mouth of yours that babbles like a brook."

"Oh, Clayton," Hildegard crooned. "What have you done? She really doesn't know what she's gotten into, does she?"

Yanking her arm from Nina's grip, Casey shrugged her off. "What have I gotten into?" What else was there after being turned into a demon?

Clay gripped Hildegard's shoulders, his eyes flashing all sorts of mysterious messages at her. "Go *now*, or I'll see to it you burn in Hell. It'll be worth my own demise."

Hildegard's last glance before she disappeared into thin air held just a hint of fear—something Casey was sure she didn't want anyone, least of all Clay, to see.

But an explanation was in order. "That was the most cryptic conversation I've ever heard. You people are like Stonehenge or crop circles—a bunch of questions and no answers. But after that, I think you owe me an explanation. What exactly have I gotten myself into besides the demon game?"

Nina's hands jammed into the pockets of her jeans as she rocked back on her heels. "Yeah. You know what? I wanna know what the fuck, too. And there's something else I wanna know. Dude, she didn't smell like vampire." Turning to Wanda, she asked, "Did you smell vamp on her, Wanda?"

"Nope. Though everything happened so quickly, I'm not sure what I smelled."

Nina clucked her tongue at Wanda's admission. "As a matter of fact, she smelled like Casey does."

Wanda sniffed the air. "Oh, yeah. Huh. So what's that about, Clay?"

Clay stared down at all of them. "That's because she is like Casey. She's demon."

Nina slapped him on the arm with an affectionate hand. "Shut. Up. You're mated to a demon? How the fuck did that happen? When I found out you had a mate, I just figured she was vampire like us."

Yeah. How. The. Fuck? Casey had just assumed Hildegard was a vampire, too. She looked to Clay, waiting.

His gaze was weary, his jaw tight. "It's a long story, Nina—long and *personal*. Now, I think tonight's been enough for Casey, and we really should get her home." He took hold of her arm, guiding her toward the parking lot behind the club, but Casey wasn't ready to go home yet. Casey wanted answers.

Digging her recovered high heels into the pavement, she shook Clay off. "Casey's right here, and she's tired of everyone speaking for her, or telling her she's tired, or talking her off a ledge that, had you been compassionate people, you'd have just let her jump from after her behavior tonight. Now, something's going on, and I want to know what it is, Clay. What else, besides this demon gig, have I gotten myself into? I'm not budging until I have an answer." So, yeah, no more pushing her around.

"Then I'll budge you myself," Clayton said before grabbing her by the waist and stalking off to his pickup as if he was carrying a suitcase, with Wanda and Nina in tow.

Her shoes fell one by one as Clay stomped along the rutted pavement while her legs dangled and her ribs crashed against his tapered waist. "Put me down! I have a right to know what your wife was talking about!"

When they reached his parking space, he dropped her to her feet. His hands went to his waist when he glowered down at her. "Hildegard loves to create chaos. She spews bullshit for the sake of spewing bullshit, and that's all I have to say on the matter. From now on, she's off limits. So let's get one thing straight in this mess. I'm not discussing her. I'm not answering questions about her because it's none of your business. My mating is my problem. I'm here to look out for you until you get the hang of this—to protect you from any harm because this is my responsibility. But that's as far as it goes. My personal life is mine and yours is yours." Clay bent his head toward her, roaring his final word. "Clear?"

As mud. Pulling her arms behind her back, Casey wiggled her toes, toes that were relieved to be out of cramped shoes that were as unfamiliar as her pole dancing. "Boy, you are a cranky one today. And I guess I'd be cranky, too, if I was married to someone I didn't want to be married to. I'd also be cranky if I was turned into a demon by some guy who was carrying around demon blood like he was toting bottled water! And I'd be super cranky if the guy who did it to me acted all offended by some silly little questions I wouldn't be asking if not for his crazy-ass, fire-breathing wife. So if my wanting answers about the utter lunacy your Gigantor wife spews upsets your sense of personal space—I. Don't. Care! Got that, crabby?"

"Niiiiice," Nina admired, holding her fist up—*way up.*

For the love of. She was like a hovercraft.

Nina flicked the bottom of Casey's short skirt and grinned up at her. "C'mon. Knuck it up, Princess. Well said."

Casey growled in frustration. She ran a hand up and down the length of her body, shooting Clay a scathing look. "And you have the cubes to yell at me because I want answers. Look at me. I'm levitating. Doesn't that deserve some answers?"

Clay's return glance was unruffled. "Your levitation has nothing to do with my marriage to Hildegard. Now give me your hand."

Turning her nose up at him, Casey scoffed. "I'd rather float home."

"So help me, Casey, I'll tether you to my antenna. Now give me your hand."

"When you give me my answers."

"Okay—enough," Wanda ordered, running a hand over her eyes. "Casey, give him your hand—now, because he seems to be the only one who can get you pavement bound. When I'm less frazzled, I think I'd like to know why Clay's the only person who can keep you grounded. For now, I want to go home. I want to go to bed. I want to forget I ever met a boy named Ice Cube."

"Cherry-Ice," Nina corrected with an affable smile.

Wanda threw her head back with a roll of her eyes and a snort. "Cherry-Ice, Ice Cube, Shaved-Ice, I don't care anymore. I want to go home. This instant. I'm tired. I'm cranky. I miss Heath. Now give him your hand, Case, or I'm going to pitch a hissy fit and shift right here in this parking lot for everyone to see. It's not pretty. Ask Nina. I'm hairy, and sometimes I drool."

Casey immediately regretted her behavior. Wanda and Nina had chased her around all night while she'd behaved just as badly as the twins ever had—minus the removal of her clothing. It was unfair to drag them into her argument with Clay. She'd just wait until they'd gone to bed; then she'd have at him, because she wasn't giving up on what she was sure was a detail Mr. Put Upon had purposely omitted.

With reluctance, she held out her hand to him and vaguely wondered exactly what Wanda had said out loud. Why was Clay the only person thus far who could stop her levitation? She forgot about that when he took her fingers in his because she was fighting off the shiver, the warmth it brought her, the reassurance it gave. Those emotions were the emotions of an infidel. And after meeting Hildegard, she'd decided she valued her hair far more than she'd ever anticipated. Not to mention her life.

Unlife. Half-life. Whatever.

When her feet touched the ground, grabbing hold of Clay's shirt collar, she stood on tiptoe while Wanda and Nina got into the backseat of the truck. "I'm acquiescing for now, but this isn't over by a long shot. I don't care what you say. Your story has more holes than Swiss cheese. So just because I'm doing what I'm told right now doesn't mean it'll last. Clear?" she finished, mocking his earlier order.

His raised an impervious eyebrow. "Like that's a surprise? Get in the truck."

"Get in the truck," she mimicked in a mock imitation of his tone, swinging the passenger door wide, and climbing in. "I'm not answering any of your questions, Casey. My business is mine and yours is yours. I'm just here to be your personal thug and protect you. Blah, blah, blah."

Entering the driver's side, he smiled at her with a wink, hoisting himself into the seat. "I think we've reached that place called understanding. Took you a while, but here we are."

"Oh, we're here," she muttered under her breath, scrunching down in the seat with the posture of a scolded two-year-old.

Clayton tugged at his earlobe before sticking the key in the ignition. "Vampire," he pointed out, grinning wider. "I can hear you."

"Then hear this," she whispered. "You have no idea the grenade of whoop ass I'm going to launch at you."

"Could you launch it with your fucking mouth closed?" Nina asked from behind her. "I never thought I'd say it, but all that banging around in that club, not to mention chasing after those two blond sticks on heels who think a Tic Tac is calorie-a-cide has worn me. Oh, and yeah, we can *all* hear you. So clamp it."

"I hate to do it, Case, but I'm going to second Nina's request. Hush. Please," Wanda pleaded.

Casey slunk farther into the seat, leaning her head back and closing her eyes.

But she was like a snake, waiting to strike her prey.

Yeah. A snake.

Hissssssssssssssss.

PULLING her blanket up over her, Clayton watched Casey and the slow rise and fall of her breasts in the moonlight.

Exhaustion, and no doubt the constant unruly hormonal shifts she'd been experiencing, had taken over, leaving her unable to make good on her threat to launch her grenade of whoop ass.

He could only duck those for so long.

She was right. To a degree, she deserved the truth. Not that an explanation would make any difference to her predicament.

Or his.

He was mated to Hildegard.

Against his will—without his consent—but mated he was, and vampire law was crystal clear. No matter your mate, vampire or not, you were in until someone was dead.

Tonight, more than ever, he'd wished to be free of Hildegard, and not just because she was like a knife in his fucking gut.

Rather, it had to do with Casey and that kiss.

A kiss that had stirred something in him he wasn't aware he was capable of. It went beyond the lust of it, beyond the silken blend of her tongue with his. It even went beyond her hot, lush body pressed to his.

Butterflies.

Or some facsimile thereof. His smile was wry. He'd actually experienced what he supposed were butterflies. A strange shift of organs he knew rationally no longer existed. Yet there it was. A sharp surge of not just desire, but of longing. The longing to protect her, followed by emotions he didn't know the first thing about giving names to because they were so long forgotten.

With more regret than he cared to admit, Clay knew the kiss initiated by Casey had more to do with the uproar her body was in, changing and adjusting to her new demonic state and those sexual side effects Darnell had talked about. He'd been an available set of lips for another set of lips that had not only grown adorably mouthy, but would have been satisfied planting themselves on any other man's.

But that didn't change what those lips had done to his.

It didn't change how enraged he'd been when those men, drooling and guffawing assholes, had been howling like the dogs they were over her pole escapade.

It didn't change how much he would have liked to have been that pole.

Jesus, Gunnersson, who the hell are you? he mused, running a hand over his jaw. It was just a kiss. One kiss that could never happen again, if he hoped to keep Hildegard at bay.

But it'd been a helluva kiss, and it was keeping him from the sleep he knew he'd need if Casey still planned to launch her grenade of attack.

Stirring, she sighed, tucking the corner of the blanket beneath her chin while rolling to her side to burrow deeper into the mattress.

Watching her sleep dredged up some more as yet unlabeled emotions, and it mesmerized him, transfixed him. The slope of her hip, the curve of the underside of her breasts, made his mouth water, made his hands almost shake with the need to trail his fingers over her skin. To find out if the rest of her was as soft as her mouth.

He wanted to sit at the edge of her bed, push back the blankets, and drag his hands over the outline of her body. He wanted her to bury herself against him in the same way she huddled under the covers.

Yeah. This was some bad shit.

Shit he had to leave alone. He couldn't allow his focus to shift. Not now. Not when he was so close to ending this charade with Hildegard.

But for whatever reason, he found himself hoping—hoping he could get his hands back on that elusive jackass who'd coaxed him to that bar the night he'd met Casey. Hoping he could find him in time to sever his bond to Hildegard without his ultimate demise.

Then maybe he might stand a chance at giving names to what he was feeling about Casey.

And a fucking kiss.

It was just a kiss, you asshole.

Let it go. He'd let it go and stay as far away as he could until he was sure she was safe.

So, in the spirit of letting go, what would one more minute spent watching her sleep while trying to figure out exactly what was so goddamned special about her hurt?

Or ten.

He could probably keep his eyes open for another ten minutes.

"WELL, it is a good picture of her, don't you think, Wanda? I mean, just look at her legs—they're gorgeous. All long and nicely toned. Plus your hair looks fabulous. I don't know what came over you when you went from frumpy librarian to sex bomb, but you look fantastic." Marty patted Casey's leg with an approving smile and returned to running her fingers through the fringe on her admiral blue knit scarf, staring blankly off into the alleyway.

Nina peeked out from beneath the blanket that covered her sunshine-sensitive eyes, her long legs splayed in front of her. She tipped her head back to rest against the pile of boxes she leaned against. "Marty? Pipe down. There's no somewhere-over-the-rainbow side to this. So quit with the chocolate-covered-goodness bullshit. And I can't fucking believe I didn't catch every one of those motherfuckers with cameras. Goddamn it, kiddo, I really tried."

Casey nodded numbly. That Nina was apologizing made everything so much worse. It meant that even someone as hardened as Nina, when the chips were really down, could have a sympathetic bone. Which meant her chips were really down. Like, way.

Wanda grabbed the morning paper from Marty and slapped it on her thighs. "Okay—so we're in a pickle."

Blowing out pent-up air, Casey pinched the bridge of her nose with her free hand. The other held her beloved Shark, swirling impatiently in his goldfish bowl. "No. *I'm* in a pickle, Wanda. Not you, not Marty, not Nina. I appreciate everything you guys have done for me so far, but this is my mess. I'll handle it."

Wanda's expression went from helpless to cross. "What about

this don't you get, Casey? We're here to help you. I use the word
we because you're my sister, and I'm not going to desert you when
you so obviously need me. I've included my friends because they're
just as willing to help. I know you're all about your independence
and taking care of yourself, but it really is okay to borrow my
shoulder. This demon thing didn't happen because you were foolish and reckless."

"No, it happened because *I* was," Clay, ever the accountable
one, said. He leaned against a streetlamp, hot and rumpled from
his rudely awakened vampire sleep. Thank goodness he'd only been
out for about an hour, or there'd have been no waking him until
twilight.

"And so did this." Casey grabbed the paper, shoving it over her
shoulder at Clay, who took it from her shaking hand. She set Shark
down on the concrete to rise, yanking at her brown jacket and
tightening it around her neck.

Though his face didn't change, his eyes did. She could see just
the corners of them from behind his sunglasses. They turned dark
and his eyebrow lifted again. "I hadn't seen the pictures yet. That
sucks. I'm sorry."

"Well, thanks for the condolences. They mean so much at a time
like this," she replied, letting the sarcasm drip from her words,
moving away from him to avoid contact. Fuckall, if she shouldn't
hate his guts right now. He was the one who'd landed her here,
and still, that wasn't enough for her to quell the tap dancer in her
stomach, and douse the fire he created in her loins by just standing
there. He wasn't even doing anything interesting, for the love of.

"And he fired you for this? Isn't that, like, the pot calling the
kettle black? His daughters aren't exactly the Virgin Mary. Or
hasn't he seen one rip off her clothes in public? I know you said
you were going to quit, but I thought maybe that was just a heat-
of-the-moment thing," Clay said.

No, the notion hadn't been heated by the moment. She'd meant to quit, but she'd hoped to do it without the kind of blemish this left on her résumé, and she'd hoped, for the girls' sake, their father would finally realize the impact of their shenanigans had led to Casey, Miss Patience and Understanding, quitting. That could hardly be the case now, seeing as she'd behaved so badly. "Yeah, he fired me. In a loud, screaming, litigious way. And he's right. I'm supposed to be a good example to them. This hardly constitutes good or an example of anything but blatant debauchery."

Clay shrugged, his smooth skin wrinkling at the forehead. "I don't think they're *that* bad. . . . In this one here, your smile's really nice."

Her smile. "Uh, have you taken a good look at that picture of me?" She flicked the full-color photo of herself with a half-crazed smile and the caption "Naughty Nannies." "See that?" She pointed to the pole her leg was wrapped around. The pole she'd hiked her leg so high up on you could see just a hint of the bottom of her left ass cheek. "That's my ass. Oh, and look," she said, pointing at the swell of her breast. "That right there—that's the miracle part of the Miracle Bra. Works wonders for a B cup, don't you think?" *Or have you forgotten the miracle of those puppies in your big, burly hands?*

She gulped. Her life was in ruin and the best she could do was recollect the bliss of jamming her tongue down his throat.

Clay's gaze fixed on her. She felt it even from behind his sunglasses—dark and stormy. But then he leaned down and said, "If it's any consolation, you were definitely having a good hair day, and, in that one right there"—he pointed to the third of four pictures—"you exert exceptional control hanging on to the pole the way you did. I was impressed."

As though that made everything better.

Wanda rose then, too, her face a mask of outraged anger on Casey's behalf. "I cannot believe the audacity of that man. I wish you'd been able to quit before he fired you, so he'd know what train wrecks his children are! What a loud-mouthed hypocrite—the jackass. I can't believe how rashly he behaved."

Rash was an understatement.

At the very wee hour of 7 A.M. sharp, Calvin Castalano had arrived on her doorstep with steam coming out of his hairy ears while she trembled before him in her bathrobe and footie pajamas. Where her demonic temper at that point was, could only be chalked up to the kind of luck that seemed to have befallen her as of late. Then he'd reminded her that her job was to prevent little messes like these, not create them. Loudly. Obnoxiously. With vigor.

He hadn't even given her the chance to say good-bye to the girls, and while they'd created the better part of this mess, she didn't want to leave without at least telling them she wanted only good things for them.

Casey cast Wanda a tired glance, defeated. "You know what? It's okay. I was stuck in a shitty job. Now I'm not. Maybe this was just the thing I needed to motivate me to move forward. So onward-ho."

Shortly after Calvin's tirade, much like any staff member who was dismissed, he'd sent in his hired henchmen to remove all traces of her from her cute apartment, leaving her and the girls and Clay on the sidewalk in the back alley.

The moving van her boss had hired, and would likely bill her for, pulled up with a grind of gears and tires.

Ah. Vinny and Guido, aka the hired movers, had arrived.

"Dude, if you break one fucking thing, you'll be using prosthetic fingers to put all that shit in your hair," Nina threatened the bulky mover with the darkly slicked-back mane.

Marty was up and at her side, a falsely bright smile on her face. She pushed an unbrushed strand of Casey's hair out of her face.

"It'll all be fine. We'll put your stuff in storage, and you can stay at our apartment here in the city—rent-free—no obligations. Until you get on your feet. Okay?"

Clay had offered his home, wherever that was, but being on his turf left her feeling upside down. Casey gratefully patted Marty's arm. There was nothing she hated more than charity, but in lieu of homelessness, she had no choice.

Just then, Roosevelt stuck his head around the corner of the building. "Oh, Miss Casey. I'm so sorry."

Her smile was warm. She'd miss Roosevelt's grin each morning. "It's all going to be fine."

He cupped his gloved hand around his mouth. "Ain't nuthin' fine 'bout you takin' the fall for those girls. I just wanted to tell ya to come back and see old Roosevelt sometime, okay?"

Pushing past Clay, she gave Roosevelt a hug, patting his cheek. "I will. Promise. Would you do me a favor? I wrote a quick note to the girls, in case they need me. Will you get it to them?"

"You know it," he said with a said smile. "Oh, and just one more thing. Man stopped by here today."

Her antennae went up. "A man?"

"Yes, ma'am. Got his name written down right here in my coat pocket." He fished around in his jacket, pulling out a slip of paper. "Name's Rick. Rick Mason. I didn't let him up, 'cause he's not on the approved list, but I tol' him I'd pass on his name and number to ya."

Casey gulped before thanking him.

Clay strode up behind her, his voice rich and gravelly. "Who's Rick?"

Her temper flared. How come he could ask questions and she couldn't? "Remember the Hildegard speech?"

A smirk spread over his lips. "Which one? There've been several."

"The one about my personal life is mine and yours is yours?"

"I do."

"Good. Take heed."

He grunted his objection, leaving her with a brief, satisfied smile at his dissatisfaction that she wouldn't reveal just whom Rick was.

But she'd rather have her skin peeled off at high noon than explain Rick. Her sobbing into her pillow for more nights than she cared to count, left college because of, duplicitous, lying ex-lover, Rick.

The one she'd run away from and hadn't seen in nearly six years.

CHAPTER
11

"You really don't have to stay."

"Oh, I disagree. I *really* do," Clayton said, plopping down on the poofy cream-colored leather couch in the middle of Marty and Keegan's lush apartment, throwing his long legs up on the dark wood of the coffee table. Wanda had finally relented and gone home to Heath for the time being, after Clay's solemn vow he'd watch over Casey. However, she'd promised to return in a couple of days, and she'd sent Heath's manservant in her place. So that he could keep an eye on her—for all the good it would do, seeing as he was no longer a paranormal. Yet Wanda had divulged that Archibald had been around a long time, and his knowledge of folk-lore and the mythology of the supernatural was extensive. Though, Casey had to admit, she still wasn't sure how a manservant who was an *ex-vampire* could lend manpower if it was needed.

And what was a manservant, anyway?

"It is someone who tends to all your needs, Miss." Archibald, stately, balding, dressed in a black suit, smiled upon offering the answer to her question.

He must have caught her staring at him, bewildered in his formal suit and tie. "I'm sorry, Archibald. I knew of you, I just didn't know any of the details."

His nod was curt, but his smile warm. "'Tis a great deal to absorb, I'm sure, Miss."

"So you were Heath's servant when he was . . ."

"A vampire, and before, Miss. Indeed, I was. And for the time being, I shall be yours. I may no longer have the power of the clan behind me, but I do have the power of knowledge, many years of it, in fact, and far more Heath experiences than I care to confess."

"You really don't have to do this, Archibald. Not that I don't appreciate Wanda sending you to be her eyes and ears. Surely you have better things to do than babysit me."

"Oh, indeed, I do. I'm, right at this very moment we speak, missing *Emeril Live*. He's making wild boar this evening with a garlic glaze that is simply to die for, you know. A devastation no greater has ever befallen me."

Her laughter filled her ears. It felt good to laugh. It felt better to see someone look at her with a twinkle in his eye and an almost smile. "There's a TV in the spare bedroom—go get your Emeril on." Casey hoped he watched closely, because whatever the frig he was brewing in the kitchen smelled like something had died. It definitely didn't smell gourmet-ish.

"If you're certain there's nothing more? Something to eat, perhaps? I'm happy to cook you something."

Oh, God. Starvation had a new appeal. "I'm fine, and thank you again. You really didn't have to come." She covered her cringe with a warm smile.

"There isn't anything I wouldn't do for the fair Wanda, Miss.

When she asked that I offer you this TLC of which she speaks, while keeping my eyes and ears open, I didn't hesitate."

Again, there was that twinge of sadness way deep down in her gut. Wanda had surrounded herself with an incredible amount of devotion, and she'd missed it playing Super Nanny. "Thanks again, Archibald. You go get some rest."

He took the kitchen towel from his shoulder, swiping it along the back of the couch as he left the room. "Wild boar and Mr. Lagasse it is," he chuckled on the way to his room.

That left her and Clay alone.

With the residual of last night's kiss.

In more silence.

Awkward.

"I really can take care of myself." Why reminding him she could take care of herself had become such a bone of contention with her left her baffled. The need to do so just ate at her.

"I really want to believe that."

She plunked down on the farthest end of the sofa, as far away from him as she could. The entire day had been spent in close quarters while they dragged her things in, rubbing her already fragile nerves to a heightened frenzy. "Then go away and let me. Archibald is here. He can have the night shift."

"Not on your life."

"My half-life, thanks to you."

"Petty."

"Truthful."

"So how about we talk about Rick."

She paled. "How about we don't."

Clay didn't look at her when he spoke. Instead, he let his head fall back on the cushiony leather and closed his eyes. "In light of the fact that I'm looking out for your best interests, I think it's wise you share with me anyone of suspicion."

Yeah. That was what this was about. "There's no suspicion about Rick. He's someone I knew a long time ago, and he has nothing to do with me being a demon now." The end. "Now, I'm going to go take a shower and wash away the day's dirt. You know, the kind of dirt that involved me losing my house, my livelihood, my *job*?" Why, along with stating her independence, she was also so intent on backsies tonight left her confuzzled, but for some unapparent reason, she wanted to twist the knife in his gut. Remind him she was unemployed and homeless over and over until his eyes rolled to the back of his head.

If he wouldn't—no—couldn't stop being so utterly wonkable, yet unattainable, then she wanted him to suffer in unspeakable ways.

"Blame, blame, blame," he retorted, the lilt in his voice teasing.

Leaving him and his smart-ass remarks behind, Casey went to the bedroom she'd chosen and grabbed some bubble bath.

The shiny gold of the taps on Marty's sunken tub made her cringe at her reflection in them. Her hair, still sticky from last night's gallon of hairspray, stuck out at varying angles, and her eyes had more bags than an airport carousel. She flipped the taps on and dumped some scented bath oil into the swirling water.

Realizing her mood was sour, Casey plunged into the suds, hoping to cleanse herself of her foul disposition. Leaning back, she let the silken glide of water swish over her belly, threading handfuls of soap through her fingers.

But the soothing water didn't calm the sudden sharp, searing pain in her gut. Bolting upright, she pressed a fist into her abdomen, letting out a squeal of pain. The compression didn't ease the sting and the sudden heat glazing her cheeks and forehead left her dizzy and disoriented.

That itch on the top of her head, the one that signaled her

newest ornamental hair accessory, crisscrossed along her scalp. Reaching an arm over the edge of the tub, she tried to haul herself out, only to flop back down with a resounding splash of water and bubbles. The moment she fell back, attempting to brace herself for impact, a fireball flew from her fingertips, bouncing off the opposite wall and nailing some dried flowers on the vanity.

Fighting a scream of agony, Casey focused on getting out of the tub. Sweat dripped between her breasts, soaking her forehead, and the ceaseless burning of her scalp revved up a notch.

Clay's knock at the door was sharp. "Casey? What the hell's going on?"

The white-hot heat of spasms in her belly intensified, taking her breath away.

"Casey?" Clay's voice grew urgent from behind the tall oak door.

Once more, she made an effort that seemed damn near monumental to lift herself out of the tub. This time when she fell back, she cracked the side of her head on the faucet. A sharp cry of pain-filled surprise escaped from between her lips. Christ, it felt like she was being split in two. Flames crackled, rising higher until they wended their way toward the decorative towels that hung near the sink.

The door exploded open in a burst of splinters and groaning wood.

The blurred motion of Clay's large, imposing form filled her watery eyes. He dunked a towel into the tub, throwing it onto the flames, tamping out the fire. Then strong arms plunged into the water, lifting her out as though she wasn't a size twelve at all.

Hiking her up against his hard chest, he asked, "Casey? What happened? What's wrong?"

She heard the strain of his voice, the concern, but she couldn't answer for the invisible knife that sliced through her intestines like they were warm cream cheese.

Holding her close to him, he rocketed from the bathroom, grabbing fluffy dark green towels on the way. Water dripped down the front of his sweater, making a squishy mess of the marble-tiled floors. Clay braced her against the granite kitchen countertop while reaching for his cell phone.

The irony of this being, she couldn't even enjoy the fact that she was pressed to the crush of her libido's lifetime—naked, because the ricocheting pain had her doubled over.

Clay barked something into the phone she couldn't quite catch for the fight she was having with herself to keep from screaming.

He flipped the phone shut, tearing the towels off his shoulder and tucking them under her, around her. Carrying her into the living room, he set her on his lap while she shivered uncontrollably, rocking her back and forth, pressing his lips against the top of her head.

Her organs felt like they'd been put in a microwave on high, the seizing, burning pain sending her muscles into spasms Clay tried to massage.

And then, out of the dim light the living room lamp cast, Darnell appeared while Clay shouted at him to help.

Kneeling in front of Clay, Darnell put a beefy paw to her head. "Shit, man—it's happening."

"What—what's happening, for Christ's sake?" Clay barked, gruff and tight with panicked impatience. He cupped her cheek, tilting her head back to look into her eyes.

"The change, boy. She's changin'. Look, her horns is pokin' out. That's a sure sign. Her bellyache is, too. It'll pass in a minute or two. Always does. Just happened later for her 'cause of her special circumstances."

"What the fuck are you talking about, Darnell?"

Her breathing had begun to even out, the agonizing pricks of pain easing. So yeah, what the fuck was Darnell talking about?

The towel Clay had so carefully tucked around her butt was lifted, cool air wafting over her exposed skin. "You look and tell me if you see the mark," Darnell prompted, turning his initialed head the other way.

The mark?

Clay didn't bother to ask; he hoisted her up, craning his neck around her shoulder. His response was a long, low whistle.

Casey struggled to maintain her dignity. This *was* her ass they were dissecting. Between clenched teeth, she gritted out, "Talk to me about the mark, Darnell."

He scrubbed a hand over his dark head. "The mark a the demon. We all get one when the change happens."

Hold the phone. If she had the numbers 666 on her ass—it was on. So on, Clay would never forget she had some flipped-out demon's nuttiness running through her veins. "First, and I ask with much hesitation, what does the mark look like?"

"Uh, it's a letter."

"Representing?"

"Who owns you," Darnell muttered, shamefaced.

Casey's eyes narrowed. Pushing sopping wet strands of hair out of her face, she searched for words. "And *who* owns me, Darnell?"

There was a long pause—long and rather dramatic. When he finally spoke, it was on a ragged sigh. "The devil."

Spankin'. "So I have a letter *D* on my ass?"

"Actually, it's an *L*. For *Lucifer*. It ain't no thang, really. Just a way for the mutha to show his muscle."

A hysterical giggle escaped her lips, forcing her to cover her mouth. "Could have been worse, I guess. It could have been a *B* for Beelzebub on my *be*-hind. Thanks, vampire." She slapped Clay on the back with mock gratitude.

"Happens every time with the change, Casey. Everybody gets the mark."

"I thought the change had happened by way of fireballs and horns?"

Darnell's full face scrunched in irony. "I thought so, too, for you anyway. But it looks like that ain't the case. You turnin' full on. Least ways that's what it looks like. It's how it happened with me and everybody else I know who's demon."

Struggling to sit up, Casey clung to the towels that covered her. "Explain 'full on,' please."

Darnell rose, backing away, the clunk of his high-tops echoing against the hardwood floor. "Means you gonna get your demon form, I think."

"Why do I get the feeling this won't be like a favorable case of *Extreme Makeover?*"

"Oh, it's extreme, aight," he muttered, looking down at his rings.

"Spit it out, Darnell," Clay demanded, still holding on to her, raising her temperature in a much different way than the microwave experience earlier. But his concern touched her, and it probably shouldn't, but there it was, touching her.

"Weeeellll, it's like this, man. When you become a demon, you turn into, well, a demon. You know, scales, talons, claws, whatever your demon form 'sposed to be."

"Hang the hell on," Casey cried, her spine now rigidly pressed to Clay's chest while he kept her securely in his grasp. "You said I could take on any form I wanted, once I practiced, or whatever. How did I go from choosing human forms—which, if you ask me, is fun and sort of exciting to anticipate—like anticipating a new outfit—to turning into some scaly beast in a fairy tale gone awry?"

"I dunno, Casey. Like I told ya when I last saw ya, I ain't never met nobody like you before. I just know now you showin' all the signs of a normal shift from human to demon."

"So in the end, the probability that I'll be just like you is likely."

Darnell's glance was sheepish. "Looks that way."

Turning her body, she stared at Clay straight on. "And all this because you couldn't resist the temptation of demon's blood."

His expression went sheepish. "Yeah. Angry?"

She let her head bend low, pushing her forehead against his. "No. Not at all. I'm struggling to find new and innovative ways to thank you for my pending scales and talons. It's not easy to express that kind of gratitude, you know."

"We've arrived at the blame portion of our relationship, then?"

Casey's eyes narrowed. "Buddy, you have no idea."

His gorgeous, "get lost in the depths of" eyes met hers. "Apologizing again would probably seem disingenuous, I suppose."

Tucking the towel between her breasts, she pushed off with a jarring jolt to his scrump-dilly-cious chest. "Ya think?" Turning to Darnell, she forced a smile she didn't feel. "I appreciate that you came so quickly. I just have one more question. Will this happen again? I hate to be a complainer, because the good Lord knows, this demon gig has been an LOL ass load of fun, but what just happened hurt. A lot. So if I need to prepare to be split in half, I'd like a heads-up."

Darnell's face was riddled with sympathy. "Won't be so bad time number two—gets easier and easier. Hard part is learning how to get back to your human form. But I'll show ya, Casey. And if you need me, all ya gotta do is think me up. Us demons can contact each other through our minds. Picture me in your head, and I'll come runnin'."

Stellar.

Composure, despite her nekidity, took over. "Thank you,

Darnell. You've been very *honest* and *upstanding*. Traits I value in a *man*." She shot a pointed glare at Clay. "And now, I'm going to go clean up the mess I've made of Marty's bathroom. I'm here only a day, and I've already torched the place. So woo-hoo fireballs." She pumped her fist in the air, turning on her heel, fighting to maintain her dignity.

She had the letter *L* on her ass.

Where was the dignity in that?

"Oh, c'mon, Casey!" Clay yelled. "Don't be mad. Why can't you just admit how cool fireballs are?"

If the letter on her ass didn't fuel her anger, his idea of joking did.

In the bedroom, she closed the door, without slamming it, then patted herself on the back for avoiding a fit of rage. Letting the towels fall to the floor, she stood before the mirror on the dresser, looking over her shoulder at her ass, something she'd avoided for the better part of her adult years.

And indeed, there it was. An *L*.

In a scribbly kind of script normally used for wedding invitations.

She'd been branded like so much cattle.

Squeee Lucifer.

Searching for some clothes, she dragged on a pair of old jeans and a sweatshirt, but she stopped cold when she heard raised voices. Running to the door, Casey pressed her ear against it like she once did when Wanda had her friends over, and they'd excluded her from their sleepover. It was childish, but stopping herself would have been like stopping a screaming freight train.

"You better tell her, Clay. I told ya she deserves to know whose blood's runnin' through her veins. I knew there'd be trouble. Knew it, man!"

Hmm.

"It doesn't change what's happening to her, Darnell. So what's the point?"

"Aww, c'mon," Darnell said with such gruff irritation, it took Casey by surprise. "The point is, that she-beast knows some unsavory dudes, and they gonna come callin' on Casey. One already did. You can't watch her forever."

Yeah. What Darnell said. Then a thought occurred to her. The *Matrix* guy in the coffee shop must've thought she was the demon whose blood ran through her veins. He'd mentioned how different she looked. If he wasn't unsavory, then she didn't know who was better qualified. So who was the owner of said demon blood? She jammed her ear against the door.

"Damn it, Darnell, Casey's demonic origins don't matter as long as I'm here to protect her."

"The hell you say, brotha! You better tell her she got that crazy-assed bitch Hildegard's blood runnin' through her veins, or I will! I can't hardly sleep knowin' that shit, thinkin' one of those really accomplished, fucked-up demons might come callin' on her. Hildegard plays with the big boys. Now you do it, Clay, or I will!"

Casey gasped—shrill and raspy.

It had been Hildegard's blood Clayton had spilled on her.

Dum-da-dum-dum.

The plot thickened. So that was why the *Matrix* guy in the coffee shop had thought she was capable of sexual acts reserved only for circus employees. He thought she was Hildegard in another form. And then, like a thunderbolt of awareness, everything was clear. Hildegard obviously wasn't afraid to take her sexual needs into her own hands—scratch that, she was clearly a slut, which meant Casey now had slutty breezing through her bloodstream—and that was why she was having hormonal attacks to challenge any nympho.

The son of a bitch had known all along. Knew the kind of

danger he was putting her in because Hildegard had nefarious connections.

And he'd lied.

Thus, the fuming began. Clenching her fists, shoving one into her mouth, she battled for self-control. Oh, she'd kill him. Yep, yep, yep. Set him on fire—rub garlic all over his hotter-than-lava body—turn on the church channel and superglue his eyes open so he was forced to watch a full Catholic mass.

"I know you heard us, Casey." Clay's voice from behind the door didn't hold a hint of resignation, or even an apology. He was merely stating a fact.

Flinging open the door, she poked a finger into his wet chest. "Oh, you bet your dark and dreary ass I heard you. You know something, Clayton Gunnersson, I've taken this pretty well thus far, don't you think? I haven't cried or carried on or blamed, not much anyway. I've been a real peach. A total champ. In the meantime, I lost my job because I could barely keep my clothes on while I humped a stripper's pole like it was my reason for living. I'm doing and saying things the old Casey never would have done or said. I'm ready to take on anyone and anything without thinking it through before I blow a gasket. I'm hot and cold—cold and hot with no in between. And all because I have your promiscuous, schizophrenic wife's blood running through my veins!" Flicking his shirt collar, she stomped to the dresser, grabbing her purse.

Flying past Clayton and a very concerned-looking Darnell, she rushed to the front door. "I just knew something else was going on, and all I asked for was your honesty. I mean, really, how much worse can it be than horns and levitation? So no more playing nice, quiet, noncomplaining Casey. You got that, you demon maker! You dumped that blond, very angry, very jealous, homicidal nutcase's blood on me. Now all of her partners in felonious acts could crawl out of the woodwork, looking for me, and you didn't have the common courtesy to tell me. Nice. Very nice. So hear this: I almost don't give a rat's ass why you were carrying around Hildegard's blood. It's probably just another wing-nut paranormal ritual I'm better off not knowing about. In fact, you can stick your demon blood up your lying ass! I'm going out for some personal time— away from you and your hokey bullshit. And I warn you, stay far away—far, far away!"

With a grind of her teeth, and a tingle in her fingertips, she rushed out the door, pumping her knees high to get to the elevator and escape Clay.

Punching the button, she seethed while she waited, not caring where she ended up, not caring who she ran into on the way. So help her God, if she came up against one of Hildegard's sexual liaisons, she'd fry his jingle bells.

Out the lobby door and into the frosty night air, Casey clomped along the sidewalk, and headed straight for the nearest bar.

While probably not the wisest choice when one was tweaked beyond reason, reason wasn't involved in her decision making at this point. Though, the farther she walked, the less appealing getting snockered seemed. It would be stupid to get shitfaced if she needed to have her wits about her should one of Hildegard's former partners show up. Jesus, it sucked to always be the one with your head on straight.

Well, for the moment anyway. Who knew if there wasn't another demon delight she had yet to experience, and her head wouldn't be crooked from spinning around on her neck.

So she settled on a diner instead. The neon flash of its sign hurt her tired, gritty eyes. This demon business was work.

Reaching for the glass door, a hand stopped her. Clinging to her purse, she lifted it high in the air, preparing to clock the living shit out of a man she thought surely was Clay. But a long-ago-familiar voice stopped her.

"Casey?"

When she heard his voice, throwing herself on the ground and kicking her feet became very appealing. "Rick?"

Rick's chuckle had that same old deep timbre to it. Like it'd been washed with a warm cinnamon glaze over freshly baked buns. "In the flesh."

Her eyes rose, meeting his, green and fringed with thick, dark lashes. The gray at his temples had spread, but not enough to make him anything less than distinguished—as was the usual for Rick Mason. College professor, teacher of all things pre-law, not to mention bed-sport-like, liar, married with two-point-five kids, a golden retriever named Winston, and a fucking cheat.

She'd had lots of time to think over a meeting like this. Years of creating scenarios in her head where she told him to crawl back to the hole he'd crawled out of for humiliating her. "Does your *wife* know you're here in the flesh? Because as I recall, she wasn't too happy about your flesh being around my flesh."

Rick laughed, the amusement reaching his eyes where they crinkled at the corners. "You've grown spirited, Casey. I like that."

"And you've grown old, Rick. I'm not so much into that."

Thumping his chest with a closed fist, he shot her a mockingly pained look. "You hurt me. I wasn't too old for you back when."

With eyes filled with venom, she cast him a cool glance. "No. You were too married for me back when. You just forgot to mention that." *And the devastating humiliation I'd suffer all over campus because of it.*

His reply was as smooth as he'd been. "Why don't we let bygones be bygones and start over? I'm not married anymore." To prove it, he held up his now-barren left hand. He said it as though she'd waited all these years to hear exactly those words.

As if.

"Did the wife catch you at the dorm panty raid?"

"Why so angry, sugarplum?"

The use of his old endearment for her made her skin crawl. "Look, I'm not much for revisiting the past. How did you find me and what do you want?"

"I have old friends at the private school you ran away to. They led me to your prior place of employment. After that it was cake."

But no one knew where she'd gone once Calvin Castalano had booted her out on her ass. . . . She kept her body rigid, shrinking away from the warmth he offered. "Which still begs the question, what do you want?"

Rick's smile was wide, infectiously so. "You, of course. I've never stopped thinking about you in all these years."

Tipping her head back, she feigned disinterest. "I can't see how I could possibly interest you now, Rick. I'm not a nubile college student anymore. I'm much too old for the likes of you. You like 'em virginal, right?"

"You've grown sassy, too."

Yeah. And I can float. "I've grown up. The grown-up me doesn't like the same old you. So go back to whatever college dorm you hang your tighty whities in now, and leave me the hell alone."

"Now don't be like that, Casey," he teased, reaching out a hand to gather hers up in his warm one. He pulled her to him, taking her by surprise when he clamped his lips on hers, pushing his tongue between her teeth with a vigorous thrust.

One hard shove later, and he was almost across the street. Next, she'd set all that distinguished hair on fire.

Casey ran the back of her hand over her lips, stalking him. Cornering him against a tree, she lifted him by the lapels of his smart tweed jacket and rammed him hard against the base of the trunk. "If you ever touch me again, I'll kill you. You trashed my entire fucking life back when, you lying puke. So go the fuck back from whatever hole you slithered out of, and leave me alone. Feel me, *Rick?*"

"Caseyyyy," a low, husky warning called.

A roll of her eyes left her forgetting about Rick, who she dropped like she'd just been caught with her hand in the secret money jar. He slumped to the ground at her feet at an awkward angle, mashed up against the tree. Jamming her hands into her hair in utter frustration, she said, "Didn't I tell you I needed some personal space? Personal has only one meaning, and it has nothing to do with together time."

Clay shot her his best sad face. "Oh, c'mon, now, Casey. We've been apart for at least twenty minutes. Admit it. You missed me."

She crossed her arms over her chest and snorted. "I missed you and your lies like a dog misses fleas. Like a girl misses that thingy her gynecologist uses in an examination—or a—"

"I think you're not being truthful, and you're hiding your deep longing for me by hurling insults. No doubt, a very fetching attribute in a woman." Clay chucked her under the chin with a laugh.

"Like you'd know truthful if it slapped you in the face."

His smile teased her. "I'm hurt."

Her lips thinned. She would not be won over by his humorous attempts to cajole her out of her foul mood. "You're infuriating."

"But cute, right?"

Ugh. Right. All the more reason to resist. "Would you just go away and let me have two seconds of peace?"

"Yeah. I could do that. But you know that guy you had by the throat?"

"What about him?"

"He's awake."

Movement at her feet rustled along the pavement. "So what? I think I just proved I can take care of him, didn't I?"

"I know that's what you'd like to think. I'd go on letting you think that but for one small fact."

"And that is?"

"I don't smell a human." Rick had risen and scrambled to his feet, backing away, but Clay caught him with one sharp snap of his hand, his eyes blazing when he hauled him upward with one hand. And she'd be impressed with his Conan-like strength if she wasn't so hacked off at him. "Who do you think this is?"

She sighed in aggravation. "This is Rick."

"The Rick you childishly refuse to talk about?" Clay asked, suspicion succinct in his tone.

Takes one to know one. "The one and only."

Clay's nostrils flared when he sniffed the air. "Who the fuck are you?" he shouted.

Casey frowned. "I told you who he is, now put him down. He's just a pathetic, aging lothario." She glanced at Rick. *Take that!* Tugging at Clay's arm, she tried to pry him off Rick. 'Cause he was older now—brittle-bone disease could be a factor here, and she wanted no part of whatever they called senior citizen abuse.

But Clay only clamped his fist around Rick's shirt that much tighter. "Who are you—speak now or I'll drain you bone dry."

Sinister. He threw that threat around often. Could you really drain one dry? "I said let him go, Clay! He's my ex—nothing more, nothing less."

Cocking his head in her direction, Clay's sharp jaw shifted. "No, Casey. He's not Rick. Not the Rick you knew. He just looks like the Rick you knew, and if you'd quit with the dramatic 'I want to be alone' thing, you might have noticed. Now, c'mere."

She was wary. "Why?"

"Because school's in."

Huh?

"Give him a good smell, Casey," Clay ordered, tipping his head in the general vicinity of Rick's armpit.

She looked at Rick, pondering. "Did you use deodorant today?"

"Casey—I meant sniff the air *around* him, damn it."

She moved in with a tentative step, taking a deep whiff. Oh. Oh, yeah.

"Do you smell that?"

"I think I do."

"Good job, grasshopper. Now. A couple of things—first, kiss me."

"*What?* I can't kiss you. You're married. Kissing isn't allowed when you're hitched."

He grabbed hold of her waist with his free hand, hauling her close. "It is when dire circumstances are going to prevail."

She placed her hands on his chest. "Dire circumstances?"

He grinned. "Yeah, like when a warrior's going into battle, the fair maiden kisses him for luck. Now shut up," he ordered, laying his lips on hers and blowing her already fragile mind with the firm, tantalizing press of his mouth against hers. Just as her breathing became ragged, he tore them apart. "Now, second—back away, and don't give me any lip or your alone time will be spent chained to something. Something hard and uncomfortable."

Casey did as she was ordered without question due to the force of his demand.

Clay eyeballed Rick. "Now who are you, and what the hell are you doing pretending to be someone you're not?"

Wowzers. He looked exactly like the Rick she knew—a carbon copy. Right down to the mole by his left eye. If he wasn't Rick, these demons had cloning hands down.

Clay shook him again, like a rag doll who was about to lose its stuffing. "Who are you, you bastard? *Who—sent—you?*" he roared, deep and blaring.

As still as the night had been was as loud as the night became in a flash of light and booming sound. Chaos erupted in the way of a harsh wind that began to gust in swirls, leaving Casey fighting to remain erect and Clay still clinging to her ex-lover. The Rick look-alike made a grotesque twitch of his limbs. The crunch of bone and the tear of flesh left Casey battling blowing chunks. A thick, gooey substance ran in rivers along his morphing body, oozing and dripping to the ground in fat globs of black, oily puddles. The shape he took didn't remotely resemble anything human.

Mouth agape, knees buckling, terror struck her motionless.

When his horns popped out, Casey's first wild thought was, she'd never, ever complain about her wee protrusions for as long as she was forced to live. Ringed with ridges that were deeply cut and deep purple in color, they sprang from his head like a jack-in-the-box. So tremendous in size, they caught the limbs of the oak tree she'd just had him pressed against.

He was bald, the skin on his head taking on a deathly chalky pallor, his eyes a silvery green that held a raging malice she wanted to fly low under the radar far away from.

Hookay. It was time to bail. "Clay!" she screamed over the howl of arctic air the demon summoned, blowing it from his gaping nostrils. "Let him go!" Bowing her head to the wind, Casey fought her way to Clay, hurling herself at his back to pull him off this thing that had once been Rick. Circling his neck, she tightened her arm and pulled upward. "Let—goooooooo!"

However, Clay clearly wanted a piece of demon ass, so he clung that much harder, rearing a fist up and jamming it under the demon's jaw with a crack so loud, it jarred Casey with a hard jolt.

Then things got sorta hairy.

The demon smiled, his pointy, rotting teeth hanging from gums that were black and veined. With a war cry that surely was as good, if not better than, any she'd ever heard, he screeched. The howl so loud, it physically stung her eardrums.

So not a fighter, Casey put her hands to her ears to defend their sensitivity, thus dropping off Clay's back to the ground like a brick thrown from a rooftop. She hit the pavement hard, scraping her hands when she braced her fall, and tearing a nail.

And just as terror had been her closest friend, fury took its place. A broken nail pissed her off. Not just because she had an owie, but because she'd just had a manicure, and she wasn't sure when she'd be able to afford one again—if ever.

A well of out-of-control anger showed up by way of her fingertips. Twisting her wrist, she rolled it until her palm faced upward, then fired her first shot.

Okay, so she missed, but she'd been damn close to landing one in the demon's mouth. Except for Clay, who clearly was a stubborn ass and had moved his head at the wrong time.

The back of his scalp lit up in orangey blue flames. Yet still, he hung on to the demon.

All reason gone, she was in the air, hovering above the two engaged in a roaring match of wills and superhuman strength. For all the good floating would do her. If only she'd learned how to summon icky things like snakes and big, ugly bugs. Panic was swift, while her thoughts raced. She wasn't a force to be reckoned with. A lame fireball and some midair hovering were hardly an arsenal of pain waiting to be inflicted.

Fear sliced through her when Clay's body arced in the air, shot with such force she felt the whiz of wind when he flew past her.

But then Clay was in the air, too, howling his rage, and steamrolling the demon, knocking him to his back. Dirt puffed up around them when they hit the ground, clouding her view. Panic had handed off its torch to desperation while she tried to think of what she could possibly do to help Clay.

"Evil be gone from this plane!" someone screeched, the words clear and drifting to her ears by way of the whistle of the ferocious wind.

The slosh of water and the howling hiss of the demon as he literally deflated and disappeared made Casey lose her concentration and flop back to the ground, though a pat on her back was well deserved for landing on her feet.

Clay grimaced, knocking the back of his hand against his jaw.

Darnell. It was Darnell. Oh, thank God it was Darnell.

He danced around, stomping his high-tops on the pavement and shaking off his hands. "Man, you know the kind of risk I run even bein' near some holy water? Gives me the hives just thinkin' on it."

Clay clapped him on the back with a jovial grin. "Nice shot. Totally missed me. Who said you couldn't play the majors?"

Darnell chuckled. "You okay?"

Casey launched herself at Darnell, throwing her arms around his thick neck and squeezing him. Never had she been so grateful to see someone. "Thank God. I didn't know what to do! And this stubborn numbskull wouldn't let him go."

Darnell gave her an awkward pat on the back, reaching around and prying her locked fingers from his neck. She slid down his round body with a grunt. "I just gotta know, Darnell. . . ."

"What's that?"

"Is that what I'm going to look like when I do this full change thing? Because I have to tell you—even having the ability to eventually look like Megan Fox isn't ever going to make up for that. Did you see . . . *it*?" A violent shiver ran the length of her body.

"He's a bad dude, Casey. Hardcore demon."

"Then I never want to be hardcore."

"And he's not Rick," Clay reminded her with obvious pleasure. "So who's Rick, Casey? I think I deserve an explanation. I did just beat him up for you."

She gave Darnell a pointed look. He shoved his fingers in his ears and looked away, whistling a tune. Glaring at Clay, she spilled. "Oh, fine. He was my college professor. We had a brief fling; then I found out he was married and because of it, I ended up labeled a slut all over campus, okay? I didn't know he was married, and if I had, I wouldn't have gone there. I'm no cheating enabler, which is why I'm so adamant about staying away from *you*. I left college to be a teacher's aide at a private school because of him, met Lola and Lita, and that's when I took the job with the Castalanos. Have we reached satisfaction?"

He smiled, smug due to his coup. "Yeah. I'm good."

Casey pulled Darnell's fingers out of his ears and shot Clay a disgusted look.

Darnell looked to Clay. "You find out what he wants?"

Bending at the waist, he placed his hands on his knees. "Obviously Casey. He appeared to her in the form of her ex-boyfriend."

"Oooooweee, my man. Somebody messin' with you two. Somebody that don't like Casey."

Duh. "So do you suppose Hildegard sent him?"

"I'd stake my eternity on it." Clay's confirmation made her shiver.

Casey threw her hands up in frustration, looking to the sky. "*What* does this woman want? I don't get it. I told her I was hands-off. No hanky-panky. Does she need it in writing? Blood?" And there hadn't been any hanky-panky. Not the kind that warranted this kind of warning. It was a kiss. Okay, two now, and the second time he'd made her kiss him.

Darnell clucked his tongue. "You a threat to her, Casey."

Her snort was loud. "Oh, I can tooootally see that, Darnell.

I mean, look at me. I'm, like, five inches shorter than her on a good day—my legs couldn't be that long if you slapped me on a rack and stretched them. Never in a trillion years could I fill out a sweater the way her and her hooters do, and to top it all off, she slinks when she walks. Me? Not so much. I stumble and occasionally even trip. I already assured her nothing was going on between Clay and me because I'd never risk his immortality by boinking him! I don't go where another woman has tread—nuh-uh. So how the hell am I a threat to her?" And staying away from Clay and all his yumminess hadn't been easy. Now to find out she had that sex-on-heels Hildegard's blood running through her made her doubly impressed she'd managed not to haul him off to the nearest available bedroom.

"Darnell—don't. Shut up now," Clayton warned, long gone was his look of playful cat and mouse.

Casey waved a cautionary finger at Clay. "You be quiet! Darnell's just trying to do the right thing. We demons have to stick together, right, Darnell?" She slapped him affectionately on his shoulders. "So go ahead. Spill it. Spill it alllll!"

Darnell looked from Clay to Casey.

Now Clay was the one to throw his hand up in an act of defeat. "Far be it from me to tell you what to do—even if it'll only add to an already miserable situation."

Now he thought she was miserable? "Of your own making," Casey reminded him.

Darnell looked torn, but valor won. "You know what, Clay, I ain't playin' with y'all no mo. Casey deserves the truth, and I need to sleep at night." He turned his broad back on Clay and placed two hands on her shoulders. "I'm gonna try an' be all delicate here. I didn't put it together, either, and that makes ole Darnell not on his game. But I got a friend who was once one a them forensic guys and he explained that DNA shit. Crazy is what it is, but this is what he said. You got *Hildegard's* blood in ya, right? That means you just like her. If you an' Clay get to . . . well, you know." He wiggled his eyebrows for effect. "It's okay because it ain't no different than if Clay was usin' his matrimonial privileges with her."

Her mouth fell open. So it was like wonking by proxy. If she and Clay whipped some satin sheets into a passion-slicked frenzy, he wouldn't expire because essentially she was Hildegard's demonic clone?

Casey cocked her head.

Yep. Those were definitely angels singing on high.

She mentally slapped her hand. She was gloating. He was still married—mated—hooked up. She'd been down that route before—it always ended with her eyes puffy and her nose dripping with snot. No matter. "I still don't see the big deal, Darnell. She wants Clay about as much as a girl wants a case of the clap." She grimaced in Clay's direction. "Sorry. And he feels the same way about her. They did this mating thing out of convenience. So what difference does my being anywhere near Clay make? How jealous can one woman be about a man she wants nothing to do with?"

Clay looked puzzled as well. His posture had gone from bent over to ramrod straight. "It's been a long day, and maybe it's just me, but I'm lost, too, Darnell."

Darnell's grin was Cheshire. "'Cause you purty powerful now, Casey. All you gotta do is work at the skills you got and you'll be just as strong as Hildegard. That means you might keep her from drinking from Clay. If she can't drink from him, she cain't stay here on this plane. That means one a you got to go."

Oh, hell's bells. That was badder than bad.

"Fuck," Clay shouted. "This woman and her hold on me. Damn it, Casey, I had no idea how deeply intertwined you were with her. I was under the impression you would just share characteristics—traits, whatever—with her. I had no idea you'd share me."

The conviction Clay showed in his face was enough proof for her to believe his statement. And what was this drinking thing about? Wanda had told her she and Heath drank each other's blood, but she hadn't gone into details, and Casey hadn't asked because it squicked her out. And if a demon needed to drink a vampire's blood, how did Darnell manage to stay on this plane? Oh, Jesus, how would she? Casey crossed her arms over her chest in doubt. "So how do *you* stay on this plane, Darnell?"

His face held many mysteries. "My contract's not up. Lucifer lets you do what you want as kind of a 'see what a great guy I am' gesture, but when the time comes to make your appearance for service in Hell, if you ain't got no other options, it's downstairs you go. That witchy woman's contract was up long time ago, but then, she knew that, and she found a way to get out of it through Clay."

Casey was instantly worried for Darnell. He didn't belong in Hell. He belonged in the biggest baseball field Heaven had to offer. "So someday, when your contract here on Earth is done, you have to—to—"

His face wore resolve. "Yes, ma'am."

Reaching for his hand, she squeezed it. "I hate that. You just made a bad choice, and it wasn't even about you as much as it was about helping your family."

"Oh, I wanted that fame, make no mistake, but I done wrong—cain't go back."

God, that was so fucking ominous. "I'm sorry. . . ."

"Don't be sorry," Clay said. "As long as I'm around, Darnell will always have what he needs."

Darnell held up his knuckles to Clay. "Aw, man, you aight."

Clay thumbed his finger over his shoulder. "Tell her that."

Fingering her forehead, Casey massaged her temples. "So let me assimilate this. What you're saying is—now Clay is kind of mated to me, too. So he's sort of gone Mormon in a paranormal way. Not only that, but I have the ability to keep Hildegard from drinking from Clay because his blood lets her keep her ability to stay here on Earth."

"Yep. That's the size of it."

But the question was . . . "What happens if she ends up in Hell, Darnell? Then what happens?" She closed her eyes with a cringe, unsure of whether she wanted to hear the answer or not.

"She has to serve him—Lucifer. Means she'll probably be mated to another demon. *For eternity*."

Ahhh. Now she got all the twisted malice—the hype over her being in Clay's presence even though the two of them appeared to despise each other. Casey was just collateral damage, and Hildegard wouldn't hesitate to kill her to keep herself firmly rooted here. Casey was a risk she couldn't afford to take.

It also meant she had the ability to save Clayton Gunnersson's ass.

Not to be forgotten—she was also the *only* person in the universe he could wonk besides Hildegard.

Cue maniacal laughter.

CHAPTER
12

"I'm tellin' ya, it din't work, womon. He showed up an' it got wicked. Dat mon you mated to is a mean one. Now be off wit ya an' stop naggin' at me!"

Hildegard grabbed a waist-long braid from her cohort's head and yanked. "I want her gone. Understood? If we don't get rid of her, if Clay succumbs to her pathetically fresh, innocent charm, and those puppy-dog eyes, I'm doomed. And there is no way I'm hitting the Highway to Hell and ending up mated to one of those disgusting hole dwellers. No. Way. Have we an understanding, Marcus?"

He ducked from her grasp, twisting her wrist and hauling her close to him. "Yah, I understan' ya. But she a tough one. She got your blood." Marcus cackled in her face, his white teeth glowing against his dark complexion.

Running a finger along the craggy planes of his cheek, her look was thoughtful. "I'd like to know how she got her hands on my blood. An enemy? I certainly have plenty of those, don't I, Marcus?"

His eyes, olive black, avoided hers. "Yah."

"Maybe, while I figure out who would betray me in such a vile manner, you could figure out how to get rid of Holly Hobby!" Her voice raised ten octaves, ending on a screech of a demand.

She'd leave this plane when she was good and ready—and that equaled *never*.

BLOWING her tangled hair out of her face, Casey fell to the couch. "Wow. I'm beat. Battling demons is daunting work, don't you think?"

Clay grunted, but didn't speak. He'd been very quiet since their walk back to the apartment together. The couch sagged when he flopped into place beside her.

"Sorry I set you on fire. I didn't mean to. My aim's been pretty good so far, but I was panicked."

A long-fingered hand rubbed the back of his head. "I'm fine. It grows right back."

She was too tired, still too much in awe that the supernatural truly existed to beat him down, but it had to be said. "You should have told me it was Hildegard's blood. It explains so much. Like, why you're the only person who can get me to stop doing my impression of the Goodyear Blimp. Because we're all mated-like."

His expression clouded, his eyes somber. "You're right. I should have. I would have, but I hoped to have solved my problem with Hildegard by now, and she wouldn't have factored in to any of this. Her cohorts might have, but once word got around that I was here to protect you, they'd have eventually gone back where they came from, and you would have gone about adjusting. It just isn't working out according to plan. Just know that my intention wasn't to continue to hide things from you, but rather to find a way to fix this before adding one more worry to your already full plate. But it looks like we have a much bigger problem now."

For now, the grave look on his face left her feeling like it was time to let some of the details alone. "So how does it feel to not just be chained to one woman, but two?"

"I really had no damn idea, Casey. I didn't know the implications involved in you absorbing Hildegard's blood." His genuine remorse made her joke fizzle.

"I'm sorry. I didn't mean to make light. It isn't me who's mated to that lunatic, it's you. My issues have only made things harder on you. It well and truly sucks."

"It wasn't your fault. It was mine. I was careless."

With *Hildegard's* blood. Why in all of fuck had he been toting her blood around? Yet another detail she was willing to forgo until a later date. Strangely enough, she had almost no doubt his reasons had nothing to do with wicked intent toward anyone but Hildegard. "But you know what this does mean, don't you?"

"I have two support checks to write each month?"

Laughter flowed from her lips. "No. It means I can help you."

"Uh, no. I don't need anyone's help, Casey. It means you're in danger, and while by proxy you may have inherited some of Hildegard's powers, you're nowhere near as strong as she is. I won't put you in danger to keep her from getting what she wants."

Nudging his shoulder, she teased. "Oh, c'mon. You heard Darnell. I have Hildegard all up in my DNA now. Why couldn't I become just as powerful as her? I can learn. I'm a quick learner." Just ask three college professors about four switches in her major.

"I don't want you involved."

Sitting forward, Casey eyeballed him. "But I *am* involved, and if Hildegard sticks around because she's pissed, I'm in danger any-way. So why not eliminate the danger?"

His lean fingers reached out, pulling pieces of tattered leaves from her hair. "Because this isn't your battle."

"Au contraire. It is now. She's as much a detriment to me as she is to you. It's either her or me, right? If what Darnell says is true, and Hildegard and I are attached by some freaky DNA connection—one of us has to go. And I promise you; the one you want to stick around isn't a leggy blonde. It's the mousy brunette. So get over yourself, vampire. Stop with all the He-Man tactics and let me have a shot at her." *Look at Miss Nonconfrontational talk shit like you don't have Hildegard's blood running through your veins, but Mike Tyson's.*

"It isn't going to happen."

Placing her hands on his thighs, Casey made a face at him. "I don't necessarily need your help. In fact, I don't need it at all."

He snatched her wrists up, drawing her in close to him. "If you get involved in this without my knowledge—"

"You'll what?" Yeah. She was daring him to stop her. Making this an exciting battle of wills. Cocky, cocky, cocky.

His face shadowed with a tense unease. "Don't. Push."

Pulling a hand from his grip, she shoved at his chest and thought quite childishly, *neener, neener, neener.*

A long growl let go from his throat. A warning growl, she suspected.

"Ohhhhhhh, we've resorted to grunting. Very caveman, but very sexy, too." She knew she was walking a fine line here, egging him on for the sheer enjoyment of seeing his sculpted face go all hard and scary. This time, as she poked, she was very aware of said poking, and it thrilled her to the bone. Pitching forward, Casey smiled in arrogance. "What's the matter, control freak? Are you having trouble coming to terms with the fact that I hold your fate in my incapable, little—"

Her breath stalled in her lungs when he cut her off, throwing her under him, and pinning her to the couch with his full weight.

Oh, Jesus, Joseph, and Mary—every hot, hard, long-limbed, bomb-diggity inch of him.

Well, my fine she-warrior—who's cocky now?

Her breath came in pants, short and choppy, and though he didn't breathe, he didn't need to for the unwavering gaze he'd locked with hers.

Casey's discomfort had nothing to do with how heavy he was, or even that he'd challenged her to a stare-off—but it had everything to do with how unbelievable, amazingly good his body pressed to hers felt.

"Just a warning," she whispered, shaky and uneven.

"And that is?"

Okay, cocky was back in his court.

She gulped.

"And that is, Casey?" he taunted, clearly enjoying his power over her.

"My libido," shot out of her mouth like a cannon ball.

"It's arrived?"

"In spades."

"Suggestions?"

Goddamn him. She lifted her chin. Pride—remember you once had some. "I'm open."

Moving in closer, letting the slightest whisper of his lips touch hers, he said, "To?"

Jolts of overwhelming heat skittered over her skin. Her stomach clenched. "Suggestions . . ."

Clay nipped her jaw, making her hips rear upward. "This is a dangerous thing, Casey."

Dangerous is as dangerous does. "How?"

His hands began to knead her hip, rolling his palms over it, inching ever closer. "You're still adjusting. It's the last thing you need right now."

Said who? "Apparently, so are my hormones," she replied on a soft moan when his tongue slid out to glide along her lower lip.

"Your hormones could bring you a lot of trouble."

Yeahhhhh. "Trouble doesn't always have to have a bad connotation attached to it."

His other hand slid under her ass, hoisting her hard against his lower body. "I've been fighting this since that kiss in the club, and you're not making it easy. We're opening a can of worms here, Casey."

"Do you want me to be the can opener, or will you?" Ballsy. Big and ballsy. "You do know what I'm considering doing with you goes against every single thing I believe in."

Clay nodded. "This is going to sound like a line straight out of Cheaters Anonymous, but I'm not mated because I want to be. It's out of obligation—nothing more, nothing less. And technically, if it makes you feel any better, you're my mate, too. But no pressure," he joked, gazing at her with amusement.

It was like she'd just gotten a day pass to Disneyland. "That's true, but what if what we just found out is entirely wrong. You could be shunned. I couldn't live with that because I couldn't keep my panties on."

"I think I'm willing to take the risk."

"What if what Darnell said is wrong? What if—"

This time, when he cut her off, it was with his mouth, driving with force against hers, stealing the last bit of breath she had from her lungs. A hot, electric current sparked between their mouths, awakening every nerve ending along every part of her body.

The lush, full push of his lips, the heated slither of his tongue along hers, drove her to the edge. Low in her belly, a tight coil of desire began, making her wind her arms around his neck, push at his sweater so she could finally feel his naked flesh.

As her hands found his back, she almost pulled away. Contrary to the hot flush of her overheated skin, his was cool to the touch—cool and dry. Lifting her shirt, then tearing off his own, when Clay repositioned himself against her, Casey luxuriated in the sensation his cooler skin brought to the fire of her own.

He popped the front clasp on her bra with expertise, shoving aside the satiny cups to palm her breast. Clay's hand pushed upward, using a surprisingly callused thumb to bring her nipple to a sharp peak. All the while, his lips moved over hers effortlessly, skillfully, sipping, tasting, devouring her mouth.

And then his tongue was slashing the undersides of her breasts, working in agonizingly slow licks to her nipple, a nipple he captured and pulled tight between his lips.

Flashes of color exploded from behind her eyelids, a rush of moist warmth pooled between her thighs. Her thighs strained against his, shaking while her heart clamored in her chest so hard, she heard it in her ears.

Clay trailed his wet tongue along her ribs, rasping over her ribcage, stopping to explore her navel. Fists clenched, jaw locked, Casey bit back the scream of anticipation his mouth wrought. The pop of the button on her jeans, the sharp sound her zipper made when he slid it downward, sent her hips in motion. She lifted them so he could relieve her of the clothing that had now become a bothersome barrier.

Through half-closed eyelids, Casey peeked at him just before he wrapped her thighs around his shoulders and dipped his head low. The light from the end table lamp haloed his frame, strong, powerful, sharply planed. He had thin white scars across his chest, and one along his shoulder, only adding to the mystique of his granite good looks.

Casey reached out to touch him then, laying her palms flat against his pectorals, gliding them along the deep slashes of his abs. His groan was earthy, guttural and satisfying to her ears before he buried his head between her legs.

A gasp of pure, unadulterated delight spewed from her lips as he parted her wet flesh, tracing the swollen nub of her clit, circling it, each pass creating a new level of awareness.

She felt raw, on edge, decadent, unnerved by the harsh yet scintillating sensations he drew from her with his mouth. Not at all ashamed to revel in the feel of his tongue, her fingers found his thick hair, curling into the strands, lifting her hips higher when he finally wrapped his lips around her most intimate place. Licking, tasting, he moaned, sending out a vibration of heat along every erotic zone on her body.

Her teeth clenched when orgasm came, her chest heaving upward, her hips straining to feel every last swipe of his tongue. The depth of release robbed her of her breath, of reason, of anything but capturing and clinging to this out-of-control tidal wave of pleasure.

A long moan slipped from between her lips when he moved from between her thighs and slid off the couch to rid himself of his jeans. Her vulnerable naked form didn't flinch when his eyes scanned her length with greed. Where this unabashedly confident stance had come from, she was unsure, but the sheer overconfidence of it was sexy and empowering.

Casey held a hand out to Clay, pulling her to him, encouraging him to finish what he'd begun. They both grunted their pleasure when he lay over her, the length of his cock brushing against her belly. He was rock hard, cool and thick with his desire for her.

Cupping his face in her hands, her eyes sought his in question. There was no going back if what Darnell had said wasn't true. Clay's answer was to plant his mouth on hers again, spread her thighs wide, and press the head of his shaft at her entrance.

She was as desperate for his entry as she was afraid.

They each paused, the silence interrupted only by her harsh breathing.

Well, so far, there hadn't been any thunderbolts—no cosmic realignment.

But they hadn't consummated anything yet, either.

Fear warred with desire. Fear for his safety won out. She unburied her head from his thickly corded neck. Her lips trembled, her words stuttered. "What . . . if . . . what if what Darnell said is wrong, Clay? Nothing is worth you being shunned—losing the security of your clan."

He paused, too, poised above her, his eyes glazed. His lips compressed, becoming a thin line, his sharp jaw tensed. "I don't care," was the last thing he said before entering her, his passage made easier by the slick wetness he'd created with his lips.

He stilled inside her, she put off the unbelievable ecstasy of his shaft buried deep within her to look over his shoulder.

Silence greeted her ears.

The world hadn't crumbled—the Earth hadn't shifted.

Casey fought a squee of delight and instead succumbed to the first stroke of his cock, hard, thick, and thrusting upward.

His hands found hers, entwining their fingers, pulling her arms high above her head, making her arch up high against the solid width of his chest.

Her head rolled to the side of the couch, thrashing with each powerful thrust he made within her. Casey raised her knees, positioning her heels against the couch to grind upward, to get closer.

Her nipples grew unbearably tight, chafing against his chest, begging for release.

Her mind was blank but for the need to quench her thirst for him. Clay rolled his hips, letting go of her hands and gripping the rounded flesh of her hips. He rode her hard, crashing against her, grinding into her until the tension that spiraled toward out of control pushed her off into the dark abyss.

Dizzying flashes of heat coiled in her belly, letting go like springs, releasing one at a time. Each snap of her self-control made her teeth clench, made her grab at him, reach around him and cup the cheeks of his ass, pressing the heel of her hand to the hard flesh so he'd plunge deeper, harder.

And then she was there, no warning, no time to savor the sweet fall of release. She came hard, just as Clay did, with a guttural, almost feral roar. Pumping in and out of her until he had drained every last bit of her energy, they collapsed, his body sinking into hers.

He rose on his elbows, bracketing her head with his large hands, but she couldn't open her eyes. Sated, exhausted, she filled her lungs with much-needed air. Clay ran his index fingers over her eyelids, tracing abstract patterns across them.

All while she pondered the second coming.

And how close that coupling had been to it.

Whether it was the demon in her, rearing its head, or she'd just never experienced sex like that before, she wasn't sure. She had never been so terrified, so lust-riddled, so consumed by anything—ever.

Her eyes were slow to open, and when they did, Clay's gazed back. What did you say to a man who'd not only turned you inside out, but had just dipped his wick in a place he hadn't been for a long, long time. *"Hey—was it worth the wait?"* But how long was long? "Soooo, it's been a while, huh?" Casey bit her tongue. Good gravy—how insensitive and crass.

He grinned, winking a dark eye at her. "Huh. I thought that went pretty well. I didn't think I showed any signs of rust."

Giggling, she rolled her eyes. "That's not what I meant. I meant . . ."

"You want to know how long it's been since I made love to a woman and what woman that was?"

No. Yes. "No. I just wondered—I mean—I don't know what I wondered. I don't even know all that much about you. I just know that you clearly hate the blond giant's guts. That can make for great sex—or no sex."

"So what you're asking is if I've ever done Hildegard."

Fine. Yes. That was what she was alluding to. No, she'd rather have her tongue cut from her head than admit it. "Forget it. I'm prying, and I shouldn't be. The situation is just so unusual, it begs questions." Many.

"You have every right to pry now, Casey. You're my mate." He grinned again, leaving her off balance. Gone was the serious, moody Clay, and in had strolled this lighthearted tease. He yawned, openmouthed and long.

"I'm your second mate—your first one wants to kill me. And speaking of, can you help shed some light on this drinking-from-you thing? Wanda explained a little of it to me, but it's still sort of hazy."

His eyes began to sag, his words to slur. Pulling her to his side, he rolled to his back and muttered, "Tomorrow . . ."

She planted her elbow on his chest, leaning up on it to grab his chin with her fingertips. "Don't you dare fall asleep on me now." Trailing her fingers along his ribs, she frowned.

So clearly cuddling was out.

Very convenient, this vampire sleep.

Laying her head on his chest, Casey let her swirl of questions subside to a dull roar in her head.

The day had been long, the revelations, brutal.

But the sex had been fucktacular.

Her libido could thank her later.

A sharp crow of laughter startled Casey from the first sound, peaceful sleep she'd had in what seemed like forever. "Hoo boy. I wouldn't wanna be you if Gigantor gets a load of the two of you."

Casey popped an eye open only to have Nina chuck her shirt at her. Nina turned her back to them. "Your sister's right behind me. If I was you, I'd get the fuck up and put some clothes on. You know this shit ain't gonna go down smooth. Not to mention, there's that shunning thing which Wanda'll be more than happy to get a good freak on over—"

Wanda's scream pierced her ears, shrill and so Wanda. The slam of the apartment door made Casey jump, the crumple of bags to the floor making her stomach lurch. Her mouth hung open in shock with no signs of closing.

Nina backed up, giving her an "I told you so" look, letting Wanda have the floor.

Archibald entered the room with a wrinkled hand over his eyes, and cleared his throat. "Ah, Miss, I see you've awakened. Fantastic! Shall I prepare a hearty breakfast? Certainly after last night, your energy levels won't be satisfied by something as unsatisfying as a mere Monster energy drink? What say I whip up some eggs for you? I have the most wonderful frittata recipe I've been dying to try." He split the fingers over his twinkling eyes, peeking out at her with a question written in them.

Nina slapped him on the back. "Hey, Arch—how's it goin'?"

His grin was wide. "Ever so famously, Miss Nina, and you?"

Nina snorted, peeling two fingers away from his eyes. "I'm frickin' fantastic, Arch. Everything quiet here last night? Well, I mean, except, you know . . ." She wiggled her raven eyebrows in Casey's direction.

Archibald blustered, slapping his fingers back in place. "Since the change, Miss, I find I sleep like a baby. Sometimes right in my chair as I peruse the Home and Garden channel. I am what one would call dead to the world," he offered with his typical discreet tact. "Shall I assume Miss Wanda has breakfasted and won't be needing a rare sirloin? Maybe a pint of blood—she looks as though she could use it."

A long chuckle fell from Nina's lips. "You go make that frittata, Arch. I'll slap our fair Wanda in the face, you know, just to jump-start her." She took him by the shoulders, aiming him toward the kitchen.

Archibald threw his head back and laughed. "Oh, Miss Nina. Truly, you tickle my funny bone." He paused just before passing Wanda and said, "Miss Wanda, do close your mouth." He pulled a handkerchief out of his breast pocket and brought it to her mouth, pressing it against her teeth. "You've smudged your lipstick."

Wanda's mouth remained open, but nothing came out. Her eyes were like large full moons, fat with disbelief.

Casey groaned. How could she have forgotten Archibald was just in the other room last night? Would she have cared in her passion-washed frenzy? Wiping the drool from the sides of her lips, Casey struggled to disentangle herself from Clay and sit up. "Wait, Wanda. Before you freak out—let me explain."

And then her sister was all sound and motion, waving her finger in the air, her eyes lit up like a bonfire. "Don't you even give me that baloney about 'this isn't what it looks like,' young lady! I see two naked people. Na-ked!" She gasped. "Omigod, you're naked! Have you no shame? Do you have any idea what you've done? I leave for one whole day—one damn day, so I can see Heath—and you do this?" She spread her hand above their bodies, wrinkling her nose in obvious distaste. "Oh, Jesus, Casey! Clay's going to be shunned. They'll throw him out of the clan. He'll be forced to wander the cold and lonely streets without any support from the others, and all because you couldn't keep your frilly panties to yourself!" Spittle had formed in the corner of her mouth, and her eyes had taken on a maniacal glaze.

"I can't believe this, but I'm going to be the voice of reason here," Nina said. "Wanda—sit your dramatic ass down, and let your sister speak. Casey—dress or my eyeballs will fall out of my head."

Clay never stirred as she gathered her clothes and put them on, looking around for something to cover him with. Vampire sleep was a fucking cop-out, if you asked her. Especially now when it left all the explaining up to her. She settled on some of the damp towels that were left strewn on the floor from the night before, throwing them over him before turning to face Wanda.

Licking her lips, Casey gulped. Jesus. This was ridiculous. If she wanted to screw—then by God, she could screw. She was well over the age of consent, damn it. But then she caught the narrow-eyed, scathing glance her sister was giving her, and she cowed. "This isn't what you think, Wanda. I mean, well, the naked part is, but not the rest. . . . Clay can't be shunned. I promise you. I would never, ever take a chance like that."

Her eyebrow shot up somewhere near her hairline. "Really?" Her tone was ultracondescending. "Did you find the magical key to breaking a bond with one's mate? Have you done something akin to discovering the answer to world peace?"

You know, maybe she had. Maybe she was a closet rocket scientist gone paranormal, and she had all the answers, by fuck. Did anyone—*anyone*—think she could make a sound decision? "You know, Wanda, would it be so hard to believe I might actually have everything under control?"

Wanda made a face and scoffed. "Not when you're naked. That didn't take a lot of control."

Casey crossed her arms over her chest, feeling childishly spiteful. "Well, I guess it's okay to be naked if you're naked with your *mate*."

Silence, awkward and uncomfortable, ensued.

She strode over to Wanda and propped her once-more-gaping mouth closed, then turned to Nina and did her the same favor.

Yeah, thass right.

Her mate.

CHAPTER 13

Nina, clearly recovered, flipped up her sunglasses. "Hang on there, Princess. How can he be your mate? He has a mate, and as far as I know, you can only have one of those at a time. And let me tell you something, if I find out my man can have some other broad—I'll pluck the hairs off his balls one by one."

Casey winced. "I think this case is special. So technically, I guess the one-mate thing is true, but according to Darnell, I have Hildegard's blood running through me."

Wanda gasped again, but Nina slapped a hand over her mouth.

"I know. I was shocked, too, Wanda, but Darnell said because I'm essentially Hildegard's sort of twin, Clay's safe. So you don't have to worry he'll be shunned or lose the safety of the clan because we . . . you know." Her eyes slid to the floor.

Nina shook her head, the ponytail at the back of her head swaying. "I swear, every fuckin' time I think it can't get any kookier—it does. Every fucking time."

Wanda pulled Nina's hand from her mouth with a grunt. "So you're Clay's mate? Forever? Oh, Casey . . . Wait. Nina, call Greg. He'll know what to do. He'll figure this out." She rooted through her purse while Nina flipped open her phone.

Casey was at Wanda's side in a heartbeat. "No!" *No? No what? Dude, you're mated to this guy, and you didn't have word one to say about it. You didn't even get a decent proposal. Though the indecent one wasn't half bad* . . . Yet, she found herself stopping Nina from calling Greg. "No, Nina. It's okay." And it was—though it shouldn't be. But it was. Why was it okay?

"All right. How the fuck is this okay, powder puff? You didn't get a choice in the matter. I totally know what it's like to be slapped up against a wall, but I didn't have to mate with Greg. I *wanted* to."

And who said she didn't want to mate with Clay? A lot? All the time, in fact? Who said she didn't want to be joined at the hip with him?

Wanda threw up her hands, jumping to her feet. "Hooooold on there. How come you're not freaked out about this?"

If she had the answer to that, they could all rest knowing the exact date of the apocalypse. Casey's shrug was as bewildered as her reply. "You know . . . I don't know. I—I don't. It just seems like it's okay."

Nina's smile was snide and knowing. "It was the sex, wasn't it? I know, I know, a good vampire toss is like standing at the doors of Heaven. Don't think we don't get that. But, dude. This is *for-ev-er* and ever, and fucking ever. You see what that did to Gigantor, don't you? She's all uptight over it, sneering and drooling like she was the other night. That's probably because she had no choice but to mate to survive. Same with Clay. It's much different for Wanda and me. We *chose* to mate. You? Not so much."

For the moment, and with Clay comatose on the couch, Casey decided it was best to leave the matter of who made what choice alone. All Wanda needed to hear was that Hildegard had to feed from Clay—or whatever that was about—in order to stay on this plane, and she'd surely flip a fang over it. "I know I didn't choose this. I didn't choose any of this, but didn't you both tell me it is what it is? Don't try and kid myself otherwise?"

Wanda sighed, deep and jagged. "Point. But we had no idea it included a mate-for-life deal, honey. You're in way deep, and we have to find a way to get you out."

Her sister's statement pricked a new level of irritation. "I don't need you to get me out of this, Wanda. I can take care of myself."

She shook her head, making a compressed line of her lips. "I don't doubt that, Case. But I think we have a case of puppy love here, and puppy love does not a mating make! I saw it from the beginning, you all big-eyed and swooning over him. Yes, he's an incredibly attractive man, but you know next to nothing about him other than he has a hot ass. Come to think of it, we don't know a lot about him, either. We all thought he was a swinging bachelor who flits from beauty queen to socialite. So how can you possibly tell me you can take care of this yourself?"

"I'm not twelve, Wanda. I'm thirty-one, and I didn't say a word about love, puppy or otherwise." Lust—wee doggie, oh, yeah. Maybe a major crush. A severe case of the "I like yous." But love took time, cultivation, wooing. A hamburger. A movie. Maybe Rollerblading. It didn't involve demons who showed up looking like former lovers, or big blond women who wanted you dead because you threatened their food source. This wasn't love, but what if it could be?

"Wanda?"

Casey flashed a look of irritation at her friend. "Nina?"

"Enough. Let's go."

"Not on your immortality. I'm not going anywhere until we figure this out."

"Get up, Wanda, and move your ass. We're going home. *You're* going home and letting Casey be a big girl for the time being. We'll go find Greg and see what this is about. Then we're going to present Casey with her options. Whatever they are—or if there are any at all—not solutions. Because it isn't up to us to decide what's right for her. It's up to *her*. So step off and give the kid some room to friggin' breathe. For now, she's safe. Clay's here. Back the fuck away."

Wanda's disbelief was evident. "Did you suck on Marty's neck?"

Nina gave her the finger. "Are you fucking kidding me?"

"Are *you* kidding me? Exactly when did you get so reasonable? You just gave me perspective. The only person who comes close to that besides me is Marty."

Nina popped her lips, pointing to the door. "Go."

Wanda, lips pursed, vibrant anger simmering just beneath her calm exterior, gave Casey a hug, but said nothing.

"Let me know what you find out from Greg, okay?" Casey kissed her sister on the cheek and smiled, trying to offer a reassurance she wasn't sure she felt. "I'll be fine. I promise. Just let me figure this out. I swear, if I need you, I'll call."

Her sister pivoted on her low-heeled boot and headed for the door.

Before Nina followed her, Casey stopped her. "Um, Nina?"

"Yep?"

Casey's feet shuffled, her eyes cast downward. "Thanks. I know I've been anything but nice to you, and now I'm guessing that's because of this transference thing, but I appreciate you getting Wanda off my back. I don't think she realizes I'm not so little anymore."

Nina grabbed her by the chin, tilting it so Casey's eyes gazed into her own. "I don't think Wanda realizes me and Marty aren't her kid sisters, either. She can be crazy overbearing with her reason, and doing the right thing. All she wants to do is help you be-cause you're her kid sister, ya know? But I get that sometimes you just need space. I also get that you need to find your way out of this on your own. I'm not sure why you're so fucking determined to do it, but that's how I read it. You've got some kind of chip on your shoulder about being a big girl, and taking care of your own shiz. We just want to help because no matter how big you are, this paranormal crap needs a shoulder to lean on every now and then 'cause it's kooky. But I'm warning you, this isn't an easy road to travel. With everything else you've got going on, adding a mating to the mix just ain't kosher. Now the advice portion of this convo is over. So go be the big girl you say you are, and call us if you need us, okay?"

Casey smiled, warmth lighting it. "You're not nearly as scary as you'd like everyone to think, are you?"

Nina popped her under her chin with a finger. "Yeah? Well, you oughtta see me when I'm around a bucket of chicken wings I can't eat because I yark 'em all up. That's scary. Check ya later," she said with a gruff laugh.

Casey shut the door behind them, leaning her forehead against it, taking a deep breath. Space. She definitely needed space to figure out the most amazing sex she'd ever had—and what to do about the fact that doing more of what they'd done last night would only deepen what she was feeling when she looked at him lying on the couch fast asleep. She wasn't the kind of woman who could hide feelings like that well. She wasn't the kind of woman who was able to detach herself about something so intimate. Whacked-out hor-mones or not, making love with Clay had meant something.

What was the question.

"I didn't think I'd ever see the day."

Casey whipped around to find Clay awake, a green towel wrapped around his waist. Her inside voice groaned. Did this man not need any primping to look good? Was it fair that she had morning breath and bedhead and he was just as perfect as he'd been the night before? Rippled abs, lean hips, thick thighs, and all. "See what day?"

"The day Nina actually extended a hand in kindness. Showed a little sympathy. Each time I see her, she continues to grow into someone almost likeable. I think Rapture is closer than we think."

Casey threw her head back and laughed. "So look who's conveniently awake. How ironic that you could sleep through all of that screaming, and only wake up when it's all over."

He cocked his luscious head, the long sweep of his sandy hair falling over his eye. "Screaming?"

"Forget it. Wanda was here with Nina, too, but everything's okay. So now that you've slept—we have to talk."

"Can't it wait until I shower?"

She looked at the clock on the wall and smiled. "You've got twenty minutes, and then you're spilling everything, *mate*."

He turned toward the bedroom he'd chosen without saying a word, letting the towel drop along the way.

God, he was arrogant. And he had a fab ass—an arrogant, fab ass. "I mean it!" she yelled after him, running to her own room to grab a quick shower and, well, primp.

Soaping up, Casey tried to stop picking apart last night. So Clay hadn't had sex in a long time. She refused to flog her ego with that fact. And she wasn't going to dwell on it, either. It had been a pretty awesome encounter, this vampire sex. She had to leave well enough alone and not psychoanalyze it to death.

Though, while she dressed, squeezing into the tightest jeans she owned, jeans that actually made her ass with the *L* on it not look half bad, she did what she was trying so hard not to do. Torture herself with all sorts of questions only a jealous lover should be asking.

Like—how many women had he done *that* with before Hildegard? Had he done *that* with Hildegard?

'Cause *that* had been amazing.

Pulling her hair up into a ponytail, she made a face. She certainly wasn't slinky like Hildegard—she looked like a teenager. That she was comparing herself to Hildegard made her want to heave. Clay didn't even like Hildegard.

Yeah, but that didn't mean he didn't like fistfuls of blondeness with legs longer than a Celine Dion note, now, did it?

Throwing her brush down in disgust, she grabbed her knitting bag and headed for the couch, forcing a casual entry into the living room.

Clay was already there, watching a football game, remote in one hand, newspaper in the other.

He cocked an eyebrow. "You knit."

"Yep. Wanna make something of it?"

"Not unless we're talking crocheting, then I'm all about a good smackdown."

Laughing, she unwrapped the yarn, drawing calm from the comforting familiarity. "You ought to try it—it's very soothing." Her knitting needles clacked together in a calming rhythm of knit one, pearl two.

"I can't think of anything I'd less like to do. Except maybe decoupage."

"It might take your mind off your troubles."

"I don't have any troubles—well, except you, *mate*." He smirked at her over the newspaper.

Ire prickled her fingers. "I don't want to be a repetitive nag, but it wasn't me who dumped demon blood on you, then turned me into your mate, *mate*."

His eyes remained fixed on the paper, refusing to look at her. "You win. I give."

Hellz, no. He wasn't going to put her off by playing dead. "So, you wanna talk?"

"About?"

"About your marriage made in Hell. Like, the literal Hell."

"Nope."

"Why not? Don't you think it might help you to let it out?"

"I don't."

"You'd much rather be all brooding and sulky about it?"

His laughter was sharp. "Is that what I am?"

"Please. All this secrecy—all this dark glowering at everyone whenever they mention your wife. Yes. That's what you are, and it's grown old. Lighten up."

"I'll try and make a more meaningful effort to be all sunshiny." His amused sarcasm was clear

"Good. Because you did say I had every right to pry. Consider this prying. So let's start with how this went down."

"No."

"Oh, c'mon. Maybe it'll be therapeutic."

"And maybe not."

She crossed her legs beneath her—not an easy task in jeans she could hardly breathe in, but she hoped to come off casual, chatty, versus confrontational. "Okay, so how about this. How did you become a vampire? How old are you? I can't believe I'm asking that and someone hasn't come to carry me off to the local mental hospital, but I have to admit, I'm eaten up with curiosity. So what's your deal? Wanda told me about Greg and Heath—was it like that for you?"

"In many ways."

"Okay, let me just clue you in on this thing called conversation. If we're going to spend all of this time together mated—or at least until I'm properly trained in the ways of the demon, and we figure my predicament out—it'd be nice if we could *talk* to each other from time to time and not have to avoid certain touchy subjects. So, here we go, and I'd like at least a full sentence. Please. How old are you?"

"A lot older than you."

She nudged his arm with her finger, sending him a teasing smile. "Look at you, participating. Okay, so *how* much older?"

"Centuries."

"How many—and I warn you, I want a full sentence."

"I was turned in the year 798."

Her eyebrows shot up. "Turned into a vampire?"

He gave her a bland look.

She sighed. "Sorry. Of course you meant a vampire." Casey frowned, then smiled with mischief in her eyes. "Boy howdy. You're old. You want me to see if I can hook you up with a wheelchair—maybe some Ben-Gay?"

"You want me to hook you up with a roll of duct tape and a gag?"

Casey giggled. "Holy cow—the man's sense of humor's returned. So this is good, right? Us all communicating. So, next question. Who turned you into a vampire? I mean, why would someone do something so ugly like that?"

"Revenge."

"It's full-sentence time. Revenge for what?"

"A Viking raid."

"Omigod—you were a Viking?"

"I was."

"Wow. Who'd you piss off?"

"A vampire."

"Who was a Viking, too?"

"Your powers of deduction are amazing."

"Don't be a wisenheimer."

"Don't I get credit for using a full sentence?" He chuckled.

"You're back in black. So what did you do to make this Viking vampire angry?"

"I stole his lunch money."

"Be serious."

"I raided his ship."

She winced. "Oh. I'm guessing that went badly."

"Well, no. The raid went off without a hitch—it was the aftermath that became a shit wreck."

"He was tweaked you raided his ship, huh?"

"Nah—he was in love with it. So much so, he spread his happiness near and far."

She rolled her eyes. "Fine. Lame question. So, you were turned into a vampire. . . . I guess you did all the typical stuff like 'boo hoo—this sucks. I can't believe I'll never eat oxen again. I'm going to live forever, blah, blah, blah.' Then what?"

"Oxen and I had a sorrowful parting?"

"Stop making this so difficult. How did you end up with Hildegard? If you had to mate with her on your five hundredth birthday, that means it was 1298—which was more than seven hundred years ago—and I'm not going to linger on the math of this because I still can't wrap my brain around it. So I repeat, in 1298, how did people get together?"

His wide shoulders shrugged. "How does anyone get together with anyone?"

Her shoulders hunched in a shrug. "I don't know? Nowadays, it's the Internet or speed dating. Both a complete waste of time, by the way. So did you date? Did people even date back then? Oh, wait! Were you betrothed? You know, the whole dowry thing?"

"No."

"You're headed for the red zone, pal. How did you and Hildegard end up in this not so connubial bliss?"

"I was turning five hundred. My choices were few."

"Yeaaaah. That's been troubling me. Wanna know why?"

"Do I have a choice?"

"Do you want one?"

"Yes."

She giggled again, gazing at him from hooded eyes. "Then no. You have no choice. So here's what's been bugging me. You just don't seem like the kind of guy who'd cop to marriage—even if it meant death to get out of it. Being all stoic and serious like you are with all these principles and such, you seem much more like the kind of guy who'd rather be dead than hitched to some woman for eternity. You joke a lot but when it comes to Hildegard, you're not laughing. So what's the dealio?"

"Maybe I'm not as principled as you think. Maybe I'm just an egotistical asshole who wants to live forever?"

"Nice. That was two sentences. But maybe you're lying to keep me from finding out something. I just can't figure what it is."

"Then here's my suggestion—stop trying."

"Why are you making it so hard to be friends?"

"I don't need more friends. And friends don't do what we did last night."

Her face flushed, but she wouldn't be daunted. "You didn't need another mate, either, but here we are. Besides, you can never have enough friends, and if we have to be chained to each other until I'm deemed independent enough to strike out in the demon world on my own, would it *kill* you to be my friend?"

He gave her another bland stare.

"Right. Sorry. You're already dead. Forgive my insensitivity."

"Forgiven."

Christ, there was just no budging this man when he didn't want to budge. "Good. So seeing as you're not budging on Hildegard I'll let it be—*for now*. But that's all in the spirit of friendship. Friends do that for each other when they need space."

"Thank you for recognizing my spatial needs," he joked with that disarming grin.

"So now that we're friends, I'll tell you something meaningless and inconsequential about me—like, not super-deep stuff—and you do the same. Deal?"

His silence was deafening.

Casey rolled her eyes. "Okay—like this—here goes. Let's see. Oh, I know. Music . . . I like Yanni. No. I *love* him. Nothing beats a bubble bath with Yanni in the CD player."

"You mean the guy who plays the piano?"

"Yes."

"I don't find that at all surprising."

Oh, really. "Why?"

"The romantic in you is pretty obvious. I'd bet you have a deep affection for kittens and snuggling on the couch, too."

And if she did? "So what you're saying is you don't like kittens? Who doesn't like kittens?"

"That's not what I'm saying at all. I like animals just fine. I especially like your goldfish, Shark. What I'm saying is you're a romantic—easy to spot."

He said it like it was a disease. "What's your problem with romantics?"

His wide shoulders rose and fell. "Oh, I dunno. Could it be that I'm mated to someone who drives me bat-shit? It doesn't get any less romantic. And I don't have a problem with romantics. Don't pick fights where there are none."

Team Clay—one. "Okay—so forget the romance thing. What kind of music do you like?"

"Nine Inch Nails."

"I don't find that at all surprising."

"Why?"

"Because you're as bipolar as their music. All fun and games one minute, serious as a heart attack the next."

"I prefer to think of it as music that makes you think."

"Or want to cut yourself."

He laughed and conceded, "Okay, it definitely has some darker elements."

"What kind of food do you like?" She frowned. Shit. He didn't eat. "Never mind, scratch that. It was insensitive of me." So much for small talk. What did you talk about with a vampire? How many knots per second he could fly?

"No, actually, I can eat from time to time. I just have to be careful, and I don't do it often. I love the smell of Italian food. Especially pizza. Ever since it was invented. There was this place down in the village called Angelina's and every time I had to walk past it, I wanted to go in and get a slice, but I never got around to it, and they ended up closing."

"I love pizza, too, but not quite the way I love French food. I love escargot. Love it."

Clay made a face.

She waved a hand at him. "I know, I know. It's not like a bag of chips and a beer. It's for the discriminate food connoisseur. Of which I am—and I'm very happy as a demon I can still eat food. I'd be very sad if I couldn't still eat."

He shuddered. "It's not discriminate, it's disgusting. Snails are slimy and they live in dark places."

"Speaking of dark, I guess when you've lived as long as you have, you've seen some pretty dark stuff. Like Hildegard . . ."

"Casey . . ."

"Look, fair is fair. My past isn't what started this—it was yours with the big blonde. So just tell me what happened because it's

clearly what led us to where we are. Mated. You know, like an episode of *Big Love* gone awry."

"Okay. You're right. Fair is fair. So here it is. Hildegard forced
me to mate with her. It had nothing to do with survival and everything to do with happening against my will. Now that I've debased
my manhood, do you want to try and make me cry, too?"

How did anyone force this man to do anything? It was prepos-
terous. "Forced . . ."

Clay gave her the white flag look. "Yes, Casey, *forced*. I was fully
prepared to end my immortality on my five hundredth birthday.
Hildegard wasn't exactly above letting me know she wanted to
mate with me just prior to. But I didn't want to mate with her. So
much so, I was willing to go to my death because of it. She didn't
much like that. So she took matters into her own hands and fed
from me while I was in vampire sleep, thus mating us—for eternity. And here's something else that, while ironic, doesn't exactly
work in my favor. I think, before I was turned, I had what is now
called narcolepsy. I was prone to drifting off during the day when
I was human. Right in the middle of everything."

"Damned inconvenient if your ship's being raided, huh?"

"Exactly. But to make matters worse, I think being turned ex-
acerbated my narcoleptic issues. It's why I warn you that when
I'm due for vampire sleep and I'm a couple of hours into the process, there's just no waking me. Becoming a vampire seems to have
magnified my narcoleptic attacks, and my vampire sleep can't be
thwarted like it can with some."

"So she was already a demon when she met you?"

"She was."

"And she basically planned this, knowing you were the force
that could sustain her? That's sick." Jesus. Casey's stomach roiled.

"She sold her soul to the devil. It doesn't get much more twisted
than that."

"So this feeding thing—that troubles me a little. Okay, a lot. It freaks me out. What does it mean? How does it work in Hildegard's favor? Wanda told me a little, but she didn't give me the deets, and it had nothing to do with it keeping her here on Earth. She made it sound almost . . . sexy, for lack of a better word."

"When you're mated like Wanda and Heath, it can be the height of a sexual encounter. But in this case it's anything but. Feeding from me, a vampire with eternal life, thereby gives Hildegard eternal life. She has to drink my blood to do it. If she doesn't feed from me at least once a year, she'll be sent to the bowels of Hell to serve her time, something she's escaped all these centuries. She certainly won't be shopping and partying—which is what Hildegard loves to do."

Casey's knitting needles stopped clacking. She just couldn't wrap her head around the concept. "But—how—I mean, *how* does she feed from you without you knowing? Why do you let her?"

The look of contempt on his face spread from his eyes to his full lips. "I don't *let* her, Casey. She comes when I'm asleep—the kind I just explained to you. When I'm in my deepest state is when I believe the effects of my human narcolepsy are transferred to my vampirism. That's when she comes."

She nodded solemnly. The coma. Freaky. Then anger reared its familiar head. What a sneaky, fucked up thing to do. It was akin to putting sperm from a condom in a turkey baster and inseminating yourself. What. A. Hardcore. Bitch. Casey put down her knitting needles and clenched her fists at her side.

"I have no control over it, and to my detriment, Hildegard knows that. Clearly, the advantage is all hers."

"So basically, you're just a pawn to her. A means to an end."

"Yes."

"Yet, if you mate with anyone else, you'll be shunned? How absolutely insane."

"It is what it is, Casey."

"Do the same rules apply to Hildegard?" How could that be if what the man in the coffee shop said about their encounter was true?

"They do."

And then it hit her, and she spoke before thinking. "Well, that explains Bendy Bob." She remembered what the demon in the coffee shop had said about his and Hildegard's sexual encounter. Hildegard might not be literally consummating anything, but wasn't she the creative one?

"Bendy who?"

Her face flushed. "Never mind. So there's no way out? You'll have to live for an eternity like this, after she duped you? There must be someone to appeal to."

His face grew dark. Big surprise.

"Do not clam up on me, Clayton Gunnersson. Don't. We've come this far, let's go all the way. From the look on your face, there is a way out. Spill."

"Her demon blood mixed with some concoction whose origins are unknown—at least to me. An antidote to this fiasco—or at least the hope of one—an antidote that took a hundred years to perfect, according to my source."

"Holy shit! That blood you dumped on me at the club was the antidote?" Oh, Jesus Christ. She'd stolen his one opportunity to free himself from that whack.

"Yes."

"And how do you know for sure it was going to work?"

"I didn't. Look, Casey, I'd searched a long time—several hundred years—for a way out of this mess. The clan doesn't want to hear about trickery in mating—they're not interested in sob stories. Your mate is your mate—no matter the species. I'd exhausted what I thought was every avenue, until I heard about this shaman who claimed to have an antidote. I'd just met him at the club when I ran into you."

"But wait—if you needed Hildegard's blood to make this antidote, how did you get it? If she's, er, drinking from you when you sleep, how did you get some of her blood to make this antidote?"

Clay's smile was wry. "I know some demons—demons who don't like Hildegard. That wasn't the hardest part. It was getting this shaman to help me make the remedy for this shit pile. That took time, and research, and a fuck load of patience."

"So call him up, for shit's sake! Get some more."

His laughter was brittle, leaving Casey desolate and not so hopeful. "Easier said than done. I haven't been able to find him since that night. It isn't like he left me his name and address. The demon world is very secretive. I imagine he wouldn't want many to know about him."

"So it was me who ruined your chance to be free of Hildegard." The pit of her stomach bubbled in discontent.

"No, Casey. It was circumstance that ruined my chances—not you."

"So what are the chances you'll ever be able to find this shaman again?"

"I've had Darnell on the lookout for some time, but he can't get a line on anything. No solid leads."

"Okay, so here's another question. If being mated to Hildegard has sucked hairy balls, why didn't you just end it all like you wanted to in the first place? You know, have a friend stake you—hit the beach at high noon?"

His eyes didn't waver, but his face grew softer, a contrast to his next statement. "As foolish and vengeful as this sounds, it became about beating Hildegard at her own game."

Men. Win at all costs. "So you've stayed mated to her all this time, never had another relationship, can't, you know, get jiggy with anyone—well, besides me now—all just to spite her?"

"Everything's so much clearer now."

Rolling her eyes, Casey scoffed. "I'm just talking this out. I'm a mere ex-human, feeling her way around in the dark closet of the paranormal. You guys have some absolutely mind-boggling rules and regulations. I'm just trying to understand. So here we are."

"Here we are."

"You're not going to make this easy, are you?"

"I have no idea what you mean," he said on a grin.

"You do so. With that in mind, I'm just going to say it. Since you've been mated to Hildegard, have you, you know, exercised your marital rights?"

Finally, his eyes met hers. "Nope."

Holy celibate. "You mean, you and—and—"

"Hildegard and I have never consummated a physical relationship. Only the one etched in blood. Close your mouth, and be careful with those needles. I wouldn't want you to poke yourself with one."

Squeeeeeeeee! "So last night . . ."

"Was a long time since 1298. Or maybe it was 1295. I can't remember when I last engaged in the art of the humpty-hump."

"But that's centuries. . . ."

"Again, your talent for stark realism astounds me."

"That you haven't killed Hildegard astounds me."

His look was pointed. "It wasn't for lack of at least trying to be free of her. Besides, our clan has a strict policy about violence unless it's warranted. Unfair acts of mating don't qualify. And I didn't necessarily want her expunged, just gone. But she's always with me."

"With you? You mean that metaphorically, don't you? And I only ask because this kooky gig has some pretty strange nuances."

"No, this kooky gig means it's literal. When you're mated by blood, you can always sense your mate. Sometimes it takes time to develop, but I can always feel Hildegard with me."

Her mouth fell open again.

"Your mouth's open again."

She snapped it shut. "Explain *feel*. . . ."

"I can feel her presence, and sometimes her emotions."

"Ah, well, that explains everything. Now I know why you're always so cranky when it comes to the topic of Hildegard. Your cranky plus hers is cranky-palooza. So I guess that explains how you knew I was having trouble with the guy in the coffee shop?"

"Yep, and I should have suspected then that this went deeper than just you sharing some blood with Hildegard."

"So you don't just have one woman on your back, but counting me, two?"

"They say there's strength in numbers," was his flippant reply, riddled with sarcasm.

Hold up, now. How dare he make her seem like the burden here? How dare he be so fucking put upon—like she was anything even remotely like Hildegard. Okay, so she was similar in that she wanted to slam him until his brains fell out of his head—but that was where the similarities stopped and the hinky reigned free. And if need be, she could control those urges, and she sure as fuck wasn't going to trick him, then stalk the living shit out of him so she could drink from him once a year. . . .

Uh, whoa—if she had Hildegard's DNA, that meant she was in the same predicament Hildegard was in. If she didn't want to end up in Hell, she'd have to drink from Clay—which made her far too much like Hildegard to stomach. Oh, the hell she'd be beholden to some man because he had what she needed.

But that meant . . . ding-dong—Hell calling.

And after all that, he had the clangers to make her feel as though she'd only added to his burden because of what *he'd* done?

Uh, no.

Casey dropped her knitting and popped up from the couch. "You know what? I don't much like your tone. I didn't do this— *you did*. I didn't sack myself with another woman—you did. And to even hint I'm anything like that spiteful, twisted, blond horror show makes me want to pull your fangs out with—"

She was silenced—quite rudely, and definitely before she was done reading Clay the riot act.

But there were other things to attend to.

Like the cloud of red dust swirling around her.

And the hand on her mouth.

And the skin-blistering heat.

Jesus, she hated the heat.

CHAPTER
14

All righty, then.

Turned out, everything Sister Theresa had said was true.

Hell was hot.

Which meant a condo in Boca was out for retirement.

"Ya got yourself in a fine mess, eh?"

Casey whipped around, her bangs plastered to her forehead, her tight jeans and sweater clinging to her in sticky discomfort. The next time she wanted to impress a guy, it was going to be with loose clothing.

A man, graceful and slender, sauntered into the room, wearing a billowy T-shirt and brightly printed Bermuda shorts. The clack of his flip-flopped feet echoed in her ears, his long braids swayed with an invisible gust of hot air. "Who are you, and am I where I think I am?" Casey looked around in disbelief—not only was it butt-fuck hot, the air was filled with desperation, a helpless vibe that gripped the marrow of her very bones. It seeped from every surface of the room, spilling from the pores of the walls, suffocating her.

His laughter startled her, jarring and distorted. "Ya, mon. You where you tink you are. Where you be for eternity if you don figure dis out."

Figure it out? Who the fuck could figure anything out in this heat? Shoving a hand into her matted hair, Casey pushed it out of her face with an impatient hand. "Figure *what* out? Who are you and what could you possibly want from me?" *And make it snappy before* puddle *and* grease *become synonymous with my name.*

He winked a large brown eye playfully. "One of you has to go. Dat mean you need ta find da key."

Or an air conditioner. Fuckall, she really hated the heat. "The key? Look, I'm not sure what this is about. . . ." And then it hit her. He must be another one of Hildegard's flunkies—and enough was enough, already. First the fake Rick, now this weird version of Jamaica gone wild. A spike of irritation followed her next question, complete with language she thought only Nina was capable of. "Do you know that fuck-nut Hildegard? Have we knocked each other around on some sheets with something called a Bendy Bob?"

She'd caught him off guard, his look of confusion said as much.

Fear spiked. "Okay, so did Hildegard send you? Because I'm really okay with telling you that it's the weenie way to do things. It's like the head cheerleader, sending all the other cheerleaders to beat up the class dork for her or something. And if you *are* here because of Hildegard, give her a message for me, would ya? Tell her Casey said—I went buck-wild all up and down her man, and but good, sistah." Frowning at her bold statement, she wanted to regret speaking so crassly, should regret it. Yet, 90 percent of her thought—*fuck. That.* It was Africa hot here—there was bound to be a certain amount of cranky.

He shook a finger in her direction, backing her up against a wall that shifted in a bulky, gooey mass, billowing in and out, emitting low groaning moans. His accent, thick at times, changed and was disturbingly clear when he said, "You betta watch your sass and focus on da ting you need to fix dis."

Moving in closer to her, Casey held her body very still, keeping her gaze on par with his in enraged defiance. The walls groaned again, then began to mingle with pitiful wails, soaring and screeching in her ears. His body, pushing her against the wall that now swarmed, bulging and hot, pissed her off. "Look, Mr. Tallyman— how about we quit dickin' around and you get to the point so I can go back home and you can get to those bananas. What *the fuck* am I fixing?"

Drawing a finger under her chin, he walked it up along her jaw and to the corner of her mouth. His eyes glowed red, spearing her to the wall. "Do you wanna be here foreva?"

She bit his finger—hard, but it only made him chuckle. "You got da spirit. I like dat."

Lifting her chin up and away from him, Casey bowed her spine, trying to avoid the wall and touching this man. "What do you mean by forever?"

"Eternity."

With a roll of her eyes, she sighed. She'd just gone ten rounds with a man who spoke in one-word statements that answered next to nothing and made about as much sense as electing a Kardashian for president. Her eyes narrowed, her fingers twitched, her head tingled. Hacked off and Casey were about to become one. "Get— to—the—fucking—point."

"If you don wanna be here foreva, you gotta do sometin' 'bout it."

Running her tongue across her bottom lip, she cracked her neck. "Like?"

"Like get rid of Hildegard. There's more at stake dan just Clayton."

Those balls she seemed to acquire when reason took a backseat to her fury grew. Invisibly swishing between her thighs. "Who *are* you?"

"Das not for you to know. Jus know, you don know everyting."

This had become like a bad episode of *Unsolved Mysteries*, and she was beginning to lose control of the manners she'd once so prided herself on. She gave him a hard shove, pushing him from her personal space. Her hands ached when she clasped them together to keep from placing them around his neck. If she could get some information from him that made any sense at all, it wouldn't behoove her to get it while she slung fireballs and in general did the exorcist thing. If there was some way she could help Clay—help herself—then by fuck, she wanted to know. The fight for calm was on. But it was becoming a monumental task to hold it together. Yet she gave it another shot. Her teeth stung from gritting them when she asked, "What's at stake?"

"Where's da fun if I tell you dat? All you gotta know is Clay knows what I say, and so does someone around him. Ask him, why don't ya?" He smiled then, sly with a secret only he had the answers to. Like they were playing a game of Clue, and she had to find the answer to who killed the maid in the wine cellar.

And it was the last thread of the very tenuous rope she swung from. "You motherfucking piece of shit! I said—tell me what you *knowwwww*!" she shrieked, lifting her hands high in the air, aiming for his head and launching a fireball.

Unfortunately, he was way better at ducking than Clay was. It crashed against the wall behind him, splattering and spewing hot sparks. If he was at all afraid, it didn't show by the way he shoved his hands into the pockets of his shorts and raised his eyebrow. Rather like he was asking if that was the best she could do.

So yeah, that made her crazier. His superiority chewed its way through every nerve ending in her body, raking at her overheated flesh like claws. A cry of utter frustration, total, full-on fury, exploded from her lips. Gasping from her escalating rage, the air that filled her lungs made her choke. It was thick and had a bitter taste like the noxious, gaseous scent of rotten eggs.

"Listen up! It's fucking hot here. I hate the goddamned heat. If you don't tell me what you mean, I swear by all that's Kentucky fried, I'm going to wail you with a fireball the size of a meteor!"

Her impassioned threat didn't faze him—not one itty-bitty bit. Because the son of a bloody bitch laughed again—this time with hearty abandon.

Something inside her broke free—tearing away and revealing a dark, dark door she couldn't seem to keep from entering. Nay, instead she ripped through it, skipping and screaming.

Raising her hands shoulder level, she let 'er rip, lobbing off a slew of fireballs, letting them shower the room like rain. They shot from her fingertips like baseballs from a pitching machine. Eyes that had once been clouded by sweat now were glazed with the desire for vengeance, sweet and tangy. A long, whistling howl erupted from her mouth as her feet lifted off the ground, leaving her a vantage point from high above whoever this man was.

If he wouldn't tell her what she wanted to know—all she could think about was making him tell her—twisting the information out of him until his eyes bulged and his breathing became staggered. She'd haul him up by his colorfully beaded braids and shake it out of him until he was left limp.

And that was when the vermin appeared.

Rats, fat and slick-haired, scattered in a million different directions, squealing and squeaking on the floor below her.

Wow. She'd summoned pestilence. If only Darnell could see her now.

Day-o.

While patting herself on the back she, of course, lost her focus and crashed to the floor below.

The very last thing she heard was the demon's freakish laughter and the words, "De servant always knows."

"CASEY? Casey—wake up!"

The rough demand rudely invaded her eardrums, but her body wouldn't cooperate with the command. It was buttery soft and lifeless, and after what had just gone down—it might be better to play dead. Or at least unconscious.

His tone was edged with a hint of panic. "Casey—c'mon. Wake up, honey."

Honey?

Heh.

It sounded like Clay, but then, the demon the other night had looked just like Rick. Her nose caught a whiff of Clay's cologne, leaving her almost reassured—but not totally.

She heard the shuffle of feet, and what she really hoped was Clay's voice, telling Archibald to call Wanda immediately and let her know to call off the search. Then he spoke again. "It's okay, Casey. It's really me. Clay. Open your eyes."

Like you could believe your eyes with this bunch of morph-tastic nuts. Though, to his credit, wherever she was, it wasn't hot. Her hands felt beside her—touching what felt like Marty's leather couch, but feeling wasn't always believing.

"Casey. *Open your eyes.*"

Okay, yeah. That had to be Clay. Only Clay could have that stern, no-nonsense tone of voice when surely she was half-dead and could use just a small "poor baby." And if it wasn't Clay, she knew how to summon vermin. She smiled. The motherfucker better be prepared to hit Walmart for some rat poison.

Letting her eyelids drift open, she struggled to clear her blurry vision. Swiping her fingers across her eyes, she massaged them, popping them open once more to indeed find Clay sitting next to her on the edge of the couch.

He ran a thumb under her chin, concern streaking his eyes. "You okay?"

Every square inch of her body moaned in protest. "I feel like I did a few rounds of Extreme Cage Fighting, but otherwise, yeah, I'm okay. What the flip happened, and how did I get back here?"

"Ironically, you reappeared in the same spot you left. You've been gone for almost twenty-four hours, Casey." His gravelly voice was tight upon his admission.

"Like, unconscious?"

"No. Gone. One minute you were giving me shit. The next you disappeared into thin air. I tried to be grateful because I thought it was just you needing a time-out, and you were getting loud, but after a couple of hours, I got worried."

An ironic chuckle passed between her lips. Clay had been worried about her. That gave her a nice, warm squishy she'd address later. She gave him a playful poke on his wide chest. "*You* worried about *me?*"

His eyes were teasing. "Sure. You are my mate."

A girly sigh bubbled, then was stomped down by her practicality. Yeah. He'd worried Wanda'd eat his balls for appetizers if something happened to her. "You deserved shit, pal. That you would even compare me to that—that woman was a real shot at my moral compass."

A small smile formed, making the dimples beside his cheeks deepen. "Okay. It was unfair, and I shouldn't have made you feel like a burden. How will you ever forgive me?"

"I don't know, but it might involve a trip to a masseuse on you. My back is killing me."

Clay's eyes dusted over when she made light of the serious situation. "Where have you been? What the hell happened?"

"Did ya miss me?"

"Casey . . ."

"Hell."

"What?"

"I said Hell. I was in Hell. I swear, in all my years of catechism, I don't know that I was 100 percent convinced I believed some of the stuff they fed me until I landed there. It really is hot."

"How did you get to Hell, Casey?"

"I have no clue. I know for sure it wasn't by way of Julie the Cruise Director."

Concern lined his eyes. "Stop joking, Casey. This is serious. What happened?"

"It's like you said, one minute I was preparing to give you the reaming of all your lifetimes put together, the next I was in Hell—or at least that's what the guy called it. Yep. He said it was Hell."

Narrowed and riddled with suspicion, Clay asked, "What guy?"

"A guy with long braids and a Jamaican accent, and he said I needed to find the key if I didn't want to end up in Hell forever. Our conversation didn't go very far because I got pretty pissed off—the heat makes me very cranky, for future reference. And then, you know, the usual stuff began to happen. Fireballs, levitation, but this time, I made rats appear. I have to admit I was rather impressed with myself—until I was facedown on the floor, that is. That's all I remember."

Clay's jaw tensed, his mouth forming a sneer. "I'll kill the bastard."

"So you know the Tallyman?"

"He sounds like one of Hildegard's cohorts, Casey, and he's a pretty rough one at that. His name's Marcus. Jesus, you could have been hurt."

Nah. She hadn't gotten that feeling at all. It had been more like he'd wanted to play with her—to taunt her with what he said he knew. "You know, I don't think he wanted to hurt me, but he sure wanted me to know something—something he wouldn't tell me. Something he said you knew about. Something that's at stake . . ."

As was typical with Clay when they talked about anything relating to Hildegard, his face closed up, devoid of emotion. "Demons are all about deception and big orchestrated games. He was toying with you. Nothing more, nothing less."

Uh-huh. She'd heard that same sentiment before, and it was always *almost* the truth. "Well, news flash—I hate to be toyed with—I hate the heat even more, and if my destination really will be Hell, then something needs to be done—soon. Look at my hair, for the love of God. I can't spend an eternity in Hell. Period." She made a joke of it, but that shit wasn't funny. The reality was this— it was either her or Hildegard who was going to be mated to some pitchfork whore who probably ate fireballs in his Cheerios.

"I won't allow that to happen, Casey."

Her eyebrow cocked. "Here's a thought—you're big on not allowing things to happen, but happen they do. So how do you suppose you can keep me from ending up in Hell?"

"You'll drink from me, but only one of you can do it. Hildegard drinks me almost dry in order to sustain herself. It's like storing up on my essence. But I only have so much to go around."

"So why wouldn't I do it now—like, right now, as squicky as that makes me feel. If I do it now, Hildegard can't do a damn thing about it, right?"

"If only it was that easy. We're talking vampire law here, Casey. She has to drink on the anniversary of our mating, and that's when you'll have to drink, too."

Oh. Ick. "So do we have a plan B?"

"No."

"Are you sure I have to drink from you to stay here?"

"Darnell assures me that's the case. The blood of a vampire is what's required."

That made her dizzy. "So it's only once a year." That wasn't so bad. It was like having to get a shot, or going to the gynecologist. You sucked it up, no pun intended, and you did what you had to do for life-maintenance purposes.

"Thankfully."

"Okay. I'm going to be brave here and ask when exactly this year will be up?"

Clay looked resigned. "Next week."

Grand. Her stomach rolled. "So it's me and Hildegard—head to head. Like Kong versus Mothra or something."

"No, Mothra. I won't let that happen. I'll make sure you're protected."

"I'd rather be Kong, thank you, and you can't stop it. She has to feed from you. And that makes me wonder something else. Why don't you just have a big paranormal sleepover when it's your anniversary? Invite, like, ten of your toughest werewolf friends and make them stop her from feeding from you when you're defenseless? If you can do it to protect me, why can't you do it to protect yourself?"

Clay's laugh was bitter. "The irony of that is if I kept her from feeding from me, it would in essence be killing off my mate. That's purposeful intent."

Her head spun from all these rules. "That still means someone has to take out Hildegard, right?"

He gave her the grimmest look she'd seen on him since their first meeting. "Yep."

"And what if no one else can?"

"I know I sound repetitive, but I won't allow that."

"Right. But you do know what that means, don't you?"

"You're going to think up some ridiculous plan B?"

"Hey, have a little faith, would ya? I did summon rats."

"Rats won't keep Hildegard from getting what she wants, Casey."

"No, but if all else fails, maybe I can."

"Absolutely not. You'll be kept safe until it's over. Period."

"Got a question."

"Hit me."

She'd sat up now, her feet dangling to the floor. Gazing at him, she asked, "Do you take anyone but yourself into consideration? Anyone? This isn't just about you—it's about me, too. I'm the one who's going to end up mated to a demon in Hell—*H-E*-double hockey sticks—if I don't get rid of Hildegard. Not that I have a clue how to do it, but I'm willing to find out what needs to be done because this is my unlife, too. The worst that can happen to you is you stay mated to a maniac, but you do get to keep your undeadedness, your home, and your pretty blue pickup while you wait around another year for her to come skulking back. Nothing that hasn't gone on for centuries changes. Boo-hoo. But me? Not so much. A choice has to be made—there can't be two of us, according to Darnell. Someone has to show up in Hell to represent the Hildegard faction, and it ain't gonna be me." Her anger that he so carelessly wanted to handle everything himself was escalating. She had the power to help, and she found it wasn't just herself she wanted to help—she wanted to help him, too. No one deserved to end up with the fate he'd been dealt.

And yes, it was because she liked him. She didn't know a lot about him other than he was one extreme or the other, and when she was actually able to turn his mood around when he was scowling thrilled her. It made her want to keep right on trying.

She looked to see his eyes had narrowed. "Casey Schwartz, I feel threatened, and I have to say I don't much like it. There's no way in hell I'm letting you go one-on-one with Hildegard. So forget it. You're not going anywhere near her. I'll figure something out."

Casey pushed off the couch, tugging at her sweater that still clung in uncomfortable clumps to her skin. "I just have to say this—you are the most difficult, pigheaded man to ever live. I can help you, Clay, and in the process help myself. This isn't just about you anymore. The hell I'll end up spending an eternity with some demon king. So you've got two choices, me as your mate or Gigantor. And be very careful what you say here, pal. I've been insulted to high Heaven on more than one occasion and all because of what you did. So if being mated to that homicidal, supernatural lunatic is what you want—you'd damned well better be prepared for the smackdown of your eternity, because I am not—*am not*— ending up taking Hildegard's place downstairs. Let me reiterate all slow so you get it. I hate the heat. At all costs, no matter what it takes, I'll kill the bitch before I'll let her leave me with a fate I neither asked for nor was given a choice about. So unless or until you have a better plan—there's nothing you can do to stop me." Turning with an exasperated huff, she planned to make a stomping, rage-fueled, hissified exit.

But Clay grabbed her arm, pulling her to him so that her spine bowed and she fit against his rock-solid frame. "Temper, temper, Ms. Demon. Look, I'll give you that an eternity spent with you as my mate has a far less bleak outlook than it does with Hildegard, but what I can't get past is, you have absolutely no choice in the matter. You're a young woman, Casey—you deserve more. You deserve better than what mating with me offers. Not that I'm a bad catch"—he cocked an eyebrow at her—"but I shouldn't have to be your only one."

Her eyes blurred, her throat clenched. Maybe she'd be okay with him being the only one. "But those choices aren't on the list of boxes to check off anymore. So it is what it is. I've always been practical, and I do understand what I'm getting into, and while I don't want to insult you, you beat Hell hands down." He was definitely much better in bed.

A throat cleared. "Excuse me, sir." Archibald held up Clayton's cell phone between two fingers. "This has been vibrating precisely every fifteen minutes. I thought I must make mention of it, as it seems someone wishes to reach out and touch you."

Clayton let Casey go, nodding at Archibald and flipping open his phone. He frowned.

Sooooooo unlike him.

"I have to take this, Casey. We'll finish this later."

Casey sighed at Archibald. "Men."

Archibald's eyebrow rose. "Indeed, Miss. We're all rotten scoundrels of the worst order."

She threaded an arm through his, directing him to the kitchen. "Not all of you—definitely not you. So how well do you know Clay?"

"Is this a fact-finding mission you're on?"

She threw up her hands. "Well, I have to get the dish on him somehow. He sure isn't talking. And no one seems to know much about him."

"Ah, then I won't be of great help to you, either. What I can tell you is this—Master Clay and myself don't know one another very well beyond social gatherings of the trio from Hell. Their words, not mine, Miss. However, I'm pleased to tell you that I sense he is a man beyond reproach, forced into a very sordid liaison, not of his choosing. I also sense a deep and abiding honor in him, and his promise to the fair Wanda was that he would protect you at all costs. And I believe him. No one was more worried than Master

Clay when you were absconded with. He went, as you young call it, ape-shit."

Which told her next to nothing, but sent a shiver up her spine nonetheless. She battled with the thought that it had everything to do with his taking responsibility for her demonic state, and nothing to do with anything emotion based. So she decided to cast her line and fish. "So he was worried?" *Over me? Of course he was worried, Casey. He's not such an ass that he wouldn't be concerned when you were snatched out of thin air right in front of his eyes and all because of what he did to you. He may not be Mr. Ray of Sunshine, but he has compassion— oh, and the wrath of Wanda.*

Archibald busied himself with the contents of the refrigerator, pulling out shelves and wiping them off. "Oh, indeed. I do believe I recall a point when I thought we all might have to stake him through the heart to keep him from finding that horrible woman Hildegard and killing her himself. Which, as you know, would only bring more harm than good to his plight. Master Clay may behave as though he's callous and uncaring, lobbing jokes about when he wishes to disguise his feelings, but that is decidedly not the case. Especially where *you're* concerned, Miss."

Yeah, yeah. But that was all out of obligation and duty. She'd never seriously thought he didn't have morals or that he wasn't willing to own what he'd done to contribute to this mess, but there was a big part of her that wished it had to do with other things. Mated things . . . "Thanks, Archibald. I think I'm going to shower and maybe take a nap."

"You'll find fresh towels in the bath along with a Yanni CD. Master Clayton asked that I purchase it for you so that you might enjoy his fine instrumentals whilst bathing. He said yours were all in storage until you're able to find another place of residence."

Casey's stomach lurched. He'd actually listened when she'd told him she loved Yanni. . . . He was just being nice. Because she was Wanda's little sister, because he'd doomed her in a deadly demon bloodbath, because he felt guilty. Yet, she muttered, "That was nice."

"Oh, undoubtedly." His profile, glowing from the light of the fridge, twitched with the lift of his lips in a smug smile.

To believe there was some hidden message from Archibald, like he'd picked up some kind of man-signal where Clay's worry about her was concerned, was only reading into things she was better off not reading into. "Okay—off to a shower. When I say my day was Hell—I can't believe I'm really not kidding."

Arch gave her an amused glance over his impeccably suited shoulder. "Then I can safely assume our girl-talk is over, Miss?"

Grinning, she patted him on the back. "Sorry, that must've been uncomfortable."

"Oh, not at all, Miss Casey. I watch *The View*—I'm very"—he swiped two fingers on each hand in the air—"in the know."

She went to the stove, where something hideous simmered. The smell accosted her nostrils. She was almost afraid to ask. "What is that, Arch?"

His hand went up in the air in dismissal. "A poultice of sorts, Miss. I'm an old man with many aches and pains. It's an old recipe from many years ago. Bloody awful on the nostrils, don't you agree?"

And the eyes. Hers watered. "It's pretty distinct."

"But soothes my muscles. Arthritis can be a demon." He frowned. "No pun, of course."

Her giggle followed her out of the kitchen.

Closing her bedroom door, she took a quick shower and changed into an old T-shirt, taking the Yanni CD with her out to the bedroom. A smile, secretive and all feminine, tugged at her lips when she put it into the CD player on the nightstand.

Oy.

Stretching her facial muscles, Casey fought the impending grin.

She would not read into a Yanni CD. She. Would. Not.

It was foolish and impetuous and something so small, it was almost unnoticeable. She was never going to mistake a gesture so simple for real interest in her again.

Ever.

Exhaustion clung to every surface of her body. Dragging the blankets up, she tried to stop the swirling images of where she'd been, and what else was at stake besides her future and Clay's marital un-bliss. Those words that demon Marcus had spoken meant something.

Yanni's soothing fingers, sweeping over ivory keys, coaxed her, calling her to rest her tired thoughts.

Her lips sleepily lifted once more.

Yanni.

Clay had bought her a Yanni CD.

No, he'd had Archibald do it.

Does it really matter how the transference of money occurred and whose hands touched it?

Yes. No. Yes.

Clay just felt guilty.

And a Yanni CD wasn't going to make up for being the Bride of Frankenstein's twin.

Not even John Tesh live in her living room could do that.

CHAPTER 15

She woke to the sound of Clay on the phone, gruffly informing someone that he'd come see them soon. Sliding from the bed, admittedly she was curious to know who he was always talking to all secretive-like. The bits and pieces of conversations she'd heard gave her no clues if he was talking to a man or a woman, but whoever it was, he talked to them often, and from time to time, his expressions warmed.

And it was driving her insane.

Rationally, it didn't make much sense that Clay was the kind of man who'd toss her, yet still be involved with another woman.

But no one was giving her kudos for her rationale these days.

Sneaking toward the door, Casey pressed her ear to it just in time for him to snap his phone shut with a quick "good-bye" and for the door to crack her in the head. "Ow!"

Clay stuck his head inside with a crooked smile, tamping out the throb of her head and replacing it with the warmth his smile brought. "If you weren't listening at the door, you wouldn't be developing that lump on your head."

"I wasn't listening," she said, way too heavy on the indignation.

"How are you feeling?"

She ran a hand over her rumpled T-shirt. "Better, thanks."

He tilted her chin upward, forcing her to look at him. "Good. You hungry? Arch outdid himself in the kitchen in your honor. I could heat some up for you."

She leaned into his hand, closing her eyes with a girly sigh. "First, no thanks. Have you smelled whatever it is he's cooking up in there? It smells like something died a toxic death. So I'll pass. And second, who are you?"

His grin was wide. "What?"

"You just offered to heat my dinner up. Warm and nurturing you're not."

"I've been hard on you."

And in me . . . heat painted her cheeks, making her swoon. "Is that an apology?"

"Yep."

"Wow. What brought that on? Did Venus and Mars align? Is the world ending?"

Clay laughed, and they were right back to the lighter side of him. "Your sister's tirade about my insensitivity with a little of Nina's browbeating me thrown in for good measure."

"Nina?"

"Yeah, I know. Crazy that, huh?"

"Crazy that," she mumbled. "I'm sorry. Wanda can be very protective. I don't understand how our roles reversed. I used to be the one who looked out for her. Suddenly, she's very fierce and winging it all over the place." Which should be a huge indication as to just how far she'd sunk since she'd begun working for the

Castalanos. She'd lost her backbone somewhere between running away from Rick and taking the job with the twins.

"You looked out for her?"

"Yeah. I know it sounds crazy, but there was a time I was a take-no-shit kinda girl."

"And what changed that?"

Degradation. Humiliation. Age. Rick. Her eyes flitted to the rounded top of his shoulder. "Life, I guess. I didn't realize what a pathetic minion I'd become until just recently."

He ran a finger along the length of her nose, making her fairly purr. "Well, you did say you could summon vermin. I'd say you're a force to be reckoned with now."

Her body trembled under his touch, as slight as it was. She found herself melting toward him, standing on tiptoe to get closer. Her hands fought a war with each other, fisting together, pulling away, reaching out, moving back, wanting to keep him where he was, but afraid she'd say something stupid and send him packing. "Did I say thank you for the Yanni CD?"

"Not properly," was the husky reply.

Casey's hormones kicked into overdrive, revving their engines. The flirtatious, kittenish half of her wanted to claw her way along his body. The other half, the one that never shut the fuck up when she was about to do something with total abandon, wanted to understand what had brought about this change of mood. This man made her head spin.

Hot, cold. Yes, no. In, out. He was like that Katy Perry song.

It was bipolar.

Which was okay by her—she could relate.

Her eyes burned when she looked into his with a haughty arrogance she had no qualms about calling upon. "What would be the proper way to thank you?" 'Cause given an op, she could think of at least twenty sexual positions that would do the trick. Oh. God. Stop, stop, stop!

Bending his head nearer to hers, Clay cupped her face, forcing her to lean into him. "I can think of a few things that might work."

"It's the lack of nookie for all these years, isn't it? Now that we've freed the beast, so to speak, you're all hog wild."

He looked almost offended. "Do you really think that's what it is?"

"Look, I won't kid myself into thinking it doesn't have at least a little something to do with it. I mean, centuries is a long time to not . . . well, you know. And even if no one would label me beautiful, I'm not butt ugly. So yeah, I think that's what it is. And I'm an adult. I consented, and I have no regrets." There. Nice and tidy.

"After all the years I was celibate, and despite the fact that Hildegard isn't ugly, either, I never caved to even her. That should tell you something. Not all men think with just their junk."

Warmth curled her toes, and threatened to get carried away. "It tells me you want me to believe that you're really spiteful and you held out with Hildegard because you hate what she did to you. But you are a man and I haven't done to you what Hildegard did. I'm the lesser of your two evil mates," she joked.

His hand found the curve of her hip, kneading it with a gentle motion. "So what would you say if I told you I'm a man who finds you very attractive? I'm not sure who or what made you think that you weren't. And there are other ways to find relief, Casey. All-out screwing doesn't always have to be a part of that," he murmured close to her lips.

Right. Bendy Bob.

"So how about you just let me find you attractive, and we'll go from there."

"You just want to wonk again. It's like potato chips, you know.

Once you have one, you want to eat the whole bag," she half teased, allowing his tongue to run along her lips, welcoming the shiver he created.

"After last night, I won't deny you're addictive," he muttered, gravelly hot, squashing any words she might have left by dragging her to him and suckling her lower lip until her arms slid up under his.

Her moan was of need, a need no one had fulfilled thus far quite like Clay. His return groan was thick, heavy with his own needs as he slipped his hands beneath her T-shirt and ran them over her ribs. Delicious ripples slid along the surface of her skin while he skimmed her hips, the tops of her thighs, teasing her, taunting until she squirmed.

Instead of waiting, Casey took the initiative, dragging the zipper of his jeans down, tugging at them to push them to his feet. He kicked them off, leaving him in his boxer-briefs and tight-fitting sweater. Her hands skimmed his pecs through the material, relishing the hard planes of his chest, grazing the top of his underwear, trailing a finger along the hair that led to his groin.

His hand wrapped around her wrist, guiding her to his shaft, encouraging her to circle it, stroke it. Clay stiffened as she made contact, moaning his pleasure when she knelt before him, hooking her thumbs on the top of his briefs and tearing them from his torso.

The thick length of him was long, silken, as she ran her cheek against the smooth skin, brushing it before tasting him.

Clay's hands went to her head, threading his fingers through her hair, clinging to it when she finally took him in her mouth. With a slow downward pass, she licked at him, caressing the length of his cock, pulling him between her lips, then letting go while his hips rotated, grinding against her mouth.

Cupping his testicles, she rolled them between her fingers

while she took long drags of his cock. His murmuring became unintelligible when she gripped him with firm hands, dragging her tongue along him, over and over until he hissed, yanking back and hauling her upward.

Their eyes met, glazed and stormy—locked as he drew her T-shirt over her head and pulled off his sweater. His hands were everywhere all at once, light, hard, fast, slow, hauling her to him until her aching nipples crushed against the smooth skin of his chest. His lips found her neck, nibbling, sucking the skin in his mouth, wetting it with his hot tongue.

And the tension in her grew, coiling in her belly, anticipating. Casey jolted forward when he took her nipple into his mouth, wrapping his lips around it while sliding his tongue over the rigid surface. A hot moan slipped from her open mouth. She gasped when Clay's hand slid into her panties, spreading her sex, thumbing her clit, making her lift her leg higher to experience every sensation he offered. Her arms encompassed his head, pulling him closer, driving her breast into his mouth, begging for more.

Limbs entwined, Clay bent at the knees, taking her with him to the floor. He spread her thighs, scanned her body with wicked eyes, hot in the dark room.

For the first time in her limited sexual experience, she didn't shy away from Clay's molten gaze. She let him look his fill, cried out when he dipped his head between her thighs and took a long, heated lick of her clit. He raised his head to capture her eyes once more. Catching the light, they held emotions she didn't recognize, swirling and fiery just before he took her in his mouth again, making her rear up against the raspy silk of his tongue.

Clay's strokes were urgent, a mingling of light and soft, bringing her to the brink of orgasm, only to ease back. The word *please* was on the tip of her tongue when he drove a finger into her, and then she lost all sense of reason. Bucking her hips against his tongue, she came with a hard swell of blood pulsing to her ears, and lava running through her veins. Her back bowed upward, her nipples tightened to unbearably stiffened peaks while she rode out a climax that engaged all five senses.

Clay didn't give her time to recover. He was under her in seconds, setting her on the thickness of him, driving into her, tearing the breath from her lungs. The muscles of his chest tensed when he entered her slick passage, tightening beneath her fingers. Fingers that dug into his skin, clinging to him while their hips ground out a rhythm toward completion.

Her clit scraped with decadent friction against the crisp hair surrounding his cock, adding another layer of sensation to an already mounting need. He allowed her to take control, moving as one with her until she saw his teeth grit, his fangs grow. Rather than frighten her, it aroused her beyond measure.

Reaching out, Casey touched them without thinking, shivering at his wild, bucking response. Leaning forward, she licked one with a tentative tongue, not even knowing what prompted her. They were erotic to the taste, and when his tongue snaked out to touch hers, she rocked on him, groaning at the flaming pull between her legs.

His hands spanned her waist, driving her to accept all of him. The clap of their flesh, the hot thickness of him inside her, the deep moan from his chest, consumed her.

Wild abandon surpassed all modesty when she lifted her hips and took a final plunge, a quest for relief. His arms went around her completely, pressing their bodies together until they gyrated as one entity. His teeth grazed her shoulder, and in her daze of pleasure, the unbelievable desire to have them sink into her flesh was almost more than she could bear.

Clay roared his release in her ear, encouraging her to let go, too. The tightening of her belly, the clench of her thighs, wrought flashes of colored light as she came, pounding into him until she was replete.

Her hair stuck to her head with perspiration, her hands feebly clung to his biceps while they each found relaxation in each other's arms. Clay's lips went to her ear, caressing the outer shell, whispering his pleasure before he scooped her up and placed her on the bed.

Climbing in beside her, he pulled the covers over them, tucking them under her chin and spooning her from behind. That simple gesture made her heart throb. The security he brought with the shield of his chest against her back made her sigh with a contentedness that came from her soul.

Casey didn't understand the emotion, and she wasn't willing to investigate the whys or wherefores. Instead, she closed her eyes and burrowed against him with a deep satisfaction she wanted more of.

Over, and over, and over.

CASEY rolled to grab her phone. Seeing Wanda's number left her debating whether she should pick it up. But she hadn't talked to her in two days. If she didn't answer, Wanda'd just barrel on over anyway. And catch her playing naked vampire games. "Hey, Wanda," she mumbled, forcing an informal casualness to her tone.

"What are you doing?"

Soaking up the afterglow of a wild toss with a vampire. "I was sleeping."

"Well, get up, and do it without the vampire."

Casey glanced over at Clay, deep in vampire sleep. "Wanda, it's six in the morning. Why am I getting up?" And what for? She had no job, no purpose.

"I want you to get up, get dressed, and meet us at a diner called the Grub Shack. It's right down the road from you."

"Why?"

"Because I said so."

"Wanda, I'm tired. I don't want the meatloaf and mashed potato blue-plate special. I want to sleep."

"Casey!" she hissed into the phone. "Get down here now or suffer my wrath."

Her wrath . . . "Wanda? What's so damned important it can't wait until later today—you know, like, after I've had a decent amount of sleep? Or have you forgotten I went on a little adventure called Hell?"

"I haven't forgotten, and that's why I'm calling. Now—"

The shuffle of the phone switching hands grated against her tired ears. "Casey? It's Nina. Get the fuck down here so I can go home and go to fucking sleep. Do you have any idea how much blood laced with caffeine I had to drink to keep my eyes open this long? I'm cranky and goddamned bloated. Get down here now."

The click of the phone and the resulting dial tone forced her from her bed. It had to be serious or Wanda would have just come to the apartment and forced her to listen to whatever this emergency was about. Throwing on some jeans and a sweater, she gave one last glance to Clay, smiling at his bizarre slumber.

This time, taking in his peaceful frame, it wasn't her loins that burned uncontrollably. Her heart did, shifting in her chest with a flippy-floppy jump.

She turned away with a swift jerk of legs and feet, freaked out by this sudden warmth she experienced for a man who was, at best, a cranky pants wiseacre, and at his worst, Genghis Kahn new millennium style.

The unbelievable sex could not be the glue with which she

mentally put some fake relationship together full of her wishful delusions.

Pulling her coat from the back of the chair, she tiptoed out of the bedroom and ran for the door, rushing to the elevator and out of the building.

Her feet carried her to a hurried halt in front of the Grub Shack, where Wanda paced by the bubbled, oval doors. She pushed it open, ushering Casey in with a firm hand.

Nina sat at a table not far from the diner's entrance with a man. A very good-looking man who was as dark as she was. Their fingers entwined, and when Nina looked up at him to listen to something he said, she glowed. How odd to see the look of love, so blatant it made you look twice, on Nina's face.

Nina . . .

Yep. Jesus was due to arrive and order a cheeseburger deluxe at any minute.

Casey trudged behind Wanda with slow feet. Unsure she wanted to hear what they had to say. A powwow like this meant it wasn't good. "Wanda? What's going on, for Christ's sake?"

Wanda scooted her along the aisle to the table. "Sit. We have to talk."

The man rose, extending his hand to her, his handsome face pale and solemn. "Casey, I'm Greg Statleon. Nina's mate—er, husband. Please, sit, and we're sorry to have dragged you out of bed."

"Not as sorry as I am. Jesus, this blood's wigging me out," Nina complained, her almond-shaped eyes wide and darting around the diner.

Casey shook his hand, sliding in beside Wanda, who looked harried and panicked, thus transferring her emotions to Casey, whose stomach took a dive. "What's going on?"

Wanda slid an arm around her shoulders, pulling Casey's head under her chin with a dramatic huff. "Do you remember the Band-Aid analogy I gave you when I had to tell you about your horns?"

Now her stomach roiled. "Uh-huh . . ."

Her sister stroked her head. "Figuratively speaking, we're going to have another Band-Aid moment."

Casey's head popped up. "Okay—so just do it. Things seem to be on a downward decline—so give it to me straight." Brave, brave words, Warrior Princess.

Greg spoke up then, his words so obviously measured. "Casey, what's Clay told you about his former life? Or has he told you anything at all?"

Hah. Asking Clay anything personal was like trying to get an appointment with God. "He's pretty tight-lipped, but I did manage to wrangle a few facts out of him. He was a Viking, turned in the late seven hundreds."

"Did he mention how he ended up mated to Hildegard?"

She bristled. "Yeah, he told me all about Hildegard and how she forced him to mate with her when he was vulnerable in vampire sleep—which I thought was nuts because he's so stubborn until he explained the possible narcolepsy thing. He said next to nothing can wake him when he's in the later stages of it." Not even a life-force-sucking bitch like that blond nightmare.

"That's true—his vampire sleep isn't on par with the rest of us. Both Nina, Wanda, and I can stall it, if necessary. It isn't easy, but it's manageable. But did he tell you why Hildegard force-mated with him?"

"Are you kidding?" Disbelief was the clear emotion lacing her tone. "Getting him to talk about Hildegard is like calling up the White House and asking for the president's home phone number. He didn't go into details, and to push Clay about her is always dangerous, and usually ends with him more angry and impatient than he was to begin with. I might as well just save myself the trouble and throw myself off a cliff. It might be less painful." Excruciating was more like it. The more closemouthed he was, the more eaten up with curiosity she became.

Wanda's cheeks puffed outward. "Well, here's the scoop about the union in Hell. Hildegard bartered for her soul. Apparently, and it comes as no surprise, she's pretty vain. As a human, she was getting long in the tooth. Back in the day, you married very young, and she wasn't getting any younger. So her father planned to marry her off to someone she didn't much want to be married to. To save herself, she sold her soul to not only get out of marrying this guy her father'd picked for her, but to retain her youth and beauty. When she found out she'd been tricked into selling her soul, and that she'd be young and beautiful, all right, it just wouldn't be here on Earth, she found a solution."

Oh, Jesus Christ in a miniskirt. This woman was a maniac. "I know that much. Clay was the solution. Because if she drinks from him once a year, she's drinking from someone who has eternal life, and that means she does, too."

Looking at Nina, you'd never guess she was a woman with balls the size of church bells that clanged when she walked. Her face was softer right now, even in the harsh glare of the diner—softer and riddled with sympathy, leaving Casey almost breathless and definitely panicked. "Did you ever wonder why Clay stays mated to her instead of doing something drastic like vampiricide?" Nina asked.

Casey nodded with a slow movement. "Yes. I even asked him. He said it became about besting her. I bought it because men can be pretty competitive, and he's not exactly the kind of guy who'd lie down and play dead. Figuratively speaking, of course." And now, from the looks on their faces, she was feeling like a stupidhead for falling for it.

Greg grunted his disapproval at Clay's predicament. "He can be very competitive. You should see him slaughter my ass at golf, but if you know anything about Clay, you know he's not the kind of man who wouldn't rather go to his grave than be mated to someone he despises."

Clay played golf? Did the wonders never cease? Golf was such a placid, structured game—with plaid pants . . . Clay was anything but placid. "I totally agree. He's stubborn and pigheaded and difficult, all while he cracks jokes. Sorry. I know he's your best friend, but if that's the case, then you know I speak the truth. He's the most difficult, domineering man I've ever met, and then in the next breath a real wisecracker. He's like the Two Faces of Eve, the Knuckle Dragger version."

Greg's laughter filled the empty diner, rich and full. "Yep. That's Clay. So then a man that stubborn has to be sticking around for something, wouldn't you agree?"

Casey winced. It was another woman. Fuck it all if she didn't suspect it. All those hushed phone calls he'd never answer in front of her. He might be stubborn, but that didn't mean he was honorable— so while she'd been a convenient orifice, his heart, or whatever was in his chest, belonged to someone else he couldn't nail because he'd be shunned. The motherfucker. She tightened her jaw, reaching for the glass of water by Wanda, and took a gulp, hoping it would douse her flaming, irate gut.

"It's not what you're thinking, kiddo," Nina said.

"Then what the fuck is it?" she whisper-yelled, slamming her fists down on the table as she leaned forward, her eyes darting about the diner.

Wanda's voice hitched when she said, "A child."

Her temper went from a hundred to zero. "A child?"

Nina's head bobbed up and down. "Yep. Clay's got a kid."

Casey reached for the paper napkin and dipped it into the water, wiping her forehead with it. A child. She turned to Wanda, confused. "Remember our 'how to be a vampire' conversation? I thought you said reproduction was impossible for vampires?"

"It is, honey. Here's how it went down. When Hildegard made the moves on Clay, he was staunchly against it. He really was willing to go to his grave before mating with her. But here's the catch. When he was turned, so was his child—the vampire who turned him obviously had some serious vengeance on his mind."

Casey's throat began to clench. "But wait, I thought you guys had strict rules about this turning thing?"

Greg's eyes held hers. "That evolved over time, Casey. And that rule does exist in most clans nowadays. But there was a time when it was like the Wild West. There were very few who felt the way we do back then, but they existed and Clay was one of them. When he joined with them, it was under the strict rules that he'd never harm anyone the way he was harmed. But at the time of his forced mating with Hildegard, he had no idea a child existed."

Her stare was blank. Oh, sweet Mary, Mother of God.

"Clay thought his entire family was killed during the Viking raid he was turned in. But that wasn't the case. This plan to snare Clay had been in motion for far longer than anyone suspected. Hildegard stole the child during the raid, and kept it hidden from Clay. When the time came to mate with him, and he refused, rather than using the child as a bargaining chip, which almost makes more sense if you're a greedy bitch like she is, she used it *afterward*—to ensure Clay wouldn't do exactly what you thought he'd do, being the kind of man he is because, Hildegard needed him to stick around. Hildegard bet on the fact that Clay wouldn't find a way out of his immortality because he had a child, and she was right. No way would Clay ever leave one of his own if he could help it."

Holy deception. Fighting the rising tide of her anger, Casey focused on control. Her heart ached, clenching so tight, she almost couldn't ask her next question. "So where is the child?"

"With Hildegard."

Casey was on her feet, pushing her way out of the booth the moment she heard the words. "Then let's go get it. The hell I'll let that psychopath hurt an innocent child! In fact, I'll kill the whore myself. There's no rule about a demon killing a demon. And even if there is, I don't give a shit. Any law that says you can't jack up the bitch that's holding your kid hostage is bullshit!" She looked at them all, unmoving. Angry bolts of lightning in all shapes and colors seized her. "What—is—wrong—with—you? There's a child at stake!"

"Casey, calm down. Now, before all of the Grub Shack is ablaze," Wanda urged with a harsh whisper. "Wait—sit and listen, Case. Here's the rest of the story. The child hasn't been harmed. In fact, she's rather unaware of what's gone on all these years. She doesn't know Hildegard's mated to her father, and she sees Clay on a regular basis. Hildegard, in all of her fucked-up-ed-ness, was at least decent about that much. The girl only knows she lives in a big house with a father who travels often and a friend named Hildegard who pops in to check on her every now and then. Not so uncommon in this day and age, and perfectly plausible to a kid. Especially one who's been around as long as she has."

The vision in her head of this poor little girl chained to some chair fled, her bitter fury didn't. "How old is she?"

"Vampires age slowly. In human years, she's about fifteen. A very difficult age for a child, worse for one who's been around as long as she has," Wanda added, her features softened by concern.

And people complained about their teenagers. Imagine having one who was a teenager for centuries? "What's her name?"

"Naomi."

Naomi. Her heart fluttered in sympathy. That could explain all the mysterious phone calls Clay received. Teenagers could be very difficult, especially at fifteen. Being a young adult with all those conflicting emotions teen girls suffered couldn't be easy—especially when it went on and on with no end in sight. "So how's Hildegard able to keep her claws in Naomi? I don't understand the hold she has over the child. I definitely understand why Clay wouldn't off himself now, and why he lets Hildegard feed from him makes even more sense, but I don't get the relation to Naomi."

"Naomi is basically Hildegard's. To make doubly sure Clay wouldn't take his immortality into his own hands, just before she mated with him without his knowledge, she bound the child to her with some sort of binding ritual. She made her a demon companion. At the time, Naomi was a toddler—unaware—innocent. But here's the real trouble. If anything happens to Hildegard, Clay could lose her to Hell forever because you can bet your bippy, Hildegard might not have hurt the girl till now, but if she's forced into Hell—Naomi will go with."

Casey's head spun so fast, she had to cling to the edge of the table. Everything was so clear, but so fucked up now. "She's holding a child hostage? A *child*? Someone wanna explain to me why we're sitting around here looking at each other? Let's go fucking off the bitch," she growled under her breath, this time not at all surprised by her howling rage.

Nina reached across the table, grabbing Casey's hand. "Take it down a notch. I know this half of you. I know it well. I had the same reaction when Greg told me about Clay. I just wanted to choke the bitch. But if there's one thing I've learned since I was turned, it's to fucking think about your next move—carefully. This paranormal crap isn't like the human world. If you fuck up, you'll end up only making it worse."

Casey fought tears. This wasn't about Clay or even her anymore as far as she was concerned. It was about an innocent kid. "Okay—so the question then becomes, how do we get Naomi from Hildegard without creating more trouble for her or Clay?"

Greg's face was grim. "That's the dilemma. If Clay doesn't allow Hildegard to feed, because Naomi's bound to her, Naomi will end up in Hell, too."

"But if I'm Hildegard's DNA twin, that means in essence, Naomi's bound to me, too, right?"

He nodded. "Technically, that's true. But first, you're nowhere near the level of skill that bitch possesses, and to stop her from feeding from Clay, which would end her life on this plane, you'd have to be. Believe me when Wanda tells you, she is maniacal enough to drag that poor kid back to Hell with her if Clay or you try to stop her."

There was always a fucking technicality, wasn't there? But it didn't mean she couldn't try, and when she got a hold of Clay, she was going to flame the living shit out of him. Literally. And that was that. No way was she letting some kid take the fall for this— no matter whose fault it was. "I have to go," she said, wooden and flat, nudging at Wanda to let her out of the booth.

Wanda gripped her arm, her eyes blatantly filled with fear and worry. "You're not going anywhere, Casey. From here on out, we're like twins—the Siamese kind. The fuck I'll let you end up in Hell because of this craziness that wasn't even your fault."

Casey was floored, her response was shaky with unshed tears. "But you'd let an innocent child end up there? A kid who has no idea what this all means? A kid whose whole life will be turned upside down because of some fruit loop with an ego the size of the Ukraine?" Casey shook her head with a violent twist. "I don't know about you, but if I have to live an eternity with that on my plate—it'd be just like Hell anyway. No can do."

Wanda's eyes filled with tears. "Casey—I won't let you do this. Hildegard's too strong for you to take on. I absolutely won't let you risk sacrificing yourself. You didn't ask for this!"

"And Naomi did?" she squeaked, brushing a hot tear from her cheek.

Greg reached across the table and put a hand on her arm. "Clay would never allow this. Never. It's why he didn't tell you himself, but if he didn't find a solution, I certainly wasn't going to let you be blindsided. I have to believe he would have come to you because that's who Clay is. But my lovely wife overheard me talking to another clan member who knew something about Hildegard, and if you know my Nina, you know there's no stopping her. She said we had to tell both Wanda and you. I've already apologized to Clay in a voice mail he'll have when he wakes. But promise me this, Casey. Don't do anything rash until I poke around some more, okay? We've got some time before Hildegard's due to feed. Let me see what I can come up with before you do anything, understood? There's no way we'll let you go into this alone."

"It'll be all-out war, Greg," Nina warned. "That freak'll bring reinforcements, maybe more than we have. Do you really think the clan's going to get involved in matters of mating? I think we both know how that fucking goes. If we do it, we do it rogue."

Greg turned to Nina, his serious eyes softening in her direction. "I know what has to be done, honey. I know it means employing those who're willing to go against clan law, but there's a kid involved. At this point, I don't care what the clan says."

"I appreciate all of this, but right now, I really have to go."

"Where?" Wanda asked.

Casey's eyes narrowed. "To kill a vampire." She pried Wanda's fingers from her arm. "And Wanda, you have to let me. I'm not saying I don't want your help, but I am saying Clay has a lot of explaining to do—to *me*. Not you."

Nina was the first to relieve some of the tension by laughing. "You give him shit, kiddo. He deserves it for keeping that kind of crap from you."

Greg's brow furrowed. "Hush, woman. Don't encourage violence."

Nina made a face at him. "Yeah, except everything that goes on in this kooky world you dragged me into has something to do with violence. It's always the endgame. You know it, and so do I. Wasn't it you just planning a rematch of the Sharks and the Jets? Clay deserves a good lickin' for not telling her. You do remember the part about not telling me what needed tellin' until it was almost too late, don't ya, honey?"

Greg made a face back at her. "Yes, precious. I remember, but it was for your own good, if you'll recall. I didn't want you to feel pressured into doing something you might regret."

"Hah! And look where that landed our asses—in the middle of a crazy smackdown with a fucking maniac. What is it with you bunch anyway? All these secrets and bullshit. It always leads to the same thing—a fucking throwdown. So don't you tell me not to encourage Casey to kick his night-dwelling ass, pal. He should just bend over and let her have at it."

Greg ran an impatient hand through his hair. "He was only trying to protect her, Nina. So she wouldn't be any more pressured than she already was. Adding Naomi to the mix is a fucked up twist that Casey didn't see coming. If she offers herself up—it's suicide for her. If she doesn't, she's the bad guy for putting herself before a young girl. That's more than a rock and a hard place. One Clay didn't want her in."

Nina spread her hand over the table in a wide arc. "And look how that's workin' out, life mate," she observed with a wry expression.

"Look," Wanda intervened, her blue eyes watery. "Go confront Clay. I'm all about getting things out in the open, but don't do anything stupid, please. Don't do anything until we can try and find a way out that's best for everyone. I *know* there has to be a way. I won't believe otherwise. We'll figure out how to take her down."

A steely determination had gripped Casey. Nothing Wanda or her paranormal friends could say would stop her from doing what had to be done, but she knew it was prudent to keep her convictions to herself. "I'll do that, Wanda. And please, don't worry, okay? Everything will be fine." She paused, turning to Greg and Nina. "Thanks for telling me. I know Clay won't like it, but that's too damn bad. You did what you thought was right, and it's appreciated."

Nina held up her knuckles to Casey, and Casey cracked them with hers. "Go home and go to bed. Your eyes look like they've been on a five-day bender," she said.

Greg rose as she exited the booth. "Casey? Call me if you need me. Don't hesitate."

Casey nodded, letting Wanda take her hand and walk her to the door. The warmth of it comforted her. "Honey, promise me . . ."

She fidgeted, moving from foot to foot. "I promise I'll be careful."

"Wait, one more thing."

"What?"

"This has more to do with Clay than you're letting on. You've developed feelings for him."

She'd developed something. "I won't lie and tell you I don't find him wildly attractive, Wanda. I do. I also won't tell you that I wouldn't have considered stopping Hildegard even if I didn't find him attractive, because I probably would have. It's unjust and sick what she's done to him and now a child. I couldn't walk away from that. It'd be like leaving a puppy to starve. If I have the power to help, then I'm in. Do I wish I'd met him under any other circumstances— oh, believe me, I do.

"But here we are. That there's a young girl involved makes me want to wretch. It makes me want to hunt that crazy slut down and set her ablaze while I roast marshmallows over her. So the answer is yes, this has to do with Clay. I like him. I like him even though he's cranky and funny all at the same time. He's also impatient and impossible to talk to, and I know very little about him. But I think now that I know about Naomi, now that I know the lengths he's gone to in protecting his little girl—I like him a whole lot more. But not even Clay's immortality is as important to me as Naomi's."

Wanda bit her bottom lip, her eyes full. "If I could take this away, I would. You know that, right? You know I'll do whatever I can to protect you. I saw this coming. I saw how googly-eyed you were over him every time he walked into a room, but I just kept telling myself it was your overactive hormones, and that he was the best option to protect you from things I know next to nothing about. This isn't how I'd want you—anyone—to begin a relationship, Case. Not with this kind of cloud hanging over it."

Casey swallowed hard. "Well, it isn't the way I would have liked to do it, either. Match.com doesn't look like as much of a ridiculous long shot as it once did. And we haven't started a relationship. We slept together. I'm not so far gone that I don't know where that leaves me, especially with a guy who hasn't had sex in centuries. I know the score. But you know, at first I thought my instant, almost uncontrollable attraction to Clay was based solely on this freaky transference thing with Hildegard, but not anymore. My hormones might be in an uproar because of it—magnified—but the rest is all me. Hildegard doesn't want Clay for anything else but the life he gives her on this plane. She never wanted him. And from the sexual escapades she's had, she'd go on living the way she has forever. She's just a snake—a coldhearted, vain, bottomfeeder—and if there's something I can do to prevent her from having what she wants, I'm just in. Period."

Wanda squeezed her hand hard, her face shaded with a mixture of fear and sympathy. "You're falling, Casey. Maybe it hasn't happened yet, not totally, but you're falling."

"Maybe so. I can't seem to stop it. But I'm not falling anywhere until I break Clay's legs. Oh, and maybe an arm just because."

Wanda pulled her close with a shaky whisper. "*Please, please* be careful, Case. Please. This is the most time we've spent together in years, and I don't want to give that up because you've gone and gotten yourself dead."

Casey pinched her cheek in response. "Dead would suck after all this, huh?" She laughed, pushing her way out the door and storming back to the apartment.

She didn't stop storming until she reached the bedroom where Mr. Vampire slept the sleep of the comatose. A glance at the clock told her he wouldn't be awake for several hours.

But that was okay.

It gave her time to plan his demise.

CHAPTER 16

"Look who's awake," Casey chirped from the couch.

Clay smiled. *Smiled*. Funny that. "Hey," he mumbled back, sleep making his tone sexy-gruff. He came to stand in front of her and pressed a hand to her forehead. "How ya feelin'?"

"I feel great. Superb. Fantastic."

His eyes instantly became leery. "Do I detect sarcasm?"

"Do you?"

"I think I do."

"Huh." She shrugged with a casual shift of her shoulders.

"Huh. That's it? No way. I just know you have something on your mind."

"Me? Whatever could be on my mind?"

"Spill."

"Like you spill?"

"Casey."

She mocked his tone. "Clay."

"Clearly there's a bug up your ass."

"Yeah, it's called my pending death."

"That won't happen. I've said it at least ten times."

"Right. Because you're not going to *allow* it. Yep, you've told me that like you have some say in it."

"So we're back to angry?"

"Nope."

"Then where are we?"

"Right here on the couch." She patted the buttery-soft leather.

"Casey—knock it the fuck off and speak your piece."

"Are *you* back to angry?"

"I'm losing my patience."

"This is me all surprised."

"Okay, so in an effort to try and get somewhere, I'll concede I can be quick to snap. I'm sorry. Are we all better now?"

"We were never not better."

"Where are we going with this?"

"I dunno, Clay, why don't you tell me? Oh, wait. How 'bout you don't tell me. Because you know, you've marketed the corner on not telling me stuff."

"What am I missing?"

"I think the question should be what am *I* missing?"

"If you keep it up, I know what you won't be missing."

"What's that?"

His grin turned playful. "A good spanking."

But that wouldn't work. She wasn't going to be wooed by a rare gem of a smile from him. Not likely. "Yeah. I bet you're good at those. I mean, if you're into that kind of punishment. You've had *lots and lots* of practice." Emphasis on lots.

"And you would know this, how?"

"I can tell you for sure, I wouldn't know it from *you*."

"So who do you know it from?"

"Listen to your voice mail today?"

He grinned again. "Nope. I rushed right out here to see how you were feeling when I realized you weren't in bed with me. Which, if I have any say in the matter, is a much better place to be together than the couch. But the couch'll work." He slid closer to her, letting his eyes take on a suggestive slant.

She used her hands on his naked chest to brace herself and slide back. "Then I think maybe you'd better hurry up and check your messages. I'll wait." She pointed to the empty space between them. "Right here."

"I assume there's a point to all this?"

"Assume all you like. It's what our relationship was founded on. Assumptions. Mine. Because that's all I have to form any kind of opinion on anything where you're concerned."

He grunted, heaving himself off the couch and picking up his phone from the kitchen table with a fast and angry hand. He flipped it open and pressed some numbers, slapping the phone near his ear and shooting her one of those looks.

Casey watched as his face went from total aggravation with her to an "aha" moment.

Clay closed the phone, throwing it on the table. He hooked his thumbs in the loopholes of his jeans, rolling his head from side to side. "So you know."

"Uh, yeah. I know."

"We're back in the bad place, I take it?"

"See, here's the thing, Clay. I don't know that we ever really left the bad place. Just because we cranked each other doesn't mean we left entirely. It just means we found some relief from a bad situation temporarily. The bad place won't go away because we yanked some covers up over our heads. Now, I've had a few hours to think about this. In the beginning, when Greg told me, I was pretty steeped. While you slept, and I simmered, the anger came in waves—sort of short and spiky, coming and going, coming and going. Now that you're awake, I can safely say, it's returned—full throttle. In fact, it's all I can do not to stay right where I am versus get off this couch and clock you in the head. You *lied* to me."

"No—"

"Psst! Quiet." The moment her fingers made the motion was the moment Clay's lips stopped moving. As though someone had stolen his voice and paralyzed his mouth.

Their eyes went wide simultaneously, and then his narrowed— at her.

Oh, shit. She had the ability to just think him quiet and it happened?

Niiiiice.

Her grin became cocky when he gave her his best "fear me" look. "Well, Mr. Gunnersson, lookie-loo. Now that I have your full, uninterrupted attention, listen up! Don't feed me the bullshit about how you didn't lie, and it was just that you just didn't tell me. That's lying by omission. You blow chunks for not shooting straight with me. I asked you—a lot. You said nothing—a lot. You have a little girl, Clay. A little girl who could be hurt for an eternity—no exaggeration—and yet you chose to keep that from me? What. The. Fuck. Is. Wrong. With. You?"

Oh, wait. He couldn't answer that if he had no voice, could he?

Bumma.

But as swiftly as it had disappeared, it returned.

Eek.

Yet instead of turning on her with his usual anger or even deni- als, he simply said, "It ups the ante, Casey. I didn't tell you because it isn't your problem. It's my fault you and my daughter are where you are. And don't ever do that again." He pointed to his lips.

"No, it's Hildegard's fault, Clay. You had no idea Naomi existed until after you were turned. And I didn't mean to—it just happened," she defended. "But I won't hesitate to do it again if you don't shoot straight with me." She held her fingers together in a threatening gesture.

Clay ran a hand over his hair, ruffling it. "While it's true I didn't know Naomi had survived, I did involve you in something much bigger than just the initial forced mating. Telling you about Naomi only added to the pressure you're already faced with if Hildegard feeds from me."

"She's bonded to Hildegard. Do you have any idea how much I want to scratch that bitch's eyeballs out for doing something so heinous to a child?"

His jaw hardened and twitched. "I think I get it."

"Crap, I'm sorry. Of course you do. But don't you think telling me you had a daughter involved in this was the right thing to do? That if I did manage to take that blond wing nut on, I wasn't just fighting for my own immortality, but Naomi's, too? Do you have any idea how scared I am for her? She's fifteen. Jesus, she should be going to school dances, dating boys that are all wrong for her, but instead there are some goddamn dark things going on that she has absolutely no idea about."

His chin lifted, his dark eyes swirling with an emotion that could only be attributed to a parent, he said, "You're a helluva good person, Casey."

"What?"

"That you're more worried for Naomi than yourself speaks volumes."

"Forget that! Just forget about me entirely and focus on Naomi and what we can do to fix this. We have to find a way. I'll be fucked and feathered if I'll sit back and just let this happen. And whether you like it or not, I'm going to do whatever I can to stop it."

Silence ensued while Clay stared at her.

When he finally spoke, he said, "You know what I regret?"

"I can't imagine the list."

"I regret not having met you sooner. I would have asked you out, Casey, if I were free to do it."

Her eyes went wide. "Wow. Is that a diversion tactic?"

"Nope. It's just the truth."

"And why is that? I'm definitely not the kind of woman you seem like you'd be attracted to." There. She'd said it. Ball was in his court.

"How would you know what or whom I'm attracted to? Talk about assumptions," he teased. "You're just different. You're wholesome and smart."

"Wholesome? Is there any less attractive word? I just don't see you as the wholesome type."

"Then maybe you don't see me."

Deep. Maybe not. But she'd never in a million years think a man like Clay would want someone as boring as her. There was nothing glitzy or glamorous about her, exciting or worldly. She was solid, and safe. Bookish and boooring. Yet she couldn't help but ask, "So what brought that on? Is this, like, my deathbed confession?"

His face went deadpan when he yanked her up off the couch and pulled her to him in a hard embrace. "Don't even joke about that. No matter what it takes, I won't let you be hurt. And what brought that on was the truth. You wanted more of that from me, and I figure if we're going to be mated for an eternity, I should tell you the truth. The truth is I would have made some serious moves on you."

Butterflies swirled in her stomach. "Reaaaalllly? Would you have invited me for a ride on your Viking ship?"

He gave her a mockingly stern grin. "Big-time. I might have even let you wear my helmet."

"Omigod—with the horns and everything?"

"No self-respecting Viking had horns on his helmet. That's just a recipe for disaster. Look, in all seriousness, I didn't tell you about Naomi because I knew you'd feel this way. I knew you'd want to help her. This problem, that wasn't nearly as shitty as it's become, just kept getting worse. Every time I turned around, you got in deeper, through no fault of your own. Naomi's predicament just added more stress. If it was just about Hildegard and me, I'd have done myself in a long time ago, but the fuck I'll allow her to hurt my little girl."

"I would have done the same, if it makes any difference to you." She let her head rest on his shoulder before asking, "What's Naomi like? I know in human years she's fifteen. That's a tough age."

"Hah! If you only knew. She's been sullen and moody and pouting for close to a hundred years now. It got worse when stereos were invented and she could tune me out, and now with the Internet and all the pitfalls of this day and age, it's not getting any easier. I keep praying this stage will end, like most parents, I guess, but when people say it feels like it'll never end, they really should have my kid."

She laughed. No truer words. "What was her mother like?"

"She was a good woman—we weren't married long before we conceived Naomi. We were young, very much in love."

"And Naomi never knew her?"

"She was just an infant when her mother was killed, and when I thought she'd been killed, too."

"Is it hard on her? Being a vampire? I mean, there can't be a lot of kids out there who stay fifteen for a hundred years."

"There are very few, but this is the life she's always known. She knows there are others who're different, and she's schooled in the ways of humans as well as vampires. She also very bright and very cagey. She wants to date and do all the things girls her age want to do. She's like trying to corral twenty cats."

"Oh, I bet that goes over big with you, Mr. I Won't Allow It."

"True enough. But I'm not just protective of her because she's fifteen. I'm protective of her because she lives with Hildegard lurking in the background. Though to her credit, and admitting this is like a shot to my gut, Hildegard has so far left Naomi alone."

"So where does Naomi live?"

"In my house—Staten Island. She's like every other teenager for the most part. She has a few friends who're just like her, and even a couple of human ones. She's got a fresh mouth, a chip on her shoulder the size of Gibraltar, and even with all that, she's turning into a stunning young woman, if I do say so myself, and she can wrap me around her little finger like no one else."

"This is a whole new side to you, Clayton Gunnersson. I think I need time to absorb this. I'm overwhelmed with warm fuzzies on your behalf and quite frankly, it's freaking me out." She grinned.

Clay's phone rang again, and this time, he didn't hide the face of it.

"Naomi?" she asked with a smile filled with relief that the phone calls were about his daughter, not some long-lost lover.

He shook his head in the negative before traipsing to the kitchen to dig through the fridge for a pint of blood, she was sure.

And for the moment, she was going to just revel in the notion that Clay truly was attracted to her—that given a chance without the hindrance of Hildegard, he'd have asked her out—maybe to a blood drive. . . .

And then she heard Clay's words, knowing full well he didn't think she could.

"I told you no, goddamn it, Greg, and you pass that on to the others, too. Under no circumstances will I let you all risk shunning—possibly losing your lives over my problems. You know damned well what could happen, and I'm not dragging the rest of you down with me. Period."

The high of Clay's earlier words slammed to the ground. There was no hiding from the hopelessness of this—there was no help without the risk of more than just her and Naomi being hurt. Her sister . . . she couldn't let Wanda jump into the middle of this when she'd just gotten her life back. When she had Heath and the happiness she so deserved. Not to mention the other casualties involved.

Oh, God.

Thus ended the warm, glowing, reveling part of her day.

CHAPTER 17

"Why do I have to stay hidden?"

"Because if Hildegard finds you, she'll kill you—and though you have eternal life—there are ways to take you out, and Hildegard knows them all. I won't—"

Casey rolled her eyes at Clay. "Allow it. I know. So I'm supposed to sit around and wait while everyone else fights my battle for me."

"*Our* battle, Casey. And in truth—mine. You should have never been involved. So yeah, you're going to behave, stay put, and wait for me to come get you. Greg and the others will handle Hildegard." He spoke the words, but he didn't look her directly in the eye.

"I bet I could take her."

"I bet you could. But here's the thing—your powers are new, your control is flaky—when one goes into battle, they should make sure their battle gear's in working order. Take it from a former Viking."

"Okay, so run the plan past me once more. Greg and the others are coming here to lay in wait for Hildegard while you sleep. Naomi's with people you know can protect her. I'm going to be at some unknown destination, heavily guarded, while everyone else does all the grunt work. I wait there until Hildegard's kaput, someone comes and gets me to feed from you—which is still a hazy affair." She winced. The feeding thing still made her dizzy.

Clay's smile softened, making the lines around his eyes crinkle. "It's not a big deal. I know the idea of drinking my blood makes you want to, what was it again?"

"Yark."

He laughed. "Right, yark. But it's what you need to survive. When the time comes, Wanda will show you what you need to do. You'll be fine."

"I won't be so fine knowing everyone's in danger while I kick my feet up and watch a marathon of *Rock of Love*."

"Casey . . ."

"No, don't Casey me. I'm not going to apologize for feeling useless. It makes me want to claw Hildegard's eyes out. I have all these new goodies, and I'm not allowed to play with the other kids on the block because they've been playing longer."

He brushed a hand along her cheek. "They're far more skilled than you. Nina alone is a force of nature. Add in Greg, Wanda, and the others, and we have some serious power to obliterate with." He chucked her under the chin, running his thumb over her lip. "So quit bitchin' and promise me you'll do as you're told."

The muscles of her stomach clenched. "I'll behave."

"Good."

They both paused, knowing the time had come. Daybreak

would arrive soon, and Clay had said he wanted to check on Naomi before he came back to sleep.

Before she spoke, Casey swallowed hard. "So this is it, right? I won't see you until tomorrow when you get up from your coma and I feed from you."

His eyes avoided hers but only for a second, then they locked with her worried gaze. "Yep."

Her heart crashed with erratic, skipping beats, but she managed to keep her voice steady. She kept her face as unreadable as possible, her hands as steady as she could. "So I'll see you tomorrow— when we're all mated and everything."

Taking her hand, he put it up on his shoulder, curving her body into his. His gaze was long, searching her eyes, and then he smiled and said, "Yeah, when we're all mated-like. You stay safe, Casey Schwartz. We have lots of getting to know each other to do. I'd hate not to get the chance to do that."

Words were pointless; she couldn't have spoken them for the hard knot in her throat. Instead, she threw her arms around his neck, burying her face in his shoulder, grateful he had a collar on his shirt to absorb the tear that leaked from her eye. There was nothing in this world she wanted to do more than have the chance to learn more about Clay. Whether they were mated or not.

His arms came around her waist, molding her to him, lifting her off her feet in a tight embrace before kissing the top of her head and planting her back on the ground and letting her go.

He winked before disappearing into the light shining in the foyer.

Her breath left her lungs in a gasp for air.

Her eyes welled.

Her hands sought the back of the kitchen chair, white-knuckled.

And then, Casey Louise Schwartz set about doing what she did best.

Fixing things.

SHE had no choice. There was no way out. If she allowed her sister and Greg and the rest of the paranormal Mod Squad to defend her, they could bring some heavy shit down on their heads—something they'd have to live with forever.

She was the only choice.

If she bartered with that psychotic nut Hildegard, no one would be hurt. Everything could be just like it was before, and while that wasn't the ultimate scenario, it beat a child landing in Hell for no reason other than some whacked woman's malice and greed.

Oh, God.

She'd never see her sister again, her mother and father.

But there was a child's life at stake.

She'd never see Clay again.

Every cell in her body rebelled against it. The very center of her existence quaked.

But a child—there's a child who would be left to fend for herself with a woman who's certifiable. A fifteen-year-old child.

She took deep, deep breaths, letting her chest expand and fill with the intake and release of air.

Never. She'd never allow it.

If Clay knew what she was about to do, he'd stop it. So would Wanda and the crew. They kept saying there had to be another way, but no one had come up with an answer that didn't involve someone losing something—a lot of "someones" losing something. But there was an answer, and only one person in this whole demonic mess had the ability to give something up.

She was the answer.

Casey Louise Schwartz.

"Darnell!" she called to her empty bedroom. He was her only hope of finding Hildegard. But he'd never agree to what she was about to do. . . . He'd stop her because of Clay's orders.

Shit.

Frantic, she stopped overthinking and acted, hoping against hope these magical powers she'd acquired would aid her.

Darnell had said all she had to do was think of him, visualize him in her mind, and he'd show up if she needed him. Was that like clicking your heels three times? "Darnell—I need you—*now*."

Darnell appeared in the shadows, soaking wet, a flowered swim cap on his head, and blue trunks plastered to his legs. His gold chains glistened in the dim light of her bedroom. "You okay? I was doin' laps at the Y."

"Find Hildegard."

Droplets of water left a trail to where she stood, his look guarded. "The hell."

"Don't make me go find someone else who will, Darnell, because I will. Find her. All I want to do is talk."

His head shook so hard, droplets of water spattered her face. "No, no, no. Clay'd have my ass in a sling if I did that. She don't talk, Casey. She ain't in her right mind. So forget that shit. Not gonna happen. I was told to keep you away from her, and that's what I'll do." He folded his beefy arms over his chest in a stance that said "not gonna happen."

"You know, I just thought of something. If I can call you up by just visualizing you, I guess I can do the same with Hildegard."

He started wagging his fingers at her, rushing at her with fear written all over his face. "Don't you do that, Casey! Don't you dare! You ain't no match for her. I ain't no match for her. She's butt-ass crazy!"

Whirling around, Casey took a deep breath, then jumped in,

both feet. "Oh, Gigantorrrrrrr! Come out, come out, wherever you are," she yelled, defying Darnell by giving him a "so there" look.

He slapped a hand over her mouth with a clap, dragging her backward. "My apologies, Casey, but I won't let you do it! She'll kill you, and that ain't happenin' on my watch!"

Casey, with mondo regret, twisted her wrist, pointing her fingers up behind her head and zapping Darnell in the ear. She winced, knowing it would hurt him.

"Ow! Shit, woman!" he yelped, but it forced him to let her go when his hand went to his head. "Casey! Stop this shit now or we gonna rumble!"

"*Hildegaaaaard*—it's let's-make-a-deal time! I know you can hear me," she shouted into the room. "You know you want a piece of this—so come on—bring it, you crazy bitch!"

"The name-calling," an amused, disembodied voice said. "Is it necessary, darling? It's so crude—so trailer park. And I'll have you know, crazy is as crazy does. I like to refer to myself as *resourceful*." Hildegard appeared, immaculate in a slinky black dress and hot pink heels. Her blond hair, scraped from her face, was twisted in a tight knot at the back of her head.

Casey's stomach revolted, but she held her ground. "We need to talk."

Her eyes twinkled with amusement when she leaned against the wall, intertwining her fingers together and stretching her long, graceful arms over her head. "You and me? Oh, I don't know. I mean, we are fighting over the same man. What could we possibly find to talk about?"

Sucking in a deep breath, Casey strutted toward her, each step she took, knowing it was a step toward an eternity in Hell.

Darnell had recovered and was up and at 'em. "Hildegard, you get on outta here, now. You leave her the hell alone!"

Casey held up a hand, palm forward, in Darnell's direction, and once more, just by thinking it, slammed him against the far wall, pinning him there. He struggled against it, pushing back with his hulking shoulders, the veins in his neck bulging from the strain. She looked down at her hand.

Wow. What a rush.

She looked up to find Hildegard's eyes on her. "Nice, right?" the blonde asked, giving her a demure wink.

Planting her hands on her hips, Casey looked up at her platinum nemesis with hatred. "Leave Clay and Naomi alone. Got that?"

Hildegard snorted. "Why would I do that? We're a *family*." She followed with a throaty laugh.

"You know what this comes down to, right?"

"Oh, I do. I know that someone's going to be mated in Hell, and it isn't going to be me."

"You're right."

"*Caseyyyyyy*! Let me off this damn wall now. You shut your mouth, miss. Shut it now!"

Casey shot him an annoyed look while she clamped her fingers together, and almost as instantly as she'd done that, his lips were literally erased from his face. All she could think was that Darnell needed to be gone. He couldn't be here to hear what she was going to offer Hildegard.

As suddenly as the thought came, Darnell vanished. Into thin air.

Dude. Double wow.

"How about you tell me what this is about? I'm bored with you already. So get on with it."

Rounding on Hildegard, Casey narrowed her eyes with determination. "I said, you're right. Someone does have to show up in Hell, and it won't be you."

She gave Casey a mock shiver. "You've got me all atwitter. Do tell."

Here. We. Go. The words left her mouth without a qualm, no second-guessing, they just popped out. "Leave Naomi and Clay alone—keep doing what you've always been doing, and I'll take your place in Hell. It has to be one of us, right? So let Naomi stay here with you—just like it's always been." She held up her hands in defeat. "No fight from me. No race to see who can get to Clay's neck first. He's all yours. Everything stays the same as it's been for centuries."

Her eyebrow arched. "Why would I believe you? We demons are infamous for deception, darling."

"No deception. No lies. I suck at them, and I haven't been doing this very long anyway. Straight up, I'll take your place. When tomorrow comes, I'll stay out of your way, and I'll make sure no one tries to stop you from feeding from Clay. I promise. You know he's the key to you being able to stay on this plane. If I throw up the white flag, nothing's changed. So tell all your demon friends I'm in."

The look she gave Casey was pensive, thoughtful. "You'd sacrifice yourself for Clay and the child? What kind of moron are you?"

"The kind who can save you a whole lot of trouble and probably a manicure, if you agree to our deal."

Her pause was long while she absorbed Casey's statement. When she appeared to have come to grips with it, her expression was incredulous with disbelief. She let a tinkle of laughter spill from her throat. "You're falling in love with him, aren't you? You've spent hours daydreaming about what it would be like to be his mate, haven't you? Did you see yourselves skipping along a sandy beach littered with seashells, and living in your cottage with a pretty white-picket fence? Nights by the fireplace, days spent swinging hand in hand along the shore. Cozy."

Well, it hadn't been on the beach—more like a nice suburb in maybe Jersey. And that made her insane. That Hildegard had pinpointed her feelings and spread them all out like she was putting them on a blanket for a picnic lunch, then had the clangers to mock them, made her want to jam both fists down her throat. Instead, she looked her in the eye. "Fuck you. Just shut the fuck up and worry about where you need to be later, psychopath."

She tsk-tsked. "Again with the names. So crude, darling, but that feisty nature? That should serve you well downstairs. They like them feisty. You'll be all the rage."

"How do I know you'll keep your end of the bargain? I want reassurance. You yourself said demons lie. . . ."

Hildegard ran her tongue over her glossy red lips. "Well, you don't, darling. That's all part and parcel of the exciting life we lead called demonic. It's all about the adventure, the risk taking, don't you think? But do think of this—Clay's the reason I can exist on this plane. The child is my insurance. Why would I give that up when you've all but handed it to me? Truly, I expected you to show up with your goons, and try and stop me. Imagine my delight."

Casey's stomach turned. Every cell in her body screamed to obliterate Hildegard, but that control she'd so longed for had finally taken hold. "Now *I'm* all atwitter."

"So I guess this is good-bye? Be well, darling. I hear Hell's hideous this time of year." She paused with a frown. "Oh, wait, it's hideous *all* year."

Hildegard left in a vaporous red cloud of smoke, her perfume the only thing that lingered.

Because she could, Casey flung a fireball into the puff of vapor.

In furious frustration.

Sitting at the edge of her bed, she watched the flecks of embers float and disappear with a resolve she didn't know she had in her.

Hookay. So Hell it was. She refused to linger on her sheer terror. She refused to spend time bemoaning what she was losing. Instead, she focused on Naomi, and a future, though still hindered by Hildegard, a far better place to fall than Hell.

Hell.

Ugh, it had been hot there.

She'd better pack some deodorant.

"WHY, Clayton, what brings you to my neck of the woods?"

"I'm here to settle this once and for all."

Hildegard rose from her chair, ready to strike, but Clay instantly held up a hand as a sign of peace. "I'm not here to fight with you, Hildegard."

Her pout was frisky and playful as she resettled herself in her chair. "But we always fight. It's my reason for existing, Clayton. What else could you be here for but to throw around threats? It's what we've always done."

Fighting to keep his hands from around her long neck, Clay lifted his chin. "We aren't going to do that anymore."

She clucked her tongue in disappointment. "I haz a sad."

Rolling his tongue along the inside of his cheek, he struggled to keep from snarling. "I think when you hear what I have to tell you, you'll be much happier."

Her slender shoulders lifted when she squirmed in anticipation, letting her smile turn flirtatious. "I'm on the edge of my seat."

Too bad it wasn't the edge of a cliff. "I'm here to make you a deal, Hildegard."

"A deal? There's a lot of that going around lately."

His puzzled look pierced the cool roll of her eyes. "It's about

Naomi. I'd like you to release her from her contract to you—
when the time comes."

A throaty laugh drifted throughout the cavernous halls of her
study. "And I'd like to rule Hell, but I have my doubts that will
happen. Naomi's my insurance that you'll stay put—so forget it.
And speaking of, have we given thought to what we'll do about
that frumpy, dreadful mouse Casey? She could put a real damper
on my anniversary, and seeing as you don't bring me flowers
anymore, it won't make me happy. I cannot believe what you
did, Clayton. Did you really think whatever that crazy shaman
gave you would abolish me? Or the real question—did you really
think I wouldn't find out? Honestly, Clayton. I gave you more
credit."

Turning from her, he fisted a hand and fought a sneer of rage.
Casey's name on her lips made him want to bloody her to a pulp.
But if he didn't play his cards right, she'd do that to Casey anyway.
"I—" He cleared his throat. "I apologize. I don't know what I was
thinking. But I'm here to make it up to you."

Her platinum head cocked to the left. "I'm sorry?"

"You heard me. I'm here to make it up to you—*in any way I
can.*"

"Does this mean, after all these years, you've come to your
senses? Why would I believe that now? It's been a long time."

"Why wouldn't you?"

"Because it's been centuries, Clay. For centuries you've re-
buffed my advances to make our mating a true one. I was so ter-
ribly hurt." Casting her eyes downward, she threaded her fingers
together.

"I was angry. Surely you can see why?"

She waved a dismissive hand. "It's all water under the bridge. It
was so long ago."

He knew he shouldn't jab her, but just one last time—for

Dagmar—his wife. The woman he'd loved and should have been able to protect. "She was your *sister*. Naomi's *mother*."

Hildegard sighed with a forlorn whistle. "I know, I know, and then I killed her because I was jealous that she had you. Yadda, yadda, yadda."

"Let's not forget the part where you let your vampire buddy turn my child—your niece. So I hope you'll consider our mating thus far a period of mourning for me. It was the right thing to do." To this day, hundreds of years later, he'd never believe that even his scheming, lying, whoring sister-in-law would go as far as she had. To this day, he wanted to strangle her—hold her down while she squirmed and begged for forgiveness.

She shrugged her shoulders, rising from the couch to saunter toward him, her eyes glowing with the look of a cat who'd just captured her prey. "Oh, right. There's that. But it was all for a good cause. So are we going to spend our time revisiting the past, or are we moving on? You said something about making it up to me. What did you have in mind, Clayton?"

CLAY listened to the plan Heath, Keegan, and Greg had hatched, and he was staunchly against it. "I already told you, Greg. I appreciate the offer, but no fucking way am I going to allow you to be shunned because of me." As tempting as the offer of help was, he just couldn't live with it. Harder still? Living with the idea that he'd lied to Casey about his intent to let Greg and the others help him. It would be the last thought she had about him when she found out what he planned to do. He was a liar.

As dawn broke, the first stirring of daylight shimmered through the window, giving Greg's determined face a sharp edge to it. "Then don't think of you. Think of Naomi. Casey. Would you really allow them to end up in Hell without at least letting us lend

support? Fuck the clan and its archaic rules, Clay. We're talking about a child here. Your child! I couldn't live with myself if
she ended up bound to Hildegard for an eternity. So how about
you let me worry about the risks, and you just shut the hell up?
You do know my wife, don't you? You know, the one who'd
beat you senseless for looking at her cross-eyed? She'd kill me if I
didn't try and stop this. I'd rather live with shunning than that—or
worse, Nina's disappointment. It's a bitch."

Clay's head moved back and forth with a violent shake. "Clan
law says you're never to interfere in matters of mating. Stopping
Hildegard from feeding from me is interfering. They'll boot your
ass out so fast you won't know what hit you."

Heath spoke then, with a grimness lacing his tone. "What's
the worst than can happen, Clay? So we don't have the support
of the clan. Trust me when I tell you, my friend, I've been there.
It might not have been purposely, but I was human for a time. It
might not be the same thing, but I started all over once, I'll just
do it again."

"The hell you will," Clay shouted. "You know it's much different
than being human, Heathcliff. You'd lose everything. All the power
you've gained over the years, the power that was transferred to
you by becoming a clan member. You'll have no protection from
rogue vampires. No resources, *nothing*. I'm not dragging everyone
down with me. That's just not an option."

Keegan slapped him on the back. "From what I hear, you won't
even know we're there, pal. You being a heavy sleeper and all."

The men chuckled, but Clay didn't. "Keegan, this won't bode
well for you, either. You know pack law. You've bitched about it a
hundred times. No violence."

Keegan's lips grew thin. "That was before a child was involved.
Because it makes me think of my own daughter, Hollis, and Marty,
too. If they were in the kind of danger Casey and Naomi are in, not

even pack law would stop me. The hell I'll allow this to go down without a fight. Not with Naomi involved."

"There'll be no fight," Clay reiterated, his jaw tight.

Greg's laughter was hearty. "Like you could stop it."

"There's nothing to stop. Hildegard will drink from me today just like she's always done."

"The hell she will," Heath muttered.

"But she will," Clay said with resignation. "I made a deal with her. She lets Casey go, and I'm hers forever. Lock, stock, and *soul*."

"What the fuck have you done?" Greg roared, the boom of his voice shaking the glass tumblers of blood on the table.

"I sold my soul to a demon."

Awed silence prevailed.

The first to shake off their disbelief was Keegan. "But I thought as vampires you had no souls. How the fuck can you sell something you don't have?"

"We do have souls," Heath said in flat response. "It's a little-known fact, but it's true—much like my reversion back to a human. It's buried pretty deep, because no self-respecting vampire wants to be someone's bitch for eternity, but it can happen. What I'd like to know is how you found that shit out, Clay?"

"Your manservant can come in handy for more than just a clean pair of shorts, buddy. He tells me that if a vampire sells his soul to a demon, he's basically fucked. I'm Hildegard's to do with as she pleases. It's just like Heath said. I'm her bitch. She shows up in Hell with me, that leaves Casey free and clear and with plenty of time to figure out what she wants to do."

"I'll kill Arch," Heath mumbled.

Clay rose. "You won't. He has no idea the kind of information he gave me. And it's true, gentlemen. No self-respecting vampire would sell his soul—unless he didn't give a shit about self-respect or anything else but the safety of his kid, and a woman he didn't plan on developing feelings for, but has anyway." And damn Casey for making him want something he hadn't wanted in so many centuries he'd lost count. His bargain with Hildegard would be far easier if he wouldn't spend eternities wanting Casey.

"But what about Naomi? If you sell your soul to Hildegard, and you have to spend an eternity in Hell with her, what about your kid?" Keegan asked.

Clay's face was stoic. "I'll still be granted the opportunity to see her. Not much will change other than Hildegard and I won't be spending centuries apart anymore. We'll live as all mated couples do." Fuck, he hated that. It made him want to puke. The very thought that she'd want him to honor her right to him as a mate made his skin crawl. But the choice was clear. It was him or Casey. Not in this lifetime or a hundred more would he risk her or his daughter. What still baffled him was Hildegard. She'd gone for his offer like a salivating dog. All this time he'd thought her interest in him was purely to sustain her existence on this plane. Yet she'd jumped at the chance to make their mating one that was real.

"We can stop this, Clay. Don't do it. Let us help you," Greg pressured.

"*No*. But do me this? Make sure Casey's taken care of, okay? She's new at this. Keep her out of harm's way at all costs." Because if someone hurt her, he'd fucking find a way to come back and mutilate them. "And keep her away from me until this is over. If I know her, she'll try to take on Hildegard, and she's not ready for that. Make sure she doesn't leave your sight until twilight. Make sure she's fed, Greg. You be the donor. Nina won't mind as long as she doesn't directly feed from you, and at least I'll know it's pure. With vampire blood Casey's life on this plane can go unhindered." He looked at each of them, men he'd played poker with, golfed with, even gone into battle with, and left them with one last statement. "I'm trusting every one of you to honor my last wish. Keep Casey away."

Heath shook his head. "This is fucked up, Clay. I can't in good conscience let you leave here without—"

Clay was gone before Heath could finish his sentence.

And he was going where no one stood a chance of finding him.

Especially Casey, who made his gut ache with need.

He wasn't 100 percent certain he could deny her if she showed up.

Because he wanted her.

And he'd go right on wanting her long after this pact made in Hell was official.

CHAPTER 18

"Casey! Casey—open this door now! We have a problem!" Wanda's voice verged on hysterical.

Shit, shit, shit. So much for a quiet escape. The plan had been to hit the bricks after Clay returned to sleep, and before everyone got here for the big showdown with Hildegard and her army of demons. But Clay hadn't returned yet.

However, if she disappeared, then called Wanda and told her the location for the paranormal rumble had changed, she could lead them all on a merry chase until she was shipped off to Hell.

And she still wasn't sure how that happened. When the hour struck, did a cab come and pick you up and take you to Hell? Was there a train station with a stop for Hades?

"*Caseyyyyyy!* I know you're in there. I can hear you and so can Nina. Now open this goddamned door or I'll open it myself!"

Damn their vampire ears. The window. She could climb out, float to the ground, and hit the bricks.

Well, okay, that might have worked if Nina wasn't such a brute force to be reckoned with. The front door split in two, wood shards exploding inward to skitter along the floor. "You move, I'll kill you, Casey Schwartz!" Nina threatened, charging at her like a rabid human rhinoceros.

Casey paused, but only for a split second before she was tackled and knocked to the ground by Wanda. Her sister sat on top of her, holding her down with but one hand. Her hair was wild, windblown and plastered to her face in spots. "Do. Not. Move. Have you lost your fucking mind?"

Fighting for air, Casey sputtered, "What . . . the hell?"

"Oh, look, girls," Marty said from above, as composed and beautiful as always, not a hair out of place. "It's the sacrificial lamb." Her face was lined with her anger.

Nina knelt beside Casey's prone form. And she didn't look like rainbows and rocking horses were going to factor into whatever was up. "You know what, kiddo? I've had about enough of this shit to last me to the next eternity. What the fuck is wrong with you, offering yourself up to that loon? Didn't we tell you we'd find another way? Didn't we say to just sit the fuck tight until we figured this out? But no. Do you listen to us? No. Why the fuck would you? I mean, what do we, the paranormal, know?"

Hell's bells—they'd found out?

"Yeah, that's right," Nina confirmed. "We heard all about your offer to take that freak's place in Hell. Are you whacked? Did you lose some nuts and bolts?"

Her breath returning in slow passes, she gasped, "But who told you?"

"Oh, Miss, I'm afraid it was me." Archibald, crisp and unruffled, appeared before her line of vision to out himself. "While I admit, and with great embarrassment, that I'm prone to nodding off due to my age, and indeed, it's true, my hearing isn't what it once was as a vampire, I do still hear. As I was on my way to the kitchen to prepare some warm milk for myself, I found myself presented with quite a dilemma—the offering of your unlife to that wretched woman. Now truly, what's a manservant to do, I ask?" He threw a hand over his forehead with a dramatic gesture. "Oh, the full five seconds spent toiling over right and wrong. But alas, I am in Miss Wanda's employ. Thus, my loyalties lie with her. Her wish was for me to watch over you when she couldn't. Hence, I let my fingers do the walking, and called Master Heath posthaste. I do apologize for, er, blowing your cover." He smiled and nodded with a curt tilt of his head.

Oh, God. No. No. Archibald had heard her and Hildegard. What kind of devious planner was she to have not checked to see if Archibald was in his room? Jesus! She was an epic-diabolical-planning failure.

But she couldn't let them stop her. They'd be shunned. All of them, and Naomi and Clay were in serious danger. A surge of terror and a side order of fear made her heave her body upward, knocking Wanda to the floor. She slid across the room, hitting the couch with a hard crack. "Get—the—fuck—off—me! I have to stop this. I can't let her hurt Naomi. I *won't!*"

Nina and Marty were on her, pulling her away with ironclad grips as Wanda leapt to her feet like a gazelle. "Casey—stop! You have to listen to me. You're no longer up for grabs. Clay offered himself up—he sold his soul to Hildegard. It's *him* who's going to Hell," Wanda yelled, grabbing Casey's chin and forcing her to focus.

Her eyes were wild, her pulse hammered beneath her skin. *"What?"*

"Listen to me. Clay sold his soul to Hildegard. She's going

to Hell, but she's taking the one thing she's always wanted with her—Clay."

"But—I thought . . ."

"I know what you thought, honey. You thought Clay was a means to an end, a meal, so to speak, but that's not what this was about. It's about Hildegard's wish to make him hers. That bitch was Clay's sister-in-law. She killed her own sister and turned her niece because she'd always wanted Clay—he just didn't want her. In her fucked up mind, she believes her sister Dagmar stole Clay from her. Now, in an effort to spare you, he's sold his soul to save Naomi and *you*."

Her eyes rolled to the back of her head, hard waves of prickling anger racing along her spine. "I'll kill him! Do you hear me, Wanda? I'll kill him. Stupid, stupid, lame, dumb-assed, difficult man. Where is he? I swear, when I find him, I'm going to do something horrible to him. I'll make him eat a rosary—lick a plateful of garlic!"

Wanda shook her head. "That's the problem. We don't know where he is, Casey. He disappeared just before daybreak after meeting with Greg and the others, and no one can find him."

Oh, the hell he'd get away with this. She'd stalk his ass in Hell. If he thought life with Hildegard was purgatory, juuuuust wait. "Where could he have gone, Wanda? It's not like I know where his favorite places to hang out are!"

Archibald poked his head around Nina's shoulder. "Oh, Miss, surely you remember Master Clay telling you he can feel you as well as that horrid piece of rubbish, don't you?"

"You heard that?"

His face was aloof and undisturbed. "If you only knew the things I hear, Miss Casey."

"So what does that mean, Arch?" Wanda asked.

"I would think it means that because Master Clayton is mated to her, it's a two-way street."

"But I don't feel anything," she cried. *Other than the need for his neck in a headlock between my thighs.*

Archibald put his hand over her eyes. "Close your eyes, Miss Casey. Summon his image. All that's required is that you grease the wheels of your new gifts. They're rusty from lack of use."

Grease the wheels of her gifts. That was the most ridiculous thing she'd ever . . . ohhhh, he didn't. She shook Archibald's hand away. "He's at a pizzeria called Angelina's in the village. He loves the smell of pizza. Angelina's is abandoned. I get the feeling he thought he could go there and no one would find him but the one person he wants to find him. Hildegard could do her dirty deed with no interference."

Wanda was all organization and orders. "Archibald, get the men on the phone. Tell them to meet us there. Hurry. Clay's only been asleep for an hour. If we time this right, we can beat the bitch at her own game. Nina—crack your knuckles. Marty, sharpen your canines. We have demon ass to annihilate."

Casey struggled against Nina and Marty, fear blazing to every screaming nerve in her body. "No. You can't do this. Please, Wanda. Please, please, don't do this—none of you. I know what can happen. Greg said you could all be shunned, lose everything. Please, just let me go alone."

"Oh, fuck that," Nina rasped. "Like I give a shit about a castle in Staten Island? It's a fucking big, drafty dust ball I spend more time Swiffering than I do enjoying. The clan can bite my skinny ass. Now shut the fuck up, and let's go."

But at all costs, she was prepared to keep them from coming. "Nina? Don't make me hurt you," she growled low.

Nina let her shoulders slump in tired defeat. "Are we gonna do this shit again? C'mon, already. I'll kick your ass from here to Coney

Island. You caught me off guard the first time you nailed me, but it ain't like that anymore. And trust me when I tell you, I've sharpened my vampire skillz—unlike you. Now could we just do this without a fight? I'd like a fucking good day's worth of sleep, something I haven't had since I met you and your fireballs. I sure as fuck don't want to do caffeine-laced blood anymore so I can keep daylight hours because it makes me hinky. So lay off already, and let's rock."

Casey balled her fist, raising it high in the air with the threat of imminent flaming.

Marty yawned, obviously bored. "Oh. No. Look," she said, wooden and bored. "Nina and Casey are going to fight. We—are—all—surprised."

"Ladies!" Archibald hollered, demanding their attention. "Please, no more fisticuffs. Honestly, if you knew the amount of time I spend clearing away the debris Miss Casey alone creates, surely you'd take pity on an old man. Now, we must hurry if we're to make the mating on time. Miss Wanda, call Master Heathcliff and have him gather the forces. Miss Casey, there'll be no more talk of shunning and interference in the matters of mating to that lowly serf. Of this I can assure you, Master Greg and the others will find Clayton whether he likes it or not. They are vampires and in an emergency are sure to use their powers of the mind to locate him despite Master Clayton's wish they leave him be. Now, do you wish to allow the men in your lives to be ambushed, or would you think it wise to find our Scooby-Doo mobile and lay in wait with the element of surprise?"

"I don't see him. Do you see him, Wanda?" Casey asked. The windows of Angelina's were boarded up. Not an ounce of daylight seeped through them. The musty restaurant was as dark as a tomb. And that made perfect sense for someone like Clay.

"I don't see him, either," Nina added. "Where the frig could he be in a pizza joint?"

Frustration and fear for Clay's safety made her yell, "Don't you two have super eyeballs? What good are you if you can't see in the dark?"

They'd made a human, er, paranormal chain in an effort to stay together, putting Casey between Nina and Wanda. Wanda gripped her hand hard. "Casey, hush. Why don't you just give Hildegard a ring-a-ling and tell her that we're here? Or maybe you'd like a megaphone. I know how badly you wanted to be a cheerleader. You can live out your dream while you lead our hunter right to us."

Instantly, Casey was remorseful. "Sorry. It's my nerves. They make me edgy."

Nina bumped shoulders with her. "And loud. Knock it the fuck off and shut your trap. Just keep walking and don't let go of our hands."

"Nina?"

"Marty?"

"Stop dragging me. I have heels on, for the love of God. If I trip and rip this dress, I'm going to pull your fangs out with a pair of old pliers."

"Oh, my God, if the two of you don't shut the hell up, I'll beat you with *my* shoes," Wanda hissed. "Now hush, and let Casey focus. Casey, honey—do you feel Clay?"

Feel him. Yeah, she felt him—everywhere. She just couldn't pinpoint it in any one direction. It was like he was all around her and nowhere at all. "I can't explain it, but it's like he's everywhere. Ever since Arch told me to grease my wheels, they've just been spinning. I can feel him, but not in any one particular place."

"Well, for fuck's sake, use more grease. I see nothing but a bunch of goddamned tables and chairs and a row of pizza ovens," Nina complained.

"Speaking of Arch, where is he?" Marty said from behind.

Everyone stopped dead in their tracks.

Nina gripped Casey's hand harder. "He was holding your hand, Marty. Don't fucking tell me you lost him. Jesus, dumb ass, he's a human—an old one at that. Left on his own, that nut'll flay him alive. Heath will kill us himself if we let anything happen to Arch."

"Why is it that everyone's always calling me a nut? I'm so disappointed with the impression I've given you all. I prefer evil genius, thank you kindly, and what a drag you all showed up. It's my anniversary, for goodness' sake. Don't any of you have a romantic bone? I can't properly celebrate with my mate if you're all here, now can I? Or do you girls swing that way?"

Each of them stood rooted in place, but Casey felt the tense tug of both Nina's and Wanda's hands, keeping her close. They could all apparently see Hildegard. Casey's eyes just didn't have that ability—not yet anyway.

Until a snap of Hildegard's fingers switched on the lights, that is.

Hildegard, dressed in jeans and a boob-hugging sweater, held Archibald by the scruff of his neck. He dangled like a rag doll, but his eyes, though they should have been frantic, sought hers with warm reassurance—one Casey didn't understand, and promptly dismissed. Nothing was going to be all right. Everyone would die because of her.

"Put him the fuck down, you ozone suck," Nina ordered. "Or I'll snatch every hair off your blindingly blond head with my teeth while I smash your face in." Nina bared her fangs with a hiss, balling a threatening fist.

Hildegard strolled toward Nina, each step a sway of confident hips. Archibald wafted to and fro, but his eyes stayed on Casey, riveted. "You are the most vile-mouthed creature. Uneducated, uncultured. I would have expected Casey to have more worldly friends—as boring as she is."

Boring this, you pissy bitch. Yet, Casey refrained from screaming her panicked wish. Maybe this could be solved calmly—so no one would get hurt. The struggle to keep her temper in check was on. "Put him down, Hildegard. Please. He has nothing to do with this."

Her eyes flashed to Casey while her free hand created a ball of fire she played with between her fingers much like magicians do with quarters. "Now why would I do that, darling? We were supposed to have a deal. Imagine my surprise when I showed up and found all of you. I have a sinking feeling you all aren't here with cake and champagne. Pity, too. I so love cake."

"Where are the damn men?" Wanda muttered under her breath, looking in Nina's direction.

"Who gives a shit?" Nina muttered back. "We can take her. She's just one floozy demon."

Marty sighed, her eyes looking beyond Hildegard's shoulder. "Weeeelll, not so much. And damn it all. I just know I'm going to lose a perfectly good pair of shoes in this. These are one of a kind. I can't believe I didn't think to change them before we rushed out the door to demon bang."

Each pair of eyes assessed the situation.

Oh.

Wow.

Casey tried to remember if there was something in her catechism class that expressed what she was seeing. A word that meant a lot and was associated with demons.

Legions.

Yeah, that was it.

A legion of demons.

That described it.

To. A. Tee.

"Look, Wanda. The Jolly Green Blonde brought friends," Nina crowed, her sarcasm echoing around them.

Casey looked at Nina and whisper-yelled out of the side of her mouth, "Yeah, she brought friends. And she has way more friends than we do. Jesus! Aren't you afraid of anything? They'll mutilate us. Don't provoke her." Swarms of demons in every scaly shape and size flocked toward Hildegard's side. Oh, this was bad. Where the hell was everyone? More important, where was Clay? He was the one they had to keep Hildegard from getting to. They'd never be able to take on so many—it was like four against four million as far as Casey was concerned.

Hildegard draped Archibald over her shoulder like a coat, and he offered no resistance whatsoever. "So who's going to be the first to apologize for ruining what was to be a lovely evening with my mate?" Her eyebrow cocked and her toe tapped with impatience.

"Fuck you," Nina seethed.

"Is it me, or do you feel a little outnumbered, Nina?" Hildegard drawled, looking around her at the forces she'd gathered. Forces comprised of hissing, horned, slimy demons, all just waiting to do Hildegard's bidding. They climbed the pizzeria's walls, breathing as one mass, the low thrum of their hatred vibrating in every corner. Webbed fingers clung to the ceiling above them, their bodies pulsing, waiting.

That flaming fireball Hildegard had been holding turned into a bolt of lightning she hurled at Nina's feet, cracking the ground open and leaving a sizzling line of charred pavement, making Nina jump back. Casey fought a scream as a demon latched onto Nina's leg, swirling around it like a lithe snake. It opened its mouth wide and snapped it shut around her leg so fast there was nothing but a blur of flashing teeth. She roared her fury, reaching down and snatching the creature up with a fist, and threw him to the ground. Marty was at her side instantly, stomping a heeled foot into its protruding belly as it screamed.

Wanda shoved Casey behind her protectively.

But Casey pulled from Wanda, taking caution as she approached Hildegard. Fear drove her footsteps. Prudence drove her words. "Okay, so I jumped the gun. Went all cocky on you. I'm sorry. What was I thinking? Let's just do this the way we planned. I'll take your place in Hell, and you feed from Clay. Nothing changes. Naomi's safe. Same dealio." She stuck her hand in Hildegard's direction, offering it to her to shake on it.

Nina yanked at Casey's sweater, and Wanda made a move to stop her, but Casey shrugged them off.

Her smile, red and glossed, was sly. "Nah. I like the new deal much better. Clay's mine. Not just sort of mine, but mine. In *every way*. The way he should have been before my sister came along and stole him from me. She knew I wanted Clay, and that didn't stop her. So instead, I stopped her. Now I can have what was rightfully mine centuries ago. So forgetaboutit." Then she laughed. Kinda crazy.

A shiver of terror spread from Casey's toes to her skull, filled with disgust for this woman. Filled with distaste at the idea that she'd be able to touch Clay with her filthy, jealous paws.

Nina rocked from foot to foot, her leg healing before Casey's eyes while Wanda cracked her neck and Marty rolled her shoulders, but Casey held up a hand to them. Maybe she could reason her way out of this. Use her people skills. "But think of all the things you'll miss in Hell. You can't shop in Hell. Oh, and you can't play with Bendy Bob. . . ."

"Bendy Bob?" her sister and her friends repeated in sync.

Hildegard drew a polished red nail over Casey's chin, then

flicked her lips. "What will I need Bendy Bob for when I have Clay? You've tapped that, right? So you know exactly what I mean. It's finger-lickin' good." She popped the very finger she'd so arrogantly drawn over Casey's chin into her mouth and sucked it with a wet slurp.

Okay, people skills now officially could be considered an epic fail.

Casey's head spun with angry swirls of light and sound while Nina jammed her face in Hildegard's, letting her fangs elongate. She grabbed a fistful of Hildegard's sweater and yanked, jarring poor Arch. "Back off, sistah. Back off now or you and this Bendy Bob are gonna be more than just strange bedfellows, you freak."

Wanda stood behind Nina, and Marty moved around to the other side, forming a protective circle around Casey.

And the mob of demons moved closer. Slithering, crawling, crowding the women until she almost couldn't breathe from the surge of raw fury. Nina growled, feral, sending out a warning signal. Archibald still hung from Hildegard's shoulder, unmoving to the point that Casey began to fear he wouldn't ever move again.

Casey's heart crashed, her adrenaline pumped, her pulse erratically punched her skin from the inside out. No matter how strong, no matter how paranormally skilled, her sister, her friends, Archibald would all be killed if she didn't act.

Oh, but they were fucked, well and good. Hildegard didn't need Casey's deal because Clay had given her exactly what she'd wanted. Hildegard would have what would never be hers without having to put the screws to Clay, and Naomi would suffer because her father would be miserable.

For eternity.

And Hildegard knew it. It was written all over her fantastical features as she arrogantly gazed at Casey.

And that made Casey want to throw her ass to the ground and stomp all over her smug, self-assured face.

Something protective, innate, wild, and furious swelled in her. At all costs, what Clay had been so against had to happen, and it had to happen now, before Hildegard could find him. Wherever the fuck he was.

And if it was the last thing she did—she'd stop the crazy bitch.

Unfortunately, from the looks of things—it probably would be the last thing she did.

But it'd be hella memorable.

Casey let out a sigh of boredom, pausing the tension as they stared each other down. "You know what, Hildegard? I think you're right. The deal thing? It's just not gonna work. But there's one thing you're wrong about. . . ."

She winked her long lashes. "Don't be silly. I'm never wrong."

"But you are. You said it was your anniversary. But you forgot to include me, and that leaves me soooo hurt. I mean, technically, Clay's my mate, too. What if I told you I don't much like to share?"

Her chiseled chin lifted upward in defiance. "I'd tell you you'd better be prepared to die for that statement."

Casey took a step closer, ignoring Archibald's wild, frantic eyes and bumping chests with Hildegard. "Okay. Well, what if I told you that you're a crazy bitch, and you'll have Clay when Hell is an ice rink in Antarctica?"

"I'll kill you," she whispered between thin lips.

"Not if I kill you first," Casey singsonged, gritting her teeth before grabbing the long strand of Hildegard's hair and yanking it, making her lose her grip on Archibald, who slumped to the floor before Wanda or Marty could stop it.

Casey watched him slither to the ground in a helpless lump.

Fuck it all if that didn't really hack her off.

And so, yeah.

More madness erupted—but she'd adjusted to this sort of thing now. It seemed it was the only way these demons liked to settle things.

She was down with that.

CHAPTER 19

Launching herself at Hildegard, Casey paid no heed to the demons that jumped from the ceiling, latching onto every available surface of her body and screeching their rage, ripping at her flesh, sinking their talons into her skin so deep she felt blood ooze from various places on her body her in a hot rush.

She didn't hear Nina, Wanda, and Marty when they roared, shifting, turning, doing whatever their supernatural bent was in order to protect her. She didn't see them taking out demons like they were dominos only to have more appear.

All she could see was Hildegard's face. The face of a woman who wanted her man—even if he was hers by proxy. He was still hers. The face of a woman who would take a father away from his little girl.

Casey, fueled by her uncontainable rage, clawed at Hildegard, shoving her fingers into her mouth and jamming them downward until she screamed her anger, tearing her jaw free. "I'll kill you, you bitch!"

Like Casey was nothing more than a feather, Hildegard flung her, sending her with a harsh crack into a pizza oven. Her neck snapped back on contact, knocking her eyeballs sideways when she slid to the ground.

That incessant niggle of rage that began as a slow, steady climb didn't waste any time today. Instead, it roared through her, jolting her body so hard, she was launched upward until she was airborne.

The carnage below her left Casey seething. Archibald lay in the corner of the pizzeria, out cold. Wanda and Marty's clothes were shredded, scattered across the floor, their shoes discarded haphazardly.

Wanda and Marty—omigod, they really could turn into werewolves. Two hairy, multicolored beasts rose on their hind legs, shooting like bullets at a group of writhing demons, canines dripping with saliva. They tore into three of them at once with bone-chilling howls.

Nina held two demons in either fist, raising her arms high and flinging them across the room only for them to crash together, then turn into one gelatinous entity. Each demon the girls attacked regenerated into something more horrifying than it originally was. They were like tribbles, multiplying by the dozens, cackling, giggling their maniacal joy at the game.

Fear turned to a hopelessness that seared Casey's quivering gut. What had they been thinking when they thought they could take on this mass from Hell? No matter how strong they were as a group, you couldn't thwart what kept regenerating and coming back in droves.

She read books all the time. Her nose had always been buried in a book. Why hadn't she researched how to kill a demon?

From the corner of her eye, Casey caught skulking shadows. Prepared to pin them to the far wall with her fireballs, she stopped just in time to realize the men had finally arrived.

A dark man, tall, imposing, hauled a long, black hose.

Which would be great if flogging these fuckers about the head and neck had any effect. Darnell was close behind in a yellow rain slicker, galoshes, and hat, with a frilly pink umbrella shadowing his head. *"Fry the moooootherfuuuuuckers!"* he screamed at the man, pointing his finger forward as though he were about to lead a charge.

"Casey, Nina, Wanda—get the hell out of the way!" tall, dark, and as yet unnamed roared, releasing the spigot and spraying the room, washing it with gushes of water.

Casey dove for the bathrooms, soaring through the air to crash into the men's room, splintering the door as she did. Scurrying to her feet, she crawled out of the bathroom sheltered by a short hallway, where she watched this man with Heath and Greg behind him wield the black hose like he was wielding a weapon.

Piteous screeching ricocheted off the walls of the pizzeria when the water sprayed them. One by one scaled, horned demons turned to trembling Jell-O like globs, plopping to the floor in gooey masses, sinking into the floorboards.

But another group cropped up by the large, boarded front window, swirling around Nina. Her mouth opened wide, her fangs gleaming under the light, she howled, charging them. And then Greg was by her side, peeling each demon off and casting them behind him with a mere flick of his wrist, to Heath, who scooped them up and chucked them toward the unknown man. "Keegan!" His bark was gruff. "Hose the assholes!" he bellowed.

She knew that name. It was Marty's husband, and whatever he was wielding rocketh.

Marty and Wanda began to pluck demons from the walls with their doglike jaws, shaking their heads with violent shudders when they threw them toward Keegan, who sprayed them until they sizzled with crackling pops.

It was like watching a sick game of Asteroids, picking off demons one shot at a time.

And then she saw Archibald, still lying in the corner, crushed
between the chairs and a table. Droplets of water from the shower
of the hose fell on her, setting her exposed skin on fire. Crawling
toward him, shoving her way with care through the toppled chairs
and tables, she latched onto his pant leg and tugged him to her,
moving him with a slow pull so as not to jar his crooked ankle.
Tears streamed down her face—he would never survive being
tossed about like this. He was at least eighty years old, for Christ's
sake.

His head lolled at an awkward angle, but his eyes opened, warm
and solemn. "Miss Casey?"

"Oh, thank God," she sobbed, pushing her matted hair from her
face to see him more clearly. She cradled his limp body against her
shaking one.

"Thank *Him* later," he replied, muffled against her chest.

"What?"

"Trust me when I tell you, Miss, all is well. I'm playing possum.
Now leave me be. Please. Go, help the others!" His face was dis-
traught with panic, his jowls quaking when he urged her to leave
him on the floor.

"Possum . . . but you're hurt! Your ankle . . ."

"I'm fine, and I've located Master Clay," he panted.

"Where the hell is he?"

Archibald gasped for air. "In the refrigerator, Miss. He sleeps
the sleep of the innocent."

Or the dead, for all the howling and raging going on. "Does
Hildegard know where he is?"

"No! But you must hurry if you're to drink from him. Now you
must go help the others!"

She ran a hand over his face, fear for him coursing through her veins. "I can't just leave you here. Let me pull you somewhere safer."

"Miss?"

"What?"

"Look—behind—youuuuu!" he yelled.

It was never good when someone said that because it usually meant there was some bad shit back yonder. It was just like when you watched a horror flick and while the too-stupid-to-live heroine went down in the basement to see what the noise was, you screamed, "Dumb ass! Don't go down there!" at the movie screen.

Yep.

That was exactly what it was like, Casey reflected.

But only briefly.

It was all she had time for before Hildegard slugged her so hard with a fist of iron, she heard bones crunch in her face.

Casey's head flew back on impact, snapping like a twig while Hildegard attacked with a rebel cry, tearing at fistfuls of hair, hauling her upward and dragging her across the floor while everyone else was distracted with the business of demon whacking.

Casey reared up against Hildegard, slapping against her long body, digging her nails into her hip, but her grip was like steel. The first tingle of her fingertips was a welcome burst of heat. Rolling her wrist, she shot upward, aiming it at Hildegard's gloriously blond, Pantene hair.

Her screech of pain didn't just bring a satisfied smile to Casey's lips, but allowed her the leverage to squirm free. Dropping to the ground with a hard thud, Casey fought for balance, rising up and steamrolling her flaming menace. With one hand, she sent Hildegard screeching into the nearest wall, holding her fingers as though she actually had them around her neck.

The wall collapsed behind her from the force of Casey's blow, and there lay Clay. Doing the narcoleptic vampire thing. Sound asleep, like the world hadn't gone mad around him.

Emotions, deep and so sharply sweet they cut her like a knife, rose to the surface of Casey's heart. This impossible man, so strong and powerful when awake, was defenseless against this heinous, spiteful monster, and she knew it left him helplessly infuriated.

Seething anger for Clay, for Naomi, whooshed through her.

And then things got freaky. Her horns shot from her head, but they felt much heavier than they ever had before, making her head wobble momentarily. When she caught a glimpse of the hand that held Hildegard in place—well, that was pretty freaky-deaky, too. Covered in shades of variegated green, her hands were no longer hands, but claws, razor sharp and long.

Her feet, which had raced toward Hildegard like she owed her money, were no longer an average size eight, but webbed and, in her opinion, butt-ass ugly. Long-toed and wrinkled, they'd stomped their way toward Hildegard, leaving gaping holes in the floor as she went.

When she screamed Hildegard's name, she sounded a whole lot like Darth Vader.

Jazzy.

Bolts of a powerful wrath she'd not known she was capable of, not even since she'd been turned, exploded in her. Determination pushed her. Incited, she slogged toward the bitch who wanted to take her mate from her.

And all this but for one goal: to keep Hildegard from getting to the opening of the refrigerator before she did.

But more than anything, to see Hildegard pay—painfully.

Archibald appeared from the debris of the littered chairs, dragging, grunting, pulling himself toward the hole in the wall— toward Clay. His eyes caught hers, sweat glistening his forehead, he held something up in a flash of coppery metal. Each square inch he covered, his ankle dragged behind him, scraping the hard floor.

The others were too busy fending off flying demons to help him, and that meant she had to get this right. Two for the price of one. Whatever Archibald was up to, his eyes had sent a desperate message she had no time to decipher.

Approaching Hildegard, Casey howled, high, screeching, throwing her shoulders back and looking to the Heavens before her gaze settled on the woman who'd wrought so much terror and pain for centuries. "Didn't you hear me when I said he's mine, you *bitch?*" The words that flew from Casey's mouth left behind a hot stench, blowing Hildegard's hair like the out-of-control wind of a tornado.

With wild defiance, Hildegard stared back at her. "I heard you, and I warned you. And now, because you just can't let things alone—I'll kill you," she raged. Cocking her hand, she flattened Casey to the floor in one fluid motion.

As Casey struggled with her new form, bulky and awkward, Hildegard made her move, leaping across the hole and straight for Clay.

Her teeth flashed in the gloom of the refrigerator, her hair flew behind her in a platinum sheet of tangled strands, her limbs like those of some demented crab.

Landing on Clay without even stirring him, she bent her head low toward his neck.

Casey rushed her, but not before Archibald rose up on one arm and flung something in Hildegard's direction with a weak but hard-won grunt.

Unleashed, it smelled of death and decay, slicing through the air in an arc of stench and a watery, unidentifiable substance.

Casey gagged from the stink, throwing a hand to her mouth. A hand that wasn't scaly anymore. Lifting her head, sluggish and heavy, she heard Archibald holler, "Be done with, you vile creature!"

Hildegard shrieked her anguish, collapsing to the floor of the refrigerator in a smoking, vaporous heap but inches from Clay.

Casey fell back on her elbows in weary disbelief, her eyes clouded by the sweat that poured from her forehead. "Archibald! Talk to me, are you okay?"

"Oh, indeed, Miss," was his drained reply, weak and trembling. "In fact, at this very moment, I'm thanking Gilad and his Bodies in Motion workout. For surely, he instilled in me a determination I wasn't aware I possessed."

Casey pushed off the floor, dragging her battered body to where Archibald lay next to Clay. He held his hand out to her and she took it, gasping for breath, pressing it to her cheek. "Arch? How? I mean, what? I mean—"

"Do you remember all the snide remarks behind my back about the stench in the kitchen and my cooking, Miss?"

Her response was a guilty wince.

"Clearly we understand each other, and I won't express the deep sadness I felt that you were so unwilling to try even one of my dishes as a result. Though, in my defense, that odor was not without reason. Suffice it to say, I know a little something about various legends. I was, after all, a manservant for many years. We listen, but rarely speak. We observe, but rarely offer commentary. For all the times I quieted a response, I have schooled myself in the ways of the paranormal. What I learned, though not always as useful as this endeavor has proven, was that there are ways to end the mating bond that have absolutely no retribution when committed by someone who is not the mated. That someone is me. I am neither vampire, nor werewolf, and certainly nothing as vile as demon. No offense to your charmingly disarming scales, of course. I'm a human, and never was I so thankful.

"All that was left was to investigate the properties that would eradicate our problem without brute force on my part, because as skilled a teacher as Gilad, no abdominal crunch in the land could prepare one for the likes of that vile creature. Thus, I brewed a potion, if you will—mixed with powerful herbs, sacred and blessed by many before you or I. Henceforth, you suffered the product of the stench in my kitchen. I do hope you won't judge my cooking so harshly and without a care for my tender feelings in the future," he finished with a rare grin.

Casey began to laugh, pulling herself up and hugging Archibald hard. "Oh, Arch, you're a genius! So what does this mean?"

He cocked an eyebrow at her. "It means we no longer must suffer the foul temper of Master Clayton due to his distress over that hateful beast. It means the tender Naomi, in all her teenage angst, can go on being sullen and pouty for many years to come. It also means that you are now well and truly mated to Clayton. I shall assume that doesn't displease you, judging from the chorus of pleasurable squeals ringing throughout Miss Marty's apartment?"

Her face flushed red. It didn't displease her. Not even a little. "You heard *that*, too?"

"Again, Miss, I hear *everything*, much to my chagrin."

"And mine," she said with a laugh.

"Jesus," someone commented from the door. "I swear to Christ, Clay could sleep through an atom bomb."

Their heads popped up to find everyone had gathered at the hole she'd torn in the wall. "You know what, kiddo," Nina remarked with a tired grin. "Today, more than ever, I'm fucking glad I'm a vampire. You might be able to eat, but you are one butt-ugly bitch all scaled and horned out. I'll stick to blood and fangs."

Both Wanda and Marty were covered with Heath and Keegan's jackets, pale and lines of weary exhaustion on their faces. Wanda's smile was warm, her eyes shimmering from the battle. "You were really something there, Case. Pretty vigilante when you're feeling protective, aren't you?"

Casey wiped the sweat from her brow with her forearm. "Me?" She shook her head, accepting the offer of Nina's hand to help her rise. "Uh, no. You two are pretty fierce all werewolfed. If I had any doubts left about this paranormal thing, they're gone. That was insane. But thank you. Thank you, all. I never would have been able to do what needed doing if not for you—most especially Arch here. And what was that in the hose? It burned." She held up her hand so they could see the red slashes.

"Holy water," Darnell said from behind everyone with his signature cackle. "Damn lucky I didn't get none of that on me, too. Shit hurts, but it sho works on those fuckers, huh?"

"So now what? What do we do with her?" Casey asked, pointing to Hildegard's crumpled body at Clay's feet.

"You give her to me, mon," a voice from thin air said.

Come, Mr. Tallyman . . .

CHAPTER 20

Casey's fists balled up. "You! You better stay the fuck away from us, or I'll blow your ass from here to Hoboken!"

Everyone smushed protectively up against Casey, but she was in no mood to be coddled. "I swear I'll do it if you don't go the hell away and take her with you!" she ordered.

Instead of heeding her demand, he knelt beside Archibald, his long braids, colorfully beaded, swinging over his shoulders. "Old mon, you okay?" His voice held concern and sympathy; his smile was warm and toothy.

Archibald slapped him on the back with affection. "I'm well, Master Marcus. You're to be commended for your potion making. Those herbs packed just the right amount of punch, lad. Now, please, do as you promised and dispose of this . . . your *intended*."

"His *intended*?" Casey asked with disbelief.

Archibald nodded. "Why, yes, Miss. Marcus was the shaman Master Clay was to meet in the bar the night he ran into you and this all began. Naturally, he appeared in a different form to Clayton so as to keep his deception a secret. Marcus here has a sweet spot for—for *her*." He pointed a gnarled finger in Hildegard's direction, distaste clear on his face. "Truly, there's nothing like unrequited love to motivate one, wouldn't you agree, Marcus?

"Marcus was the demon Hildegard signed a contract with. He was young, and alas a fledgling, willing to do whatever necessary to climb the ranks in Hell. When he made the contract with Hildegard, he fully expected she would end up having to mate like everyone else—with another demon, of course, and his hope was that she would mate with him. But she's a crafty one, as we all are aware. Thus, Marcus has waited all these years with love in his heart until the right opportunity came along. I was the right opportunity. With a little teamwork, Hildegard is now free to mate with Marcus."

"Ya done good, old mon." Marcus looked to Casey then. "I tol' ya, da answer was wit the servant, din't I? Das why I took you down there." He pointed to the floor. "To test your skills 'cause I knew a battle was ahead."

He had. Those were the last words she remembered before she woke up with Clay.

Marcus stooped to lift Hildegard's limp form. "I'll take her now. She gonna be pretty mad when she wakes up."

Upon those words, both Hildegard and Clay stirred. When his luscious eyes popped open, he looked right at Casey, drinking in her bedraggled sweatiness with a warmth that took her breath away. She fought a smile. "Well, look who's awake—*after* we've taken down Gigantor. This whole vampire-sleep thing is avoiding conflict at its best, don't you think?" she teased, her pulse doing a yippy-skippy.

Clay launched upward to his feet as though he'd never slept and pulled her close, running his hands over her face. He kissed the tip of her dirty nose, assessing her from head to toe, eyeing her ripped clothing. "You're okay. What happened? How the fuck did you pull that off?"

She smiled up at him. "Oh, don't look at me. I can't take any of the credit. It was all Arch."

Heath had helped Arch up, bracing him from around the waist.

Clay glanced at Archibald. "Arch?"

Waving a hand, he smiled. "'Twas nothing, sir. I had to stop Miss Casey from taking that awful woman's place in Hell, and I had to stop you from becoming her man-toy. It was unthinkable. However, some credit must go to your new mate. You should have seen Miss Casey tonight. Sir, she was an *animal*."

Casey put her arms around his waist and squeezed, laughing at the ever-changing emotions on his face. "I'll explain everything later."

Hildegard moaned in Marcus's arms, squirming out of them. "Put me down, you moron!" When she took note of Clayton, she threw a dramatic frown on her face. "Clayton! Did you see what they did to me? It was ghastly." She shuddered, looking down at her torn dress, smudges of black soot littering her flesh. "So tell them all to go away, and I just might find it in me to forgive you and allow you to continue our mating."

Magnanimous.

Clay lifted his chiseled jaw to respond, his eyes fiery, but Casey was the one to act. Sauntering up to Hildegard, she pointed a finger in her face. "Hey, Hildegard. Guess what?"

She regarded Casey with disdain while Marcus came to stand beside her, his hand on the curve of her hip. A hand she brushed off with angry impatience, eyeing Casey. "I can't wait."

Casey smiled. "Your mated days are over, sistah."

Her face was glacial. "You're a funny little creature, aren't you?"

Marcus's head swung back and forth. "What she say is true, womon. You must come wit me now." He grinned to punctuate his statement, planting a sloppy kiss on her cheek.

Hildegard's eyes went wild as she ran a hand over the spot where Marcus had kissed her. "But that's absurd. Neither of us is dead. Our bond can't be broken unless one of us is expunged, and if any of you had anything to do with it, you'll be shunned. So what you claim is impossible. Now, Clayton, make these awful people go away," she whined.

"The bond can't be broken by either one of us, but it can be broken by a human," Clay snapped. "And if I were you, Hildegard, for all the pain you've brought me, for all the bullshit I've suffered because of your jealous longing, I'd shut up, because now that we're not mated, I just might do what I've wanted to do for centuries. *Kill you.*"

Hildegard's eyes went directly to the only human in the room. Archibald. They oozed her rage. "It was you!"

Archibald sighed with a bored yawn. "Why yes, Miss, 'twas I. And if you wish to set me afire, please be sure you do so here." He pointed to his shoulder. "I'm told heat is good for arthritic bones, and after my superior quarterbacking, it aches."

"You old bastard, I'll kill you for this," she growled. "It's not true—it can't be true!"

Casey's grin was on par with the Joker—evil and superior. "Tell me something, Hildegard. Isn't it true that because of your bond with Clayton, you can feel him, so to speak, and he can feel you?"

She held her mussed head high, her face taking on a haughty expression. "It is."

"But if the bond is broken, he won't be able to feel you anymore, right?"

Her eyes narrowed in suspicion. "Make your point."

"Clay? Tell me if you feel *this*." Pulling her arm back, she slapped

Hildegard's face. Hard. Her head snapped back from the force Casey used, her howl ringing in the refrigerator.

Clay rubbed his jaw with lean fingers, then grinned as realization dawned. "Nope. Nuthin'. Not even a little residual." He held up a hand to her, and she slapped it. "Nice job, honey," he praised.

Turning her back on Hildegard, she eyed Clay. "Okay, so then tell me if you can feel *this*." Lunging at him, she wrapped her limbs around his waist and neck and kissed him. Soundly—thoroughly—tasting every inch of his mouth—reassuring herself that he was unharmed.

When she let him go, he chuckled. "Now *that* I felt."

A commotion had flared up as Hildegard fought to get away from Marcus. "Let me go, Marcus! What is wrong with you? We were in this together. How could you have let this happen? Clay was supposed to be mine!" she hollered.

Wrapping the length of her long hair around his wrist, Marcus's eyes glowed red when he tugged her to him, molding her lithe body against his. "Hush, womon. Nobody should know betta dan you about deception." He gave her ass a hard slap and chuckled. "Dis is all ovah now, and you're comin' wit me. You wasn't kiddn' when you said we in dis together."

She fought him, pushing against Marcus, but he seemed to find the fight in Hildegard amusing rather than aggravating. Dragging her by the hair, he pulled her into the dark of the pizzeria, his laughter, victorious and bubbling, filling the room as he went.

Casey slumped in Clay's arms, exhausted, when everyone began filing out of the refrigerator. "You need rest," he whispered against her ear, nuzzling it with his lips.

She giggled. "I need to exfoliate."

Wanda pinched Casey's cheek, Heath close to her side. "Jesus, are you okay, Case? You must be exhausted."

"Well, if she isn't, I sure as fuck am," Nina said, interrupting, holding Greg's hand, and pulling him toward the exit. "I'm out, people. Casey, I gotta give it up. You were badass today. Thumbs-up and all that jazz. Now c'mon, vampire. Take me home to my drafty castle."

Casey grabbed her and gave her a quick "non-personal space invading" hug, whether she wanted one or not. "Thank you. Thank you for helping me. All of you. I don't know if I can ever thank you for risking so much to help me—"

"Us," Clay interrupted. "*Us*," he said again, winking down at her.

Marty blew a kiss at her, scooping up her tattered heels. "I need to get back to Hollis, and I need to mourn the loss of my shoes properly," she teased, looking to Keegan. "Honey? I think tonight it's the full-body-massage package, and no skimping."

Keegan growled, nuzzling her hair before holding his hand out to Clay and enveloping it with a hard shake. "You have some little warrior here, friend. You two look out for each other."

They made their way out over the toppled chairs, leaving Wanda, Archibald, and Heath. Wanda's hair stuck out at odd angles that Heath pushed from her face with a tender hand, holding Archibald up with the other. "Well, young lady, if you think you'll be okay, I'm out, too. I just want to go home to my own bed and sleep. A lot."

Casey gave each of them a hug, cupping Archibald's cheeks in her hands, she said, "You're a genius, Arch. Thank you. I'll never forget this."

"Then I can safely assume my wild boar with a garlic glaze will be a fit celebratory feast?"

Casey laughed. "I'll eat every last scrap on my plate. Promise."

Heath helped Arch out, lifting him with care over the debris. Wanda faced them, eyeing Clay. "So—you're mated. And that's all well and good, but there's a whole lot more to this than just—

being naked. Never mind, you know what I mean. You make sure you look out for my little sister, got that? You two need to spend some time getting to know each other under circumstances that don't include crazy giants and their fireballs."

Clay kissed Wanda's cheek. "I promise to take good care of her, but from the sounds of things, she doesn't need much help after what happened tonight."

"That's because she's a Schwartz," Wanda said with a smile. "Can I trust you to explain the feeding thing, Clay?"

Casey's stomach took a dive when Clay nodded, her face green, but Wanda chucked her under the chin. "Trust me, you won't think it's so bad once you've done it. Now give me a hug, and call if you need me, okay?"

She hugged Wanda hard. "*Thank you.* I know I've been a crappy sister, but I love you, and I appreciate everything you've done. I promise it won't be like it's been in the past."

"Good. Because now that you're part of the BFF circle, I'm handing Nina off to you for a year," she said with a laugh. "I love you, honey. Go do mated things. And hurry—you'll need to feed soon." She waved a hand over her shoulder at them, picking her way through the rubble.

"Casey, you done good tonight. Made me proud to be demon." Darnell placed a beefy hand on her shoulder. "But if you evah stick me to a wall like that again, I'm gonna show you what real vermin is," he joked.

Casey hugged him tight. "Thank you for everything, and don't be a stranger."

Darnell held his fist out to Clay. "You go get you some demon, man."

Clay bumped his fist. "Done."

Darnell grinned. "Aight, then," he said. "Peace out." He held up two fingers, then vanished.

Twisting her around, Clay pulled her close. "I'm going to be very serious here for a minute. So take heed, woman, because it doesn't happen often."

"Heeding," she murmured, leaning into him, reveling in his solid strength.

"You did something so goddamned stupid, if I didn't want to throw you down and have my way with you, I'd kick your cute ass. Don't ever, ever enter into a bargain with a demon, ever again——"

Outrage assaulted her. "Stupid is as stupid does. You did the same thing——"

He silenced her with a kiss she couldn't fight the deliciousness of.

When Clay pulled his lips from hers, he grinned. "I did it because I didn't have any other choice, and I didn't want you to have to make a choice. But pay close attention. I can never thank you enough for what you did, not just for me but for Naomi. That all the nights of fearing the worst for her because she was attached to Hildegard are over. I don't know how to express how grateful I am. What you did was reckless, and stupid, and crazy, but I'll *never* forget it." He ran a gentle finger over her cheek, his eyes soaking her up.

Embarrassed, she smiled coyly. "Yeah, well, you might want to forget it when I batter your eardrums with my Yanni CDs. Oh, and then there's John Tesh and Kenny G. Can't forget Kenny."

"Oh, right. I forgot—this is an *eternity* thing." His eyes smiled his amusement.

"Yep, so Yanni it is, pal. Forevah."

He dragged her to him. "Fine. I can live with Yanni, but I'm not knitting."

"Don't be such a naysayer. Who couldn't use a nice scarf in the winter?"

"I dunno, but I do know what I could use. . . ." His grin took a steamy turn.

"What's that?"

His phone rang before he had the chance to answer. Digging in his pocket, he pulled out his cell and flipped it open, then nodded knowingly. "It's my precious, moody angel. Now officially your stepdaughter."

As Clay answered, Casey soaked in the impact of that statement. Her stepdaughter. Her *teenage* stepdaughter.

"Hi, honey," Clay answered. He frowned. "No. Absolutely *not*. What have I told you about boys at the house when I'm not there? No. Boys. Young lady. None. They're all dogs in heat. We'll talk about this when I get home. Now go do your homework. I love you."

Casey swatted at his arm playfully. "So you're one of *those* fathers."

"Speaking of, how do you feel about being a stepmother?"

Putting her arms around his neck, she curled her fingers in his hair, laughing up at him. "A little freaked out isn't a phrase I'd use fast and loose right now."

His face took a serious turn. "There's no turning back, Casey."

Nah. She was good with heading forward. "Nobody said anything about turning anywhere."

"So we're in." He didn't ask. He stated.

Yep. She was as in, as committed, as deep as she'd ever been. "We're in."

"Nice. So whaddya say I take you back to my swinging bachelor pad and we investigate the feeding thing. Wanda's right. You have to feed soon, and she's also right when she says it's a good thing. It can be very pleasurable if it's consenting."

"I say okay, but I want to know in advance if I yark on you, you won't be mad. You do have a tendency to be very cranky."

He drew her lips to his. "You won't want to yark when I'm done with you, Ms. Schwartz."

Shivers spread along her arms in anticipation—even with the feeding thing. "Isn't it Gunnersson now?"

"Yeah. It sorta is."

"Hookay, then, let's go swing," she said on a chuckle.

"Wait. One question, and this is serious—no toying with my emotions, either. I don't want to go through all this shit just to find myself dumped and drowning my sorrows in a pint of Ben and Jerry's while I look at your picture with longing and wander around my house in your old T-shirts."

Casey laughed without reservation, from deep within. "My T-shirts are too small for you, and you don't eat. So what's on your mind?"

"How do I know all this crazy passion you've been experiencing for me isn't just a result of Hildegard's blood running through your veins? The transference was much deeper than we originally thought, and as I guess you've found out, I wasn't just Hildegard's meal ticket. She was hot for me in a big way. So maybe you're not really succumbing to my incredibly sexy charm, though I find that hard to believe. Maybe, and I say this even though it's ridiculous, but maybe you're being fooled during your adjustment period. Maybe it'll wear off, and that would be tragic because I'm a crazy-awesome catch." He raised an eyebrow in question, but his smile was playful.

Nuzzling his lips, she said on a sigh, "Then I guess you'll just have to stick around to find out how you rate on the awesome scale of one to ten, won't you?"

EPILOGUE

Eight Months, Four Freaky-Deaky Paranormal Accidents, and One Mouthy, Sullen, Moody Teenage Vampire Later . . .

And stick around Clay did. In fact, Casey and Clay stuck around a lot.

Together.

So much so that they'd fallen head over heels in love. They took things slowly at first. Casey insisted they date while they got to know each other, and Clay agreed. Clay bought her tickets to a Yanni concert and almost managed to make the entire event without falling asleep. In turn, she brought earplugs to the Nine Inch Nails soiree and only winced once. Many a night found them on the couch together, Clay watching football, Casey knitting a blanket, their feet intertwined in companionable silence.

Without the pressure of Hildegard's presence, Clay was a new breed of man—fun, thoughtful, powerful, smart, and the best damned frolic between a set of sheets evah.

But most important, they complemented each other. Clay understood her need to be independent and self-sufficient. So when she took a job as a pole-dancing instructor at the Y in order to help pay for her degree in teaching, he was behind her 100 percent with the prereq that it only involve middle-aged housewives. He'd even picked up some nifty thongs for her to wear at home. "You know, to keep you feeling as one with your inner stripper," he'd joked with a lascivious grin. He hadn't offered to pay for her classes, and Casey assumed his understanding came from a sixth sense that she needed to prove to herself she could do it on her own—without the generous help from him or even Wanda. Though she knew he would if she asked him to.

And she got that he had responsibilities that involved more than just the two of them. He had Naomi. Free and clear. Though, Clay often joked had Naomi ended up in Hell, Lucifer would have never survived her ever-changing moods. Casey's level head and practicality kept Clay from continuing on the path of overbearing and so totally overreacting where Naomi was concerned.

She was the voice of reason, the flip side of the coin when Clay turned into Attila the Father.

Casey understood Naomi's mood swings better than anyone—especially after the events of the last few months—and little by little, she and Naomi had forged a relationship based on trust and a friendship only two girls can share. When Clay was off golfing, they giggled long into the night about boys while they watched horror movies and hung out. You could often find the two studying together in comfortable silence, banging out a Metallica tune on Rock Band—or listening to Nickelback while they painted each other's nails. Casey didn't force the issue of the addition of another parental unit in Naomi's life, and it was the clincher in a deal born of unbelievable circumstance, then nurtured over time.

They had become a family—if an unconventional one—and she'd never been happier—more fulfilled—more in love.

Fighting his way through four dozen pink balloons, Clay came to stand at the dining room entryway to watch Naomi greet her guests at the front door. "So how many sweet-sixteen parties do you suppose a girl can have? It's not like we can say, 'she'll only be sixteen *once*,' " Clay commented against the top of Casey's head, frowning at the arrival of two boys, one riddled with acne, and the other with braces, both almost as tall as Clay.

Casey chuckled, standing on tiptoe to kiss the corner of his mouth. "Oh, honey, I promise it'll be just one if you promise to keep your overbearing, vampire nose out of her party."

He grunted. So out of character.

Naomi turned then, smiling at Casey and Clay. Dark-haired and blue-eyed, she took Casey's breath away. She was stunning—even with two eyebrow piercings, deep purple lipstick, and her new fondness for black clothing. "Daddy? Stop freaking out. I swear. You'll always be the only man in my life."

Clay swiped a finger along her nose with a grin. "Super Stepmom told you to say that, didn't she?"

Naomi giggled, sweet and girlish. "Whatever. She's still right."

Clay winked. "I can't deny the truth. She owns me."

"Total ownage," Naomi said with a nod.

Flapping a hand, Casey shooed Naomi off. "Go—be sixteen. Leave your father's presence before he gets the chains and decides to turn the basement into a dungeon."

Naomi gave her a quick hug, and whispered, "Thank you. He never would've done this without you."

Clay mocked a hurt expression. "Would, too."

Casey snuggled against his side, breathing in the welcoming

scent of his familiar cologne. "Oh, baloney. You would not, either. But it'll be fine. Naomi's a good girl, and if she hasn't proven that to you in as many centuries, then you've got a long road ahead of you."

"Give the kid a fucking break," Nina crowed from behind the couple. Everyone was seated around the long stretch of Casey and Clay's dining room table, pretending to lie low for Naomi's sake. "Besides, do you really think shit would go down with us here? And Jesus, Clay. She's been a teenager for a gazillion years. Imagine how much that sucks hairy balls. All I can say is I'm damned glad this shit didn't go down when I was sixteen."

"Hah!" Marty cackled, bouncing Hollis on her knee to keep her distracted while Keegan blew bubbles for her from a pink wand. "I bet there're centuries' worth of high school kids who feel the same way."

"Oh, Miss Marty, can you imagine the rumbles that might have passed had Miss Nina had her vampiric powers so early on. Surely, given that kind of time on her hands, she could have made school-yard rumble history," Archibald joked, straightening his suit jacket after setting Naomi's cake on the table. True to his word, Archibald really was an incredible cook, as proven by many a meal he sent over for Casey because, in his words, "How can one truly indulge in the art of culinary delights for those whose diet is limited by rare beef and blood?"

Nina laughed, leaning into Greg's chest. "You get funnier and funnier, Arch. Must be all that hanging out with Wanda you do."

"Hey!" Wanda piped up, holding Heath's hand and smiling. "I have to have a sense of humor with the both of you. God was seriously snarking me when *He* saddled me with you and Marty for eternity."

Casey giggled, sending a warm smile Wanda's way. They'd made up for lost time since her "accident." She'd gone on shopping trips to the designer outlet mall with the girls and her sister, eaten at Hogan's Diner, and at least twice a month, you could find the four women harassing some poor waiter at the House of Hwang on karaoke night. Casey made the effort to reenter Wanda's life instead of hiding in shame with the blanket of her mistakes covering her. In fact, Casey'd even offered to volunteer her time to Wanda and Heath's relief effort for reverted vampires, and they'd begun to research a new potential for a support group for other accidentals, not just those who'd turned back into humans, but all species of the paranormal.

"Because seriously, we can't be the only fucking accidents," Nina had joked. "How much you got says there's some poor chick out there who's like a fire-breathing dragon, all scaly and shit, because she was bitten by her lame-assed boyfriend's Iguana?"

If it had happened four times in just a couple of years to a group of women not even six degrees separated, Nina said, she'd bet her left lung, if she still had one, there were others just like them.

They had all agreed she had a point—who better than them to aid and abet?

Casey sighed with contentment. Life was incredibly good, and the bit of envy she'd felt about Wanda's life had turned her into an active participant in pursuing her own.

Everything was damned close to perfect. Well, except that overprotective-father thing. Rolling her eyes, she caught Clay by the loop of his jeans when he attempted to make a getaway and a beeline for Naomi, who was dancing in the middle of the living room with, according to her, the crush of her lifetimes. "Oh, no, killa. It's just some dancing. Let them be or there'll be no goody bag for you to open later tonight," she teased.

Clay stayed put, but kept one watchful eye on Naomi. "Always with the threats of no nookie. And I signed on for life? I dunno, cupcake," he teased with a grin. "That's some harsh shit you're doling out."

Casey snapped her fingers, lighting each tip with a controlled, low-burning flame. "Not nearly as harsh as your sentence will be if I have to lob fireballs at you—and we both know how good I am at that. Now cut—it—out." She kissed his yummy lips as a warning.

Darnell poked his head between them with a grin. "Hey, we need a light," he said, pointing to the cake. "Use them fingers fo' good, Case."

Casey turned to head for the table, but Clay stopped her, pulling her to mold against his hard frame.

She gave him a questioning gaze.

"Save a dance for me later? You know, so we can do the grind thing all slow-like."

Casey gave him a saucy grin filled with the happiness he'd given her. "Like I'd pass that up. I'd grind all slow-like with you anytime, anywhere."

Or forever.

Whichever rolled around first.